The Redemption of Kindall, K.

The Redemption of Kindall, K.

Renee Nielsen

Callaei Books

Published in New Zealand by Callaei Books (independent publisher)

callaeibooks.com

First published 2019.

The Redemption of Kindall, K. (Kindall K series, Book 2)

ISBN-13 (paperback): 978 0 473 49927 3

ISBN-13 (hardcover): 978 0 473 63052 2

ISBN-13 (Kindle): 978 0 473 49928 0

ISBN-13 (ePUB): 978 0 473 57898 5

First printed in the United States of America

For everyone who supported and encouraged me
when I was writing *The Case of Kindall, K.*

KINGDOM of ARKALA

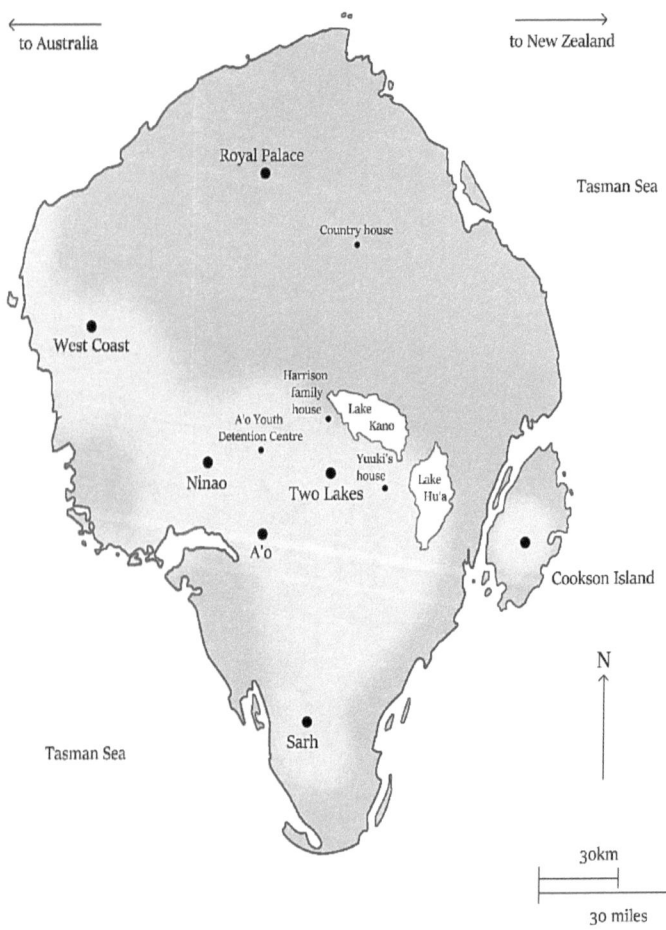

Key: Native forest
         Urbanisation

to Australia

to New Zealand

Tasman Sea

Royal Palace

Country house

West Coast

Harrison
family
house
A'o Youth
Detention Centre
Lake
Kano

Yuuki's
house
Ninao
Two Lakes
Lake
Hu'a

A'o

Cookson Island

N

Tasman Sea

Sarh

30km

30 miles

Arkala Peace Forces

Public Notice

Updated: 11.03am, 13th September 13-Tau

At 2.49pm, 30th August in the Thirteenth Year of Taularh's Reign, Our Leader Taularh was confronted and killed at the Royal Palace of Arkala. Peace Forces declared the nation in a state of emergency as soon as news of Taularh's condition was confirmed.

Peace Forces are carefully investigating the incident, however there is reason to believe that the suspected assassination was dealt by the recent group of missing persons including the Harrison family, the victim of the Ninao kidnapping and a released youth prisoner. Negotiations are in the process of being made to diminish tensions and proceed in the most peaceful way possible.

The prime suspects in this tragedy/incident are as follows:

Kindall, Kyle (17, Male, Arkalan/Arkala (Arkala'ana)): Kindall was charged with manslaughter earlier this year after an incident at Village Park on the night of 29th June left fellow high school student Daniel

Wilson dead. The Village Park homicide case was closed with Kindall expected to be detained at A'o Youth Detention Centre for at least two months, however upon decision of the judge the case was privately re-investigated by Security Officer Yuuki Takahashi. Kindall was permitted temporary parole on 13th July under emergency health conditions. He disappeared from A'o city two days later along with Takahashi.

Takahashi, Yuuki (25, Male, Arkalan/Japanese): in the weeks prior to going missing, Takahashi became involved in a private investigation of the Village Park homicide case. Takahashi was seen assisting the youth, Kyle Kindall, charged with the murder in escape in disguise of an emergency discharge, two days after which both Takahashi and Kindall disappeared. It is believed Takahashi may have led and/or assisted in the assassination.

Smith, Laura (18, Female, Arkala): niece of Kindall's youth advocate, Charlie Smith. She claims to be the passed Princess, Daughter of King Fahlu. It is believed she may have removed Taularh from the throne herself in order to claim sovereignty for herself. Peace Forces are currently investigating the claim.

Harrison, Timothy (50, Male, Arkalan): judge of Arkala Court House. Harrison was the judge of the Village Park homicide case and gave Kindall's sentence. In spite of convicting Kindall of manslaughter, arranged to have Takahashi conduct a private investigation to find evidence supporting Kindall's claims of being not guilty. No official appeal was filed. Peace Forces speculate Harrison to be one of the orchestraters of the release and fleeing of Kindall, as well as the assassination of Taularh.

If you see or have seen any of these people, please contact the Peace Force of Arkala immediately. These people are considered dangerous so do not approach them. Please see the Missing Persons page for more detail on the other members of this group: Smith, Charlie (59); Harrison, Susan (46); Harrison, Joshua (21); Sahla, Avi (17); Cook, Logan (18); and Park, Andy (51).

According to protocol, the Kingdom of Arkala shall be under martial governance until further notice. The Arkala Peace Forces ask for the nation's patience during this time.

1

The meeting room is tense and filled with sombre atmosphere. Yuuki's relieved that he's late for that reason. He's not sure how much of this air he'll be able to stomach.

Only a few people spare a glance at him as he enters, the rest of them fixated on where Andy stands leading the meeting at the other end of the room. Andy looks considerably more worn out than he did when leaving for the city yesterday, Yuuki notes. Judging by the stress written all over his face, the update on the group's situation he's come back with isn't exactly a good one either.

Yuuki quietly closes the door behind him. *Guess we aren't done fighting then.*

"Perhaps this will explain our situation better," Andy says, a deep furrow in his brow. He takes the sheets of paper he has tucked under his arm and begins unfolding them. His jacket shifts as he does so, flashing a glimpse of the Peace Force officer uniform hidden underneath it.

Yuuki instinctively tenses. He has to force himself to resist the urge to flee the room at once. There's corruption among the Peace Forces. Yuuki's been a victim of it several times, the first of which was the Ninao incident – or the 12-Tau Ninao kidnapping, as it's known formally. He's had to relive that incident day in and day out since he was rescued thanks to PTSD.

All the other times Yuuki's come into contact with the corruption since then have involved someone else getting hurt by it also. It makes it hard for Yuuki not to see a potential threat in every PFO uniform-wearing person he sees.

But Andy's not a threat; he's on their side. Kyle, sitting at the outside of the group, can testify to that: he's a victim of that corruption too, and he's been saved by Andy's skilfully made intervention before just as Yuuki has. Yuuki can still feel the seventeen-year-old watching him as he tries to subdue the adrenaline spiking his blood.

Kyle fixes Yuuki with an understanding gaze. Yuuki grimaces. It's hard for them of them to see a PFO uniform and not lose their calm about it.

His hand is still on the door handle. Reluctantly, he lets it go.

Just as Yuuki's hesitant to move away from the door, it seems Andy's been hesitant to show them whatever's on that page. Andy doesn't turn the papers in his hands around to show everyone, but instead lowers them down to the table in front of him.

It doesn't take much to see why.

Timothy is the first to break the stunned silence. "What...are these?"

It's not a missing person notice. In the centre of the page, Yuuki's face stares up at the ceiling with a neutral expression. 'WANTED' is written at the top of the page above his name. Andy straightens out the creases and steps back with a resigned sigh.

Yuuki himself isn't sure how to react. He should be troubled by this, and subconsciously he is, but not as much as he should be. No, there's something else bothering him. He replays in his head what Timothy just said and it clicks. *"...these?"* Yuuki's stomach sinks.

He's not the only one with a wanted notice to his name.

"According to the media and the Peace Forces themselves," Andy says, spreading out the papers to reveal that each of the notices indeed hold different people's pictures and names, "Yuuki Takahashi, Timothy Harrison, Kyle Kindall and Laura Smith are on the Peace Forces' most wanted list. This means they have arrest warrants issued for you four."

Which is more unsettling, Yuuki's not sure – being regarded in such a way and having his own name and face printed on a wanted poster, or the fact that the picture the Peace Forces have used for Kyle's is the same as the mugshot taken of him when he was wrongly convicted and imprisoned a few months ago. One glance at Kyle is enough to know its effect: the expression he wears is the same guarded, hopeless and angry look he had on his face when Yuuki first met him.

Without a doubt, there's still a part of Kyle that feels guilty like he'd been accused of being. It's a misplaced guilt, but it's there all the same. Yuuki quietly moves to stand behind him, shifting slightly to Kyle's right so he can rest his left hand on Kyle's left shoulder. *That's not who you are,* Yuuki hopes the touch conveys. *We have enough evidence now to prove it.*

"These names I just mentioned," Andy continues, "I'm sure you all can understand why you are our topmost priority of people to protect when we go back into civilisation. I'd say the only reason why there haven't been any orders to act on those arrest warrants is because of the severe repercussions they'll face if they invalidate the legitimacy of

Amelia's claim to the throne as the Princess of Arkala."

"So for your safety, we'll remain here at the palace until further notice, or rather until we've worked out a way to go back without putting the lives of those around us at risk. Bear in mind everyone else besides these four would likely be taken in for questioning, arrest warrant or not."

It comes as no surprise, really. The Peace Forces had been hunting them for weeks after they fled the city. The news only cements the fact that the reality of their current situation is still no different from where they were before they succeeded in taking over the palace: on the run, and with the threat of being forced into a court battle they have no hope of winning. Kyle's case is a prime example of how easy it is for the Peace Forces' corruption to rig any proper investigation into their situation against them.

"And what of the rest of us?" Logan asks. "I thought they were after all of us. Especially after we, y'know, took down Taularh."

Andy's gaze flicks across the group to him. "Accomplices. Myself included. Before we took over the palace, officially we were no more than missing persons. After we killed Taularh, we became informally labelled as criminals."

The choice of words has Kyle stiffening. Yuuki can't blame him. For the past two and a half months, Kyle's been labelled a criminal – convicted of manslaughter in an incident that he, in fact, was the victim of. They have sufficient evidence now to clear Kyle's name, but with the way things are at present it isn't likely he'll be acquitted any time soon. From what he can gather, Kyle still blames himself for Daniel Wilson's death. It was his self-defence against Daniel's own attempt to commit murder that rendered Daniel dead, after all.

At least there's more defiance in his eyes than when Yuuki had first met him. Back then he'd given up trying to defend himself as soon as he was sent to the detention centre. Now, Kyle's not alone in his defending himself anymore. Yuuki knows that means a lot to Kyle and that it has made the burden of his conviction somewhat lighter, however being accused so many times in spite of his honest pleading not guilty has long since taken its toll.

Being dubbed a criminal *again* for simply trying to stay alive is like having his face turned for them to slap the other cheek.

As if Kyle's case alone weren't enough.

Charlie, Kyle's youth advocate on the matter, clicks his tongue. "What kind of lies are have they been sowing into the public this time?"

"Misinformed ones I'd say, if they weren't deliberately spreading them," Andy murmurs. "From what I saw, they're refusing to acknowledge that the Princess still lives, instead insisting that Laura Smith is violating the deceased Princess Amelia's name instead of being she herself. To add to that, there's some people accusing Kindall of having manipulated her into falsely claiming such and subsequently killing Taularh for him."

Amelia bristles at that but doesn't comment.

"Do people hate my first name or something?" Kyle mutters under his breath. His eyes gleam.

"They're holding all of us accountable," Andy says. "To some degree at least. But in terms of who they're holding responsible for the actual assassination, it seems they're pinning that on Amelia."

"What?" Logan protests. "But I was the one who…"

Andy grunts. "Yes, I realise that, and if the investigators have picked up a search warrant and come looking for your rifle, they'll realise that too. But it's much more efficient a system of blame and public persuasion to do what they're doing, and that is to pick an easy and believable target and go with it – as opposed to going to the trouble of rooting out the truth which may turn out to be less favourable for them in their incriminating us. It also saves them a lot of time and effort they can otherwise be using to figure out how to deal with us in a culturally acceptable manner."

Timothy's expression morphs in disapproval. "Right, so they're not even investigating any of it properly. They're only pulling together biased evidence again, aren't they? Like what they did for Kyle's trial?"

"Essentially, yes. They *could* come here to get solid evidence if they wanted, but in doing so they risk drawing negative attention to themselves. *'The Kingdom of Arkala believes that peace should come first.'* Isn't that what King Fahlu used to always say? It's why our law enforcement calls itself the Arkala Kingdom Peacekeeping Forces. They'd only be earning disrespect if they marched on over here – they'd be asking for a fight they already know we'd be forced to give them.

"As this public notice here states, they'll probably continue to try to resolve this whole situation through negotiation. And, since we're way outnumbered, that would be preferable for us, too."

This earns several thoughtful nods from around the room. It's a reassurance, in one way, knowing that the Peace Forces have reason to restrain themselves from overwhelming the group. They could easily subdue them if they wanted to; they have the numbers and resources to do so. But thankfully the Peace Forces have their reputation to keep in check, otherwise there would be almost no breathing room at the palace at all.

Yuuki allows himself a sliver of relief, but it's replaced all too soon.

From where she sits beside Logan, Amelia raises her hand hesitantly. "I understand them blaming me for what happened with Taularh, and you've already explained why they're blaming Kyle, but...how come Timothy and Yuuki are being blamed as well?"

"Because in their eyes," Andy answers, "they kidnapped and let loose a prisoner who should've remained in detention."

Before Yuuki can control his expression, his lip twitches. He sees Kyle swallow hard in his peripheral and his blood boils. Timothy raises an eyebrow, sending Andy a warning look. The Peace Force officer glances at Kyle, then at Yuuki, and an apology creeps into the guilty expression on his face.

"I apologise. My choice of words just now..."

"It's okay," Kyle grits out. "I get it. Th-this is how the public see me. It's fine. Isn't l-li'...like much has changed really, anyway."

"How long before it does?" Yuuki asks lowly. It's an effort to keep the frustration out of his voice after hearing Kyle's temporary stutter, brought on by his recent head injury, brought on with the emotional stress.

Andy rubs his forehead. "It's complicated."

Timothy glances between Yuuki, Andy and Charlie, frowning. "I thought they would've lodged the appeal by now. He's eligible for a retrial. We sent all the evidence we'd gathered a few weeks ago."

"The court could be refusing to accept the new evidence for the case for a number of different reasons. I'd say most of those are just excuses to keep us labelled as the bad guys. That's who we are to the public, the way the media are warping the story – the bad guys. The Peace Forces want to keep it that way."

The corruption present within the Peace Forces isn't exclusive to Peace Force units. It's present also within the judiciary system, as Timothy, Yuuki and Kyle are so keenly aware. The two law enforcement groups have a working relationship together, after all. Yuuki's always felt that Arkala had too harsh a judiciary system, but his perspective on how messed up he believes it is sure was cemented the moment it became clear there's corruption weaving its way in Peace Force ranks.

"But..." Timothy grimaces, narrowing his eyes as he regathers his thoughts. "Surely not everyone believes what they're being told, right? The Peace Forces, too – surely not *every* officer believes what everyone else is latching onto? I mean, there's you yourself, for instance, and the other officers helping us out with security. Surely some of them are on our side."

Andy nods. "I highly doubt they can sway that many people. 'Everyone' is, after all, a lot of people to convince. The problem though is that the news is being sourced from the Peace Forces. It's considered justified. The media are simply reporting and amplifying whatever they're being fed: lies, half-truths and all.

"Of course, we'll let them know our side of the story. Amelia will be giving her speech in a couple of days. I have a contact within the media industry, so we'll record that and get it broadcasted live. Hopefully that will answer some of the public's questions, correct false answers they've been given and cause a bit of chaos by presenting a contrasting version of the story they're being told.

"If Amelia's speech is received well, that'll make things a lot easier for us. Otherwise, it's going to be a hard trust to earn and a hard fight to win. And it would be good if we could settle everything without there being any more casualties involved."

As if choosing that moment to make an emphasising point, the stub of Yuuki's right arm flares in pain. Pins and needles take over his nerves. It's uncomfortable and slightly nauseating, and he can't help but wince.

Prompted by the pain, emotional flashbacks threaten to flood his mind. Yuuki tries to distract himself by concentrating on what Andy's saying, but the flashbacks are too vivid, too recent. He's standing in the meeting room of the Arkala royal palace and yet he's also kneeled on the floor of the house he lived in in the city, pinned against the wall with his left arm twisted behind his back and his right arm being shot once (a warning), twice (a consequence), *a third time* –

"Yuuki."

Though it's low enough to avoid drawing anyone else's attention, Kyle's murmur of his name is enough to yank him out of the memory. If he's speaking then he's not gagged like he was less than a minute further into that memory, and his voice – clear and steady – reassures Yuuki he's not injured or in any imminent danger. There's no way that flashback can be reality again if that's the case.

Kyle's safe, in other words. If Kyle's safe, then Yuuki's safe too.

But it's a losing battle, believing that.

You think you're both safe? questions the voice of Yuuki's PTSD derived anxiety. *He's still recovering from the head injury he sustained those couple of weeks or so ago. What happens if something else happens while it's still affecting him? What happens if someone tries to kidnap us again, or attacks us and we're powerless to fight back like last time, and the time before that?*

There's no guarantee it won't happen again. History repeats itself, and somehow Yuuki always ends up dragging others into whatever mess he gets caught up in. Every time: first it was Timothy and Joshua, then it was Kyle, and then Kyle again…

Without realising it, he's dug his fingers into Kyle's shoulder. Yuuki hastily withdraws his hand and curls it into a fist at his side instead.

"…so with all that in mind," Andy is saying, "it's likely we're going to be forced to base ourselves here for the next several weeks, maybe even months. I've sent some of the officers who sided with us when we confronted Taularh to various stakeout positions. They'll keep us informed of what's going on in the city and report to us any signs of incoming attack. They'll be rotating shifts with the officers remaining here for security around the palace.

"Until we can return to the city without the threat of attack or arrest hanging over our heads, the palace is our safest place to be."

Safest, he says, but not to the extent that we can lower our guard completely.

Yuuki wonders if he'll ever be able to lower his guard again. Hypervigilance is a curse enough on its own without it needing to be utilised as the survival mechanism the brain designed it to be. Constantly being on guard is exhausting, draining, and Yuuki's beyond tired of this constantly feeling on edge. It's wearing him thin.

But at least it isn't such a bad thing to be hypervigilant here: it keeps him in a state of caution he doesn't have to mentally prepare for; it keeps him ready for the unexpected; and it reminds him of one crucial thing to remember in these times.

Nowhere is safe.

2

After it's clear Andy has nothing more to add, everyone disperses. Charlie and Amelia are the first to leave with the mission of finalising and practising a validating speech. Andy calls Avi after him to help him carry in supplies. The two leave the room with a squeak of door hinges and floorboards creaking under their feet as they walk down the hallway. The other three head out soon after, leaving Timothy, Kyle, Yuuki and Susan alone in the room where they linger.

Timothy leans forward in his seat, props both arms up on his knees and leans his head into his hands. "I thought we had it."

Yuuki walks around Kyle to grab a now vacated seat. He spins it around with his foot and drops into it. Timothy's defeat is a shared one. Yuuki reciprocates it with silence.

"So…I'm not really clear then, after all?" Kyle asks quietly, shoulders tight.

Timothy sighs. "Technically, yes. Legally, no." He sits up again and leans back in the chair. "I'm really beginning to question the likelihood that the current laws have been made to be rigged against people in situations such as ours."

"No," Yuuki mutters. "It's just that those people are jerks."

Outside, the clouds shift and the light coming in through the windows dims. Kyle laughs at Yuuki's deadpan tone, though there's little mirth in it.

Susan taps Timothy on the shoulder. "I'm gonna take a nap," she says, voice congested with the cold she caught last week. She looks up at Yuuki, assessing. "Your arm giving you trouble again?"

"It's fine," Yuuki answers curtly.

Kyle betrays him with a raised eyebrow.

Timothy's wife's mouth quirks at Yuuki's responding expression. "Do you want me to get some more painkillers? You've probably run out by now, am I right?"

"Save them for someone who needs them," Yuuki says.

"You need them."

"Someone who needs them *more*. We don't have enough for me to be having them so often. I can manage without them. I can put up with it."

"I asked Andy to see if he could get some more painkillers while he was out, so you can't use that excuse," Susan retorts. "Yuuki, you're dealing with enough stress as it is. Give yourself some relief from that while we have the resources for it."

Too tired to argue any further, Yuuki relents. "Alright, then. But don't worry about getting them for me now. Go get some rest first. I can wait till later, or get them myself."

Susan muffles a cough in the crook of her elbow. When she lowers her arm, she nods wearily. "Okay then. You know where they are if you need them."

With that, Susan excuses herself and the conversation lapses into silence. In it, Yuuki feels the weight of their defeat come crashing down all over again.

They thought they'd won something. But all the group has really gained is one small foothold in a giant rock wall with seemingly no more foot or handholds above them. And as they wait there, presently stuck, Yuuki can feel himself beginning to fall backwards. He can't rest. His PTSD is relentless and exhausting. No matter what he does, he keeps getting knocked down by one thing after another.

It's like everything he is and has done is coming undone.

It's unfair. It's unfair on Kyle, too. Yuuki fought so hard for Kyle's case, Timothy too, and now they find that the court won't even accept the evidence for it. No wonder Charlie didn't get very far as Kyle's official defender in the courtroom. No wonder Kyle gave up on himself, gave up on *hope*, so easily.

Yuuki narrows his eyes. All this talk of police corruption suddenly has his mind whirling with a renewed suspicion. "Timothy," he says. "Do you reckon, with Ninao, they haven't done any more investigating on *purpose*? As in like, not bother with looking into it more because they don't want the Peace Forces looking bad if they find out the people who attacked us were actually also Peace Force officers?"

Timothy grunts. "Once I would've argued, but now I must say I think I agree with you. Though we don't know for sure those men were PFOs."

"Maybe that's because they don't want us to know for sure."

Which raises the question – was there perhaps something else going on behind the scenes that they didn't know about? Was there another reason for the Ninao kidnapping besides the Youth Rehabilitation Trust potentially marking Yuuki as rebel to Taularh's reign? Yuuki's unnerved to realise he's starting to fear there might be.

But if there was, it might be near impossible to find it out. The people involved in all this have proved themselves well-versed in covering their footsteps. Yuuki might never know.

Kyle's brow creases. "Did they do any investigating at all?"

Yuuki shakes his head.

"They did some," Timothy corrects, "but only enough to cover themselves during news reports and interviews. The most they did for us was monitor the vicinity of our homes and Yuuki's hospital room for a couple of weeks after the incident. Security was tighter for our family during the three days when Yuuki was missing – in between the incident at the office and when we finally found and were able to rescue Yuuki. So I'm guessing there had to be at least *some* genuine effort going on there. From the PFOs not affiliated with the corruption, that is."

Yuuki's throat tightens. "They tightened security but didn't do so much about looking for me."

Confusion clouds Kyle's face for a moment. "But then how did...?" He tilts his head questioningly, but Yuuki averts his gaze and fixes it firmly on the floor. "How did they find you, again?"

"Andy gave us a tip," Timothy murmurs. "I don't know if you remember him telling us that first night he joined us, at the cave?"

"Oh y-yeah..."

"Joshua and I ended up searching for Yuuki ourselves. It was in the middle of that that we got the anonymous leak of co-ordinates. We were unsure of how much caution we should be responding with, but I think – seeing as it involved us and that it had been a full three days since Yuuki went missing – ...we were a bit reckless."

Yuuki lifts his gaze to stare at him, pleading him to stop. Timothy's eyes flick to his, and the horrible memory reflected there is enough to reassure Yuuki that Timothy doesn't wish to recall it any more than Yuuki does – which, at the end of the day, is not at all.

"At the end of the day," Timothy concludes slowly, "whoever's in charge of the investigation was probably called to bury it, with the excuse of having more urgent cases needing investigating."

Yuuki forces out a laugh. "Or they could've just been putting on a show to make it seem like they cared."

The cynicism loaded in his tone has Timothy frowning deeply. Yuuki tries to brush off the concern but instead feels a pang of guilt. He bows his head and lets his hair shield his expression for a moment.

"Sorry," he murmurs. "I'm just…"

Yuuki's unable to finish the sentence. He doesn't know what he is, what he's feeling. Frustrated? Tired? Overwhelmed? All of the above and something else, something more?

Timothy briefly rests a comforting hand on his shoulder. "It's okay." *It's been a rough few months…past year…for you. It's okay to be in over your head trying to process it.*

"It sounds like what they did to me," Kyle whispers. He clears his throat. "There were Peace Force officers who k-knew I hadn't done it. Like Jeff and Deborah. They'd been the ones to send Daniel after me first, and then when the whole thing required an investigation they did nothing e-except sit quietly keeping secrets. And Yuuki, when you were kidnapped, they knew where you were – they have to have, if Andy knew – and yet they chose to remain silent 'bout it.

"How'd they manage to keep everything so quiet *both* times?"

Timothy exhales slowly. "It definitely seems suspicious when you put it that way."

A sudden insistent chirping snatches their attention. Yuuki's heart rate accelerates, images of being attacked at Timothy's old Ninao office always fresh in his mind. But when he looks in the direction of the triggering sound it turns out to be a sparrow, not a man. After seeking shelter and finding none, the bird wheels and darts out of sight.

"Are you thinking there's a connection?" Yuuki asks when his heart's settled down. "Between what happened at Ninao and what happened to you? Besides it just being the Peace Forces involved?"

Kyle hunches his shoulders a little. "It's…it was just a thought."

Timothy says, "I think it's safe to say there is some sort of connection between the two. Andy said Jeff was involved in the kidnapping, and he was also involved in your case, Kyle. Then there's Deborah." He glances at Yuuki. "Though she wasn't, as far as we know, involved in the Ninao incident, she was there at your house when she hurt you and tried to kidnap Kyle, and she was with the two guys you said you recognised from Ninao."

"What rank were Jeff and Deborah?" Kyle asks.

"Same as Andy, I think. Jeff was, at least."

Yuuki says bitterly, "When Deborah came to my house, she bragged about being Jeff's lead interrogator. Whatever that means in terms of rank."

"I think she might've been above?" Kyle fidgets with sleeve of his jersey. "When Jeff caught me at the Checkpoint A hut, h-he and Andy seemed to regard her as slightly outranking them?"

Timothy frowns. "I doubt she would've been higher than a commander. She might've been working as part of a separate agency, if you think about it. One working more closely with Taularh, even. I wouldn't be surprised if she was part of some sort of special task force assigned by Taularh to go about these things."

Yuuki raises an eyebrow. "Under the guise of being a part of the Peace Forces?"

"Technically it could still count as Peace Force. Managing threats to Taularh's reign and quietly dealing with those deemed a risk? Seems like it fits the definition of a Peace Force officer to me."

"'Deemed a risk', huh? Like us."

Timothy hums.

None of them want to think about what could've happened to Kyle if Deborah had gotten another chance to deal to him. She almost had at the hut. Who knows what she would've been willing to do to Kyle to get the cooperation she wanted out of him? They've seen how effective and efficient her plans are. They've also seen and experienced how helpless it is to be ensnared in them.

Timothy nudges his glasses up the bridge of his nose. He pinches the shadows beneath the inside corners of his eyes. "I wish we knew who's behind all of this, who's orchestrating this. Sure would make exposing them and defending ourselves a lot easier."

They're at a loss here with what limited information they have. At this rate, they'll continue to be oppressed and the truth surrounding them will continue to be suppressed and replaced by white lies. Meanwhile, the Peace Forces will continue using corrupted means in their peacekeeping efforts, whether they're aware of it happening or not, and people like Yuuki and Kyle will have to suffer because of it.

Bringing it all to light is what they need to do to stop it, but any attempt at doing so would be immediately shut down. They'd need to expose everything all at once if they wanted any chance at succeeding, or at least be able to bring *something* to the table that can't be covered up so easily. Unfortunately they aren't in any position to properly investigate.

Deep in a profound sense of helplessness and thoughts leading nowhere, Yuuki stares blankly at the wooden floorboards in front of his feet. Timothy's doing much of the same.

Neither of them notice the contemplative flash in Kyle's eyes.

3

Old books, some worn and some seemingly never read. The palace library is filled with them, though they're likely more a collection of King Fahlu's than they are of Taularh's. The air has a certain musty quality to it, and there's dust gathering on the shelves. It seems this place was at least dusted and aired out while Taularh was here, but not recently.

Not since we killed him. Kyle doesn't like to linger on that thought.

He weaves in and out of the aisles of bookshelves, searching. The archives he's looking for he finds near the back of the library. Conveniently, that's also where Sam and Joshua sit at a table messing around with a laptop and everyone's phones.

So much for going about this on my own, Kyle thinks.

He's somewhat annoyed, having hoped to keep this researching private – at least until he can be sure he isn't making a fool of himself, looking for clues in a place where actually *trained* people have certainly already looked and found none.

Exactly what clues he's hoping to find in newspaper article, he has no idea, but maybe this isn't so much about finding answers as it is about reminding himself. He scans the boxes lined up neatly on the shelf before him. After finding the most recent collection of papers, he traces the dates back to the month he's looking for. Kyle's skin chills as he finds it: *June, 12-Tau*. Copies of all the newspapers containing articles about the Ninao kidnapping case are in there.

Those are exactly what he's after.

Kyle reaches up to grab the filing box, but his fingers won't grasp the filing box properly and it falls with a loud *thunk* on the wooden floorboards. He winces and bends down to pick it up with a hiss of frustration at himself. Recovery takes time, he understands that, but he's had enough of all these things still affecting him from his head injury.

"You all good there?" Sam asks from her seat at the table. When Kyle glances in her direction, he sees her staring at him over the laptop screen in mild curiosity.

Kyle grimaces. "I'm good, thanks."

In truth, he's not, and it takes a few failed attempts before his fingers work enough to get the filing box it up off the floor into his arms. Thankfully Sam doesn't call him out for it, instead jerking her chin in the direction of the filing box.

"What are you looking for?" she asks.

Kyle hesitates, regarding her warily. He glances between Sam and her older brother, weighing up whether or not to tell them in case they tell him it's stupid, just as his mind's telling him. But considering the subject he's researching, as well as all they've been through together over the last couple of months, it's highly unlikely they'll react in such a way.

He trusts that they won't.

Breathing out slowly, Kyle carries the filing box over to the table and sets it down beside the scatter of smartphones lying all around the laptop.

He spins the filing box around so that Sam and Joshua can read the month and year written in red permanent marker on the spine.

Joshua's eyes flash.

"Ninao," Kyle says with a small nod.

While he finds the wording he's looking to describe what he's doing, without any needless stumbling through an excessive amount of words, Kyle shifts the box to the side and opens it. The particular date he's looking for is at the start of the month, so he digs right to the bottom of the newspaper pile. He stops when he finds the issue dated *June 5, 12-Tau.*

Kyle tugs the newspaper out of the pile. "I wanted to see if I could find anything that might give us a hint as to who's behind all this. What happened to Yuuki, what happened to me – I think there might be a connection between the two? I thought m-maybe if I read over the articles again we might be able to see something. I know it's probably stupid, but…I don't know."

The chair Sam's sitting on creaks as she leans forward and hooks a finger over the edge of the box. She drags it closer to her, half-shuts the laptop and fishes out another newspaper. "You'll want to be looking at this one."

Right, the kidnapping happened on June 5 so they wouldn't have had written any article on it until the next day, on June 6. "Thanks…"

It's on the headlines. Discomfort coils in Kyle's stomach.

June 6, 12-Tau
Kidnapping at Ninao Law Office: One Man Missing

One man is missing after an assault at Ninao Law Office yesterday. The incident occurred at 12.35pm yesterday, with twenty-four year old youth detention officer Yuuki Takahashi kidnapped from Judge Timothy Harrison's office within minutes of the assault. Takahashi's current whereabouts remain unknown.

The four assailants, yet to be identified, also attempted to kidnap Harrison and his son, twenty-year-old Joshua Harrison. Fortunately, the father and son's quick thinking alerted people nearby of the kidnapping in time for Peace Force officers to thwart it. The two suffered minor injuries but were otherwise unharmed.

Peace Forces have teamed up with the Arkala Search and Rescue team to locate Takahashi. Peace Forces are investigating the scene of the incident for any clues that may suggest Takahashi's location and or the location of the four perpetrators.

If you know something that could help to track down Takahashi's whereabouts, Peace Forces ask that you do so confidentially either by calling the national police services line or approaching a Peace Force station directly. Thank you.

Kyle frowns hard. He turns the page but there's nothing more overleaf. "That's it? I thought there was more."

With a grunt, Joshua rubs a hand on the back of his neck. "They mentioned more in the news on TV, but not much more."

"I was just talking with Yuuki and Timothy. They did say that there wasn't much effort put into the investigation, but for some reason I thought the news reports at least covered more than this."

The expression in Joshua's eyes grows dark. "They didn't elaborate on much. Pretty sure all accounts besides mine and Dad's witness statements were disregarded. I mean, they failed to mention that I was thrown in the boot of the car Dad was tied up in. It's like they were trying not to draw everyone's attention to the incident by not going into detail about it."

Kyle feels the blood drain from his face. "What?" He'd thought it was only Yuuki who the kidnappers had gone to such lengths with, not Timothy as well. "Did they…did they tie you up as well?"

"Hmm? Oh – nah, I was an extra." Joshua's mouth quirks. "They didn't bring enough rope, apparently. Boot was enough, they thought – until I kicked out both tail lights."

"It's because they weren't expecting you there," Sam murmurs, studying the cover of the laptop. "When they went in there to get Yuuki and Timothy, they weren't expecting a third person to be around the corner about to try to stop them."

"Saved us, really," Joshua remarks.

Kyle swallows. *Saved most of you,*

Hearing it all for the first time, Kyle can't help but stare at them in astonishment. These kinds of details would usually be in the news, right? Didn't reporters generally cover this kind of thing? Of how fortunate victims made their escape? But instead the focus was all on Yuuki remaining missing, Peace Force investigations turning up no evidence as to who the perpetrators could be, and the assumption drawn that Yuuki was targeted because of the Youth Rehabilitation Trust.

He can see it now, what Yuuki was talking about: this lack of coverage was deliberate. It's hard to distinguish exactly what that feels like to think about.

"One thing I don't get, though," Kyle wonders aloud as the thought comes to him. "How come they tried to kidnap Timothy as well? Wasn't whoever it was after Yuuki? Because he set up that that charity or something?"

The corner of Sam's mouth pulls. "That's what we all *think*, anyway."

"Well, Dad helped him through the legal stuff," Joshua says. "If they saw Yuuki as a rebel to Taularh's rules when he set up the Trust, then they could've seen Dad in the same way. A judge actively disagreeing with the laws he studies?" He grunts. "Although I don't see how 'Youth Rehabilitation Trust' echoes any sound of rebellion or whatever from it. And that's not even mentioning that the Trust was a charity, for crying out loud."

Kyle's brow furrows at the tense. "'Was'?"

"Yuuki signed off the management of the Trust to someone else while he was in hospital. He realised pretty early on that he wasn't going to have the energy or headspace to think about it for a good while."

"Is there anything happening with it now?"

Joshua crosses his arms over his chest and exchanges a glance with Sam. "I'm not sure. He had a few sponsors who kick-started it, but I'm not sure if they're still sponsoring it. They might've decided to withdraw from donating after hearing what happened to Yuuki. You know, with what happened to him due to his involvement with the Trust."

"Chickens," Sam mumbles, but the hard look in her eyes says she thinks otherwise. *Good call.*

This is all so messed up, Kyle thinks. He folds the newspaper back up and returns it to its place in the box. As he pulls out the next one, he can't help but wonder if there's more to what the Peace Forces were trying to hide – kind of like with his own case, with how Jeff was in the middle of hunting down Amelia. If that's true though, in that there *is* more to the story than the one they think they know, then it's going to take a lot more investigating to figure out than simply reading through newspapers.

Still, got to start somewhere. Right?

The next article, issued June 7 – the second day Yuuki was missing – essentially just builds on the first. It features on the front page again, this time with the headlines reading, *Security Tightened Around Harrison Family Home, Takahashi Still Missing*. The article mentions the Peace Forces upping security around the Harrisons' home like Timothy had described and includes a comment from Timothy about how alarming the whole experience was, but otherwise just reiterates what the previous day's paper said. It finishes curtly saying that the Peace Forces are still searching for Yuuki's whereabouts and asking for any further information the public might be able to give them.

"They made it seem like they really were out there searching for him," Kyle murmurs, astounded. "But…they weren't, were they?"

Joshua grimaces. "We could've easily fallen for the illusion that they were, what with the officers they stationed outside our house. But… I don't know, I guess Dad and I had a bit of survivor's guilt going on too. We felt guilty we'd made it out of there and Yuuki hadn't."

"So you wanted to make it up to him by finding him yourselves."

"Yeah."

"I think we kind of sensed it too," Sam says. "Even if we didn't fully realise it at the time, it sure *felt* like the Peace Forces weren't doing enough. Mum said we were just wound up from the whole thing and that the

29

search and rescue team were doing their best, and that we needed to stay calm and let them handle it. I think she was just trying to make sure we didn't do anything stupid."

Joshua raises his hands in the air. "I have no idea what you mean."

Kyle watches with amusement as mischievous grins grow on their faces. The joy in their expressions quickly fades, however.

"Only it was pretty futile, what we ended up doing." Joshua murmurs. "We wouldn't've found Yuuki if it hadn't been for those co-ordinates Andy gave us. I mean, where on earth do you look for kidnapped and missing person when you also have no idea who took him in the first place?"

Sam grunts. "And those who *did* know probably influenced the search. They probably sent those the search team to look for him in all the places he wasn't."

Kyle thinks of Yuuki lying there bound up in that shed for three days while all this was happening and he feels sick to the stomach. Another parallel between his case and the Ninao one: Kyle was deliberately kept from being found not guilty just as Yuuki was deliberately kept from being found where he was. He wonders if Yuuki's already made this connection after their discussion. For Yuuki's sake, he hopes he hasn't.

Not wanting to linger on the thought, Kyle hastily drops the newspaper on the table and grabs the next one: June 8, the third day of Yuuki's ordeal and the day on which Timothy and Joshua found him.

This next article speaks a shallow urgency when appealing for any information regarding Yuuki's whereabouts. Concern is raised over Yuuki's condition and statistics are given on the probability that he will be found uninjured or even still alive after so many days missing. The probability significantly decreases with each passing day after that 72 hour mark, or as the interviewed Arkala Search and Rescue team leader says, with each passing hour.

Last year, Kyle hadn't been anything more than mildly concerned hearing this. Though he certainly hoped that the guy called Takahashi was found, he hadn't experienced the gut-wrenching angst the Harrisons would've been feeling. Back then Yuuki Takahashi had been no more than a name and picture in a newspaper.

Pulling out the paper issued June 9, Kyle doesn't bother reading the headlines. He knows what's happening. He isn't, however, prepared for the spear that stabs straight through the chest nor the way it paralyses him from the moment it strikes.

He'd anticipated feeling sickened by reading this, now that he knows Yuuki and has come to regard him as a close friend. He hadn't anticipated it being the news of Yuuki's survival rather than the news of his disappearance that gets at him the most. In particular, it's the pictures accompanying the article that do it. A nervous glance at Sam and Joshua informs him that it's the same for them.

On the front page are two pictures: one featuring an old battered and rusty garden shed, and the other a person lying on a stretcher being loaded into an ambulance, their face obscured by an oxygen mask and the paramedic holding it in place. Black hair peeks out from behind the paramedic's hand.

Shaken, Kyle loses the grip he had on the newspaper and it slips out of his hands. He wants to blame the lingering effects of his head injury.

31

Not knowing if his legs are steady enough to bend down and pick the newspaper up off the floor, Kyle leaves it fallen as it is.

Kyle remembers this. He remembers everyone talking about it. The story was all over the news and social media, and the subject of almost everyone's conversation at school. He remembers Yuuki's last name being mispronounced over and over and having to stop himself from correcting each time, *"it's ta-ka-ha-shi, not ta-ka-HASH-i."*

But he doesn't remember it hurting so much.

The mild concern and empathy he'd felt back then now all morphs and melds itself into something far more intense.

He knows Yuuki in person now. Kyle's seen the severe stress he has to deal with as a result of what he went through. The media might've moved on after a couple of updates regarding Yuuki's recovery in hospital but Yuuki, because of his PTSD, isn't able to do that.

None of them really can: not Yuuki, not Timothy and not Joshua. Because that kind of thing can't simply be moved on from. Perhaps that's why Kyle's doing this 'research', then. To find answers, to help them find closure in the hope that they can.

But Kyle's research turns up nothing. It's not like he was expecting to really find anything, but it still feels mildly disheartening. Closure won't heal them, and it won't relieve Yuuki of having PTSD, sure. But it could at least bring them one step closer to making sure Yuuki doesn't get hurt like that again. Like any of the times he's been hurt, in fact.

"Guess I won't be finding anything with this, huh," he mumbles aloud.

Across the table, Sam frowns. "We actually started researching ourselves," she says. "God knows there wasn't much, if any, investigating being done by the Peace Forces behind the scenes. Joshua had to go back to studying at uni, but before he did we compiled a whole bunch of stuff onto a USB drive. I tried to see if I could find more after he left but then Dad found out and basically shut the project down. He was worried about what might happen if we were found snooping."

She pauses, scratches the back of her neck and returns to fidgeting with her sleeve. "After what happened with him and Yuuki investigating your case, I can understand now why he wanted to keep us quiet about it."

Kyle quietly digests this. He's starting to feel a little dizzy and nauseous, and not just from the topic at hand and the information he's learning. He ignores it. He'll need to go lie down soon but he's not quite ready to be left alone with such a torrent of screwed up thoughts.

"Do you still have the USB?" Kyle asks.

Sam shakes her head. "Not on me. I left it back at home. We were in such a rush to pack what we needed when we left to get to Yuuki's in time. I didn't think to bring it."

Before *that* series of emotional flashbacks assails him, Kyle asks, "What's in it, exactly? The USB, I mean."

Joshua looks at Sam, thinking. "All the photos and video evidence I took, digital copies of things like our witness statements, Yuuki's medical records from the hospital…"

"You…you t-took photos?" Kyle swallows down the nausea rising in his throat. "Why?"

"Evidence. To make sure no one decided to write us off as suspects in the kidnapping." When the horrified expression doesn't ease from Kyle's face, Joshua winces. "I know. I hated it myself. But it was Dad's idea, and he's a judge. He knew what he was doing when he asked make record of it."

"It would've also been good for the prosecution," Sam says, "if the whole coordinate sending thing had been a trap."

Kyle pales at the thought. He knows the angle they're coming from.

Joshua nods. "Thankfully it wasn't a trap. I mean, when we went in there, at first we weren't a hundred percent sure we *were* gonna find Yuuki at all, or even *how* we were going to find him." He grimaces. "But yeah, since we were first on the scene and had no witnesses, we needed something besides our own word to show the exact state and situation we found Yuuki in. The video showed our live reactions of breaking the shed door open and finding Yuuki inside."

"No one could've faked those reactions," Kyle murmurs.

Joshua nods grimly. "I filmed everything up until Dad asked me to call the ambulance, after which I switched to taking photos and helping Dad with first aid." Softly then, for Kyle's sake, Joshua adds, "He was conscious when we found him, but barely. Honestly, I don't think Yuuki remembers much of us being with him out there. But we've never asked him and he's never said. Me and Dad though…yeah, we remember it very clearly."

Kyle takes a deep breath. He closes his eyes a moment and nods. "Yeah. I can imagine you would."

Abruptly, Sam clicks her tongue. "I just remembered – Marina gave me that list of all the on and off duty PFOs who had any potential of being one of the kidnappers."

34

"Who? Marina," Joshua says, "as in your PFO friend?"

"Yeah! Her team was in charge of investigating the case but they got called to drop it. She got suspicious after that and snuck me this massive comprehensive list of every officer on and off duty that day, where they were stationed and what they were doing."

Joshua blinks. "Oh. Wow. How on earth did she get a hold of that?"

"Without letting anyone know."

"Uh, yeah. She'd lose her job in an instant if they knew."

"And I'd be willing to bet," Kyle mutters, "that the ones who would be firing her would be the ones who would be losing *their* jobs if everyone knew. If it proved the corruption going on, that is."

Joshua sighs. "Not necessarily. The corruption stuff could be happening in every rank. Anyone could be involved, and they have ways around things they don't like. They'd just act like Marina was falsely accusing them."

All of a sudden Sam stills. It captures both Kyle and Joshua's attention, unsettling them as they wait in apprehension for whatever Sam's running through her head. The silence drags on.

"Sam," Joshua says. "Kill the suspense already."

"The corruption – it could be anyone, right? And these people who willingly participate in it – they'd have to be good at acting to be able to pull it off and not raise suspicions among the people around them, right?" Alarm flares in Sam's eyes. "We need to get that flash-drive."

Kyle stares at her blankly. "Huh?"

"That file Marina gave me, on it she highlighted a bunch of names she'd narrowed down into more likely suspects. We can't know for sure if any of them were involved in Ninao, but we can cross-check with Andy to see if any of them are here at the palace. You know, just in case."

Joshua's whole body tenses. "What do you...? Wait, you mean...oh, dear God."

Brain in overdrive, Kyle's vision blurs and tilts. *Here at the palace.* They haven't seen them themselves, but Sam's right: people involved in the Ninao kidnapping could very well be present at the palace with them without them knowing.

Before a passing vertigo can pull him to the floor, he grabs the edge of the table and leans his whole weight into the palm of his hand. A chair scrapes back and then there's two hands on his shoulders steadying him. Beside him, Sam uses her foot to drag a chair over and helps him sit down in it.

"Sorry," she says. "I should've said that in a better way."

Kyle grits his teeth against the wave of dizziness. "No, it's fine. It's not th-that, it's... just my head."

"You sure?"

"Yeah."

All three of them know that's a lie.

Joshua taps the table top, eyes wide and staring into space with a severe look on his face. "Andy would know though, right? He interviewed them all after the fight and sent the ones iffy ones back to the city."

"Andy might've done a good job at keeping himself undercover before he joined us," Sam says, "but that doesn't mean he can't be fooled by someone else's."

"True, that."

The worst of the dizziness subsided, Kyle raises his head to look up at Sam. "You said the USB with all the files on it is back at your house though, didn't you?"

Sam nods.

"Then there's no way we could get it even if we w-wanted to."

Joshua locks eyes with Sam, questioning, then looks away and bites his lip. "I can't believe I'm saying this, but technically there is."

"What?"

"I could drive us there."

Kyle slumps forward against the table. "Are you actually suggesting going into the city to get it?"

"I'm stupid, yes, I know. I'm aware."

"Were you not present when Andy was giving us that team talk earlier?" Kyle waits until Joshua meets his eyes and then stares at him hard. "I don't know about you, but I don't want to go back to prison."

Sam's eyes flash. "If it means we stop trouble from catching us unawares here, it's worth the risk."

The seriousness thickens the air to the point it's suffocating. Kyle's throat burns with all the emotional distress he had to endure while he was imprisoned. It'll choke him to death if he has to go through all that again.

"In all seriousness," Joshua says, voice tight, "I think this is something we need to do. It's okay if you don't want to come. I understand why you don't like the idea. But like Sam says, it's worth the risk."

Kyle tries to control his breathing. "You could get caught."

"We could. But the Peace Forces know it's far too risky for us to be in the city, so they won't be expecting us. They won't be wasting manpower on an excessive amount of security and patrols because of that. So long as we don't run into some scheduled patrol, we're all good."

"And what if they set up a burglar alarm inside the house? Or some surveillance system?" Kyle counters.

Sam tilts her head. "I doubt they'd think that necessary since they know we're stuck out here. And as far as they know, there's nothing valuable enough in the house for us to need to run back in for."

"Yeah, that's what I was thinking," Joshua says. "They'd have patrols going about here and there in the streets every now and then, but until we show up in civilisation again ourselves that probably suffices."

"Are we going to tell Dad what we're thinking? Or Andy?"

"You think they'll let us go if we do?"

"Good point."

In other words, no – they won't be telling anyone.

Kyle exhales slowly. His emotions are conflicted inside of him, but his gut is telling him one thing: "Safety in numbers, right?"

Joshua and Sam exchange a glance. That mischievous grin returns.

"You're in?" Sam asks, her eyes gleaming.

I hope I don't end up regretting this. Kyle nods. "When are we going?"

4

Kyle spends the seven hours until rendezvous desperately trying to keep his anxiousness under control and internalised. Nine p.m. at the car park, they'd decided. He's just got to play it cool until then.

After he, Sam and Joshua leave the library, Kyle makes a point of avoiding everyone he can. He's not sure how well he'll be able to pull off pretending he's not about to do something stupid and reckless. He doesn't want to risk compromising the mission because of it.

There's one person in particular Kyle's worried about being caught out by: Yuuki. Two people, if counting Timothy, but Timothy's not as well versed in reading Kyle's body language as Yuuki is. Timothy might be a judge but Yuuki by nature is discerning. It wouldn't be surprising if Yuuki's hypervigilance adds to that too.

And so as much as he hates the symptoms of his head injury he's still experiencing, he finds himself mildly grateful for them. It means the shaking of his hands and the occasional slip up of speech can be passed as that, not as the nervous display they really are. There's also the remnant behaviours he'd been forced to develop to protect himself at his foster family's house, such as not allowing himself to eat until everyone else has. Everyone knows not to question it, and so no one bats an eye when Kyle slinks in late for dinner and well after mostly everyone is already finished.

Running into Yuuki around this time would be unavoidable, he'd thought. But Yuuki's not even here. Usually he stays and leaves when Kyle does, but tonight he's nowhere to be seen. The absence of a plunger left sitting on the table implies he hasn't even been here yet at all.

Kyle hopes that Yuuki's not ill. If he is, then Kyle's going to feel tempted to stay behind, for Yuuki's sake. He technically doesn't have to go along with Sam and Joshua tonight, after all. They did also say it was fine if he doesn't come.

But the thought of them going out there, just the two of them, makes him feel unsettled. 'Safety in numbers' is what he'd said earlier, but there's more to why he'd said it than just common sense: whenever something really bad has happened to him and Yuuki, it's always been just the two of them.

Sam and Joshua will be safer if there's a third person going with them. If Kyle's got to be that third person, then that's what he'll be. And if it turns out he needs to stay behind for Yuuki's sake, then he'll just have to ask the two siblings if they don't mind postponing their mission until another day.

If, of course, it comes to that.

When Kyle goes to get his new second-hand jacket Andy supplied him with, he finds Yuuki in the infirmary napping. His presence is no more than a dark shape lying on his stomach on top of the duvet, and Kyle – thinking he's awake – flicks on the lamp that sits on the table between their beds. As it turns out, Yuuki's actually fast asleep.

Startled, Kyle hastily turns it back off. His heart pounds. He stands rooted to the spot, waiting for Yuuki to wake at any second, mumble something in irritation or flinch at Kyle's unheard entrance. But Yuuki doesn't even stir.

Concerned, Kyle nervously creeps forward until he can see Yuuki's face more clearly. There's nothing notably wrong. Though it's hard to tell in the lamp light and that of the night light by the door, Yuuki's skin tone doesn't appear to be any paler than it has been. His breathing is normal and easy. When Kyle raises a hand and softly touches Yuuki's forehead, his fingers find a normal level of warmth and no sheen of sweat that might suggest a fever.

I'm worrying over nothing, Kyle scolds himself inwardly. Still, he can't help but feel anxious. Selfish, even. Maybe it's because he's afraid he might be unintentionally neglecting Yuuki when he needs Kyle with him. That could be another reason why he feels so guilty about going on this USB-fetching mission. Thinking about that further, he realises why that guilt is so heavy in the first place.

It's because he blames himself for Yuuki's condition.

The shadows beneath his eyes are dark, charcoal smeared beneath both bottom eyelids. They weren't this prominent the day Kyle first met Yuuki a few months ago. And seeing him as he is now, sleeping seemingly without any nightmares where sleep usually evades him altogether, Kyle knows Yuuki must be feeling absolutely shattered.

What have they done to you? is the first question in his head, but then bitterness washes over him. His eyes take in the remnant limb of Yuuki's right arm, the stretched lines beneath his eyes and the way the sides of Yuuki's face have thinned. He didn't look like this in their first meeting.

41

Kyle tightens his grip on the jacket. *What have I done to you?*

Before he leaves, Kyle takes the pen and paper lying on the table, scribbles a messy note and tucks it beneath his own pillow. He checks it's sticking out a little so that it's noticeable but not in plain sight in case it's found before he's left with Joshua and Sam. He then takes a spare blanket from the chair on the other side of the room. Somehow Yuuki doesn't wake even as Kyle lays it out over him, though as the blanket settles over his body he shifts a little and groans.

With a deep breath, Kyle sets the pen and paper back down, dons his jacket and leaves.

"Are we really doing this?"

Joshua tests the switch on his torch. "Seems like we are." Satisfied, he slips it back into his pocket. He precedes to double check the multiple pockets of his jerseys and jacket for everything else he has on him. "If you're having second thoughts, all goods if you want to back out. It would be good to have you come along with us, but I know your head's still bothering you, too. So no biggie if you'd rather not come."

"N-no," Kyle says, "I do want to come. I just…" He swallows and shifts his weight from foot to foot. "It feels like we're doing something *really* bad, and the consequences of us getting caught *are* really bad and I seriously do not want to end up back in prison. You know I don't say that lightly."

His heart races every time he thinks about what'll happen if they're caught out there. Scenes run through his mind as his imagination takes over and brings that anxiety to life – his brain warning him, preparing him, *reminding* him of the various possible outcomes that could become of this.

This isn't general anxiety, after all.

"But like you said earlier," Sam murmurs, "safety in numbers, right? More people means more eyes to watch each other's backs. It'll be better that way."

Kyle grunts. "That's what I keep telling myself."

With a sharp exhale, visible in the night air, Joshua brandishes a set of car keys. "Alright. Everyone good to go?"

"Did we leave a note to say where we're going?" Sam asks, glancing between them.

"I did," Kyle answers. He shivers.

"I was going to leave one on the table in the library, but after our conversation, I didn't feel comfortable letting whoever wanders in and sees it know what we're up to. Last thing we want is some PFO who isn't really on our side seeing it and letting a patrol in Two Lakes know we're coming."

"I left a note on my bed under my pillow. I don't know if Yuuki will see it when he wakes up, but it's there."

Joshua gives him a thumbs up. "Sweet. And you've got our phones, eh, Sam?"

His sister nods.

"Cool. That's us, then. C'mon, let's go."

"Yeah," Kyle mutters as they start crunching the rest of their way across the gravel to the vehicle Joshua's chosen. "Before I have second thoughts."

The car is at the end of the row of Peace Force vehicles, between the last of the four-wheel drives and Harrisons' car retrieved from the country house. It's not the Harrisons' car they head towards though – it's the common, nondescript one that is Charlie's. They hadn't gone with the family car as it would've been too likely that Timothy would've noticed them taking the keys. Unfortunately, they underestimated Charlie in the process.

They haven't even reached the car before a fourth set of footsteps join the gravel crunching and an amused yet weary voice calls out to them from behind. "And where do you lot think you're going?"

5

The three of them skid to a halt. Kyle's blood spikes with adrenaline. The guilt that washes over him isn't misplaced in the least. Sam stops beside Kyle sharing the same frustrated expression as her brother.

In front of them, Joshua throws his head back in defeat. "Charlie. What are you doing here?"

The older man raises his eyebrows. "Me? Oh, I just saw you three heading out for a bit of fresh air and I thought I'd join. If you don't mind, of course."

"Maybe another time? We're, uh…not exactly going for a walk, as you can see."

"Oh, yes," Charlie says. He chuckles. "I'm quite aware."

Sam digs the heel of her shoe into the gravel. "So…guess our mission's a bust, guys. We tried."

An awkward, somewhat stiff silence falls between them. Kyle's heart is beating too fast from being caught, his breathing a little uneven. He waits for the yelling, the reprimand. His body is tense with the anticipation of being dragged back into the palace for a serious lecture or whatever kind of punishment Charlie and Timothy and Andy find suitable.

He's trying his best not to think too hard about that. It wouldn't be so bad if they'd actually succeeded in getting the USB first before getting caught, but now they have nothing to validate their reckless intentions with. Kyle doesn't know if they can count on Charlie to defend them here – just because he's been Kyle's advocate in court doesn't mean he'll be willing to let this slip. That's not even mentioning how Yuuki's going to react.

But what Kyle's not expecting is for the corners of Charlie's eyes to crease in mirth.

"So is that a no or a yes?" Charlie tucks his hands into his pockets, shoulders slouched casually. "'Safety in numbers', I believe I heard you saying? Care to take a fourth person along on this little adventure of yours?"

Kyle, Sam and Joshua stare at him in astonishment. Joshua clears his throat. "You mean, you want to come with us? Is that what you're saying?"

Charlie hums. "So long as I'm not going to disrupt any long thought-out plan you've constructed."

"Well, we don't…we don't exactly *have* a plan."

"As of yet," Kyle quickly adds.

Charlie shrugs. "Spontaneous suits me fine. Though we'd best think of one on the way, eh?"

Pressing the button to unlock the car, Joshua nods. He laughs. Orange light briefly flashes around them. "That's likely a good idea."

Their exit is not a quiet one. Charlie drives, having driven these windy corners and bumpy stretches of gravel road many times before. Sitting in the back with Sam, Kyle thinks he sees someone watching them from the edge of the car park as they drive off, but when he looks again there's no one there.

Kyle scowls at himself and rubs the back of his neck. *Great, now I'm seeing things.* He hopes the darkness hides the flush of embarrassment that spreads across his cheeks.

"You okay?" Sam asks quietly, noticing the stress on his face.

He blinks. "Yeah, I'm f-fine." He bites his lip at the conveniently timed stutter. "I'm fine."

He can't blame his head injury this time. It's simply his own anxiety getting the better of him.

"Alright, folks," Charlie says, shifting the car into gear and into motion again. "If we don't meet anyone we don't want to meet, we should be at the house in about an hour and forty-five minutes."

Sam sits up straight. "A how long?"

"Andy was telling me about a couple of roadblocks on the main roads outside of A'o that our lovely policing friends have set up. To avoid them we'll have to take a bit of a detour."

"We have enough fuel, right?"

"Enough to last us the trip there and the trip back. Hopefully we don't run into trouble, but by taking a detour we should, by rights, avoid it."

Kyle leans his head against the window. "On the road at least."

"On the road, at least."

Gravel gives way to tar beneath the tyres. Everyone breathes a sigh of relief as they at last pull out onto the open road. The road is clear – clear of PFO vehicles and any vehicles besides theirs, full stop – so Charlie puts his foot on the accelerator and brings them up to speed.

Kyle gazes out the window at the native trees flashing by, these ones characteristic of northern Arkala. He hadn't realised until now just how far out they'd come. They'd hiked through forests to get to the palace but it feels different when travelling via the road. Even though he knows where the royal palace is on the map, somehow it didn't feel like they travelled as far from the city as they did.

Coming into the city, beneath street lights and on roads signposted with weather warnings and Peace Force announcements, makes the feeling of just how removed they've been from civilisation even more known. Familiar streets look foreign through a lens of shifted perspective and circumstance. It's something Kyle's experienced before, one day out of prison and still dressed in his prison clothes – the day Yuuki took him to his home from Harrisons'. It's a strange feeling.

Kyle turns his face away from the window when they drive past his foster home where he used to live. He doesn't look when they pass Village Park either. He's not sure if he'll be able to keep his rising anxiousness under control if he does. He's nervous and feeling sick enough as it is. Flashbacks and thinking about all that isn't going to help in the least.

Everyone's holding their breath as they turn down the last street to their destination. They've been lucky; they've yet to run into any trouble and the only Peace Force vehicle they saw on the way in was parked at a petrol station they drove by. Perhaps things would've been different had Charlie not taken them the long way in, but for all the warnings Andy gave them it almost feels wrong that they make it the whole way unseen and unpursued. It's uncanny, and more unnerving than it is relieving.

"Anyone else not sure about how they feel with how easy we got out here?" Joshua murmurs, vocalising Kyle's thoughts.

Sam leans sideways in her seat and peers over her brother's shoulder. "Well, it looks like there's police tape in front of the house. Guess that's something."

"Yeah, but all that shows is that they've been here. But there's like…no one around keeping watch. Did they seriously think we'd not be game enough to come back to the city?"

"It would cost them a lot of man hours," Kyle thinks aloud. "If they were going to prepare for us as though we might come back at any moment, then they'd have to PFOs stationed all over the city – A'o, Two Lakes…maybe not Ninao."

Joshua grunts.

Pulling the car over to the side of the street, close to the Harrisons' but still several houses away, Charlie hums. "It would make Ninao an ideal place to hide."

Joshua grunts. "Unless we get chased from the palace like we did the country house, I don't think any of us will want to head that way."

"It's likely the Peace Forces will have thought about that too," Kyle says. "Reverse psychology."

The four of them stare through the windshield at the house. Rain splatters their view, seconds later beginning to rain in earnest so Charlie flicks the window wipers on. The car engine rumbles.

Sam huffs out a breath. "Well…guess we're getting wet."

"Better cover for us," Joshua says. "And hey, look, guys! It's the water we forgot to bring on our trip with us!"

Kyle feels the corner of his lips curl in amusement.

They share another minute of silence, observing the scene around them – waiting, rather, for any sign of someone coming or any kind of reason they should abandon the mission. But there's nothing of such concern. The rain pours down. A cat pelts across the street, its fur gleaming in the headlights of Charlie's car. A blackbird lets out a loud squawk from a tree on the other side of the footpath.

Everything is, as far as they're aware, all clear.

"I'll drive you down," Charlie says, tone low and serious. He slips his phone out of his pocket, frowning at it dubiously. "You tested these things, right?"

Joshua nods. His eyes are sharp. "Works all goods. Sam and I tested the connection again before we left. The 'network', so to speak, that our phones are set up on now is exclusive to us. Any PFO with eyes – *ears* – on the cell phone networks won't pick us up."

Kyle blinks. "Oh, is that what you guys were doing when we were in the library this afternoon?"

"Yep. Took a bit of work getting them all set up, but we did it."

"Wait...can't they still track us via GPS?"

"That's already disabled," Sam answers. "Dad did that part of the job while we were at the country house. He had to turn the phones on to do it though, so that's probably how the Peace Forces caught wind of our location without physically coming by to scout the area first."

"So," Joshua says, "by rights, they don't know we're here."

"Yet."

"Hmm. Which is why we should go in now. We'll be wasting time if we sit here observing any longer."

Glancing at everyone to make sure everyone's ready, Charlie shifts the gear stick and they drive on. Sam undoes her seatbelt in advance, Joshua doing the same a few seconds later. Nervously, Kyle releases his as well.

Sam takes her own phone out of her pocket. "Kyle."

Kyle accepts the phone, cradling it between two hands. He tightens his fingers around it lest he accidently drop it. His nervousness increases. He sees Joshua adjusting the brightness level on his phone, and Charlie's phone sitting nestled between his thigh and the seatbelt on the driver's seat. It's all beginning to feel real now, what they're doing. As an afterthought, he wishes he'd brought his knife along with him. If the Harrisons' weren't so close to Village Park, maybe he might've.

When they reach the end of the street, Charlie doesn't stop, instead turning around in the cul-de-sac and driving up to where a reserve access makes a path between two houses to the reserve behind them – their entrance.

As soon as Charlie brings the car to a halt, Joshua, Sam and Kyle fling their car doors open and pull themselves out into the rain.

6

They slam the car doors and make a run for the reserve access. The walkway gets plunged into darkness when Charlie pulls away from the kerb, but they keep moving. Behind them, Charlie drives off back down the street to head to their arranged rendezvous point.

Since the streetlights and the lights shining through the windows of neighbouring houses are the only light they have to see by, Joshua pulls out his handheld torch and flicks it on ahead of them. They narrowly miss running through a large puddle. As they skirt it instead, Kyle wonders if splashing through it would've made much difference anyway. They're getting soaked in the rain as it is.

Joshua leads their way, guiding them left as they exit into the reserve. They head straight for a row of native trees. Their path has them jogging alongside them for a hundred metres before they turn in and duck into their cover. There's a half a minute of picking their way through the trees and slippery leaf-littered ground, and then they're breaking out into the Harrison family house back garden.

A sheet still hangs on the washing line. There's a rusty rake lying near a now unmaintained vegetable garden. Kyle almost trips up on it. The three of them stop by the back of the garden to collect the spare key buried here, and as Joshua sets about finding it, Kyle's hit with a sudden melancholy.

Since he only ever saw the interior and the front of the house, he doesn't recognise the Harrisons' home from this side. But Sam and Joshua do; this is their family's home, after all. The Harrisons abandoned this place willingly, Kyle knows, and when they abandoned it they'd done so for him.

He feels bad about it yet simultaneously grateful. Deborah would've gotten away with kidnapping him if they hadn't left when they did, but Kyle still can't help feeling ashamed. It's his fault the Harrisons had to leave here. It's his fault for inadvertently getting them involved a predicament that should've been his own to deal with the consequences of.

Stop blaming yourself for everything, Kyle reprimands himself. He watches as Joshua grabs a stick and digs a hole in the side of the compost pile. *When they made the choice to leave, it was because they were worried about something happening to me and Yuuki. Something like what happened with the Ninao incident – something they were already affected by and feared happening a second time.*

They were right – something did happen. And while Kyle and Yuuki were the primary targets of Deborah's attack, who's to say she wouldn't have stopped by here to come after Timothy as well?

Kyle doesn't like the realisation of just how likely that would've been.

"Aha! Guess they didn't think of the worms and beetles being accomplices too, huh."

The torchlight doesn't show Joshua's face, but his grin is audible. Mentally, Kyle laughs. Physically, he's too distracted by how much he's shivering to be able to express it. Emotionally, he's too distracted by trying to dismiss unwanted memories.

The three of them head over to the back door. By the time Joshua unlocks the door and yanks it open, they're all well and truly soaked. Their shoes squeak on the floor as they enter. Their dripping clothes leave small puddles in their wake. It's a trail of traces of them being here, but there's little they can do about it. *Get in, get out* is their mission plan at its most basic level; there's no time to be worrying about finding a towel.

No alarms are triggered on their entrance. The house is quiet – a peaceful yet haunted kind of quiet, the latter amplified by their nerves. The three of them stand still for a few heartbeats, doing nothing except for listening and shivering. Outside the rain comes down louder. They have to strain their ears to listen for noise that might be inside.

Deciding they're good to go, Joshua waves his hand. "Let's go."

Just as he takes the first step forward, both his and Sam's phone's ring with a heart-lurching vibrate. Joshua visibly flinches and Kyle nearly chokes on air. The phone Kyle has tucked against himself in his attempts to shelter it from the weather is lit up with Charlie's name.

Joshua gestures for Sam to move forward and raises the phone to his ear. Sam goes ahead and eases open the laundry door. After a pause, she slips out into the hallway.

Kyle follows them, pressing the green call button on Sam's phone and as he goes. His heart races. The darkness they move in is unyielding and unbearable. It reminds him too much of his prison cell at night. *You're not there*, he tells himself. *You're fine.* He has to force himself to focus on breathing and concentrate hard to hear what's being said.

He tunes back in in time to hear Joshua whisper, "Yeah, we're in. Making our way up to Sam's room now."

Sam and Joshua disappear upstairs as per the plan. Kyle remains on the downstairs, on guard. With Joshua's torchlight gone, Kyle turns on the torch on Sam's phone. He moves it about the room, scanning.

The light grounds him, calms him if only slightly. His eyes flick about the lounge, his shoulders tightening with every object the light lands on. Vaguely, he recognises the couch he'd slept on the night he stayed here, but everything is otherwise unfamiliar and it gives Kyle's mind opportunity to make him see people in the place of furniture.

But there's no one here. With Sam and Joshua upstairs, it's just him. Alone. In the dark. With only his thoughts and the anxious workings of his mind to keep him company. *To keep him sane.*

Kyle lies to himself that the shaking of his legs is just shivering. He knows full well it's not. *Just breathe. They'll be back down in a sec. Sam just has to find the flash drive and then we'll be gone. Just stay calm. We'll be out of here soon.* But this is too reminiscent of being in isolation, and there was no escaping from there.

He instead tries to distract himself with the grounding exercises he's learnt from Yuuki. It starts off near impossible. He can't see anything besides what the torch shows him in the dark, and focusing too much on his other senses only gives permission for his adrenal glands to go crazy. But he tries again, needing *something* to distract him lest he wind up having a panic attack.

Concentrating hard, Kyle focuses on finding the things that differentiate being here to being locked up in the cell: it had been cold in the cell where it isn't so cold in the house; his clothing is soaked with rain, something he hadn't been able to experience while imprisoned; he has light in his hands where he didn't back there; and he has friends nearby and there's no locked door between them to keep Kyle removed from them. He's a lookout, not a prisoner. He's the one monitoring, not the one being monitored.

Nothing really works though. His body's at the Harrisons' but his mind's back in solitary confinement at A'o Youth Detention Centre. Kyle even thinks he hears someone quietly fiddling with lock on the front door, something he sometimes heard on the worst of his sleepless nights. Of course, there'd been no one there; the door had stayed shut and no one had come in –

The front door opens.

Streetlights, the pouring rain, the silhouette of a *person*. From where he stands at the foot of the staircase, Kyle can see them. His eyes stretch wide, unblinking. He hastily turns the torch light off. The door closes, shut with such carefulness it's obvious this person isn't just here for a visit.

An involuntary noise of terror escapes his throat. His veins flood with adrenaline. Kyle covers his mouth, trembling.

The flashbacks don't have his mind trapped now.

"Kyle?"

He can't move. His legs are paralysed. His vision whites out and dizziness sweeps over him. He's too weak with terror – if he moves, he'll risk stumbling into something or his footsteps being heard.

"Shit, Sam. I think someone's here. We gotta hurry."

No light is turned on. A floorboard by the front door creaks.

56

"Kyle," Joshua says. "Can you tell us how many people are here?"

The phone volume is down low enough that it doesn't mask the person's footfalls approaching. There's just enough light coming in through the windows of the kitchen to be able to see the silhouette making its way closer.

They know I'm here. They saw the phone light on. They know I'm here. They know I'm here.

"Okay. Plan B. We're leaving from up here. Sam's – oh no, she's just found the USB so try get yourself up here and we'll –"

Kyle shoves the phone in his jacket pocket a moment before hands reach out to grab him.

7

Yuuki wakes with a jolt. Abruptly he pushes himself upright. The pillow gets dragged up beside him, his fingers curled tightly into the fabric of the pillow cover.

He stares across the room, wide-eyed and disoriented. This isn't his usual reaction to a nightmare. Usually he'll gasp awake mid-dream. Usually he'll remember, at least for the first minute or two after waking, what he'd been dreaming about and it would take several minutes after that to dispel the fear from the front of his mind.

Right now, there's none of that. Yuuki doesn't even think he'd been dreaming. No, this something else. He realises his hand's shaking then, and that his leg muscles are tense and he's agitated.

Why does it feel like something's wrong?

His first thought is Kyle. The bed opposite Yuuki's is empty, but that alone isn't a cause for alarm. Whatever time it is – it hadn't yet been dark when Yuuki settled down for a nap, so he's not sure – it's probably simply too early for Kyle to want to sleep yet. Yuuki's not the only person who can't sleep till late around here.

Stifling a yawn, Yuuki scrambles out of bed. Despite the grogginess of having just woken up, he's itching to run, or to flee, or something. He stumbles through the motions of getting his jacket on and mentally prepares to leave the infirmary. Staying here isn't going to help shake this anxiousness. He needs to find Kyle or Timothy or someone who can reassure him that the nervousness in his gut is a product of his own stress and nothing else.

Yuuki's about to leave when something catches his attention and he stalls. The blanket lying on his bed, the one that he'd just been sleeping under – he hadn't fallen asleep with it over him. Yuuki wonders for a moment if he just can't remember grabbing it, but no, he hadn't. He'd all but collapsed on the bed, pulled himself into a comfortable enough position and let his exhaustion claim him. He hadn't meant to sleep as long as he had – hadn't expected his brain would even let him – but he had, and so it must've been sometime during that nap-turned-sleep someone had laid that blanket out over him.

His gut tells him that it's something Kyle would do. Timothy might too, as would Susan, but Susan's sick and has likely made herself scarce, and Timothy probably wouldn't have come here unless he ended up getting concerned about Yuuki's longer than usual nap. It's then that Yuuki's gaze falls on the bit of paper sticking out from under Kyle's pillow.

Yuuki doesn't remember covering the distance. One moment he's standing by the door looking back over his shoulder, the next he's standing beside Kyle's bed reaching out to take the paper. His hand's shaking as he unfolds it.

It's a note. Yuuki narrows his eyes at the paper, at the unsteady handwriting scrawled on it. His stomach sinks.

To Yuuki – or whoever finds this

In case you're looking for me, I'm with Joshua and Sam. We've gone to the city to the Harrisons'. We'll be back late. Sorry we didn't tell you before, but it's an important mission and we didn't want to risk getting stopped from going.

We'll explain everything when we get back.

See you later,

Kyle

"Yuuki?"

Yuuki flinches. The light switches on, blinding after the softer light of the lamp and the nightlight. He squints, eyes adjusting, and finds Timothy staring at him with his eyebrows furrowed.

"Sorry, just came to make sure you're okay. Haven't seen you all night."

"Uh, yeah…" Yuuki lets out a shaky breath. "I-I…"

Timothy approaches slowly, carefully.

"Y-you haven't seen Kyle at all, have you?"

"No? Joshua and Sam aren't around either, so I figured they must be out on a walk or something together. They were hanging out in the library earlier."

Yuuki raises his hand to his face and presses his fist against his forehead. His palm is clammy, his fingers cold. The knowledge settling over his chest is colder.

"Hey…what's wrong?" Timothy asks.

Swallowing hard, Yuuki shakes his head. "They're not out on a walk."

Gritting his teeth, he shifts the note in his fingers and lifts his hand up in front of him. He locks eyes with Timothy as he does so, and the older man's concern suddenly bears more weight behind it. Timothy takes the note and uses both hands to flatten it until he can read past the creases. The infirmary is silent as he reads what Kyle wrote on it, so silent that Yuuki almost forgets to breathe.

Yuuki lets his arm drop back down to his side. He doesn't know what to do, doesn't know if there's anything they can do. If anything happens to Kyle, Sam and Joshua while they're out there like this note says they are, there's nothing anyone can do to help if they meet any trouble.

In other words, if they get caught, the three of them are basically screwed.

It's the first time Yuuki's ever heard Timothy swear.

8

Kyle rams his hands into the person's shoulder and shoves them backwards with all the strength he can muster. He's too shaky, however, and the push has little effect.

"Guys!" he yells. "We –"

The warning is cut off by a large hand clamping down over his mouth. Before the person can secure a grip on his clothing to hold him, Kyle brings a knee straight up into the guy's crotch. The hand slips away from his face.

He tries again. "Get out of here! Someone's here!"

Joshua and Sam already realised this but it's not them he's trying to warn – it's this person. *I'm not alone,* Kyle's trying to say. The man isn't deterred, however. He just hisses at Kyle's alerting the others and then lunges at him.

Kyle's tackled to the floor. The impact shocks him. His head smacks into the floor and he chokes on a gasp. He lies there, stunned. There's only enough time for him to draw in a breath before adrenaline surges through him and he's sent into a panic of fighting to keep himself from being pinned.

So much for this being a stealth mission, he thinks dimly.

It takes a great amount of adrenaline-fuelled thrashing and writhing, but finally Kyle manages to throw the man's weight off him. Unfortunately the shove lacks the strength he needed it too, and Kyle's barely able to get his feet under him before the guy reaches out, grabs his hood and yanks him back down to the floor.

"You ain't getting away this time," the man mutters.

Something about the tone of his voice has Kyle feeling freshly nauseous. It's like he's heard this voice before. While he can't determine from where exactly he's heard it, he knows for certain that the buried memory it's associated with isn't a pleasant one.

"Who the heck are you?" Kyle forces out.

"Someone who got tipped by someone who knew you were coming."

Kyle's too distracted trying to process those words. The man takes advantage of it.

A hand latches onto his wrist. With a spike of adrenaline, Kyle tries to twist his wrist free but finds he can't. Panic fills him. He lashes out with his free hand, but the man catches that too and wrenches it sideways. As he's rolled onto his back, Kyle swings his leg up and catches the guy in the elbow with his knee. Kyle's able to get his arms free again then, but the man makes his next move before Kyle has a chance to.

Tactics are switched. Instead of trying to restrain him, the man wraps one hand around Kyle's neck. Kyle freezes. The kick he'd just been about to deliver drops. A chill runs up his spine. Cold fingers tighten and the hand begins to press down, but it's nothing compared to the constricting fear that encloses Kyle's throat.

Flashbacks come – sickening ones. Daniel's gloves hadn't been cold but the fear had been. The memory of what happened at Village Park replays itself: memories of being pinned down, the handle of a knife forced into his hand, *trapped there,* and then –

An angry and mildly blood-curdling scream erupts above him. A grunt, and the weight bearing down on his throat vanishes. Kyle coughs. He weakly rolls onto his side, trying to gasp in air. Noise and movement surround him, but all he can do is lie there clutching at his throat, eyes wide, breath hitching.

Though it's too dark to get any proper aim, Sam's the one landing the most hits. All he can really see of her is a shadow, but she's an infuriated Harrison shadow at that. Sam doesn't even give the guy a chance to do as much as touch Kyle again.

Then one of Sam's hits misses and the man catches her in the abdomen. Kyle hears the sharp exhale as she staggers sideways. It's in that moment that Kyle's mind catches up to him. The stranger was about to strangle him, wasn't he? Harm is intended here, or at least threatened, and now Sam's directly in the way of it; even if it's Kyle who the man's after, Sam's standing directly between them both.

I need to do something.

Telling her to just leave him and run isn't an option – she won't listen if he does. He'll need to help her fight, then. Kyle reaches into his pocket. His heart lurches when he realises he forgot to bring his knife with him. Instead his hand falls on the only weight in either pocket: Sam's phone. That won't help him. Not unless he throws it, which he doesn't think Sam will appreciate.

But as Kyle gets to his feet, his legs shake. His palm grows clammy around the phone. When he gives his head an abrupt shake to flick his wet hair out of his eyes, a sudden light-headedness overtakes him. He tries to take a deep breath to steady himself, but it only makes him more conscious of the ghost pressure of the man's hand on his throat.

There's no way he'll be able to put up a decent fight like this. But they need a chance to run. How else is he supposed to get the man to leave Sam alone for long enough for them both to get out of here?

An idea occurs to him. He fumbles to get the phone out. Head spinning, Kyle jabs the home button. He squints hard, swipes the screen brightness all the way up high and hastily turns the phone away from himself.

It's sufficient a distraction. The man stalls. Instead of throwing a fist at Sam, he pulls the same hand up in front of his eyes to block the light. Kyle catches a glimpse of his face as he does so and the same unsettling fear returns.

Somehow he *knows* this man. Knows as in has seen him before, has heard him before. Kyle's skin chills more than the rain soaked clothing is doing. He catches himself on the side of the couch. A heartbeat later, he slips and crashes to the ground.

Danger! his mind screams, for reasons Kyle's not entirely sure. His brain remembers something he can't. It instils a terror in him that he can't explain.

Sam doesn't give him the option of digging through his memory on the Harrisons' house floor to figure it out. She grabs Kyle by one arm and hauls him to his feet.

Kyle's legs are weak. He's too shaky to walk straight. He's too dizzy.

It's a struggle to breathe let alone walk fast. Sam catches onto Kyle's difficulties soon enough and slings Kyle's arm over her shoulders. She wraps her other around his waist and pulls him forward, a strong support. On the verge of panic, Kyle focuses on that support – on that physical contact providing a point of anchorage in his inability to find any grounding.

Kyle's back prickles as he and Sam reach the stairwell. Their backs are exposed, he realises too late. Heart hammering, he grips Sam's phone harder in his hands. He squints against the light of Sam's phone in his hand. Before the man can reach them, Sam hastily releases Kyle, grabs her phone out of his hand and switches the torch light on.

She shines the light shines straight into the man's eyes. "Get lost!"

With a yell, the man freezes. While he's busy rubbing his eyes and trying to see again, Sam hands the phone back to Kyle and takes up her support again.

They clamber up the stairs as fast as Kyle's unsteady legs will let him, the weaponised torch light now used to guide their way upward. When they reach the top, Sam lets out a nervous breath.

"Do you trust me?" she asks.

Downstairs, a light switch is slapped on. The stairway lights up. Kyle can't get his voice to work to answer her, but the question might as well be rhetorical anyways.

There's no time for Kyle to give any words or nods in answer.

They run across the once organised chaos of a mess of Sam's room to the window. They need to leave, but they can't escape through any of the main entrances. Looking at the wide open window and judging by their current trajectory, Kyle gets the gist of what they're about to do.

Sam lets go of Kyle long enough to pull herself up onto the window sill. Pocketing the phone, Kyle pulls himself up beside her, feet braced and hand gripping the window frame. His stomach lurches. His instincts yell at him to find a safer way to get down from this second story window. But his body's filled with adrenaline to escape, Joshua is yelling at them down below to jump (he already has) and the man is now in Sam's room shouting at them to wait. This isn't safe, but neither is staying inside.

Sam grabs a hold of Kyle as they do, and Kyle a hold of her.

They jump.

Kyle's consciousness recalls a similar memory to this that his brain can't – of falling, of wrapping himself around the other as best he can to protect them. That's all the time he has spare to think before they slam into Joshua.

The impact drives the breath out of all of them. Kyle's head throbs, spins – almost as much as it did in the first couple of weeks after his head injury. He tries to get enough air into his lungs but it's hard. It scares him. They've got to keep moving and yet he can't tell up from down and he's on the verge of spiralling into a panic attack –

Sam rolls out of Kyle's arms and Joshua shifts out from under him with a groan. Kyle doesn't have time to process what's happening when the two of them take one of his arms each and get to him on his feet. His knees buckle. The world tilts.

"It's okay," Sam says. "We've got you."

They're moving. Running, even. Sam and Joshua end up having to support most of his weight with how uncoordinated he is, but they do it.

The rain increases its intensity. A house door slams. Kyle clenches his jaw tight against the panic. They pick up the pace. As best he can, he forces his legs to run with them.

They duck into the cover of the native trees and weave their way as best as they can through them and out into the reserve. "We're going where Charlie's waiting for us," Joshua shouts above the weather. "Just got to get to the other side of the reserve!"

They tear across the grass, feet slipping and sliding. They splash through great puddles of mud, water and grass, though since they're already drenched and cold they don't really pay that much heed. Kyle stumbles as they run through one such puddle. He's expecting to end up face planting into it, but Sam and Joshua tighten their grip on his wrists so that he doesn't. They pull him into motion again and a moment later they've resumed their pace again.

Kyle's fighting for breath by the time they reach the other side of the reserve. It becomes an effort to keep his head up. He doesn't register arriving at the car, only that the sound of an engine rumbling draws incredibly close all of a sudden. Their momentum stops. A door is opened. Joshua loosens his grip on Kyle's wrist but Sam doesn't, though she switches to wrapping her arms around his chest. In an awkward yet hurried action, she hauls him into the back of the car with her. Joshua helps manoeuvre Kyle's legs inside and then slams the door.

Sam slumps against the seat. Kyle shuts his eyes and lets his head fall back into Sam's lap, chest heaving. His ears are ringing. As soon as Joshua's in the passenger seat, another door slammed closed, Charlie chucks the car in first gear and they're driving.

9

Charlie is speechless, focusing solely on hightailing it out of the city. He drops the clutch on almost every gear change. Kyle bites back a groan of discomfort each time.

"May I…" Charlie begins as they pull out onto the highway at last. He clears his throat. "May I ask what went wrong back there?"

As they navigate their way back to the Kano-Hu'a Road, Charlie does a good job at maintaining normal speeds in spite of the urgency of their situation. It's somewhat calming, and it works to diminish the adrenaline still humming in the air between the four of them.

"Someone saw us leave," Kyle rasps. "Thought I was seeing things, but…"

Sam shifts in her seat a little. "What do you mean?"

Kyle hesitates. He contemplates sitting up, admittedly embarrassed to be using a female friend's lap as a headrest. But Sam seems okay with it and Kyle's not sure he trusts himself not to get motion sick. He's feeling bad enough as it is. Lying down as he is, legs propped up knees bent for lack of room to stretch out, it's easier to breathe and endure the dizziness.

In other words, it's better to stay as is.

"When we left," Kyle explains, "I thought I saw someone s-standing there watching us. Didn't see him next time I looked though, so thought…so I thought I must've been imagining it."

"You mean it was the same person?" Sam asks, bewildered.

"No, different. The man who attacked us just now said he'd been tipped, remember? I think that's who he might've been talking about – a spy or something at the palace."

"That would explain why you didn't get a good look at him, then. If there's a spy then they wouldn't want us knowing about it."

Kyle murmurs in agreement. "They obviously did a good job at hiding themselves. None of us saw anyone."

"You did," Sam points out.

"Yeah, but they made me think I was seeing things. They vanished that quickly."

Joshua heaves a sigh of exasperation. "They're trained in stealth, then. And here I was stressing back there that someone among *us* gave whoever that dude was a tip."

"I thought that too," Sam murmurs.

"No offence to us and out stealth capabilities, however. We're learning."

"I thought that you all would think that and blame me," Charlie says quietly.

"What?" Joshua exclaims. "Charlie, no."

Charlie frowns. "Well, you know. I show up just as you're all about to leave, ask if you don't mind me going with you. And then after I drop you all off so I can go wait for you on the other side of the reserve, that unfriendly, sneaky chap shows up and…" He coughs. "Never mind. You fought him bravely, Kyle. And Sam. I heard pretty much everything."

"Including me freaking out," Joshua mumbles.

Kyle risks opening his eyes but quickly decides that's a bad idea for now. "But I di'…I didn't…?"

"You all did," Charlie says. "You all did very well tonight. You evaluated the risks, prepared yourselves well for a spontaneous mission, and when you made a proper plan you took into account each other's needs. When things went wrong, you worked together to get yourselves out of there."

"We achieved the mission objective, too," Sam says, smiling. "I got the flash drive."

Joshua grunts. "Yeah, only after you found it again after you misplaced it. No wonder Mum always asked you to clean your room."

"It was dark, okay? And I hid the USB on purpose, so it was, you know, *hidden*."

"Hidden also to yourself isn't the point."

There's a brief lull in the conversation. In it, Kyle sighs. "D'you think Yuuki found the note by now?"

The lull turns into thickened silence. Dread taints the emotional atmosphere and Kyle fears it sharpen itself in his mind and stab him in the stomach.

"Won't be just him," Sam murmurs. "Dad will have definitely noticed we're gone. Mom, too."

Charlie hums. "Not to mention it's now past twelve. One of the patrolling security guards likely noticed the car's missing."

"Urgh, and it took us about two hours to get out here. We won't be

71

back 'till two, huh? They'll definitely have noticed we're gone."

A drop of water slips off Kyle's hair into one eye. Kyle shivers. "Think they'll be waiting for us?"

No one verbally answers, but the general consensus is clear: yes. Yuuki and Timothy will most definitely be waiting for them. And none of them – even Charlie who isn't drenched, injured or exhausted as Kyle, Sam and Joshua – are looking forward to finding out what kind of reception they're going to get when they return.

The group return to the palace just after 1.30am. Sam nudges Kyle awake as Charlie brings the car to stop. He blinks, confused, not realising he'd dozed off. With a groan, he rubs his eyes and pushes himself upright.

"We back already?" The unintended nap eased his dizziness, but now he's left feeling completely out of it.

Sam hums. "Yep."

Kyle lets his head drop, only to bring it straight back up again when the action restricts his breathing. He groans again, this time in mild irritation. "There ain't any way to teleport inside, is there?"

"I wish."

Before Kyle had started drifting, they'd discussed sending Yuuki and or Timothy a message to let them know they were on their way back. None of them had been particularly keen on it. The main reason they'd hesitated was because it would alert whoever received it to their secret mission.

But as it turns out, they'd already been found out – the many text messages and calls from Timothy silently bombarding each device had announced that clearly enough.

Yuuki found Kyle's note, in other words.

At least they know their phones survived the weather and their escaping.

Unsurprisingly, everyone's reluctant to move. The heater's been on the whole drive back, so it's warm inside the parked car. If he doesn't move too much, Kyle can almost forget about the uncomfortable sensation of damp clothing pressing against his skin. Knowing that Yuuki and Timothy are awaiting their presence only makes the physical process of moving even harder. Kyle looks around to see Joshua and Sam likely thinking the same thing.

In the end, it's Charlie who breaks them out of their reverie. "Better not keep them waiting," he murmurs, unclipping his seatbelt. He switches off the lights and the sighs. "Sooner we get out, sooner we'll be able to hit the hay."

Sooner we'll be able to get this over with, Kyle thinks. *And stop having to linger in this nervousness.*

Frowning, Sam slaps her hand on the door handle. She shoves the door open with a weak push and swings her legs out of the car onto the ground. "Oof, it's cold."

With the cold air rushing into the car, crisp and fresh and rain-laden in contrast to the stuffy yet warm interior of the car, she doesn't even need to announce it. It rouses the rest of them and one by one they get out, albeit grumbling, sighing and shivering as they do so.

Kyle crawls out Sam's side, staggering as he goes to shut the door. It only half-closes. He grimaces. It almost seems like too much effort to shut it properly. Maybe it is, because the moment he shifts his weight to put more power into his arm, one knee gives way. He braces himself against the car before he falls.

"Here," Sam says, coming in beside him. She gently takes the arm closest to her and Kyle lets her lift it over her shoulders. She places her free arm around his waist.

Kyle ducks his head. He hates to admit that he needs the support again, but so long as Sam's willing to offer it it's easier to get past the shame. "Thanks," he whispers.

The four of them begin their way to the main door, the gravel beneath them loud and their breaths fogging in the air as they go. It's not raining here, but the puddles everywhere say it has been.

The sensor light comes on as the group approach, revealing Yuuki and Timothy standing outside waiting for them. Apprehension shoots through Kyle's core. Yuuki stands stiffly, tension lining his shoulders and his hand shoved in the pocket of his jacket. If he'd had both arms, he likely would've been standing with his arms crossed over his chest much like Timothy is beside him. Kyle assesses Timothy's expression, wary, but the stance is a way of warding off the cold than a display of dominance.

"You're back," Timothy remarks, voice flat. His gaze flicks over each of them.

Kyle tugs the collar of his jacket up a little higher.

Joshua scuffs his shoe. "We're back."

"Everyone accounted for," Charlie says. His tone lacks enthusiasm.

Sam's arm around Kyle tightens slightly.

Yuuki's gaze is severe. His eyes are narrowed, and his whole body

74

language burns with an anger that makes Kyle feel colder than his wet clothes do exposed to the night air. Beside him, Timothy's expression bears a hint of that same anger, but it's nowhere near as fierce as Yuuki's.

Kyle decides it's better not to look directly at either of their faces at the moment.

"Did something happen while you were out?" Timothy asks, looking at Kyle.

For a heart-stopping moment, Kyle thinks he's already found out about the man attacking them. But Timothy gestures to him in general, his gaze on the arm he has slung over Sam's shoulders as she supports his weight. Kyle lets out a shaky breath. He doesn't want to upset Yuuki or Timothy any more than they already are right now.

"I'm – ...I haven't been feeling that great," Kyle says. It's not a lie.

"Okay. Well, that's a good thing. But seriously, guys, may I ask who thought it would be a good idea to –"

"It was me," Kyle interrupts before the blame falls on anyone else. In his peripheral, he sees Joshua open his mouth to argue but Kyle stops him with a hard glance. "It was my idea that led us to go."

No one speaks for a moment, no one really knowing what to say. A thick silence falls between them. It's an atmosphere of strung tight tension, and Yuuki, already worn out by high levels of stress and exhaustion, is the first to snap under it.

"What the heck, Kyle." The sentence isn't phrased like a question.

Kyle lifts his head to look Yuuki straight in the eye. It's a mistake. Fear plunges itself in his gut. Yuuki's furious. It's hard to maintain eye contact, let alone breathe while doing so. Self-consciously he swallows.

The pain that causes helps to distract him from the nervousness coiling in his stomach.

"W-we did it for you," Kyle stammers. His voice wavers badly. The rasp of it is obvious. "For…for everyone."

Yuuki's nostrils flare. "You think getting freaking arrested would help anyone? Or getting kidnapped? Or killed?"

Kyle's never been on the receiving end of Yuuki's anger, and it's frankly terrifying. Not just because of how intense it is, but also because he's scared of the rift driving itself between them with every sharpened word that passes. He's scared Yuuki will decide that's it, he's had enough, and shut Kyle out for good.

A rush of wind hits them from behind. Kyle locks his knees, leans a little more into Sam. "Didn't happen though, did it?"

"Being that stupidly reckless is asking for it to."

"Maybe being stupid and reckless was worth the risk?"

"Do you want to go back to prison?"

Kyle's upper lip twitches. "Y-you don't even know why we went yet, so what gives?!"

Yuuki falters. He freezes on the spot, no words to add to the argument. Initially Kyle thinks it's because of what he said. But then he realises where Yuuki's now looking and he mentally kicks himself: Yuuki's eyes are locked on his neck. In the arguing, Kyle forgotten to be conscious about keeping his skin obscured.

The abrupt change in expression and mood attracts Timothy's attention. As soon as he sees what Yuuki does his face hardens. "What…did you run into trouble?"

Everyone looks now. In the visibility that the outside light provide, they can see what Kyle can't: scratches lining the sides of his neck. He vaguely remembers frantically clawing at the man's hand as it pressed against his throat but he doesn't remember harming himself in the process.

Kyle pales at the memory of that close call. He opens his mouth to answer Timothy's question but finds he can't.

"We did," Sam says instead. "But we got away from it. Some guy showed up as we were getting the USB. Attacked Kyle."

No one needs to comment that the scratches on Kyle's neck look self-inflicted. The implication of what that attack involved is clear.

Timothy shifts his feet. "Are you okay, Kyle? And what USB?"

After Kyle nods, Sam answers the second question. "Forgot to bring it with when we left."

"And what's on there that's so important that you felt the need to risk yourselves getting caught for it?"

Charlie clears his throat. "Later."

Timothy purses his lips, looking like he's about to ask them to elaborate. But then he catches the subtle warning Charlie and the rest of them are trying to convey and he stops. *This isn't something to talked about out in the open where they might be overheard.* He nods instead.

Yuuki, who has been glaring at his shadow on the ground in front of him, shifts his gaze back to Kyle. Kyle meets it. Much indescribable emotion is passed between them, a gut-wrenching mix of something conflicted, heated, apologetic, concerned, and *frightened…*

With a sharp inhale, Yuuki tears his eyes away and clenches his fist.

He opens his mouth to say something but instead just blinks hard, pivots and marches back inside. He bangs into the door in the process. No one comments at the harsh shove he gives it.

Kyle instinctively wants to go after him. To apologise for his recklessness and his being so secret in going about. To explain why they did what they did, why they considered it important and worth the risk. To reassure Yuuki he's fine. But watching him leave right now, movements jerky and emanating frustration, Kyle decides it's probably best to give him some space. He's learnt that Yuuki prefers to process such conflicted emotions on his own, in private. That needs respecting.

Timothy watches Yuuki disappear in the shadows of the hallway, overwhelmed. He raises a hand to the side of his face and rubs his temple. He looks like he might be revising his words for a lecture he's about to give the group, but instead he just sighs.

"Come on, let's just go inside, get you guys warmed up," Timothy says tiredly. "We can talk about this later."

They follow him inside, weary. Inside the temperature isn't much different, but it's certainly better than the chill of outside.

Even so, Kyle finds it hard to relax. He can't shake how unnerved he is. At first he's not sure entirely sure why. They made it back safe. They're back in a sheltered place where they can rest. Why then won't the muscles in his neck and shoulders loosen?

He feels his situational awareness increase with the anxiousness. His ears hurt as they strain to listen harder. His mind burns in protest as his gaze flits about the space around them, hyperaware. *Calm down,* he tries to tell himself. But the silence inside makes every noise loud, and Kyle's on edge half-expecting a stranger to jump out of nowhere and feel fingers tightening around his neck –

We're back now. That guy isn't here.

No, he isn't, but the person who reported to him that they'd be coming most likely is.

Kyle presses against Sam as he kicks his shoes off. "I'm worried," he whispers.

Sam's brow furrows. She slips her own shoes off in a similar manner. "What about, in particular…?"

"The guy back at your house who attacked me. He said he'd been tipped, right?" Charlie shuts the door behind them and Kyle flinches. He struggles to remember his train of thought. "He never said anything about knowing what we went in for."

"You're thinking they might be keeping an eye on us?" Sam asks. "Wanting to find out what we're up to?"

Kyle clenches his jaw and exhales sharply through his nose. He nods. "I'm worried they might try something."

What exactly that something may be, he's not sure.

Maybe he's just overreacting, letting the nervousness he's currently experiencing get the better of him. His mind churns. No, his mind's not overreacting here – it's warning him.

History repeats itself. What if that kind of thing happens again? The Ninao kidnapping, the Village Park incident that had Kyle arrested and imprisoned, the attempted kidnapping that cost Yuuki his arm – all those attacks came out of nowhere. The people who planned them did so in such a careful way that none of their targets had any idea they were coming. In other words, if there were an attack being planned right now, they wouldn't know it until it was already happening. By then it would be too late to do anything, and everyone supporting Amelia would be at risk.

That's why the USB retrieval mission was important to do, right? We're trying to figure out who's involved in these attacks. If we're able to, then we'll be able to prepare for any further incidents before they have a chance of happening.

That's the idea, at least. Whether or not they'll be able to do so prior to anything else happening is another story.

10

The scratches on Kyle's neck look worse in the morning light. Yuuki has to remind himself that he can breathe while looking at them. Kyle's hair is long enough now to hide the reddened scratches on the sides of his neck, but there's no hiding the strained undertone that was present in Kyle's voice when he spoke earlier.

Yuuki hadn't slept at all last night, bar the few hours' worth of a nap yester evening. All too recently Kyle sustained an injury that could've cost him his life. He's still recovering from that, and now this? He feels as though fate is taunting him, saying that his hypervigilance isn't vigilant enough. That this survival mode which PTSD has him stuck in needs to elevated even further. He dares relax his guard just a bit and then something bad always seems to happen.

Yuuki takes a deep breath in and out. Thinking about all this before they've all had time to debrief and discuss it is only making his head hurt and muscles tense. He has to force himself to unclench his jaw and to relax his brow. It's difficult, to say the least.

Someone strangled Kyle last night. They'd done so with the full intent to kill him – or at least make clear that they *could*. If they'd actually succeeded in bringing him right up close to death or even to it, then

Joshua and Sam could've been next, and that could've been it for the three of them right then and there. Gone. Not coming back. Over an unnecessary mission.

Yes, but it didn't come to that, Yuuki reminds himself. He watches Kyle's chest rise and fall. *No,* argues another part of his mind, directing his attention the desperate scratches on Kyle's neck. *It didn't but it could have.*

Yuuki doesn't get it. One moment Kyle's fine and hanging with Joshua and Sam in the library, and then he wakes up from a nap to find the three of them are off on some reckless outing they dubbed a mission. While Kyle could almost be forgiven for his recklessness due to his head injury possibly affecting the way he thinks, what of Joshua and Sam? Sure, they're the type to get up well-intentioned mischief if they see a need arise for it, and sure, Yuuki doubts they wouldn't be careful about it, but...

Kyle knows the dangers. He of all people should be wary of getting caught. What's so important that he, Joshua and Sam felt the need to do something so dangerous?

Trying to relax proves impossible. He decides to take himself off for a morning shower in the vague hope it'll distract him from all this, even alleviate it. But though the hot water helps loosen the tension in his neck and shoulders, it does nothing for the fear swirling in his mind and in his gut.

What made that person strangle Kyle like that? There has to be a why: there's always a why. Like what happened to Kyle at Village Park, is this another 'they know something they shouldn't and so it's better they aren't alive to pass that information on' kind of situation? Maybe Kyle recognised the man who snuck into the Harrisons' last night, and that's why they'd decided to kill him instead of trying to take him away or turn him in for arrest?

Soon, Yuuki reminds himself. *I don't have to figure this out myself. This isn't Kyle's case.*

He shuts off the shower water. A sudden and overwhelming sense of ineffectiveness washes over him in its place. He used to be able to do something *useful.* He used to *be* someone useful. Now, idly sitting around at the palace doing nothing, he feels ashamedly worthless.

Back when Kyle was still in prison, Yuuki had promised him he'd fight for him. He and Timothy had committed to doing whatever they could to protect him. But now Kyle keeps getting hurt and Yuuki's not been able to do anything to stop it.

I've failed Kyle, he realises. It's a horrid feeling.

"You guys did *what?!*"

Yuuki flinches and drops the coffee plunger in the sink. Kyle's gaze is on him immediately, wary.

Beside him, Avi ducks his head in a hasty apology. "Sorry."

"It's fine," Yuuki murmurs. He scowls at the plunger like it's done him a personal offense, and tries to keep the frustration off his face as he awkwardly navigates getting the coffee ready.

Kyle's gaze lingers but Yuuki determinedly ignores it. He can't tell if Kyle's watching him to decipher his mood (and whether or not he should be scared of it) or if he's simply watching out of concern and waiting in case Yuuki needs a hand with preparing the coffee. It could be both. While that hand would help, Yuuki's stubborn: he'd rather do it himself if he can, lest his missing arm become more apparent a disability.

"You are kidding though, right?" Avi says incredulously, glancing between Yuuki and Kyle for confirmation. "Going into the city? You didn't actually...?"

Kyle grunts. His shoulders hunch defensively. "We did, and we got what we went in for."

"Which was?"

"A flash drive. It's got all of Sam's research she did re the Ninao ki-... *incident* on it."

Yuuki pretends not to be affected by almost hearing the word *kidnapping*. He lifts the plunger to his mouth and grabs the knob in his teeth. The shaking of his hand as he opens the coffee bag betrays him.

Avi raises an eyebrow. "Research?"

"Yeah. Sam tried investigating the case herself. She said all the stuff she compiled is on that USB, including a list of names of potential PFO suspects who might've been involved. After that meeting we all had yesterday, Sam thought it might be worth it to get that list in case any of those potential suspects are here at the palace with us. Me and Joshua agreed."

Far too much coffee ends up in the plunger cup. *Here at the palace? They wouldn't be though, right?* Surely Yuuki would have seen and recognised them by now – the men who kidnapped him – or else Kyle might have. So unless they *are* here and have simply been concealing themselves really well...

He feels rather than sees Kyle step into his personal space. If it were anyone else, except for Timothy and maybe Susan, Yuuki likely would've flinched away. Instead he's drawn out of the anxiety-ridden imagining and back to the mess of coffee on the bench.

Don't get ahead of yourself, he reprimands himself. *Andy's thoroughly questioned every Peace Force officer who's remained here. He'd have noticed if someone or something was suss.* And yet the apprehension coiled in his gut refuses to unwind. Yuuki covers his spark of anxiety with an irritated huff.

In his peripheral, he sees Kyle tentatively reaching for the cup, eyes wide in careful questioning. Yuuki regards him blankly for a moment before taking the plunger back in his hand and stepping to the side, defeated. Kyle quietly sidles over and fixes the quantity of coffee for him.

Some of the tension between them dissipates. It hasn't gone unnoticed, the stiffness in the air between them. Thankfully Avi doesn't question them. He merely stands as he is, observant. Cautious yet respectful. When Yuuki goes to get the jug, he catches Avi's not quite subtle glances at the scratches and slightly inflamed skin around Kyle's neck.

Kyle catches him looking too, and before he can draw conclusions that aren't true, says quietly, "I was attacked at the Harrisons' last night." He hunches his shoulders as though to hide the evidence. "Some guy showed up and came at me."

Avi's much better at masking the concern on his face than Yuuki is at present, but the emotion comes through in his voice. "Oh, o-okay. So you went on a dangerous mission and got attacked by dangerous people."

"Someone told him we were coming. We would've come and gone with no trouble at all if it weren't for him."

"Do you know who?"

"No."

"And I'm guessing that's what this meeting today is about?" Avi asks. "About the possibility there might be some not so great people around here?"

Fear stabs Yuuki in the gut.

Kyle nods. "Timothy told Andy about it this morning. Andy said it would be best if everyone was there for the debriefing, that way we all know what's happening."

"Makes sense."

The toaster pops and Yuuki flinches again. He grimaces at his reaction and tightens his grip on the jug handle.

Avi points to the toast he's just put on a plate. "Did any of you want some toast? I'll put some more bread in?"

Kyle winces. "I'll pass, thanks. My throat... it kind of hurts to swallow."

With a short shake of his head, Yuuki declines also. He should eat, but what with his lack of appetite he probably won't be able to do so anyway. Not for a while, at least. *Maybe after the meeting.*

"We should head over," Yuuki says curtly, finishing preparing his coffee.

Kyle murmurs in agreement. There's a hint of reluctance behind the rasp in his voice. *He must be nervous,* Yuuki realises with a pang of guilt. *He's waiting to be scolded. Sat down and lectured. Or... yelled at.* Because of how Yuuki reacted last night, Kyle might very well be anticipating this meeting to be more like a trial and the meeting room a courtroom.

And who's mostly to blame for that?

He's barely a step out the kitchen door when Kyle calls after him. "Yuuki, wait."

Tempted as he is just to keep walking, Yuuki stops. Leaving Avi to finishing his breakfast, Kyle follows with a cup of steaming tea cradled in his hands. It smells like ginger.

"Um," Kyle says as they start walking again. "C-can we... I just – ..."

Yuuki bows his head. "I'm sorry."

"What?"

"Last night."

A series of emotions pass over Kyle's face.

"I was scared," Yuuki confesses. "But I should've waited to hear you out first. I'm sorry. I shouldn't have yelled at you."

Kyle self-consciously rubs his throat and then goes back to holding the cup of tea in both hands. His hands are shaking a little. It's not exactly visible but neither is it intended to be – that's why Kyle's using both hands to support the tea, not just one. That's why his fingers look so stiff holding it. It's not just because Kyle's been having some minor difficulties with his precision grip. Yuuki knows the signs from experience.

"You didn't yell at me," Kyle says softly. He grunts. "I've been yelled at plenty of times before, and that I wouldn't classify as yelling."

"Still..."

Yuuki's at a loss for what to say. The closeness they'd built leading up to coming here already feels fractured and again he feels like he's let Kyle down. Yuuki's aware that his isolating himself from everyone is partly at fault for that. He knows he's even been distancing himself from Kyle who at this stage probably knows him even better than Timothy does, so really it's Yuuki's own fault for driving them apart.

I'm sorry I'm not the person perhaps you'd hoped I'd be, he wants to say, but he can't apologise over and over without sounding ridiculous. Doing so would just make Kyle uncomfortable.

He feels selfish, yet helpless in that none of this is happening by intention. *What exactly am I so afraid of?* Not being able to interact well with the others is one thing, but this has far more to do with shame. Shame of how messed up his PTSD has made him, and shame for all it inconveniences and discomfort it must bring to the others.

"Yuuki?" Kyle asks quietly. He glances nervously at Yuuki's expression before fixing his eyes on the meeting room door just a few paces ahead of them. He lowers his voice even further, and the question scrapes with emotion and pain on the way out. "Are you okay?"

And there it is: such a simple question. An opening, an invitation. But one that is perhaps the hardest to know how honestly to answer.

Yuuki schools his expression, neutralising any emotion in his eyes and frowning hard as he contemplates how best to answer. *No,* is the most direct and truthful response. But what with his PTSD, he's not really been okay for a long while. The fact that Kyle's even asking after him means that he's already noticed that Yuuki's not okay, so is there really any need to confirm it?

'Do you want to talk about it?' is what Kyle's really asking. But how does Yuuki explain it? Does he say that he's been struggling with confusing and complex emotions, ones that can't really be described adequately enough in words? Or that he's been dealing with things that a lot of people just wouldn't be able to understand from a PTSD-anxiety point of view? That

he's become increasingly paranoid, progressively worse and unexplainably anxious for reasons he's yet to be able to pinpoint with clarity?

Kyle wouldn't judge him if Yuuki told him all this. It's Kyle. He'd understand. He'd support. He'd offer to help him figure out exactly what's got him feeling so on edge, to process whether or not it's general anxiety built on shadows of past fears or if there's genuinely something setting him on edge for whatever reason?

Even if Yuuki could find the words he needs to explain all that, there's still no quick way to do so. Now's not the time or place: they're already at the meeting room door.

"I'm fine," Yuuki murmurs finally, avoiding Kyle's eyes.

Kyle doesn't press. He takes in Yuuki's expression a moment longer before opening the door and going in ahead.

Inside the meeting room, mostly everyone's already gathered. Yuuki sets down the plunger on the table that's been pulled to the centre of the room. Kyle makes to sit down in the vacant seat next to him, but he's called away by Sam and Joshua waving him over. The void Kyle leaves in his wake has Yuuki feeling isolated anew.

Resigned, Yuuki simply sits and waits. Timothy and Andy are deep in conversation with Sam and Joshua, Amelia's sitting quietly beside Susan and Logan's getting a projector set up and connected to Timothy's laptop. Avi comes in a minute later with the cup Yuuki forgot to go back to the kitchen to get. Yuuki quietly thanks him as Avi slips into a seat beside Susan.

While they wait for Charlie, and for Logan to finish setting up the projector, Yuuki's mind drifts. So much has happened up till now, and it's clear it's not over yet. He wonders if it's possible for them all to go back to living a normal life after all this is finished. He wonders if he'll be able to. Will there even be anything left of himself to go back with?

They still have so much to work through and to be frank, Yuuki's not sure how much more of it he can handle. He's exhausted. They all are, he knows that, but this is something beyond exhaustion. It's a relentless fatigue, and it feels like it would only take one more thing to push him over the threshold, to push him past breaking point into a place or a state he won't be able to come back from.

Yuuki presses the plunger down and pours the coffee into the cup. A muscle in his brow twitches. It scares him. It scares him more than he's willing to admit.

11

"Alright, meeting time. Can I have everyone's attention, please?"

Timothy doesn't really have to ask; everyone's already waiting to finally start the meeting. They're all too tired to want to be here having a meeting at all. Yuuki's on the same page. They just had a long, intense meeting yesterday. No one's exactly in the mood for another.

"We'll try keep this short," Timothy says, "but there are some things that need talking about."

Behind him, Joshua ducks his head sheepishly. Sam and Kyle shift uncomfortably. Charlie's posture where he sits is reminiscent of a mischievous school kid who's trying to act like he's done nothing wrong.

"I'm not going to bother going over the first, but I will say this: *please*…if you feel the need to do anything reckless for the greater good or go on an adventure of sorts, tell someone before you do it. Preferably verbally, so we know what's happening when it's happening, and so if something happens and you don't check back in by the time you expected to return by, we can respond accordingly."

Timothy removes his glasses to rub at the shadows in the corners of his eyes. "Secondly, and a more pressing issue to deal with, we might have to think about upping security measures in and around the premises." He puts his glasses back on and sighs. "Andy, if you will?"

With a fake cough, Joshua steps forward with a raise of his hand. "Do we want to maybe tell everyone else exactly what happened? In detail too, now that Kyle and Charlie are here?"

The Peace Force officer hums. "I think that would be a good idea."

Cue given, Joshua relays their mission objective and recounts the mission itself. Sam interjects with a comment of reasoning here and there in their defence. When they pass the explaining to Kyle regarding the man who attacked him, the concern for raised security around the palace becomes clear.

"I think he was communicating with someone," Kyle explains. "Someone at the palace who saw us leave, I mean."

Hearing this has Andy frowning deeply. "This is indeed troubling."

"Proves the mission was worth it," Sam says. "We never would've known otherwise."

"That's assuming," Timothy says slowly, "that there definitely *was* someone who witnessed you leave."

Kyle tugs on the sleeve of his jersey. "There was. I saw them. They were standing over by the car park. I thought I was just seeing things at first, but…yeah."

Timothy exchanges a careful glance with Andy. "Could've just been one of the Peace Force officers on our side taking a break. It might not have been that person who the man who attacked you was referring to."

A flicker of self-doubt crosses Kyle's face. Timothy sees it and quickly amends, "That's not to say you're wrong. It's still a valid concern. I just mean to point out that it might not necessarily have been someone here.

Someone in the city might've seen the car or a neighbour might have seen you guys sneak into the house, is what I'm saying."

Charlie taps his finger on the edge of the table. "I didn't notice anyone peering out of windows or anything when we were there. And I don't think that man who attacked Kyle would have had enough time to get to the house after receiving the call had it been one of the neighbours who reported our presence to him."

Joshua exchanges a dubious look with Sam. "Yeah, unless we have new neighbours all of a sudden, I really can't imagine anyone on our street sneaking into our house like. I mean, he was deliberately trying to keep quiet about attacking us. Plus he had a house key."

"So…a new neighbour who's a Peace Force officer?" Logan says. "It could explain why he had a house key and why he got there so quick then –"

"He said he'd been tipped," Kyle interrupts. His eyes gleam with a not-so-old hurt, a remnant anger. "H-he said that he'd been tipped by someone who k-knew we were coming. Those words exactly. Doesn't sound like just a neighbour to me."

Yuuki recognises that defensiveness. It takes him a moment to place it, but then he remembers seeing that same stiffness in Kyle's shoulders and hearing that same frustrated tone when Kyle was in prison and responding to some of the questions Yuuki had asked him. Except this time, Kyle's word is actually listened to, not dismissed or deliberately covered up like it was at his trial.

Timothy's brow pinches and Andy falls silent as he considers what Kyle's just said. Though still bristling, Kyle lets the heat die in his eyes and distracts himself with drinking his tea.

Sitting forward, Andy frowns hard. "Alright, so it's reasonable to say that it's likely someone here at the palace saw you leave and alerted the man who attacked you. Until we have other evidence, however, I think it should be regarded as a speculation. Reason being is that it'll consume a lot of our energy questioning everybody and narrowing down who that person might've been, and the time that would take could be better spent elsewhere."

Timothy weighs the information carefully. Yuuki allows a brief smile of amusement to creep over his face at the sight of Timothy falling into his work expression. It's superficial though – Yuuki's whole body is tensed up. The thought of there being people secretly spying on them out here unnerves him, and thought of them choosing not to do anything about it, even more so.

It's like that night before Deborah came and tried to kidnap Kyle. It wasn't a shadow I saw outside; it was a person doing surveillance. Of us. He feels the panic building in his chest in quickened breathes. His heart beats faster and his palm grows clammy around the cup handle. It's an effort to stop himself from spiralling.

Timothy doesn't physically glance at Yuuki, but Yuuki can feel his concern shift onto him. "I agree with Andy: we'll be using up a lot of energy if we automatically assume we're being actively watched here."

The group express various acknowledgements. Kyle looks a little deflated at having his idea somewhat rejected, but the resignation in his eyes tells Yuuki he understands the angle Andy's coming at. Assumptions are what landed Kyle in prison, after all. Kyle's well aware of how consequences can become severe if speculation is rendered in the same light as fact.

Andy stares at the table a moment, thinking. "Kyle," he says, looking up again. "While you were explaining, you said you thought you recognised the person who attacked you. Who was it you think you recognised?"

Kyle grips the cup of tea. "I'm…I'm not sure?"

"He wouldn't be someone from one of your foster families, right?"

"No. Definitely wasn't. Something about him was familiar though, and not in a good way. Also, I think he recognised me, too. He said he wasn't going to let me get away this time, so by that I'm presuming…w-we may have met."

"Well, if he's a PFO like we've been thinking he might be, then maybe you met him at some point during your trial and stuff?"

"I don't remember…"

Andy nods. "Okay. Don't force yourself to put a name and a face to him. In any case, you all mentioned that you think this guy was a PFO. Do you know that for sure, or is that another speculation?"

Kyle looks between Joshua and Sam, conflicted. "The guy wasn't wearing a uniform," he says hesitantly. "At least not that I could see."

"But he had the key to the front door," Sam says. "The only people who have any access to our house keys are people in the Peace Force, right? We don't have any extended family who have any."

Andy nods, thoughtful. "And you said he knew you were coming?"

"Told me, in his own words and with his own voice," Kyle reiterates. "As he was strangling me."

"Alright, well…that makes sense you'd end up at such a conclusion as you did then."

"So are we going to look for that person now?" Amelia asks. "The person who tipped that guy, I mean. Shouldn't we look just in case?" Her shoulders are tight. "They're obviously not on our side. What if they attack us?"

"No," Andy says. He rubs a hand over his forehead. "Looking for them might give them a reason to attack us first, if they don't vanish before that. Princess Amelia, you're giving your speech tomorrow night. I'd rather we conserve our energy for whatever response we receive after the broadcast."

Yuuki frowns. His brow furrows and he tightens his grip on his coffee cup as he speaks up for the first time that meeting. "No, our priority should be personal security."

The whole room turns to look at Yuuki. He tenses under the directness of everyone's gaze, especially Andy's, but as a trained security officer Yuuki knows the grounds he's standing on. Andy, as someone who's also gone through Arkala Police College and as someone with more years' experience, should too.

"It is," Andy says, "but if there is someone here and they figure out we're onto them, they'll only end up working out a plan to stop us from finding out more. As far as we know, they don't know what you four went to the Harrisons' for. Unless they specifically heard you talk about the USB and what's on it, it's safer to lay low. It's better we act as though we're not actively intent on discovering them."

"Yeah, and in doing so we'll be compromising the safety of everyone here," Yuuki retorts.

Andy blinks. "We'll be compromising everyone's safety if we draw attention to ourselves."

To that, Yuuki finds it hard to argue. Throughout the investigation of Kyle's case, Timothy had stressed over and over that they had to be absolutely vigilant in going about things as quietly as possible – and look what had happened when they did something that no longer had them keeping under the radar. Only a couple of days after they'd gotten Kyle out of prison, Deborah had attempted to kidnap him and had shot Yuuki's arm to beyond saving in the process.

"Still," Yuuki grits out. "Regardless of whether we act or just sit back and nothing, we can't guarantee that they're going to respond in the same manner we do."

"Therefore we shouldn't provoke them."

"They come out of nowhere. Every single time. You never see them coming, you never see them planning, and when they do strike they act without mercy. They –"

Timothy's chair creaks. "Yuuki."

No. I'm not backing down. "They operate on their own terms and in their own time. Amelia's speech is tomorrow night. They are probably planning something as we speak – or at least starting to. Are we really going to do nothing?"

The debate between Peace Force officer and security officer settles in the air like a stalemate. Both their points are valid. But while Andy's the higher ranking officer, Yuuki's been through several cases of trauma to know first-hand how the corrupt PFOs operations work. Andy's seen some of it happen in real time from working alongside some of the perpetrators, but Yuuki's been a victim of it.

It's understandable why Yuuki feels a greater need for a plan of action.

"I'll take a look at the names on the list we now have," Andy says. "But in the meantime, we shouldn't stress ourselves out any more than what is necessary. I can't promise that I'll be able to arrange any immediate action after reviewing it, however I'll keep my eye out for anything that seems off about the other officers."

Yuuki grimaces. He closes his eyes, takes a decent drink of coffee and tries to quell his frustration. He can't find the energy to argue anymore. When he opens his eyes again, he sees Kyle looking somewhat pensive as though he doesn't quite agree with Andy's course of action either. He catches Yuuki's gaze, a flicker of fear passing through his own.

They're both on edge but there's not a lot either of them can do about it. They could try argue further but Yuuki's too tired and Kyle's voice sounds a little strained. Pressing their concerns will only wear them both out and make Kyle feel like he's back in court again.

Let's just leave it. Andy's the one with the most experience here. We'll just have to trust him to make as best of a decision he can for us.

Yuuki takes a deep breath and tries not to think too hard.

"I think it wouldn't hurt for us to at least take a look at the names on this list, though," Timothy says as he plugs it in. "We can have a look over the photos, and if anyone recognises anyone from the list doing something that doesn't seem quite right, we can have another talk."

He moves his finger over the mousepad to wake up the laptop and the projector screen lights the room up in blue. "Sam, you got the USB with you?"

Sam fishes the flash drive out of her jersey pocket and hands it over.

"I believe there's also ID photos along with the names?"

"Yep." Sam shifts on her feet. "They're on the same PDF file."

Timothy nods. "Thanks." He clicks on the flash drive folder and moves the cursor over the folder named 'Ninao stuff'. "Alright, let's have a look at what we've got here…"

It isn't, however, the list that shows up on the screen. Instead it's a folder full of disturbing photos. Yuuki feels the blood drain from his face. His vision tunnels and his throat closes up.

It's the photo evidence that Joshua took of his rescue.

Without scrolling down, it's enough. The shed. Yuuki as they found him, his wrists bound behind his back and his ankles tied together. A damp piece of cloth lying on the ground by his chin where he'd spat it out. Silver duct tape hanging off the side of his face. Behind him, Timothy lit up by the flashlight going off, a pocketknife in his hands as he prepares to work on the rope.

Yuuki hasn't seen these photos before. He's never had even the slightest desire to see them. But here they are, up on the screen where everyone in this room can see them and he…

That shed, and the stifling dustiness of the air. The unrelenting tightness around his wrists and ankles, and the strain of his neck as he worked to get the tape off his mouth so he could spit the cloth out and breathe. The stench of urine creeping into the air.

Fear, and the overwhelming inability to understand.

Light entering, and the door opening as he faded, this time not a hallucination.

Warm hands on him, safe voices…then nothing.

The muted panic of knowing there were strange people around him that he couldn't get away from, of lying in a hospital bed with bandages wound around his wrists and deliriously thinking his wrists had been tied again. The unwelcome touch of nurse's fingers rubbing antiseptic cream over the bug bites on his face, neck and hands.

Questions. Too many questions. He can't remember, he doesn't know and he can't speak to describe what he does. It's too much.

It's too much.

Yuuki's body feels numb, fuzzy. Before he catches a glimpse of the panic on Timothy's face as he yanks the projector plug from the laptop, or has a chance to see the horror on everyone else's faces as they turn from the screen to look at him, he stumbles out of his seat and leaves.

12

There's no backspace button; it's too late. It can't be unseen. Everyone's already seen and the horror has already struck, and for Yuuki the damage has well and truly already been done.

Kyle starts after him on instinct but Timothy throws his arm out, barring his way. The back of Kyle's neck prickles at his path being blocked. "What are you...?"

"Let him have time to himself to process it," Timothy says, dropping his arm. He seeks out Susan, looking for some kind of affirmation to know he's making the right decision. But Susan's busy confirming with a disbelieving Avi what they all saw in those pictures.

Charlie rises out of his seat, unsure. "I don't know if leaving him alone right now is the right call," he says slowly.

"He won't want anyone seeing him." Timothy shakes his head. He shoves the laptop a little further away from himself as though disgusted with it. "Not after *that*."

A muffled silence fills the room. Logan glances nervously about the room, taking in everyone's expressions. Kyle does the same. Susan's doing a decent job of masking her uneasiness. Beside her Amelia's crestfallen. Andy sits solemnly. Joshua is pale, the tips of his ears red with guilt. Sam is hissing at herself, fingers clenched in her hair and pulling, and Timothy looks downright mortified.

Yuuki's coffee sits on the table, steam rising and swirling in the air.

Kyle's not sure what his expression portrays. He's not exactly sure what he's feeling right now. His mind's gone blank. There's doubt flickering in his mind, a hesitancy – a reluctance to go against his gut and not go after Yuuki when intuition says he should.

"Are you sure?" Kyle asks quietly. "Are you sure you he'd rather be alone right now?"

Timothy closes his eyes a moment. "No…no, I'm not. But if you'd just had all your shields torn down and highly sensitive vulnerability of yours pulled out and put on display for everyone to see, *literally*, would you want to be around those people while you try process it? I just…I don't want to risk him shutting us off completely before he's had time to process seeing himself like that. He's vulnerable at the moment. It might only make him feel cornered."

While Kyle agrees with Timothy's logic, he's not so sure. *Is space to process things really what Yuuki needs right now, though? What if he's having a bad panic attack and is having trouble grounding himself, and here we are… not doing anything to help him?*

The thought doesn't sit well with him.

When Yuuki had had that panic attack coming into Kyle's cell a few months ago, he'd accepted the hug – the *rather awkward* hug – Kyle had offered him. The fright had slowly disappeared from his eyes and the stiffness in his body had eased a little. That's not to mention the other times Yuuki's calmed down much quicker with someone there to help draw him out of it.

But I wasn't there when Yuuki was recovering in hospital. I wasn't there at the shed to see him like that first-hand. Timothy was. Joshua, too. They were the ones there by his side while he was readjusting to life; I wasn't.

Timothy has the greater insight here. He also knew Yuuki before the kidnapping and before post-traumatic stress disorder shook him into someone he hadn't been before the incident. If Timothy reckons it's best to give Yuuki space right now, and if Joshua doesn't disagree, then…

"We'll check on him after the meeting's finished," Susan murmurs. There's a contradicting shadow in her eyes that says that maybe she's feeling the same as Kyle about this.

"We needn't be much longer here," Andy says. "We'll need Yuuki to see if he can identify any of these people."

Timothy leans his head into his hands. "He isn't exactly going to be wanting to be looking for the faces of his kidnappers. It's not right to force that on him anyhow."

Beside him, Sam nudges Kyle's arm. "Would you be able to recognise any of them?"

Kyle blinks.

"Not necessarily that man from last night, but the two men accompanying Deborah when they attacked you and Yuuki, before we all fled to the country house."

"Oh, you mean when she tried to kidnap me?"

"Yeah. Yuuki's said before he recognised the two men from the Ninao incident. He sounded fairly confident. I was wondering if you might remember them too."

Timothy glances at them over his shoulder.

Kyle frowns. He scratches the backs of his hands and shifts uncomfortably. "I'm not sure. I wasn't exactly trying to memorise their faces or anything."

"Sam," Joshua murmurs. He gives her a cautioning stare.

It takes a moment for Sam to catch her brother's message, but when she does she winces. She flashes Kyle an apologetic look even as her face flushes red. "Sorry, I shouldn't be making you to remember such things. Gosh, I'm so insensitive today. Stupid..."

Kyle wants to reassure her it's fine, that he knows she didn't mean to force him to remember such upsetting memories. But then he realises she's not just referring to him – she's also meaning forgetting about the photos being on the USB like they are, all loosely dumped in the same folder as the PDF file of the list of names, and about Yuuki.

She probably hadn't thought Timothy's laptop would display the files like that though. Kyle can't find any reason to fault her. It's an innocent mistake with severe consequences, is all.

Much like my case, he thinks wryly.

"Alright," Timothy says, loud enough for everyone to hear him. He sighs. "We've pretty much discussed what we need to, so I guess we can call this meeting to a close. Andy, I'll flick you this list for you to take a look at. About what we talked about earlier, everyone – and I mean it goes without saying, but – just be careful where you go. Maintain appropriate situational awareness. If you feel the need to do something you know involves a high risk, let either Andy or myself know. Or Charlie, if he's not sneaking out with you."

With a sheepish smile, Charlie nods.

"Okay, that's that," Joshua says. "And what about Yuuki?"

Susan gives Timothy a stern glance. She raises her eyebrows.

"Maybe just give him a little more time," Timothy says. There's less strength to his voice than there was before. Less confidence.

With a resigned sigh, Susan rises out of her seat. "Alright then."

The meeting ends there and the room dissolves in movement. Logan the first out the door and Susan, Charlie and Avi soon after. Timothy reluctantly gets to scrolling down past all the photo evidence of Yuuki's rescue to find the actual file of interest. As he does, Sam mutters a curse beneath her breath and abruptly leaves looking like she's about tear some of her hair out or hit something. Joshua goes after his sister, mixed emotions on his face.

Kyle deliberates again about going after Yuuki. He still doesn't like the idea of leaving him alone after…*that*. By all means, Yuuki's strong enough to be able to get himself out of whatever induced state of panic or anxiousness he's experiencing, but Kyle knows from experience how hard it can be to do so. *Is it really worth letting Yuuki suffer through that alone in exchange for allowing him some privacy? Like Timothy says, he probably doesn't want anyone seeing him dealing with everything and he probably would prefer to have some alone time to process it all, but…*

"I'm going to look for him," Kyle announces. Before he can begin to doubt his decision, he picks up his cup of tea from the table and makes for the doorway.

Timothy doesn't call him back.

Out in the hallway, though, Kyle realises he has no idea where to start looking. He's narrowing down a list of places Yuuki frequents when Amelia wanders out from the meeting room beside him. Her movements are so quiet that her sudden presence startles him.

"I'm sorry," Amelia says, eyes wide.

Kyle wipes his jersey sleeves over the tea spilt over his hands. "No, it's fine. You're fine."

"Sorry, I…" she trails off, seemingly losing her trail of thought. She stares into space, intensely though at nothing in particular.

Not only does she seem a little out of it, she looks shocked. Kyle waits a moment before asking, "Are you okay?"

Something unidentifiable flashes over Amelia's face. She blinks back into focus, her lips parting as she tries to form an answer. After a few seconds she smiles. "If I'm honest, I'm not sure."

"Do you want to talk about it?"

"Aren't you going to look for Yuuki?"

Kyle grunts. "He could be anywhere. I'm trying to pick my search route strategically."

The laugh Amelia gives is mirthless, a defence mechanism. "Right. Okay, then. Well, it's nothing really. I'm just…I'm afraid."

She crosses her arms over her chest, eyes flicking between the floor and Kyle's face like she's afraid he'll simply shrug and tell her that everyone is. He doesn't. With a nervous breath, Amelia continues.

"My speech," she says. "So much rides on it. We're going to be recording it live tomorrow night, so it's not like it's not going to be a big deal if I mess it up once or twice. I know I just said it, but so much depends on it. Arkala's currently under martial law since Taularh's no

106

longer and people won't accept me their sovereign yet. Andy says it will remain that way if I'm not accepted."

Kyle frowns. "Which means the Peace Forces would be in charge still?"

"Yeah. It also means that it would be them deciding who the next ruler is, or at least an acting ruler."

"Yeah, we don't want that."

"No, we sure don't." She sighs, defeated. "I might be the Princess, but that means nothing. Charlie has documentation to prove my identity, sure, but that's worth nothing if nobody believes me."

Kyle hums in agreement, grim. He's had personal experience with that. They made Kyle a criminal to cover up their tracks, and now they've made them all out to be bad people even as they've been fighting for their lives and fighting to protect Amelia and everything she stands for. It'll be hard to prove herself to everyone what with the Peace Forces actively manipulating the publics' emotions against them.

It'll be a hard fight to win.

"This is all beyond me," Amelia murmurs. "If everyone does recognise me as Princess, then I'll end up becoming a queen, and…I'm not ready for that. I don't know what I'm doing. I don't know how to lead." And then, confessed in a whisper: "Could I not have just stayed as Laura?"

To that, Kyle doesn't know what to say. He understands her situation to some extent, but having the misplaced label of convict attached to your name and having the title of Princess placed on your shoulders are two different things. One bears injustice, the other responsibility. One requires acquittal, the other a coronation. And while Amelia might've been better off before all this, safer, hidden and able to live a relatively normal life, Kyle hadn't been.

If he had the option to go back in time and keep things the way they were, unlike Amelia, his answer would be no. In addition to everything that had been worse off for him before, Kyle's gained so much these last few months. In spite of how messed up everything has been, he's found family where he had none. Though it's dangerous to be in the position the group's in, and though he's been accused, kidnapped and almost died on several different occasions, now he has friends where he hadn't before.

He feels like his life matters. That's not something he's experienced in a while. But of course, as he's reminded yet again as Logan comes running down the hall towards him and Amelia, all that he gained didn't come to him without a cost.

"Glad you're still here," Logan says, a little breathless. There's a look of anxiety on Logan's face as he slows to a stop in front of them. He casts Amelia an uncertain glance before his eyes shift to Kyle and stay there. "It's Yuuki."

A spear of angst stabs Kyle right through the core. "What is it?"

"Um... he told me not to tell any of you. He's having a panic attack in the bathroom. Said he didn't want anyone to come, but I thought it might be better to tell you."

Kyle grips the cup in his hands tighter. "Which bathroom?"

"Main one," Logan says. "I didn't know what to do. I'm sorry."

"It's okay. I'll go. Thanks."

"Uh, all goods?"

Kyle doesn't waste time getting there. He's wasted enough time doing nothing already. He finds himself cursing himself like Sam probably still is. How could he have been so stupid? He should've trusted his gut. He should've pushed past Timothy and left as soon as Yuuki removed himself from the room.

When he gets to the mens' bathroom, he puts the tea cup on the floor and barges inside. It's empty. There's no one here, and both the two stalls are vacant too. *Logan had said the main bathroom, right?* Kyle exits, goes back in and double checks. No, there's definitely no one here.

"He won't want anyone seeing him like this," Timothy had said. *"He'll only feel cornered."*

Oh. Yuuki doesn't want to be found. Kyle can't find him because Yuuki's already gone and concealed himself elsewhere. He grimaces. Yuuki must've anticipated someone coming after him. He must've left right after Logan had.

Returning to the hallway, Kyle's left standing there at a loss. *Now what?*

13

An hour. That's how long it takes before Yuuki's finally fought through the worst of the panic attack. He's exhausted. His muscles feel weak and worn out, but in the least can breathe normally again now.

Yuuki heads back to the palace, nervous and wary. As much as he'd rather avoid everyone right now, they'll start getting majorly concerned if he's away too long. He's able to get back inside without meeting anyone though, and he somehow manages to evade everyone throughout the rest of the day too. It only then occurs to him why: they're giving him space.

He's not sure whether he feels relieved or dejected about that. He appreciates that everyone's giving him some personal space to do so: it'll take him several hours, maybe even several days, before he's back to relatively normal – *stable* – levels of emotions, so it's good he has some quiet time to himself to process everything.

And yet all it does is make Yuuki feel more isolated.

It's fine. He repeats it in his head until he manages to half-heartedly convince himself it's true. So long as he doesn't have to think about the Ninao incident again anytime soon, he should be fine.

All he needs to do is not think.

*

The palace is always near silent past midnight. Yuuki wanders the halls, trying to immerse himself in it. It's the kind of stillness that ought to bring peace, but Yuuki's mind, in contrast, is a hurricane of unwanted thoughts.

You're not there, he tries to tell himself. It doesn't matter how many times he does, though. The Ninao incident may have happened over a year ago, but that doesn't mean the ordeal was over once he was rescued.

It's with great grief and frustration that he wishes it was.

He clenches his jaw and tries to blink away the images, the sensations, but the flashbacks don't stop. In the darkness, they only twist into more memories. Yuuki draws in a deep breath and exhales slowly. He stops walking, leans against the hallway wall and presses his thumb and index finger into the bruise-like ache beneath his eyes.

Footsteps sound behind him, approaching slowly and calmly. Yuuki's instinctive reaction is to tense up, but the second he recognises the footfall as Timothy's, he lets his guard drop back to its previous level of vigilance.

The warm hand on his shoulder startles him nonetheless. Timothy hastily murmurs an apology, then after a brief pause, says, "No luck sleeping yet, huh?"

Yuuki grunts. "At this point, I'm not even sure if I want to sleep."

Timothy hums. Yuuki's grateful for the comforting weight of Timothy's hand that remains on his shoulder.

"You're not able to sleep either?" he asks. "It's late, for you."

"Had a lot to think about lately. Just one of those nights my brain can't seem to switch off, though I guess that meeting we had earlier doesn't help."

111

Not surprising, Yuuki thinks. Over the last two months, Timothy's had to be a judge, a leader, a father and a friend. Timothy's still basically the one leading them in all this, though now he has Andy to confer with and the leadership is shared between the two of them. It's a lot of stress, and Yuuki feels guilty to have brought on any extra to that.

"About earlier," Yuuki says, "about the, uh…t-the photos."

Timothy lets out a heavy breath. "I am *really* sorry about that. I –"

Yuuki shakes his head. "No, I wanted to say please don't make yourself feel bad about it. You didn't know they'd be there. I'm not upset with you or anything, or Sam, or anyone else. On second thought, maybe Andy, but that's a matter of conflicting opinions on how to respond to this situation, not about the photos. It's fine, really – it's not like you knew they'd be there."

"You say it's fine," Timothy says carefully, "but are *you?*"

Not having the energy to answer in full, Yuuki grimaces. "I will be."

Timothy nods, though by his expression he clearly doesn't believe it. "Okay, well…there's something I wanted to talk to you about," he murmurs. "It might be better to have this conversation elsewhere, though."

Yuuki pushes himself off the wall, brow creased. His nervousness heightens. "Is there something going on?" he asks, voice lowered.

"Nothing dire, don't worry. Just something that's been on my mind to talk about." With a small smile that doesn't reach his eyes, Timothy inclines his head in the direction of the kitchen and dining room. "I normally wouldn't suggest this, but would you like to sit down and have a drink together?"

A cautiousness has crept into Timothy's tone, whether he's aware of it or not. Yuuki frowns, unease still stirring in his gut. Timothy never says he wants to talk unless it's about something serious.

Apprehensive, Yuuki nods slowly. "Uh, sure."

Yuuki spends the walk to the kitchen mentally preparing for whatever bad news Timothy has to tell him. Perhaps it's about Kyle's past foster family situations, or the legal documentation required to get his acquittal and close his case once and for all? Something about the condition of the head injury Kyle sustained protecting Yuuki during the fall a couple of weeks ago?

He finds himself in a state of near panic, thinking about the number of ways Kyle might be taken away from him, both in the immediate and coming future. The twinging and aching of the muscles in Yuuki's back and shoulders – not to mention the stiffness in his legs – still has yet to fade entirely, and it serves a clear reminder of the last time he'd thought he was about to lose Kyle for good. He remembers the fear that had consumed him then as if he were back in that situation all over again.

Not after all this, he begs silently. *Not after everything he's had to go through already…everything* we've *had to go through.*

But maybe this isn't so much about Kyle as it is about Yuuki. Yuuki's been losing his mind over the last couple of weeks, or at least that's what it feels like and that's what he fears others might be thinking of him. Maybe this'll end up being a 'talk from a concerned friend' like his once-friend-and-flatmate Lee often gave Yuuki before he left.

Maybe this is Timothy saying he's tired, he's had enough, and where Yuuki loses another friend to his PTSD.

"Coffee?" Timothy asks when they reach the kitchen. He opens a few cupboards, frowning in thought. "Else there's whiskey, beer…and some expensive looking wine. Tea, if you feel like a change."

Yuuki curls his fingers around the hem of his jersey. "How much am I going to like the conversation we're about to have?"

"You're not."

"Whiskey, then."

"Whiskey?" Timothy repeats, raising an eyebrow.

Yuuki shrugs. "It's grounding – the aftertaste." He walks out into the dining room and tries to ignore the weight of his friend's gaze following him, reading his body language as he grabs a chair and sits down in it with a heavy sigh.

Yuuki slouches over the table. If he had two elbows instead of just one, he'd be leaning his head into his hands and hiding his face. As it is, he props his arm up on the table, palm on his forehead, and tries not to let his head drop. He's not going to want to lift it back up again if it does.

In the kitchen, cupboard doors open and close and drinks are poured. Yuuki listens, absently visualising Timothy's actions. One of the light bulbs above his head flickers. He does his best to ignore it, but when it stops flickering and flickers again he feels a surge of irritation well up inside of him. He turns his head to the side to glare at the light. It turns out to be a moth flying crazy loops at the light bulb. Yuuki watches it for a moment then looks away before the light can burn a white afterimage into his eyes for him to see every time he blinks.

After having stood in the darkness of the hallway for so long, this room is too bright and Yuuki finds himself wishing he was back in the darkness again. Sure, the flashbacks come a lot easier there and the darkness itself can serve as a trigger for them, but there Yuuki doesn't have to worry about masking the grief that he knows is written all over his face. He doesn't have to fix his expression if the shadows are hiding it. He doesn't have to fake he's okay when he's not.

Unfortunately, there's no hiding from Timothy. There's a bit of release to be found in that, but it's equally unnerving. It's not so bad around Kyle, since Kyle *knows* how he's feeling – knows as in has experienced a lot of it himself, and in a way that Timothy never had even after being directly affected by the Ninao incident.

But around Timothy he feels a lot of shame.

Perhaps it's because Timothy's always been steady throughout all of it, being able to recover from the shock of what happened at the Ninao office in ways that Yuuki can't and hasn't been able to. Maybe it's because he's always been a constant support and so Yuuki almost feels like he owes it to him to be doing better. Now that he's doing worse, falling backwards no matter how hard he tries to keep a hold of himself…

His mind tells him it's his fault. Everyone else – Kyle especially – tells him it's not. Yuuki knows in the rational part of his mind that no, of course it isn't his fault that recent circumstances have rendered him so overwhelmed, but still he can't help but feel ashamed of himself.

"What is it you wanted to talk about?" Yuuki asks as Timothy comes over and sets down two glasses of whiskey on the table.

Timothy waits until he's seated beside Yuuki before he answers the question. "You."

Yuuki narrows his eyes. At least he saw that one coming. But instead of his usual 'I'm fine' dismissal, he says nothing. He doesn't know what to say that. He's not sure there is anything to say about it. He could laugh and joke about how Lee would scold and tell him 'I told you so' if he saw Yuuki like this, but that's about it.

There is, however, no one to blame but Yuuki himself. He was warned about what taking on Kyle's case might do to his health. He was warned multiple times and by different people, so it wasn't as if he hadn't seen it coming and it wasn't as if he didn't have an out; Yuuki's undoing has to be as much his own fault as it is a product of the circumstances.

Thoughts circulating again, Yuuki furrows his brow, sits up and takes the glass of whiskey closest to him in his hand. He stares at the light reflecting off the surface of the liquor for a moment before taking a sip and then downing a mouthful. Timothy says nothing of the behaviour and simply takes a swig of his own.

The silence between them isn't comfortable.

"Are we going to have this conversation?" Yuuki mutters.

Timothy doesn't answer. His lack of words is disconcerting, so Yuuki drinks some more of his glass to distract himself and tries as hard as he can to turn his focus away from his anxious thoughts and onto the smoky aftertaste lingering his throat.

It occurs to him after a few minutes that Timothy's deliberately not talking so as to give Yuuki a chance to talk. Timothy's ready to listen and offer supportive words where he can, but he doesn't want to pressure Yuuki to find words straight away.

But Yuuki struggles to say anything. Saying those words verbally is a lot harder than it would be if he were to write them down, and even then

Yuuki's not sure how well he could explain everything he's dealing with. Some of it he doesn't even fully understand himself.

Yuuki tries to hide his frustration but fails. Timothy can see it clearly but doesn't press.

"We should probably have something to eat with this," Timothy remarks. He pushes back his seat and glances at Yuuki's near finished drink. "Would you like me to refill that for you?"

The glasses are small and so don't hold much. Yuuki's already feeling the effect of the alcohol on his mind, but it's not unpleasant and he's still aware of himself. He hands the glass to Timothy with a quiet thanks.

While he's gone, Yuuki tries to find words for everything he's dealing with. He could easily summarise it as 'PTSD stuff' and coming to terms with everything that's happened in the last two months, but it's more than that really. He knows that Timothy isn't going to be bothered if there's no conversation to be had. They can speak with their silence just as well as they can speak with their words.

Besides his current difficulty to communicate verbally, what Yuuki is going through isn't new. They've been over what's bothering him. They've already arrived at a conclusion surrounding it. So why then, is Yuuki unable to shake off the bewilderment he feels when thinking about it?

Perhaps the investigation into Kyle's case is what's been influencing his thoughts, or the recent development of events and Andy's refusal to consider Yuuki's point of view more seriously. Or, as he's coming to realise as the alcohol takes effect, maybe it's something Yuuki's felt all along but just has never really questioned for fear of finding out a different truth.

He clears his throat as Timothy returns to his seat beside him. Before he speaks, he takes another sip of whiskey and then, after struggling to break free of the grip some unknown force has on his throat, downs the entire glass.

Timothy's hand lands on his shoulder again. "Hey," he murmurs, voice tight but not unkind. "Come on. Tell me what's going on in that head of yours."

There's enough alcohol in Yuuki's system now for his tongue to loosen and finally find the words he needs. "Ninao." *Great start, Yuuki*, he retorts inwardly. *Pretty sure Timothy's already guessed that.* He tries again. "You…you ever still wonder about Ninao? A-about, um…"

"It's okay, Yuuki. Take your time."

Yuuki grimaces. He's not sure if his words are making much sense. He knows what he's trying to say but getting it out verbally is difficult. He tries again. "About…*why*. Do you still ask yourself why it happened?"

And there it is: the question that's been lurking in the back of his mind for months now, the one Yuuki's been too unwilling to let himself think too hard about.

A glance shows Timothy trying to grasp what Yuuki's getting at, his gaze full of caution and haunted by bad memories. Yuuki knows he features in those memories. Timothy had been the one to bust open the door to the old shed Yuuki had been locked in. He'd been the first person to lay eyes on his condition and the one, alongside his son Joshua, to monitor him while they waited for the ambulance.

Ninao haunts them both in different ways. Neither of them wish to revisit those memories if they don't have to, and yet here they are, the recent events and conversations having brought up the worst of it.

"Are you meaning the reason why Ninao happened?" Timothy asks quietly.

Yuuki swallows. His vision blurs but he blinks it away. "Yeah."

"You think it might not be because of setting up the Youth Rehabilitation Trust?"

"I mean, I *know* that's what everyone agreed it had to be about. I know I thought that's what it was about, too. I just...I don't know."

He's afraid of what his reaction will be once he finds out, if there is an alternate truth. It's said that ignorance is bliss, and Yuuki wonders if it's true for this situation too. Maybe he'd be better off just believing that the whole incident – his kidnapping, that harrowing experience in the shed that nearly killed him – was simply because people viewed the setting up of the Trust as an act of rebellion against the usurper Taularh's justice system.

There's just something that doesn't make sense no matter how much Yuuki thinks about it. If he asked questions when looking into Kyle's case, then surely he ought to ask questions for this too?

Timothy squeezes his shoulder. "What other reason do you think there might be? Can you think of anything?"

"I don't know," Yuuki whispers. "I don't know."

"That's okay. Your concern isn't invalid just because you can't justify it. Sometimes we know things by our gut instinct that can't really be understood with logic."

"Like when you questioned Kyle's case?"

"There was logic involved there too," Timothy says. "But it wasn't until I listened to my gut and followed it that I saw that. I *knew* something wasn't right with the case. I became increasingly aware of how disconcerted it was making me feel, but I could've just as easily dismissed it as doubt and pushed it to the back of my mind.

"So what I'm saying is…if your gut's telling you something's amiss, then hear it out. Give it a chance."

My gut's telling me we should be actively looking for whoever the spy is here at the palace, not waiting around hoping they'll be nice and not attack us, but no one would hear me out before, would they?

Timothy withdraws his hand then to give Yuuki space to think. Beneath the table, Yuuki's right leg bounces up and down uncontrollably. Yuuki narrows his eyes against the swirling of his mind. He considers taking a handful of the peanuts Timothy brought out and is now munching on, but Yuuki can't bring himself to do so. He has no appetite and doesn't have the energy or will to stop leaning on his arm long enough to reach for the plate.

Yuuki takes a deep breath and sighs. The whiskey starts talking. "So, uh…you know how they k'…kidnapped me?"

Timothy hums in acknowledgement but otherwise stays quiet.

"I've been wondering…why didn't they just kill me? What was the point of taking me if not to kill me or interrogate me or something? They could've just dumped me off a cliff or shot me. Why did they…?" Yuuki's throat constricts. The words are coming too fast for his liking. "Did they want me to die a slow death? Is that it? Is that why they left me in that shed, so that there'd be enough time for my body to give up on itself before anyone found me?"

Staring wide-eyed at the empty glass in front of him, Yuuki wishes he hadn't downed the drink so quickly. He could do with the distraction and the aftertaste is not enough.

He's trembling. He curls his fingers and digs his nails into his palm. "I…why didn't they just kill me?"

Dizziness and anxiety overwhelm him. Yuuki's breathing picks up and he's on the verge of losing himself to another panic attack when Timothy's arms wrap around his shoulders.

Yuuki blinks slowly. It takes him a few seconds to realise that it isn't so much Timothy leaning over to hug him as it is Yuuki having tilted sideways into him. *When did that happen?*

"Let's get you back to bed before you crash," Timothy says. "You're drunk already, aren't you?" He shifts to sling Yuuki's arm over his shoulders and wrap an arm around his waist. "I'll help you walk, okay? We can talk about Ninao later on."

Thinking about the nightmares that will stalk him, Yuuki almost protests. But he's still coherent enough to agree that if he's not going to have a choice about crashing into sleep, out here in the dining room probably isn't the best place for that to happen.

He lets Timothy pull him to his feet. Yuuki stumbles, but Timothy's grip on his wrist tightens and he remains upright.

"It's alright," Timothy murmurs. "I've got you."

There's a strange-sounding emotion Yuuki hears in Timothy's tone. It's strange in the sense that it carries a heavy weight that Yuuki can only identify as sorrow. For what, he's not sure. It's never been something he's heard in Timothy's voice when they've talked about Ninao before.

He tries to ask about it, what it means and why Timothy sounds so sad all of a sudden, but his voice refuses to come. It feels like the whiskey is dragging his body closer and closer to the ground; if Timothy weren't holding him up, he'd probably collapse and pass out right there. Yuuki makes a mental note not to drink again any time soon. He feels like this enough, just from being sleep deprived.

Somehow they make it to the infirmary without falling. He does his best to carry his own weight, but a few minutes of dizzy walking he's leaning so heavily against Timothy that all he's doing is keeping his legs moving forward.

Kyle wakes to the noise of them stumbling in – or more specifically, Yuuki's foot catching on the side of the doorway – and he jolts upright in his bed, eyes wide, taking everything in. It was Yuuki's choice to sleep in here when they all first moved into the palace so that Kyle didn't have to sleep alone. Now is the first time Yuuki's felt any regret over that choice.

Yuuki mumbles an apology as Timothy hauls him over to the bed beside Kyle's. Kyle watches them, his shoulders losing their tension but his eyes alight with concern. There's a lamp on a bedside table that's been placed between the two beds, and when Timothy pulls Yuuki around to sit on the bed, Timothy's face is momentarily thrown in shadow. It's because of that shadow, and Yuuki's own drunkenness, that Yuuki doesn't see the glances Timothy and Kyle exchange around him.

"What...ha'..happened?" Kyle asks. Usually there'd be a hint of frustration in Kyle's voice at the stuttering his head injury brought on, but tonight there's none. Only worry – the kind of worry that stabs the soul.

"I-is he drunk?"

Timothy's sigh carries no strength to it. "It wasn't his intention to get so. Eh, Yuuki? You just didn't realise it would have this great an effect on you."

"Hnnnnn 'f course," Yuuki mumbles. He feels his feet come free of his shoes, his legs being lifted up onto the bed. He doesn't remember lying down, but he's too tired to do anything.

"Sorry we woke you up, Kyle. I know it's been hard to sleep for you lately."

Kyle's voice, barely audible. "'s fine."

Yuuki closes his eyes. There's a rustling followed by a gentle weight settling over him. A blanket. He shifts so that he can grasp the edge of the blanket in his hand and pull it closer to himself. Timothy and Kyle talk quietly between themselves, whatever they're saying going over Yuuki's head.

The sound of the conversation, of voices that are safe and familiar, is comforting, and he finds himself lulled by it.

14

Yuuki wakes in the morning with a terrible headache and his stomach churning uncomfortably, but also with a consoling warmth spread out behind him. It takes him a fair while to drag his mind back into focus, and he belatedly realises that the weight draped over his torso is someone's arm.

Before he has a chance to freak out, he realises it's Kyle's. When he turns enough to peer over his shoulder, he sees, in the lamplight and the sunlight sneaking through the gap beneath the curtains, that Kyle's sound asleep behind him.

Has he been hugging me all night? It's not like they've never slept side-by-side this close before, so Yuuki's not bothered in any way by it. But something inside of him feels unsettled at the thought, however. It's something Yuuki knows to be true but it's not something he likes to acknowledge, because in doing so, he's also confessing how badly he's been slipping downhill.

Timothy can see his confidence unravelling. Kyle can see the ways in which that misplaced shame manifests, the ways in which Yuuki's own mind sabotages itself. So far, Yuuki's done his best to hide it from the others, but he can feel himself breaking further and further apart and he knows it won't be long before they see it too. And here Kyle is giving him a hug, knowing all this but staying beside him anyway.

Yuuki's too ashamed to admit just how desperately he needs it.

Behind him, Kyle stirs. He stills and by that Yuuki knows he's awake. Kyle props himself up on his elbow and peers over Yuuki's shoulder. With a groan, he withdraws the arm draped over Yuuki's side, sits up and moves over to sit on the edge of the bed.

"Sorry. I didn't make you uncomfortable, did I?" he asks, voice thick with sleep.

Yuuki already misses the weight of Kyle's arm over him. His back feels cold. He rolls onto it to make up for the lost warmth and tries to ignore the sharp yearning in his chest for Kyle to come back to hugging him. "You didn't."

Kyle turns and regards him cautiously. When he sees that Yuuki genuinely means that, he sighs, relieved. Yuuki wishes he could manage to verbalise his gratitude as a reassurance, but the words get lost in his throat.

"Timothy told me," Kyle murmurs. "About what you guys were talking about last night, re the Ninao incident."

Oh, so that's what they were talking about when I fell asleep. "I see."

"Yuuki?"

"You think I'm out of my mind, right?"

"No. Timothy doesn't either, by the way. He's just afraid of you stressing too much over things we can't find the answers to right now."

Yuuki frowns hard. "Yeah, I know."

"Do you want to talk about it?" Kyle asks quietly.

Yuuki drags himself into sitting upright. He heaves a sigh. "Not

125

really."

"That's okay."

And Kyle leaves it there. No pressing, no prying. The invitation is still there but he's not pressuring Yuuki to talk about something he's uncomfortable with. The tension between them recedes further.

Yuuki wonders if that's why he drank last night, instead of simply defaulting to coffee like he always does – because Timothy was concerned and wanted to talk.

Yuuki realises he's built a force field around himself. He's afraid to let anyone see just how much of a wreck he is inside, even Kyle. He's afraid to let himself be that vulnerable. These walls he's built up have perhaps always been there, beneath the surface, but now they're exposed and so he'd been making a subconscious effort to reinforce them. Beneath them, he's ashamed of who he's become and he feels the need to prove to everyone he's managing, that he hasn't lost it.

A gentle weight settles over his head and shoulders, his back. Yuuki lifts his head, bewildered, as Kyle fixes the blanket he's draped over him so that the side of it isn't hanging in front of Yuuki's face.

Yuuki stares at him. "What are you…?"

Kyle leans back away. "I, um…I find this helps when I'm going through a rough time." He flushes. "I think it's because it makes me feel like I'm hiding, or being hugged or something. I don't know."

Yuuki huffs out a breath. He ducks his head, a small smile tugging at his lips. *Trust Kyle to be so thoughtful like this.* "Thanks."

"And, uh…if you ever want a hug, just ask. Or if you can't – if that's too difficult – then…"

"I'll keep that in mind," Yuuki murmurs.

Kyle nods. He ducks his head, scratches the back of his neck. After a moment, he asks, "Are you okay, after yesterday?"

"Yeah, thanks. Don't worry, I didn't drink much. It just affected me a lot more and a lot sooner than I anticipated."

"I mean, after what happened because of the meeting."

Because of the photos, Kyle doesn't say. Yuuki wishes he hadn't brought those images to the front of his mind by mentioning them. "I didn't drink just because of that."

"I know. I just...panic attacks always leave you shaken, don't they? Feeling all worn out and not right, like your energy's unbalanced? At least, that's how they make me feel when I've had them." Kyle's brow pinches. "You had a pretty bad one yesterday. Is there anything I can do? Make you a coffee or something?"

"It's fine. Making it myself will give me something to do to distract myself. Thanks, though."

Yuuki feels bad for dismissing Kyle's offer, especially since his concern is so real and understanding. But it's true: Yuuki does need a distraction. As awkward as it is to do so one-handed, he still likes the routine of preparing coffee himself. It's helped him adjust to not having his right arm anymore, both physically and emotionally.

Thankfully, Kyle doesn't take it personally. "All goods. Just let me know if there is anything you need, 'kay?"

"Hmm."

Truth be told, Yuuki doesn't know what he needs. An involuntary mental tugging at the memory of the comfort Kyle's hug brought him begs to differ. Yuuki adamantly ignores it. He'd rather lie to himself than admit he's not brave enough to say he wants it. Sure, Kyle did offer it first. It's not as though they've never hugged or cuddled before, either. It simply feels too selfish a request, and one he doesn't deserve, to ask for such comfort.

"I think I'm gonna go get something to eat," Kyle says, breaking the silence. He moves off the bed and picks up the jersey chaotically folded on a nearby chair. He slips it on over the clothes he's taken to sleeping in. "I'll see you out there."

Yuuki slouches and slumps forward when he leaves. He sighs.

He debates trying to go back to sleep, if just to stop thinking before paranoia gets to him again. But the risk of nightmares is too high and Yuuki doesn't have the mental or emotional energy to deal with the after effects of that. He slept better when Kyle was here, too, he thinks. In any case, it's best just to stay awake.

He shrugs the blanket off his shoulders. He gets up, changes into warm outdoor clothes in readiness for a walk later and leaves the room too.

Looking at the time, it's only mid-morning. He's not feeling so great. Yuuki expects it's due to his stomach still processing the alcohol from last night, but the unease taking a hold of his limbs tells him there's something else messing with his system: anxious stress.

It's different from general anxiety, and it feels different from the residual shakiness left in him from the panic attack yesterday. Yuuki struggles to understand what it means. He tries to brush it off, dismiss it, but the feeling won't leave him and it makes him all the more nervous.

Is this a genuine gut feeling that something bad is going to happen today, or am I just paranoid? Is there a reason why I'm this on edge, or am I just letting my PTSD related anxiety get the better of me?

Yuuki can't tell anymore. He's too afraid to ask anyone else if they're feeling this too, even Timothy, despite remembering how they talking about trusting gut instincts last night. The chances he'll be invalidated and this feeling of his dismissed as his own anxiety is too high.

But the ominous feeling only grows, and it's not even reached midday by the time the walls of the palace start to feel too closed in. No one seems to be surprised when Yuuki abruptly abandons his second coffee. Again, he hasn't finished it, but like yesterday he needs out. He keeps his eyes downcast as he exits the building in a hurry.

As soon as he's out in the fresh air, his nerves calm a little. It irons out some of the prickling sensation in his blood and numbs the churning in his stomach numbs. He takes to the trail to the north-west of the palace, same as usual, letting his movements ease into a familiar steady pace.

At the end of the trail, an hour and a half's walk into the bush, there's a small waterfall. The sound of rushing water is calming, and Yuuki lets his mind get lost and thoughtless in the sound of it. The quiet surrounding it, and the slight dip in temperature here is welcome. Standing here, he's able to experience something akin to peace.

But the effect doesn't last long. Without warning, the ominous feeling that's been following him around all morning comes back to greet him. His mind pulls out of the trance and his body involuntarily begins to tense up.

What the heck is going on with me today? Yuuki thinks in frustration. The

129

tranquillity of the waterfall's atmosphere lost to him, he heaves a sigh and starts trudging back down the path.

The leaves high up in the trees rustle in the wind. Yuuki distracts himself with navigating puddles and patches of mud again. Near the end of his walk, dehydration and hunger start making him feel faint, and Yuuki considers the possibility that the reason for his feeling out of kilter could simply be that – that coupled with having had that bad panic attack yesterday could easily explain why he's so unnerved.

Yet such an explanation would be too easy, wouldn't it? The answer, as it turns out, is yes.

Fifteen minutes out from the palace, a bird lets out an alarm call and shoots past him from that direction. Yuuki's heart pounds in fright. He tries reassuring himself everything's fine and then he hears it: there's someone coming.

Footsteps are headed his way, sticks and stones crunching underfoot. They're accompanied by a middle aged man's voice, and Yuuki almost relaxes. His body stubbornly won't let him, but he tries to quell the adrenaline anyway. It's probably just Timothy. It sounds like he's talking to someone. Maybe he's with Kyle and they got concerned when they couldn't find Yuuki anywhere, and so –

"… wouldn't have happened if Kindall had been successfully dealt with in the first place."

Yuuki's vision whites out. …*what?* That's not Timothy. His blood spikes with an electric fear that turns his hearing to static.

"I mean, we could've just left him alone," says a second voice, younger than the first. "Everything started becoming messy because he insisted he was innocent."

"No, it got messy because our representative couldn't fulfil his job." A pause. "That, and it's not like we knew Harrison and Takahashi would get involved."

"They wouldn't have had the chance to if you guys and the other two hadn't failed your mission."

Yuuki's paralysed. They're talking about Ninao. They're talking about how Kyle wasn't killed as planned at Village Park. He needs to move. He needs to move.

"Really, Rob? It failed because there was an unexpected problem, not because we were incompetent."

Yuuki's eyes widen. It finally clicks. The voices, the subject of conversation. *They're the ones who kidnapped me.* Two out of three of them are, at least, and while he doesn't recognise the third, something tells him he should.

Adrenaline finally kicks in as it's supposed to and Yuuki pulls himself out of his freeze. His knees are trembling, but he forces his legs to move. He can't go back to the palace – he'll run straight into the voices if he does. He could run back down the trail, but he'd only be forced to hide again at the end of it and he has to get back to the palace urgently to warn the others.

There's not enough time. Yuuki scans the bush around him and makes a decision.

He's barely concealed himself beneath the overlapping fronds of a small native tree fern when footsteps come over the rise in the track. His muscles lock, his heart beats wildly in his chest. Yuuki clenches his jaw and waits.

"Yeah, I know. I'm just frustrated things aren't going smoothly. I guess we ought to stop beating ourselves up about all this. That group deserve some credit, I must say. Dare I say we underestimated these guys?"

"Who knew it would be so hard to take down a scraped together group like them…"

The three men saunter down the path, oblivious to Yuuki's presence. Their footsteps sound like the beat of unsynchronised war drums in Yuuki's ears as they approach. Yuuki's almost too scared to look, but he does anyway. Sure enough, it's *them*. Their faces haunt his dreams. The third man – the one whose voice he initially mistook for Timothy's – looks vaguely familiar, but Yuuki can't pinpoint why. He feels like he's seen this guy before though, somewhere…

He holds his breath, keeping himself as still as possible and tracking their movements only with his eyes and ears. They don't notice him. Their strides continue along unchanged.

That is, until they don't.

"Guys," says the oldest of the three. He stops abruptly, right outside of Yuuki's hiding place. "We need a plan."

The fern fronds are the only thing between Yuuki and them. The other two men stop too. Their shoes crunch on the gravel as they turn. Yuuki has to mentally force himself to keep breathing.

One of Yuuki's kidnappers grunts. "I thought that was why we came out here – to plan."

"It is. But I'm thinking it might be imperative we do something sooner than later. We've kept the Princess at bay with what we've told the media, but I get the feeling she and her group will figure out a way around them if we don't intervene."

Plan. They're planning? It's just as Yuuki feared – exactly what he was trying to warn Andy about earlier: these guy operate on their own terms, provoked or not.

Somehow managing to think, he slips out his phone. His heart lurches as he almost drops it. If Andy won't believe his word, then Yuuki's going to have to bring him solid evidence. Fingers shaking, he swipes the screen and fumbles for the audio recorder app. He presses record.

"Luis, didn't you say the Princess was doing a speech or something tonight?"

The other of Yuuki's kidnappers hums. "Heard Andy talking on the phone to someone about it yesterday."

"When you were out in the car park?"

"Yeah."

Yuuki swallows. Kyle was right as well – there most definitely was someone who saw them leave last night.

"Shame you failed your mission," Luis says, the smirk in his voice evident. "Would've been great if you'd succeeded, eh, Rob? I gave you a great advantage, and you let it slip."

The older man, Rob shifts his feet. "Alright, *I'm sorry.*"

"Sorry you got beat up by a girl and defeated by a mobile phone?"

"Hey."

Luis laughs. "Kidding. It was three to one. You did what you could. It's not like we had much time to organise anything anyways."

"I thought we could at least capture one of them to try to force the Princess to surrender. Honestly, that Kindall kid though. He's a fighter."

"Juun had a bit of trouble subduing him too."

The other man beside Luis huffs. "Yeah, the only way we got him was because Deborah started shooting Takahashi."

"Still reckon it was a bit extreme of her."

"Why?" Juun says. "It did the job, didn't it?"

Yuuki wants to be sick. Literally sick.

"Alright," Rob says. "Come on, we need to plan something. If we could do something today would be great – deal with this whole situation before the Princess gives that speech of hers and has any chance of winning anybody over. Any ideas?"

Juun sighs. "I know we want to try to stick to the more *peaceful* options, but maybe we ought to consider a less negotiable approach."

"It'd take too much time to plan. Besides, Deborah's the one who usually organised those sorts of things. Unless we can plan and execute something well, it's too risky."

"Taking a hostage might work," Luis remarks. "Which, you know, we could've had that if you'd managed to take Kindall."

Juun sniffs. "Well, unless we magically happen to run into someone out here on their own, ain't gonna happen. So we can rule that one out."

Yuuki's shaking. His jacket is warm but it's not warm enough. Then again, it's not the cold he's shaking from. *They'll take me,* he realises in terror. *If they find me here, they'll take me. They can't find me. Please, don't let them find me.*

His best chance of getting out of here is to wait until they've gone, but he might not get that option. If he gets spotted, the moment that happens he needs to run. No hesitation. No second guessing himself as to whether they've actually seen him or not. His knees are sore from crouching so tensely, but he's just going to have to ignore it. He can't take on all three of them.

In other words, as soon as he gets the chance, he needs to run.

"Let's keep walking," Luis says. He sighs. "We might think of something as we go."

Juun and Rob hum in agreement.

The three men start walking again, and relief washes over Yuuki in a lukewarm wave. He stays as he is though, almost rooted to the ground like the trees around him. It's better to wait until they're out of sight and far enough way they won't hear him leave his hiding spot.

But then Rob's shoes scuff the soil. His footsteps slow, and Yuuki *knows*. Rob's seen him.

"Luis, Juun."

The other two sets of footsteps slow to a stop again.

From here, Yuuki can see the broadening grin on Rob's lips as he turns.

"What's up?" Juun asks.

Run, run! Yuuki screams at his muscles but they won't move. He's frozen. He's paralysed.

Rob's gaze shoots straight through a gap in the fern fronds and locks on Yuuki's face. "I think our plan might just work."

15

Yuuki almost chokes on his breath. He launches himself out of hiding, stumbles. In his peripheral, three shapes advance but Yuuki doesn't spare them a proper glance. He just turns and *sprints*.

With blind terror, he runs. His chest is tight with panic and his throat constricts with it too. It's far worse than the panic attack he'd had only half an hour ago. It's far worse than any panic he's ever experienced. He's all adrenaline. All survival mode is now locked in flight. He can't fight them and win. Freezing and hiding already failed him.

He has to run. He has no choice but to try outrun them.

A hand snags his raincoat. Yuuki's yanked to a halt, his phone flying out of his hand, still recording, with the motion of it. It's hard to see past the white haze over his vision, but Yuuki fights. He lashes out, whirls and kicks. A frustrated hiss. The hand loosens and he darts off again.

His mind's empty. The phone's forgotten. *Escape,* is his only tangible subconscious thought. He's not sure he can make it back to the others. He's fast, especially on adrenaline, but there's three men chasing him and at least one of them is faster.

Freeze failed him. Flight's not enough, apparently. That means his only escape now is to literally fight his way out.

He's caught up to again. Yuuki trips over his own feet and while the momentum he's got going is enough to carry him forwards without him falling, it slows him down. The same hand as before latches onto his arm and pulls him sideways, sending them both careening straight into a wide-girthed tree.

Yuuki grunts. He staggers, tries to pull his arm free but fails. The man tugs him back towards him and Yuuki's met with a fist flying towards his face. He ducks just in time. The man's fist hits the tree instead.

In the same instant he yells, Yuuki's able to tear himself free.

It's a losing battle, though. He's not sure if it's Luis or Juun who slams into him then. Rob's not caught up to them yet, not that it matters though.

Yuuki's tackled to the ground. His breath's driven out of him. He wrestles with the weight on top of him, throwing himself into the wildest struggle he can manage. His fist catches the guy in the jaw. It almost feels like a fluke. Yuuki knees the guy in the stomach and throws him off of him. He rolls over, brings his legs under himself and makes to get up and run again.

But he's out of time. Another weight lands on his back. Yuuki plants his palm into the soil and tries to buck him off, but then there's a hand clamping down on the back of his neck and slamming his head back down. The elbow digging into his back leaves his spine, only to be replaced by a firm grip on his wrist. Before Yuuki can draw in a breath, his arm's wrenched behind his back and his wrist pulled right up to between his shoulder blades.

Yuuki gasps at the pain. He squeezes his eyes shut and struggles. Each movement sends pain shooting through the muscles in his shoulder and arm, pulls at the muscles in his hand as he tries to tear himself out of the guy's grasp.

It's futile, though. He's pinned. He tries kicking, but all it does is lash his shoulder with pain. The guy holding him down breathes hard, but there's no tiredness to loosen the vice grip he has on Yuuki's neck and wrist. Even when the guy shifts to dig a knee into Yuuki's spine, the hold doesn't loosen.

Yuuki failed. He's screwed. He's been caught, the bad guys are planning something – the bad guys are planning something and *now he can't warn the others* – and furthermore that something is highly likely going to involve him. If anything, it'll prove to Andy he was right, but there's no consolation in the matter.

"Nice catch," the first guy says. He laughs, a little out of breath.

Rob catches up then. He walks into Yuuki's field of vision and smiles at him triumphantly. "Nice of you to save us the trouble."

Yuuki glares at him as best he can muster, though he doubts there's anything that can be seen past the fear he knows is shining in his eyes.

Something clicks in Yuuki's mind. He *has* seen this guy before, he knows it. But the air about him is different, as though the crazy grin on his face doesn't match his character. Something about him feels displaced, like whatever memory Yuuki has of him was simply an act and now he's seeing this guy's true character revealed to him.

The revelation is disturbing. It sends an arrow of extra fear piercing through his heart. *Have these people been lurking right in front of us all along?*

"What's with that look? It's your own fault, you know. If you stopped getting in the way of things, you could save yourself all the trauma."

Stopped getting in the way of things? He says it as though it's Yuuki's own fault he's had to suffer so much. Like they're not the ones who have deliberately hurt him in the first place.

"Hey guys," the guy pinning Yuuki down says. "He had a phone on him."

Rob frowns. "Search him."

More hands on him. The first guy approaches out of Yuuki's sight, and the fear that shoots through him as the guy's hands feel around him and plunge into his jacket pockets, searching, is suffocating. The guy holding him down snickers at Yuuki's reaction.

The first guy pulls back, empty-handed. "Nothing. Must've dropped it. I'll go back up the trail and look for it."

"Wait, Luis," Rob says. "We can look for it after. We need to get Takahashi secured first. I'll run and get some stuff. You stay here with Juun and make sure he doesn't get away."

"Roger that. You know where we put our backpacks, right?"

"Linen cupboard, out the back?"

"Yep."

With one last glance at Yuuki, Rob starts off down the trail. "Sweet. I'll be back." As he moves into a run, he calls over his shoulder, "Do *not* let him escape!"

Juun, the man holding Yuuki down snorts. "Think we'll do a better job than you with Kindall!"

Rob's footsteps fade. The noise they created from the chase fades to nothing. Yuuki's heartbeat is loud in his ears. The silence presses around him like an oppressive sheet.

"You're awfully quiet," Luis murmurs, coming to crouch down on Yuuki's other side where Yuuki can see him. "What's up? You scared?"

Yuuki clenches his jaw. He makes another attempt to fight but it's useless. The hand on the back of his neck tightens and sends a shiver down his spine. Yuuki stiffens and stills.

"You should know by now," Juun says, "that when we catch you, we catch you. What is this – the third time we've caught you?"

Luis rubs the reddened side of his hand from when he hit the tree. "Third time, I believe. First was Ninao. Second was Two Lakes. Then now." He chuckles. "Though I don't think Harrison will be saving you this time."

Yuuki's trying not to think that far ahead. In fact, he's trying not to think at all. Dissociation has yet to settle in, but right now he's content with letting his overly heightened senses and core-deep panic blind him to anything else. He doesn't want to think about what will happen to him. He doesn't want to imagine what will be done to him – done to the others – once they have him secured.

No one knows he's out here. No one knows what's happening him to him right now. But when they do, Yuuki has to trust that someone will find a way to get him out. It's too early to know if a rescue is possible, but the faith that there's hope for one is something he must cling to. He has to.

It's the only thread keeping him together right now.

Luis tilts his head, a thought flashing across his face. He fixes Yuuki with a narrow-eyed stare. "Your phone. You were trying to call for help, weren't you?"

Not willing to answer that, Yuuki simply averts his eyes. It's better they don't know the truth about how he'd been recording their conversation. That'll only make them search for it harder.

"Maybe you should go check," Juun says to his friend. "If he was, then the rest of them might figure something's up."

Luis blinks. "I'd rather risk that happening than risk him getting away. Rob shouldn't be too long. I'll have a look when he gets back, as planned."

After a moment's thought, Juun leans down, tightening his fingers around the back of Yuuki's neck as he does so. "*Or* he could tell us himself." His breath is warm on Yuuki's ear and Yuuki's skin crawls. "So? Were you trying to call for help?"

A scoff. "He won't answer you."

Pain burns through Yuuki's shoulder as Juun pulls his wrist a little higher up his back. Yuuki cries out then, and his chest heaves as he struggles to keep as much fear and panic at bay as possible lest it consume him entirely.

"Juun, come on."

The pain eases, but it doesn't completely leave. Yuuki grimaces.

It's only a matter of time before Rob comes back. He's carrying a plain black backpack, bulked up with supplies that can only be kidnapping materials. Sure enough that's what the contents are, and Yuuki's stomach roils with nausea as his mind finally accepts the reality of what's about to happen.

He closes his eyes a moment, swallowing hard. He doesn't see Luis go off in search of his dropped phone, but he hears it. He doesn't see the coils of rope being pulled out of the backpack, but he hears it. He feels, nonetheless, numbed panic sweep over him as Rob ties a loop of rope around his wrist and knots it.

Yuuki begins dissociating then. His mind clouds with derealisation. Juun doesn't shift his hand. He keeps Yuuki still, face pressed into the dirt, until Rob gives the signal. Juun shifts his hold, moving his weight to sit on the backs of Yuuki's legs. He maintains a firm grip even as Rob grabs the collar of Yuuki's jacket and forces his chest off the ground. Rob wraps the rope right around his chest, once, twice, three times before tying the end off around Yuuki's wrist again. No longer needing to keep his arm pinned, the rope now doing the job for him, Juun finally releases his grip on Yuuki's arm.

The change is worse – he buries his fingers in Yuuki's hair, curls them and *pulls*. Yuuki gasps. He opens his eyes then, and when he sees what Rob's just taken out of the backpack his breathing quickens. *No...*

It's a Peace Force grade cloth meant to be used to help in restraining verbally violent arrestees. It's also what they used to shut Kyle up with in court.

"Please don't," Yuuki whispers. He's already on the verge of spiralling into another panic attack. It's hard to enough to breathe as is, but with that in his mouth... "I-I won't speak. I won't. I'll be quiet, I promise. I'll —"

Rob raises an eyebrow, hands prepped at either end of the cloth. He brings the cloth forward. "You're not in a position to ask."

Yuuki turns his head away, but Rob's hands only follow. Juun's fingers tighten in his hair and pull his head further back, restricting his movement. The cloth brushes against his lips and Yuuki whimpers. He channels all the fear gripping him to clench his teeth together as hard as he can.

"Open your mouth," Rob says, a stern warning in his tone.

Yuuki doesn't relent, so Juun gives him a rough shove. Yuuki whimpers again and screws his eyes shut, but he doesn't loosen his jaw. Rob tries to force the gag between his teeth all the same. Another harsh shove. Juun repeats Rob's instruction but Yuuki still refuses to comply.

So they force him. Fingers grab his jaw and then thumbs are pressing hard into the hinges. Yuuki tries to grit his teeth through the pain but it all of a sudden becomes too much and he's forced to loosen his jaw. The cloth is shoved between his teeth the next second, effectively muffling his cry, and either end is deftly knotted at the base of his skull.

Things move quickly after that. Luis comes back without having found Yuuki's phone, and after a brief discussion, they haul Yuuki to his feet. Before they start walking, they blindfold him. If Yuuki could speak through the gag and through the arising panic attack, he'd tell them that his legs are far too shaky for him to run away on anyways, that they needn't bother taking away his sight.

Unfortunately, it's not his decision to make. He's at their mercy. If they cared, they wouldn't be doing this in the first place.

Yuuki fights for breath, fights to stop the tears from wetting his cheeks and the fear from constricting his throat. He's unable to control the terrified blend of sobs and screams that leave his throat. He tries to quieten himself. He tries to just let himself be frightened if that's what it would take just to stop himself from making so much noise.

But panic still takes a hold of him. He's quickly lost in it, consumed by it, drowning in it.

His captors throw him to the ground and start beating him up for it. But even with fresh bruises over his body and fresh pain throbbing in his shoulder, he can't control it. The three men soon realise this, that he's not just shouting for the sake of making noise, and with grumbles of frustration they stop shoving and kicking him.

Juun makes the call to knock him out. Yuuki's thankful for it.

The last thing that crosses his mind – or rather, his subconscious mind – is that, based on what Rob said earlier, the Ninao kidnapping didn't happen because of the Trust after all.

Yuuki doesn't get the chance to follow that thought before a fist slams into his temple.

16

By 4.30pm, Yuuki's absence grows too disconcerting to ignore. *He's out on a walk,* Kyle tries to reassure himself. *That's why I can't find him around anywhere.*

But it's been a while since Yuuki left. It's not like he's never gone for long walks before, but it's been almost three hours since he left. Kyle's searched all around the palace for him, but he's nowhere to be found. The half-finished coffee Yuuki left behind in the common room is still there too, neglected along with the plunger. Kyle can't help but worry that something may have happened.

He's tempted to think that maybe Yuuki's managing to evade him by actively following him around as he searches, but that's highly unlikely. If that were the case though, someone else would've seen him by now, surely.

When he checks the infirmary again that he notices the dark blue altered raincoat of Yuuki's is missing. It isn't lying on the floor where Kyle last saw it before he left the room earlier in the day, and a careful scan of the room shows that it's not here at all.

Maybe he's worrying too much, but he can't suppress the anxiety he's feeling for Yuuki. The panic attack he'd been having must've been awful if he hadn't been keen on anyone at all seeing him. Yuuki would've known when he made his decision to leave that Kyle, Timothy or Susan would be the only ones who would come after him, and they've all witnessed him having panic attacks before.

Perhaps Timothy was right after all: despite Kyle's best intentions, maybe it is better that Yuuki's allowed his own space and time to process it all. They say it's best to trust your gut instinct, but...

"That's a deep frown you've got on your face."

Kyle flinches. He blinks out of his trance and finds Timothy leaning against the infirmary door, hands in the pockets of his trousers. Kyle feels his face heat up in embarrassment at his reaction.

"I was just thinking," he says defensively.

Timothy hums. "I just came to ask if you'd seen Yuuki around anywhere."

"No. I've been trying to find him, but I think he's gone for a long walk – his raincoat's still gone."

"Ah, that's probably the case then."

Part of Timothy's expression speaks relief, but the weighted concern doesn't leave his face and the furrow in his brow doesn't ease. Kyle can tell he's worried about the length of time Yuuki's not been around too.

"He's not usually gone this long, is he?" he asks.

"Depends. It wouldn't be unusual considering he's still...upset. Did he take his phone?"

"I think so? Joshua gave them all back to us the other afternoon before we, uh, went on our mission, so Yuuki should have his. At least, I think. I tried ringing it but he didn't pick up."

"Either he wasn't ready to talk or he didn't hear it, I'd say."

"I also sent him a message asking if he's okay, but it hasn't been marked read or anything yet."

"He doesn't check his messages much," Timothy says, mouth quirking.

Kyle nods. *Well, I guess that could explain it,* he thinks, wringing his hands.

A thought sees to occur to Timothy then, for he takes his phone out of his pocket and flicks open his messages. But whatever he's hoping to find isn't there and the small sliver of hope he'd had fades. When he sees Kyle's lost expression, he lets out a resigned sigh.

"Yuuki and I came up with a code while we were investigating your case," he explains. "It was supposed to be an SOS message, basically, in case one of us ran into a dangerous situation and had to be careful about subtly letting the other know. In hindsight, it was a good idea, but we never practised it. Just now I thought maybe Yuuki might've remembered to send one and I'd somehow missed it."

Kyle tries not to think too hard about the implication. *What if something came up and Yuuki wasn't able to think clearly enough to send such a message? Or didn't have time to?* But on the other hand, they simply could be worrying too much and there's been no need to send any such alert message at all.

After a minute, Timothy straightens up and sighs. "I guess if he's not back by dark, then we can go out looking for him." The pinch in his brow deepens. "After that, if we still can't find him…then we'll just take things as they come and respond accordingly."

There's more weight to those words than either of them realise.

147

*

Dark comes an hour and a half later, and still Yuuki hasn't shown up.

At 7pm, Kyle and Timothy take their concerns to Andy. The two of them form a search party with Joshua and head outside, equipped with flashlights and a backpack of emergency first aid items between them. Before leaving, Kyle takes his knife and slips into his jacket pocket, though it's not a tool he regards it as right now so much as a weapon.

The blade saved him from capture once. *Better safe than sorry.*

They leave Andy staying back at the palace with a shadow of self-doubt in his eyes. Second guessing himself in how he'd dismissed Yuuki's concerns during the meeting yesterday. It seems like it's now occurring to him that Yuuki may have been right in fearing a prompt attack. Kyle wants Yuuki's concerns to be validated, but he's frightened by the possibility that Yuuki himself might involuntarily be the one to his point about personal security.

His imagination's getting to him now. It's no longer general anxiety Kyle's feeling now, but trepidation. Something has happened to Yuuki – there's no dismissing that now. What exactly, they have yet to find out. Until they do, Kyle's mind runs wild imagining varying degrees of injury in which they might find him, ranging from Yuuki being too shaken up and exhausted from the panic attack to move, to finding him lying bleeding or broken or collapsed somewhere.

Kyle's not ready to include hostiles in that equation. Not yet.

The night is eerily peaceful in contrast to the mood. Timothy points them in the direction of the trail Yuuki said he likes to walk, but besides that there are no words exchanged between them. Their footsteps, rustling of jackets and silence speaks enough.

They walk, and native owls keep hooting. The breeze keeps stirring up the treetops. There's no signs they're approaching anything out of the ordinary. But none of them can relax. Not when they suspect Yuuki's out here, alone, possibly injured.

Fifteen minutes into their walk, the beam of Joshua's head torch reflects off something half-obscured in a dense bush about a metre away from the edge of the path. It's clearly not naturally occurring, and it sends a jolt of fright through Kyle's core. His fingers curl a little tighter around the hilt of the knife in his jacket pocket.

"Found his phone," Joshua announces. His voice is almost too thin to hear.

Joshua and Timothy scan the surrounding area before approaching the object. Kyle sends a nervous glance behind him, flicking his handheld torch back and forth across the path, half expecting to see a shadow slip out of the trees and morph into someone unwelcome.

No one appears, however; it's just the three of them. Joshua trudges through a patch of mud, braces a hand on a tree trunk and leans forward to grab the phone. Something to his left catches his attention, but he precedes with retrieving the phone and walking back to drier ground first.

Cracks on the phone screen light up under Joshua's headlight like spider webs. Joshua wipes the screen with his sleeve and tries turning on the phone, but it doesn't respond. He checks it over for unnoticed damage, but from what Kyle can see, it looks like it should still be functioning. The bush prevented it from smacking into the ground or a tree, so it should've been protected enough.

"Dead battery?" Timothy suggests.

Joshua grimaces. "Yeah, could be actually."

"Well, we know he was here. That's something, at least."

Narrowing his eyes, Joshua hands the phone to Kyle and turns back to what caught his attention earlier. Timothy steps forward, frowning in curiosity, but Joshua holds up his hand. Kyle's gut fills with dread.

"Stay where you are," Joshua murmurs, crouching down, "but can you guys shine your lights over here quickly?"

Kyle first takes a moment to make sure no one's managed to creep up behind them before joining Timothy in doing so. With the three beams of torch light illuminating the soil, they see what Joshua's seeing: a rend in the muddied earth, like someone skidded sideways, and other disturbed areas of gravel and dirt in the path where the ground's been slightly churned up.

With a solemn air about him, Joshua rises out of his crouch. "I think it's signs of a scuffle."

It takes Joshua's voicing his speculations before either Timothy or Kyle understand what they're seeing, however. The marks in the ground – they stand out because there's nowhere else the soil's marked up like that. It poured with rain last night, so they're fresh too. And while Yuuki's discarded phone is an obvious suggestion at who might've left them, these marks have a different look about them than they might had Yuuki simply slipped and lost his balance.

It looks more like someone danced here than simply lost traction.

"Let's not make assumptions," Timothy says carefully. "We don't know with certainty what happened here, and aside from this all we have is Yuuki's phone to go by."

Kyle's right hand goes weak and tingling around the knife. He swallows hard, takes a deep breath. Timothy helped save his life by not making the same assumptions as everyone else when it came to his case. He's right; making assumptions here isn't a good idea.

Joshua raises an eyebrow. "His phone screen wasn't cracked when I gave it back to him," he says, gesturing to Kyle who's holding Yuuki's phone in his other hand.

"Maybe he threw it while he was upset yesterday," Kyle suggests. It's a plausible guess.

Though he considers it for a moment, Joshua just frowns harder. "Possibly, but that doesn't explain why his phone's here and he's not. If he wasn't trying to get away from something or some*one*, wouldn't he have come back for his phone and not just left it here?"

That's…a good point.

"It might've been harder to see in daylight," Timothy reasons. "We saw it because it caught the light of our torches. It's been cloudy all day, so it's not like there was any sunlight to reflect off the screen either. And in regard to why he didn't come back to get it…"

"He could be hurt," Kyle supplies.

Timothy puts his hands on his hips and tilts his head in Kyle's direction. "That."

But Joshua remains dubious. "If we're dealing with a situation where Yuuki was injured instead of chased, then how do we explain this?" He gestures at the marks in the mud. "He would have to be seriously injured to slip and not even try to look for his phone. If he were injured, he

151

would've tried to call us, right? Or at least try get back to the palace?"

Silence from Timothy confirms it as a valid thought.

"I mean, *or* he could've just been having a *really* bad panic attack," Joshua says. "Could've somehow ended up going back up the trail if he was hallucinating a bit or something – I don't know, can that happen with panic attacks? Maybe he freaked himself out and now he's hiding somewhere, I don't know. Point is, Yuuki's missing and the state of his phone says it's likely not of his own choosing."

Kyle struggles to keep a hold of his emotions. He's unnerved, scared for Yuuki and angry about how he could've prevented this all from happening in the first place had he gone after Yuuki sooner. If he'd been the one to find him having that panic attack in the bathroom instead of Logan.

If somehow he's managed to keep Yuuki from running away and running into whatever this is.

"So h-how do we find him?" he whispers.

Joshua's expression is grim. He looks to his father.

"If he's been taken," Timothy says heavily, "then it's best we don't follow him into whatever trap or situation he got caught up in. Let's not take that risk. Of course, we don't have any concrete evidence to know for sure that's what happened; Yuuki might still be out here, on his own, and got himself hurt somehow. If that's the case – in fact, in both cases – I think we should head back to the palace, let Andy know what we've found."

Kyle opens his mouth to argue that they should search for him around here first, but Timothy counters him before he has a chance to speak it.

"We could search for him now, but it would be safer if there were more people out with us. We'll need more equipment too, since we'll be going off trail. We might even have to wait till daylight, as I don't know if Andy will approve of us conducting such a search in the dark when the ground's unfamiliar and slippery."

"So we're going back?" Joshua asks.

Timothy nods. "We'd better."

"Wait, what if we called out to him?" Kyle suggests. "To Yuuki, I mean?" He hates the idea of leaving Yuuki out here alone, especially if they happen to be close to where he is. Maybe he's not in the forest anymore at all, but...

"If he's been caught, we'll be alerting whoever's got him that we're coming from miles away. They'll hear us bush-bashing and talking anyways, but it'll give them more time to prepare for us if we yell out that we're coming."

"Oh...yeah."

They start heading back to the palace, falling into the same formation as before with Joshua leading and Kyle bringing up the rear. They walk slower this time, torch lights sweeping the surrounding bush and the path before them. All three of them are on high alert, and what composure Joshua and Timothy had before coming out here erodes rapidly.

This isn't the first time they've gone out searching for Yuuki, Kyle remembers. He recalls Joshua's tone and body language when he was recounting finding Yuuki in the shed, and Kyle gets why Joshua's so adamant they acknowledge Yuuki may have been taken and why Timothy would rather

153

convince himself to believe that no such thing has happened.

As for Kyle... he's only willing to acknowledge what he knows to be almost certain, and that's that something bad has most definitely happened and whatever it is isn't going to allow Yuuki to return to them in the same state he left the palace earlier in.

It's 7.55pm when they arrive back at the palace. Susan greets the three of them at the back door with a disheartened half smile. She folds her jersey tighter around herself.

"Andy's in the kitchen," she says. The slight quiver in her upper lip betrays her nervousness.

Timothy notices and wraps an arm his wife in a supporting hug. There's no reassurance in it; it's merely for comfort's sake.

"I'll go get one of the waterproof maps from the foyer," Joshua says quietly before slipping away.

Kyle trails behind Timothy and Susan. He feels like he's intruding on an old family affair, or like he's been displaced in space-time and has been sent back to the feels and atmosphere of June last year. But he didn't know Yuuki then. With the current mood as it is around the Harrisons, it feels like Yuuki's been made a stranger to him all over again.

He doesn't connect that thought the more overarching one to begin with. When he does, Kyle doesn't know what to feel. If this is what Yuuki's kidnapping felt like to be directly affected by, then this is like Ninao all over again. And if they don't find Yuuki on this next search, they're going to have to consider the possibility that he's been kidnapped again today.

Emotions well up inside him and intertwine with the anxiousness already eating away at his ability to stay relatively calm. Timothy and Joshua's calm has already broken though. Kyle knows it won't be long before his follows suit.

"Yuuki's not going to be himself for a while," Kyle hears Timothy saying in a memory he can't quite place. *"I don't know if he ever will be. If something like this happens a third time, it'll destroy him."*

This, right now, is that third time, isn't it?

Andy's not in the kitchen; the light's off and the entire dining room and kitchen is vacant besides themselves. Susan pokes her head around the corner to double check. She frowns.

"He was here ten minutes ago," she says.

They wait for Andy to return, but he doesn't. They hear a vehicle pull up in front of the palace front entrance, and car doors opening. There's a bit of a commotion down the hallway that seems to be coming from the foyer, Joshua's voice one of the louder and more even.

"Joshua must be telling the others," Kyle thinks aloud.

Timothy hums. "Sounds like it. I think that's Andy now, too. He might've gone out to the car to bring in some more supplies."

"Would he need to bring the vehicle up here though?" Susan asks, eyebrows furrowed. "Whoever's going out on the search could just collect what they need on the way out?"

Too stressed to come up with a logical explanation, Timothy shrugs.

They're going round in circles thinking and pulling at strings here. It's like Timothy said – they can't know anything for sure until they have concrete evidence. They can guess as much as they want, but unless it points them to Yuuki or at least gives them a decent clue as to what might've happened to him, they're at a loss.

At 8.15pm, they get the solid evidence they wish for. The news is delivered to them by a shaken, wide-eyed and pale faced Joshua.

"Uh, guys?" he says thickly. Joshua's hands are curled into tight fists. "You might want to come see this."

Susan's shoulders tense. "What is it?"

"I-I found Yuuki."

17

Kyle's mind blanks out. Where he'd been feeling relatively fine physically, now he's not. His legs move on autopilot and his head's filling up with a white haze that makes his vision fuzzy. He has to pocket Yuuki's phone before his fingers seize up and he drops it.

The fear crawling up Kyle's throat hurts more than physically being choked did. He's not ready, but he needs to see. He doesn't want to know, but he has to. He wishes he could run and hide from whatever sight is waiting for them, but he can't – for Yuuki's sake, he can't.

And so, as Kyle, Susan, Timothy and Joshua make their way to the foyer, the only thing Kyle can do – the only thing any of them can do – is brace themselves emotionally, mentally. When they arrive at the scene, everyone's already there, staring out the open front doors at whatever's being illuminated by the outdoor lights at the front of the entrance way.

Seeing the fear reflecting in their eyes, Kyle tries to prepare for it. But there's no way to prepare for it. Not this.

Out on the driveway, parked right in front of the palace's front doors, is a standard Peace Force four-wheel drive vehicle. Three men stand in front of it. The body language of the person in the middle is severely different from the other two. Those other two seem to be all that's holding him upright.

Kyle's vision tunnels. *No. Please, no.*

The person in the middle has their face half obscured by two separate lengths of cloth, but there's no second guessing who it is: Yuuki, a blindfold tied over his eyes and the same kind of cloth that Kyle was gagged with during his trial in his mouth; Yuuki, rope wrapped around his chest, pinning his arm behind his back; Yuuki, visibly trembling as he's manhandled further out into the open before them so that everyone can see him clearly.

Yuuki, taken hostage.

"Shouldn't our priority be personal security?" Yuuki had said only yesterday. It's their fault. It's their fault this happened. They underestimated their enemy, and now Yuuki's paying the price for it.

But why? Why does it have to be him? Of all of us, why did it have to be him?

Amelia's crying. Susan's doing her best not to. Andy's face has gone several shades paler, remorse writ all over. Sam's eyes are wild, distressed. Avi and Logan appear to be frozen in space-time.

Timothy, much like Charlie, is frozen, unresponsive, his only expression 'haunted'.

Between Kyle and Amelia, Joshua is the first to break out of the grip horror has on them all. His fear is sharpened into fury. "Care to explain what the *hell* you're doing?"

The man standing on the left of Yuuki clears his throat. He raises his chin and locks his gaze on Amelia. "Princess, we're offering you a deal."

Amelia shakes her head, sobbing.

"You can have Takahashi back if you surrender."

An ultimatum. One they can't afford to accept or deny: no one can bear to watch Yuuki suffer like this, but they can't surrender either. They *can't*. And Yuuki surely knows this too – it's not like he can tell them, but if he was allowed to speak Kyle knows that he'd be telling them not to listen to his captors. He'd tell them his life isn't worth it. He'd tell them *he* isn't worth it.

But are they really willing to watch Yuuki suffer before their eyes in exchange?

"And what if we refuse to surrender under such terms?" Andy says levelly. There's the tone of authority in his voice, but it's weak; he has no authority here.

"Then you'll pay the price for it," says the man. "Or should I say, he will."

To emphasise his point, he raises a fist and rams it into Yuuki's gut. Yuuki doubles over with a muffled gasp of pain. He probably would've sunken to his knees if the other captor didn't have a tight grip on him. Kyle doesn't miss the brief look of exasperation that guy sends the first. He doesn't miss the gleam of light off the gun in the first guy's back pocket either. Though it can't be seen from this angle, no doubt the second guy has one too.

Overwhelmed, Amelia breaks down sobbing. Her face has gone several shades lighter, off colour, her breathing is erratic. It's a natural reaction, but also a dangerous one. There's too much weight on Amelia's shoulders. She's crumbling under the pressure of it. As it is, the idea of leading the Kingdom is above her and the stress of it has her in over her head.

159

And now she's just been handed an ultimatum that's forcing her to choose between stopping a friend's retraumatisation and quitting her struggles to officially claim the throne as her own. It's obvious which one appeals to her more.

Kyle's not the only one who's realised this. Joshua, standing beside her, shoots her a nervous glance. When Amelia returns it, bewildered, his eyes flash and he presses his lips together tightly.

Don't take the bait, he's trying to convince her. *Don't let your emotions trip you into falling into the trap they've laid for us. Playing their game will only end bad for us – for all of us on this side of the driveway, and for Yuuki.*

They can't give up fighting for Amelia; surrender is not an option. Leaving Yuuki in the hands of those men is not an option either, of course, but they're going to have to figure out another way to get him back.

Yuuki's captors watch this exchange with amused, rewarded smiles. "We figured there wasn't going to be any peaceful way to negotiate with you," explains the guy who just punched Yuuki.

"You proved that to everyone when you killed Taularh," says the second guy.

"He was going to shoot Amelia first," Logan blurts out. "We were protecting her."

The first guy raises his eyebrow. "Oh, it was you, was it, who shot him? No matter. Our talk is with the Princess, not you." He turns back to Amelia. "I think you know this yourself, but you're far too inexperienced to rule. Last I checked, most of the Kingdom of Arkala thinks so too. And yet here you are selfishly claiming the throne for yourself when –"

160

"It's part of her birth right," Andy interrupts.

"– other older and more competent people could be and should be leading in your place. Birth right or not, murdering someone to get to the throne isn't what Arkala would could peaceful negotiations, is it?"

"Neither is holding someone hostage," Kyle counters. He feels the blood drain from his face as he speaks.

"Kyle," Joshua warns. *Don't provoke them.*

Yuuki's captor narrows his eyes. "You all made your way of negotiating clear. It's only fair, isn't it? If you lot aren't going to respect the Arkala culture of going about things peacefully, then neither are we when it comes to dealing with you. Since we decided it's highly unlikely you'll all listen to us asking Amelia to quietly step down, we thought you could use some incentive."

It doesn't need to be clarified that he's talking about Yuuki.

"We'll give you an hour to think about it. If you need more time to make your decision to surrender, we can give that to you, but each half hour you hesitate means your friend gets hurt. Deal?"

No one says yes, but Amelia doesn't say no either. They're not given the choice to say no, really. Not while those two have Yuuki.

With a satisfied grin and triumphant flash of eyes, the two men tighten their grip on Yuuki's jacket and walk him back to the vehicle. Yuuki doesn't resist, though he trips a few times with how roughly they shove him and how shaky his legs are.

As they take him around to the other side of the vehicle and force him into it, something sparks in the back of Kyle's mind. Anger for one, and something else – something that stokes that anger like a fire. Recognition of a kind, Kyle thinks, but he can't place it.

He thinks harder. There's a confidence with how they've carried out this hostage situation. They sound practiced, and their movements and voices are sure. It's almost like they've done stuff like this a number of times before, even like they've trained for it.

And then it clicks: these were the two men with Deborah that time Kyle was almost kidnapped. These were the two men Yuuki said he recognised from the Ninao incident, the two men who took care of his kidnapping. Kyle had wondered how Yuuki had known, but now he sees: they're brothers, these two men, and there's something distinctive about the way they move as well as a certain timbre to both of their voices that makes them easy to remember and distinguish.

Kyle's surging forward before he can stop himself. They've kidnapped Yuuki a second time. This is the second – no, *third* – time they've made Yuuki suffer and he's not standing for it. *There's only two of them; two on one. I can fight them. I will fight them.*

Strong hands catch his arm. Kyle shrugs the person off.

"Hey!" Joshua hisses in his ear. He throws his arms around Kyle's torso and pulls him to a stop.

But Kyle refuses to be dragged back. "Let me go."

"*No.* No, stop. They'll hurt him."

Kyle struggles to tear himself free of Joshua's grasp.

"*They'll hurt him.*"

Breathing hard, Kyle forces himself to still. His eyes burn. His stomach hurts. He feels like he's being strangled all over again.

"Recklessness won't save him," Joshua says, voice tight. "Okay? I…

Sam, can you help me out here?"

Hesitant footsteps approach. Kyle can hear the unsteadiness in them.

"We'll take him somewhere quiet to calm down," Joshua murmurs over his head. And then, directed at Kyle and accompanied by a gentle yet firm tug on his arm as Joshua shifts his hold. "Come on, before you do something stupid."

Kyle lets himself be lead. The fight drains away from him. In it's place he's left with only helplessness. The lights are too bright, the darkness too dim. Joshua and Sam's presence beside him is both too much and not enough. He doesn't know where they're going but he has no mind to care.

They end up in the library. Joshua switches the light on and finally releases Kyle. He gestures to Sam to close the door behind them. Joshua moves to stand right in front of Kyle, forcing him to look him directly in the eye. "Kyle, you with me?"

Numbly, Kyle nods. It feels like somebody else is nodding for him.

"I'm sorry for stopping you back there. I was tempted to do what you did, I swear. But if we want to get Yuuki back, we can't just rush in there blindly. Th-they'll hurt Yuuki if we go in there. You saw how they were treating him out there. You saw first-hand what they did to him to get to you back at Yuuki's house. Yuuki's hurting enough as it is; let's not make the situation any worse for him than it already is."

"We can't just leave him there," Kyle whispers. "We have to save him."

Joshua swallows, fights down the emotion in his voice. "I know. Believe me, I know. But we need to focus. That's the only way we're getting him back. We all need to take a moment, calm down a bit and focus. Me included."

For the next minute, all the three of them do is breathe. Sam's quietness dissolves into silent crying. Joshua puts his hands on his hips and turns about on the spot, eyes closed, brow furrowed and mouth pulled down in a frown. Kyle tries to recall what reality is.

With some internal cue, Joshua stills. His gaze is severe. He abruptly moves away from Kyle and Sam and starts sweeping the room, ducking between the rows of bookshelves, checking. Once he's satisfied with whatever he's looking for, he marches over the windows and draws all the curtains.

"Okay. We don't have much time," Joshua says, breathless, "but the fact that we're back here, out of sight and out of range of them hearing us gives us the advantage. They think we're back here trying to deal with our emotions and what's happening out there. They won't anticipate us trying to pull a rescue off."

Sam sniffs. "What are you talking about?"

"A plan. We need a plan."

"And how are we going to do that? Like you said, they'll hurt him if we try to rescue him. We don't even have a plan."

Joshua squeezes his eyes shut. "I think..." he opens his eyes again and takes a deep breath in and out. Contradicting what he'd said to Kyle just before, there's recklessness written all over his face. "I think I might have an idea."

18

Joshua takes a deep breath. "Kyle, how confident are you with being the one to go in to get Yuuki?"

The world tilts a little around him. Kyle blinks. "Um…"

"How confident are you?"

Well, I was in the process of charging out there to try rescue him just before, he thinks. *But I was running on anger and adrenaline then, so I'm not sure.* "Depends. What are you thinking?"

"There's a small bush trail that runs to the east side – the ridge side – of the palace. There's enough distance between the trail and the open field that I don't think they'll be able to see torch light through the trees. Sam, your head light has a red setting on it – maybe keep it on that while you're getting into place, just in case. Then –"

"Wait," Sam says, cutting him off. "I don't follow. Can you slow down a bit?"

Joshua grimaces. "Sorry. Mind's going too fast." He swallows. "Okay, so the trail I just mentioned? We can't approach Yuuki directly from the palace; we have to sneak in from behind. That trail will allow us to get on the other side of the vehicle Yuuki's being held in."

"But we'd have to run across an open field to get there," Kyle says, frowning.

"Yes, I realise that. But it's night, it's really cloudy – which means no moon, so it's dark – and as long as you're not wearing any reflective gear and you're quiet, you might be okay."

"'Might.'"

"Hey, we don't have time to make a fool proof plan, okay? Even if Amelia surrenders, I'll bet my life that they'll still use Yuuki as a means to get us to do what they want. They say they'll give him back to us, but I don't trust the word of someone who's willing to abuse someone like that, let alone take someone hostage who they've traumatised before."

Kyle's heart skips a beat. "So you figured it out too."

Sam glances between them, eyebrow raised.

"They're the same two guys who kidnapped him from the Ninao office," Joshua explains to his sister. "Remember how two went after Dad, two went after Yuuki?" He jerks his thumb in the general direction of the foyer. "Yeah, I'm certain that's them. I don't know if you remember, but they were also the same two guys who were…"

Joshua trails off, eyes flicking to Kyle. Hesitating, seeking permission almost. But Kyle doesn't know what the remaining words of the sentence are supposed to be, so he just stands there, confused.

"…they're the ones who were carrying Kyle away in the box," Joshua finishes.

Kyle's stomach dips. He hadn't thought about that. It's one of the memories he tries to suppress the most. He swallows. *So in other words, the same two guys who kidnapped Yuuki also tried kidnapping me. And now they've gone and taken Yuuki again…*

"You realise they could've been on that stupid list?" Sam says. Her eyes flash. "The one on the USB? We should've checked. Yuuki freakin' warned us all that sitting back and doing nothing was stupid and what do we do?"

"We didn't know, Sam," Kyle murmurs tightly.

Sam grits her teeth in frustration. She opens her mouth to argue her point, but stops herself with a high-pitched growl.

"Anyways, back to the plan," Joshua says. "We don't have much time to spare."

"So Sam and I will be sneaking around the other side," Kyle says, mind churning. A headache is growing and his concentration is beginning to flag, but he ignores it as best he can. He looks to Joshua. "What will you be doing?"

"Covering you," Joshua says firmly. "I'll take Logan's rifle up to the rooftop. My aim's not as good as Logan's, but worst comes to worst, I've got your back."

"Is it just me running in, or Sam too? Won't it be safer with both of us?"

Joshua's brow furrows. "If it looks like you're going to need both of you to get in and out there safely, then do that. Otherwise I think it would be better if you stay behind the bush line," he says to his sister. "Reason I say this isn't to invalidate your ability, Sam, but because one of you needs to be carrying a heavy backpack and that's going to have to be you. Kyle's going to have Yuuki to support. You need to stay with the gear."

"Do we even need a backpack?" Sam asks.

"Yes. Why? 'Cause we don't know what's going to happen after we go ahead with this. You guys might not be able to return to the palace, at least not immediately. We need to be prepared for that."

He's not wrong. The consequences of this mission succeeding are good for them as it means they'll have Yuuki back. For the two men using Yuuki as a bargaining chip, however…

Whatever happens, Kyle just hopes they'll be far across the field and well out of sight before anyone realises Yuuki's gone.

"Wait, what if they suspect us trying something?" Sam asks warily. "I mean, just a couple of days ago we snuck out on a mission to get the flash drive. It's the same three of us again, minus Charlie."

Joshua shifts his gaze to stare at the wall like it's challenging him to a duel. He bites his lip. "I think we're fine as long as everyone still thinks we're back here trying to calm ourselves down. We'll leave the light on when we leave. They'll buy it if we're careful, I think."

"We'll have to tell the others somehow," Kyle says. "If we're going to make sure we maintain the illusion that we're here, then we need to make sure the others don't break it."

Swinging his gaze back around to Kyle and Sam, Joshua blinks. "Oh, shoot, yeah…"

"If our aim is to get in and out undetected, then by rights the others shouldn't see us either. I'm just worried they'll see me running in and react to that."

Joshua nods. "I'll…I'll take care of it." He takes a deep breath. "Right, okay. This plan…are you guys with me?"

Kyle and Sam nod in unison.

"Cool. Now we need to move. Our window of opportunity is less than an hour. That time's already ticking, and we've already lost ten or fifteen minutes of that planning. From here, no less than fifteen minutes packing and then you guys need to be out and on the move."

Discussion over, the three of them leave the library. The light stays on, bidding them good luck, and the darkness of the hallways they walk seems to be willingly aiding them.

They grab a backpack from Timothy and Susan's room and then set to packing in Joshua, Logan and Avi's. With three of them to fetch what they need and time pressure not allowing a leisurely pace, they're done in just over ten minutes. A quick last minute bathroom stop for each of them, and they're ready in fifteen.

As they do a final double check to make sure they've got everything, Kyle remembers Yuuki's phone in his pocket. He slips it out and hands it to Joshua. "Here."

Joshua accepts it with a grim nod. "Thanks. Alright," he says. "I'll be up on the rooftop by the time you guys are in position. Go up the trail only as far as you need. You won't be able to see me, Kyle, but trust I'll have your back."

With a nervous exhale, Sam shoulders the backpack and adjusts the straps. "This had better work. Not just for us; for Yuuki. No pressure, Kyle."

Kyle grunts.

"Good luck out there," Joshua says quietly, laying a hand each on Kyle and Sam's shoulders. "And try stay safe out there."

Sam nods, her whole body lined with tension. "You too."

"Now go. Get him back to us."

169

19

After Kyle and Sam head out, Joshua makes his way back to the library and then to the foyer. He's far more nervous than he let on to them, maybe even more so than he lets on to himself. He steels himself as he rounds the last corner that brings him in sight of the foyer.

Thankfully his nervousness is actually doing him a favour here: it serves to mask the subtle confidence holding inside of him. He, Kyle and Sam have a plan in motion that no one knows about yet, and one that the bad guys won't – *hopefully won't* – see coming. Everything's reliant on Kyle's ability to sneak in and whisk Yuuki away unseen, now. That, and the rest of the group's ability to not give away what's happening if they happen to see Kyle when he runs in.

Joshua takes a deep breath. He's the one to try make sure that doesn't happen. *Here goes nothing.*

"Hey," Timothy says, seeing Joshua approaching. His whole demeanour speaks with an emotion that Joshua struggles to affiliate with his father. "How's Kyle?"

Joshua glances out at the driveway. Yuuki's still in the vehicle. *Good.* The two men holding him hostage have positioned themselves on the palace side of the vehicle, between the group and Yuuki. They stand with their arms crossed over their chests against the cold and a bored yet watchful gleam in their eyes.

Joshua's heart beats faster. *If it stays like this, Kyle's got an open run to Yuuki.* "He's, uh...yeah," he replies, and he mentally cringes. *Yeah, great start to the nothing-suspicious-going-on-here speech – not.*

But the words seem to fall in line with an expected answer anyways. Timothy nods slowly.

"Yeah, so...Sam and I are going to stay back there with him. He's quite upset."

Finally Timothy registers the odd pattern in his sentence intonation. It's flatter, more drawn out. Spoken as though Joshua's reciting lines for a play. Different than the tone of voice he usually communicates with, but in a way that's subtle enough that anyone who isn't familiar with Joshua's usual way of talking, even in stressful circumstances, won't pick up on.

It's as best a code as they have available to them right now.

Holding his Dad's gaze steadily, Joshua says, "We're in the library, if you're looking for us."

A hint of doubt flashes across Timothy's face. Joshua's relieved when the look sticks. *Dare I say,* he wants to joke, *our family raised each other well.*

Timothy himself is a bad liar, but Sam and Joshua are quite practised at it. With all the good-hearted mischief they used to get up to growing up, over the years Timothy has had to learn how to detect when his children are telling the truth or not. He's joked before that it was his first introduction to the job of a judge.

"Okay," Timothy murmurs. He seems unsure of what exactly is going on, but he's smart enough not to question it here.

Charlie leaves Amelia's side for a moment. He glances at Timothy. "Would it help if one of us was also there with him?"

Joshua's mind screeches. *Not unless you can figure out that an empty library means we're planning something.*

Seeing Joshua's hesitation and the slight widening of his eyes, Timothy says, "I think Sam and Joshua can handle it. Too many people will only overwhelm Kyle more."

Another reassurance: Timothy's gathered that *something's* going on and he's aware he needs to make sure no one goes to the library while it is. All it would take is for one genuinely concerned person to go to make sure they're all okay back there, only to find them not there and come back and tell the others that they're gone for their plan to be put in jeopardy.

But now that Timothy's vaguely aware, they can be assured he'll do what he can to make sure that doesn't happen.

Thanks Dad, Joshua conveys through an appreciative glance and a grimace. "How's Amelia?" he asks.

Charlie doesn't bother softening it. "This is far too much for her. It is for all of us, but I'm sure you'll understand the extra stress she's under. She's in control of what happens to Yuuki."

With an acknowledging hum, Joshua nods. *It doesn't have to be entirely Amelia's responsibility to ensure Yuuki's safety, though. Not if we can help it.*

Conscious of time ticking away, Joshua excuses himself, saying he's headed back to the library. Charlie and everyone who hears him believes it. The two men outside watching the interaction with keen eyes believe it. Only Timothy doesn't.

That should be sufficient cover for them in the meantime. Joshua trusts that Timothy will be able to figure out how to keep suspicions down in the event that someone starts asking questions.

As soon as he's out of sight, he lets out a shaky breath. Things are going well so far, but he's holding his breath for this to work. He's afraid to jinx it by simply thinking about it. *This plan* can't *fail* – for everyone's sake.

Joshua's realising now just how it important it is for Amelia as it is for Yuuki that they make sure this mission is successful. Thinking about if further as he's collecting Logan's rifle and spare ammunition, the reality of this situation dawns on him: the hostage situation going on out there is an act of terrorism. There's no wishy-washy way to put it. Those guys out there are trying to force

It makes Joshua frustrated. *Here those guys are marking everyone here allied with Amelia as bad guys when they're going around doing stuff like this. What's worse, they have the media and likely most of the public on their side.* The only way they're going to counteract the leverage the bad guys have against them is if they're able to bring irrefutable evidence to the table. Right now, though, that's pretty much impossible – all they have is their word.

Joshua slings the rifle over his shoulder and stills. His eyes widen.

They do have evidence: the palace's CCTV footage.

He pulls out his phone and checks the time. He has enough time.

Joshua detours on his way to the rooftop. They likely won't have this evidence if they don't get it now – it'll be wiped by the time they come back for it later, if Kyle's case is anything to go by.

When he gets to the security room, he finds it unlocked and the computer left on, most likely due to Andy having been in here recently checking the cameras for any sign of Yuuki. Everything's operating normally. Breathing hard, Joshua searches through the computer. He finds the folder he's looking for, opens up his email account in a separate window and uploads the necessary video files to his email's online storage. There's an error processing the latest one, however, as it's still currently in recording.

Joshua grits his teeth. They need that file. There's no choice.

He stops the live recording, waits a couple of precious minutes for the file to save and upload, and then he's resuming the live recording and closing down the internet browser.

He runs then. He has no idea how fast Kyle and Sam have been moving. He's somewhat relieved when he gets to the rooftop and finds nothing's changed yet. As he creeps into position, lying down near edge overlooking the driveway, he keeps his eyes open wide and watchful for any sign that it does, his gaze constantly flicking between the two men and the shadow cloaked open field.

It occurs to him then, how good a vantage point this is to watch the rescue happen. Joshua finishes setting the rifle up beside him and then takes his phone out of his pocket. He swallows. It's an even better vantage point to record it.

Just like the photos and video he took of Yuuki's rescue from the shed, they need evidence of his rescue now. He's not sure how much he'll be able to show besides Kyle's attempt to rescue him, but as long as he's able to capture that and the men's reactions when they realise what's happening, it should be enough. Having the CCTV footage as well ought to be proof enough of what's happening here, and hopefully proof enough that this none of this situation is being staged.

Evidence, he reminds himself as he prepares for recording. It doesn't help him feel any less sick.

Rifle and phone ready, Joshua waits. Though the former is for worst case scenario, it won't just be the rifle he'll be shooting tonight.

Joshua takes a deep breath. *It's up to you now, Kyle.*

It's foolish. All of Kyle's sensibility warns against this. It's stupid and reckless, exactly like Yuuki said. Acts of heroism during hostage situations are cautioned against for a reason.

But the dangers of not getting Yuuki out of there exceed the risks of what he's about to do: for one, the hostage has a severe psychological injury that's actively being made worse the longer it takes to save him; and secondly, it's checkmate for all of them unless they either sacrifice Yuuki or save him. Kyle's having none of the first. He highly doubts any of the others are either.

In front of him, leading the way with her head light on red, Sam looks like she's off for a hike. The backpack she's carrying is crammed full of hastily their prepared survival items: spare clothes, a sleeping bag, a couple of tarps and a few aluminium emergency blankets, a small first aid kit, a Swiss army knife and spare torch batteries, both Kyle and Sam's currently powered off phones, a bunch of muesli bars and two 1.5L water bottles. It's a relief they had a sturdy backpack on hand for it all.

Kyle tightens his hand around the sheathed knife in his pocket. He has a feeling they're going to need all of it.

"I think this is far enough," Sam whispers, slowing to a stop.

Kyle comes to stand beside her. He peers through the gaps in the trees. The palace's outside lights are a beacon. He nods. "Yeah, I think so."

They've followed the trail long enough that they're out of sight of Yuuki's captors' peripheral and are on the other side of the vehicle. It still feels too close, but they can't risk putting too much distance between the vehicle and where they are behind the bush line. More distance means more time they have to be spotted.

Sam directs the beam of her headlight over the ground leading out to the field. "Can you get out from here?"

Kyle assesses it carefully. There appears to be no deep puddles or patches of mud to watch out for, and there's no dense clumps of fallen leaves or grass plants to worry about making a lot of noise passing by. His only major concern is tripping, but the path Sam's spied for him appears to be relatively free of those hazards too.

"Yeah, it looks good," he says.

Nervousness spears him in the gut. It washes over him, makes his vision lose a little clarity and his muscles loose a little strength. It's hitting him now, what he's about to do. As soon as he steps over that threshold...

The open field beckons him to make himself known.

Common sense begs him to stay hidden.

Kyle draws in a deep breath and exhales slowly. *No turning back.*

Sam gives him a supportive pat on the shoulder. "I'll meet you wherever you end up coming back into the bush. When you get Yuuki, just get back here. I'll come catch up to you guys."

"Okay," Kyle murmurs.

He swaps his knife from his right pocket to his left. Thanks to the head injury he sustained from the fall a few weeks ago, his right hand is still weaker than his left. He doesn't trust he'll be able to hold his grip on the knife if he uses his right hand to wield the knife, especially not with how shaky with adrenaline and nerves he is right now.

"Wish me luck," Kyle says.

Before he has a chance to stall, he starts moving.

20

Kyle's mind blanks out as he steps out into the open. His survival instincts shout at him not to reveal himself. He ignores it. He keeps momentum. The window of opportunity is closing fast; they don't have much time left. He can go back to hiding as soon as he's got Yuuki.

The empty space around him makes him feel so small, so vulnerable. He hastens his strides into a jog, and then into something just shy of a run. The weight of his knife is jostled back and forth in his left pocket as he runs. It's uncomfortable, but reassuring. He lets it comfort him.

This is crazy, he thinks as he veers across the field, putting the vehicle directly between himself and the palace. His throat tightens and burns. Kyle realises the only reason he's doing this is because he's able to put his trust in Joshua's plan. It's the only reason he's able to get past the terror threatening to make his body seize up.

That, and because he doesn't really have a choice. Not if he wants to make sure Yuuki's returned to them alive and not additionally injured or traumatised.

Kyle's heart is beating out of his chest when gets to the vehicle. *I made it unseen.* He struggles to believe it. He ducks down, leans his back against the wheel. There's no time to make himself believe it.

The vehicle door is open. He forces himself to breathe silently, forces his legs not to go weak on him. Unsheathing his knife, he turns and peers inside. Yuuki's propped up on the seat, right in front of him. In addition to the blindfold, gag and rope binding his arm, his ankles have also been tied together and the seatbelt's been pulled across his body, securing him to the seat.

So this is why they felt it was safe enough to leave the door open then.

Kyle waits only as long as required to make sure no one is coming in that instant, and then he's crawling sideways into the space between the inside of the door and the vehicle's interior.

Sensing his presence, Yuuki recoils. Thinking quickly, Kyle reaches up with his free hand and lightly taps Yuuki on the side of his leg, then writes his name with his finger. The tension doesn't leave Yuuki's body, but the air of fear is met with an undertone of something else: trust.

Without delay, Kyle cuts through the rope binding his ankles. *The bare minimum,* he reminds himself. Once that's done, Yuuki's free to move his legs which means all that's left is the seatbelt. He can't cut through that in a hurry, though, which means he needs to get the seatbelt off and pull Yuuki out of the vehicle at the same time, or right after the other.

He might be seen as he does this. Kyle hastily gives Yuuki a warning, written as a countdown in the same manner he'd alerted him to his presence: *3-2-1.*

Here goes.

Kyle launches himself up and forward. The seatbelt he unbuckles with his left hand, then catches with his right. He hooks his left arm around Yuuki's back. Guides the seatbelt silently back to its resting position.

Then, ungracefully, leans all his weight backwards.

A muffled gasp of alarm escapes Yuuki as they fall. Kyle hits the ground first, rain-softened grass and dirt slamming into his head, neck and shoulders. Yuuki's weight lands on top of him and Kyle's breath is driven out of him.

Miraculously, no one seems to have seen or heard them. Kyle lies still, ears strained. Disbelieving. But there's no sound of gravel crunching under feet. No one's about to lay hands on them. Yuuki quietly pulls his feet down out of the vehicle from where they've been caught in the foot well. The rustle of his raincoat as he moves to do so is all the noise there is.

Kyle rolls them both onto their sides. They're clear, but they can't waste the opportunity. He hauls himself and Yuuki upright. There's not enough time to free Yuuki completely right now, but he does spare a few precious seconds to cut and tear the blindfold away from Yuuki's eyes.

There's not enough time to wait for Yuuki to adjust to having his vision back. Every second here is dangerous; they can't afford to linger here any longer. Yuuki's disorientated. He blinks hard, his eyes are unfocused and glazed. But there's awareness in them, and that's all Kyle needs to see to know Yuuki's with him.

"Run with me," Kyle whispers. He readjusts his hold.

They run.

Beneath them there's nothing but barely illuminated grass whipping by under their feet. Dips in the ground have their ankles rolling. Yuuki stumbles, and Kyle with him. Kyle somehow manages to keep them from tripping and falling over.

Half way to cover, Yuuki's breathing grows ragged and strained. Kyle initially thinks it's a result of the sudden sprint and the adrenaline. He then he remembers he's forcing Yuuki to run while still bound and gagged, and guilt washes over him. *The priority is getting back safe and unseen,* he reminds himself. *We'll have time to get those off when we're back in the bush.*

Anxiety crawls over his skin. *We might not have time at all if we get caught before then.* Kyle's expecting they'll be spotted and pursued any second now. He has to resist the urge to glance over their shoulders to check. Looking back will only slow them down.

He scarcely believes it when they do get back. It feels too unreal. They careen into the bush. Kyle remembers last second to slow them down in time to avoid them crashing through the plants and making a ruckus. They manage to leave the open field quietly enough to avoid announcing it to everyone back at the palace.

Limbs wobbly with adrenaline, Kyle does his best to guide Yuuki through the trees. His heart pounds in his chest. He struggles for breath. Yuuki's feet are dragging now. His knees buckle a couple of times and it takes all of Kyle's strength to keep him from falling.

"Just a little further," he reassures. "Just gotta…find Sam…."

With a stab of worry, Kyle realises he doesn't know which way Sam is. This isn't the same spot he left off from. It's darker here too, making it more difficult to keep steady footing since they can hardly see where they're going. They find the trail without too much hassle, which is good, but he has no idea which way to go.

Momentum lost, Yuuki falls to his knees. There's not enough strength left in Kyle's arms to keep him up this time. Kyle's mind whirls as he sinks down with him.

After running in and out, and now full of adrenaline, stopping here all of a sudden feels wrong. *But Sam did say she'll come find us,* he reassures himself. *That was the plan. And we're in cover now, so it should be safe to wait here for her – relatively safe, at least.*

Considering the fact that Yuuki's so deeply shaken and still tied up, Kyle highly doubts he feels like he's safe. Following that thought, he realises he's still got the blindfold clenched in his hand. With a jolt, Kyle flings it away.

He takes a deep breath. "Hey," Kyle says softly, turning his attention back to Yuuki. "I'm going to finish freeing you now."

Yuuki doesn't actively respond, but when Kyle moves behind him to better access the knots, he doesn't move away. When Kyle's hands touch his face and his fingers find where the gag has been knotted at the base of his skull, Yuuki stays still as he can and lets Kyle do what he needs to.

The only problem is it's hard for Kyle to see what he's doing. Though his eyes are adjusted to the dark and he can see the vague outlines of the shapes nearest to them, it's not exactly sufficient light to be able to work loose the knot. He's fumbling in the dark trying to undo it. His fingers, particularly his right hand, won't pull with enough strength and the knot's tied too firmly for any progress to be made.

Of all times to be experiencing difficulties resulting from my head injury, now is not a good time.

Kyle can tell it's beginning to distress Yuuki further. He's hunching his shoulders, unconsciously leaning forward and bowing his head – an unconscious effort to try to get himself away. His breathing's erratic.

Every tug that ends in a failed attempt to free him pushes him one step further towards the edge of a panic attack.

After a moment's contemplation, Kyle makes the decision to use his knife. It's still in his left hand; he's been reluctant to let it go. He gives a brief warning to Yuuki, telling him what he's going to do, and then slips two fingers of his right hand down between the cloth and Yuuki's temple.

The material is tough – it's meant to be durable, what with the purpose of its use and the number of washes each cloth would have to go through after each and every occasion of being used. Unfortunately that makes it harder to slice through as well.

It would all be a much faster process if he just used the torch in his pocket. Yet as tempting and far more practical as the idea might be, Joshua's warning rings in his ears. They don't know for sure if they can safely use a white torch light without being seen, and right now the darkness concealing them is a comforting blanket.

Better awkward and safe than sorry.

Still, Kyle manages to work the blade of the knife through it without injuring Yuuki in the process. The feeling of the cloth giving way under the knife and finally breaking is relieving. He sheaths the knife before shifting to help Yuuki ease the clench in his jaw and then at last Kyle's able to pull the saliva-soaked gag out his mouth.

Yuuki coughs weakly. A hysterical sort of gasping for it as his lungs realise he can breathe properly again. Overcome by the sudden increased availability of air, he makes a sound in his throat like he's about to throw up. Fortunately, nothing comes up.

Before moving onto the last thing binding him, Kyle lays an

apologetic and comforting hand between Yuuki's shoulders. "Sorry," he says. "Sorry that took so long."

He twists around to toss the gag in the same direction as the blindfold, then pauses. He could be just hearing things, but...

A twig snaps. Yuuki flinches so hard he almost falls over – would have, if Kyle hadn't been in the way. Clothing rustles. Then a pair of footsteps grows closer and closer and with it, the shape of a person emerging from the dark.

Kyle drops the cloth and hastily places his hands on Yuuki's shoulders to steady him. "It's okay, it's Sam," he says quickly. It's a verbal reassurance to both of them. "See?"

Sure enough, Sam walks forward, hands wrapped around the straps of her backpack and the red beam of her head light falling over them as she nears. "Yep, just me."

In the red light, lines pressed into Yuuki's cheeks from the gag stand out. The corners of his mouth are reddened. Dried spit runs down to his chin. Sam and Kyle try their best to ignore it for Yuuki's sake.

Sam looks nervous caught in Yuuki's gaze. Her eyes flick to Kyle, eyebrows uncertain. *Is he doing okay?*

The only answer Kyle can give is a forced half smile. Yuuki sees this exchange and looks away.

"I can't believe that actually worked," Sam says. "And..." Her voice softens. "I'm glad you're back with us, Yuuki."

Though he doesn't look up, Yuuki acknowledges the words with a small nod. He tries his best to act like he isn't half expecting Sam to morph into someone hostile and attack them.

Without further ado, Kyle gets back to setting Yuuki free. He regrets not having done this part sooner – cutting the rope is a lot easier than cloth. It only takes a fraction of the time to saw through. Having Sam's head light to see by certainly makes it a lot easier.

The last cut leaves resounding relief in Kyle's chest. Yuuki's arm slides limply down his back. Yuuki winces as it drops to his side, fingers twitching in pain.

Sam bends down and picks up the discarded bindings, including the blindfold Kyle chucked to the side. "I'm going to bury these." The flatness of her tone says she'd rather burn them.

Yuuki lets out a shuddering breath but says nothing.

While Sam ventures a little way back down the trail, Kyle gently wraps his arms around Yuuki's shoulders. Startlingly, Yuuki jerks away from the contact and Kyle instantly lets go. But before he can withdraw the embrace completely, Yuuki slumps forward and drops his head onto Kyle's shoulder. Tentatively, Kyle returns to hugging him.

"We're safe back here now, okay?" he murmurs. "You're safe now."

The darkness and the quiet is consoling. Kyle understands now that Sam's also giving them a moment of privacy: she's allowing Yuuki space in case he needs it.

But Yuuki's eerily quiet. In contrast to his reaction when he saw the photos from the Ninao incident, this isn't much of a reaction at all. Kyle had been imagining Yuuki to be overcome by the same awful screaming that had taken over *him* when Yuuki had lost his arm. But this…

It's like after I woke up at the Harrisons, after Yuuki and Timothy got me out of prison, Kyle realises. Not the loud, painful kind of processing of trauma, but the numbed, shocked, non-verbal kind.

Kyle, though he's had a taste of both, isn't sure which he finds more unsettling.

A couple of minutes pass and Sam comes back, frowning. "Hey, Kyle. I think we should think about moving. It's been almost an hour."

Kyle squints against the red light. It clicks. The 'negotiation'. "Oh, I forgot about that."

"Yeah. They'll realise Yuuki's missing any moment now."

"Okay, um…" Kyle lightly taps Yuuki on the shoulder. "Do you think you can walk?"

Yuuki doesn't answer.

"I'll support you, so you don't have to walk completely on your own."

It starts to seem like the words are lost to the night air, but then Yuuki whispers hoarsely, "I don't know."

Which is basically code for negative. "Okay. That's okay. We'll, uh, we'll figure something out. Maybe have a drink of water first, actually. Sam, do you –"

Kyle's interrupted by a harsh shout from the palace. All three of them stiffen. Yuuki's eyes stretch wide, unseeing.

Sam grunts. "I think they realised."

21

"Kyle, we need to get moving."

"Where will we go?"

"I don't know? Preferably further that way." She gestures in the opposite direction of the open field.

"That means going uphill." Kyle points out. "We're at the base of the ridge."

"Yeah, well…"

"It's too dangerous. Yuuki can't walk, and I doubt they gave him anything to eat or drink for however long it was they had him. It's also pretty much pitch black around here and we're all going to end up injuring ourselves if we try go uphill now. Don't forget it's been raining; it'll be wet and slippery."

"Well, what do we do? It's dangerous if we stay here too."

"Less dangerous than if we climb."

"Maybe, but if they come looking for us –"

"Then they can fight me," Kyle interrupts. He cringes at the anger that's crept into his tone. *What's up with me?*

"The only weapons we have on us," Sam says slowly, "are our own fighting abilities and your knife. Plus torches, if they count. Joshua can't cover us across this distance. Our best offence is defence, and that means getting the hell away from those guys as best we can – even if that's just moving into the bush a bit more so we're better hidden."

Kyle grimaces. She's right. *We need to do what it takes to keep Yuuki safe. That's the objective here.*

He looks at Yuuki, struggling to breathe beside him. Yuuki's chest heaves. His fingers curl tighter in the material of Kyle's jacket. He keeps his panic silent, but up close Kyle can hear the tone of desperation and fear in every inhale and exhale.

Moving is dangerous but so is staying where they are. So in terms of which one offers them better promise of safety...

"Okay, let's go."

Getting Yuuki up isn't easy. Kyle pockets his knife and hooks his hands beneath Yuuki's armpits. With Sam's help, he pulls Yuuki up to his feet. Yuuki's legs refuse to cooperate and won't take his weight. His body's locked up and even if it weren't, Kyle doubts he'd be able to get up on his own. If Kyle had the strength in his muscles to carry Yuuki on his back, he would. But he knows he wouldn't last more than a few steps before his own legs stopped working.

They'll just have to do the best they can.

Kyle and Sam hold onto him. Readjusting himself to give better support, Kyle slings Yuuki's arm over his shoulders and wraps an arm around his waist.

"Which way?" he asks Sam.

Sam glances behind them. "I think we should put some more distance between us and the palace first."

Kyle catches the way Yuuki's eyes flick back and forth between the ground beneath his feet and Sam, who's at the edge of his periphery. But it's not Sam Yuuki's likely bothered by. Kyle thinks about it a little harder and the realisation hits: it's the having more than one pair of hands on him that's getting to him.

"Hey, Sam?" he says. "Do you want to lead the way?"

The look she gives him is confused. "I can if you want me to, but...can you both manage?"

"I think so. I'm just thinking it might be easier for Yuuki to walk if he can see where you're putting your feet." It's not an invalid reason, but it's not the reason why Kyle spoke up in the first place. *Given the situation we're in, I guess I may as well say it for what it is.* "That, and...we saw the way those two guys were treating him. Let's not make it feel like we're re-enacting that."

Realisation dawns on Sam's face. She nods soberly. "Yeah. Okay then."

Over Kyle's shoulder, Yuuki's fingers twitch. Kyle understands it as an unspoken sign of relief and gratitude. He gives Yuuki's wrist a reassuring squeeze. Yuuki involuntarily whimpers and ducks his head.

With no designated destination, they follow the trail away from the palace. There's another couple of shouts that leap into the night from back there, the two men who kidnapped Yuuki obviously still trying to figure out how Yuuki managed to disappear on them. Kyle, Sam and Yuuki leave them to their confusion.

The further along the three of them go, the less flat the ground becomes. The path begins to curve inward, towards the ridge, and when it does Sam decides it's safe enough to switch her head light to its normal white light setting.

Yuuki's almost fully reliant on Kyle's support when they start to climbing. It's exhausting. Kyle's muscles burn. His head spins. He glances up at the looming mass of shadow above them and he can't comprehend how on earth Yuuki managed to carry him all the way down to the others. At least right now Yuuki's able to assist bearing *some* of his weight – when Yuuki had carried Kyle, he'd had to do it all on his own since Kyle was out to it with his head injury.

Is that why I'm against moving uphill? Because this is nearing where we fell or something? It would make sense. He might not remember any of it, but he might subconsciously. No wonder he's feeling so inexplicably nervous.

Kyle has no idea exactly how long they've been going when they decide to stop. All he knows is that they're all needing the rest when they do. Kyle's on the verge of experiencing vertigo, Yuuki's sagging further and further towards the ground and Sam's wearing under the strain of the heavy backpack.

Sam finds them a reasonably flat and sheltered space to rest. Kyle doesn't wait for her to pull the tarp out of her bag before lowering Yuuki down. He's afraid he'll end up dropping him if he waits even a second more.

As it is, Yuuki almost face plants the moment his knees touch the ground. Kyle's grasp on his arm is all that stops him from actually doing so.

"Hang on," Kyle says between breaths. "Ground's wet. Wait for…Sam's just…"

Yuuki groans and fights to keep himself upright.

Once the tarp is laid down, they all settle down on it. Yuuki lets the ground take his entire weight and Kyle's happy to let it. He sinks down to his knees beside him, body humming with relief that they're no longer walking.

Sam drops her backpack with a heavy exhale. "What do you think's happening?" she asks, rummaging through the bag and pulling something out.

One of the 1.5L water bottles lands on the tarpaulin. Kyle stares at it blankly. "Huh?"

"Back at the palace."

"Didn't Joshua say he was gonna call us?"

Sam swings her arms up in a stretch, back clicking. She stills. "Oh, yeah."

While she turns bends down and hunts for her phone, Kyle turns on his hands and knees to face Yuuki. He reaches out and grabs the water, then gently shakes Yuuki's shoulder.

"We have water," he says.

Yuuki's brow twitches. He mutters something unintelligible, slurred.

"You need to drink something."

"…'ll have some…soon…"

Kyle frowns. "Okay. Just make sure you do."

"Hnnngh."

At first he thinks the response equates to nothing more than tired resignation. It's not until Kyle sees the pinch in Yuuki's brow that he notices otherwise. He shuffles over so he can get a better look at Yuuki's face, and just like that, even as he's trying to figure out what's wrong, Yuuki's expression contorts and he stiffens.

Kyle puts the water bottle down. "Yuuki?"

Gritting his teeth, Yuuki abruptly curls in on himself. His leg twitches.

"Hey, what's wrong? Tell me what's wrong. Tell me where you're hurting."

Sam steps over to them, cell phone in her hand. She quickly moves the beam of the head light aside when Yuuki screws his eyes shut even tighter at it.

"Do you want me to get the first aid kit?" she asks.

Kyle's mind whirls. "Hang on…" *What if they poisoned him? Or he's got internal bleeding or something? Or…*"Is it muscle cramps?"

Yuuki cracks his eyes open. He grunts in lieu of a proper response.

Oh, well that makes a lot of sense. "It's 'cause you're dehydrated, right?" Kyle says. "Plus you've been tensed up for hours. I really think you should try having some water now. You'll feel better afterwards, even just a little bit."

Even if marginally, it's got to be better than suffering through all this.

"Are you hurt anywhere else? Do you have any injuries that need seeing to?"

Sam gives Kyle a friendly nudge on the shoulder. "You sound like my Mum."

Kyle blinks. "Huh?"

With a small laugh, Sam shakes her head and goes back to unpacking what they need from the bag.

Yuuki coughs. He answers Kyle's last question with a croaked whisper.

"'m fine."

That answer isn't all that believable, but Kyle decides to trust that Yuuki would say something if he had any injuries needing immediate tending to. It's better than fussing over him more than is necessary and stressing him out further.

By the time the cramps have eased up enough to let Yuuki sit up and take some water, it's past 11pm. They're still waiting for a call from Joshua. It's impossible to know if that's a good or bad sign. In the meantime, while they wait, Sam goes about setting up a makeshift shelter.

They packed another tarp besides the one they've already laid out on the ground – this Sam strings up above them. It's a basic shelter and doesn't really offer them much protection against the elements, but so long as the weather amounts to no more than a light wind or passing shower they should be okay. At the end of the day, it's better than nothing.

As for protection against the cold, all they have on them are the emergency blankets, the clothes they have on them as well as the ones wrapped up in plastic bags in the backpack, and a large sleeping bag between them. The sleeping bag is big enough to have taken up at least a third of the space in Sam's backpack, bulking it up and limiting what space they had available to pack other things. It is, however, far too much appreciated for there to be any lingering doubts about the room it took up in that bag.

They wait for Joshua's call with the sleeping bag and emergency blankets wrapped around their shoulders. Sam sits beside Kyle to give Yuuki more space on his other side. Once she's settled in beside him, she turns the light of her head torch off to conserve battery. The darkness is thick around them but it's quiet. With nothing small to talk about and too much to process, they sit in silence and simply listen to the night around them.

In the stillness, Kyle begins to come off the adrenaline rush, thankfully at a steady pace. Yuuki, on the other hand, is dumped off it. Whether it's voluntary or not, Yuuki slumps against Kyle's side, sinking lower until his cheek's pressed against Kyle's shoulder. A violent shaking takes a hold of him.

Initially misinterpreting it as something else, Kyle murmurs, "Are you cold?"

Yuuki clenches his jaw tighter but doesn't answer.

Kyle's not sure exactly what that means.

He moves his arm around Yuuki's shoulders to draw him in closer, careful not to make him feel restrained but close enough to hopefully have some comforting effect. His stomach churns when Yuuki presses closer still. Kyle wonders if he's even aware he's doing it. Yuuki never seeks touch like this. Unless it's been openly offered or he's the one offering it, he usually avoids physical contact altogether. Especially lately, it's like Yuuki's been denying himself it altogether.

Kyle's eyes burn. His throat hurts. *You shouldn't have to suffer alone,* he wants to tell him. *Let us help you.* But he knows it's not that simple; it's not that easy.

The tears are hot in contrast to the night air.

22

It's almost midnight when Joshua finally calls. Sam's phone lights up with it, illuminating the over-tired expression on Sam's face. She sighs, answers the call and puts it on speaker. "Hey."

"Hey guys." Joshua's voice sounds dreary. "Sorry it took so long to get to you."

"What's the situation at the palace?"

"It's been chaos. Well, more so for those couple of jerks. I wish you guys could've seen their faces. They were so confused." He pauses. "So, uh...how's Yuuki?"

Beside Kyle, Yuuki lets out an irritated huff.

Kyle clears his throat. "He's...it's not like he's fine."

"Yeah, I know. It's just..." An uncomfortable pause. "Dad and I, Mum... – and everyone – we're just...we're –"

"I'm fine," Yuuki mumbles. There's no strength to the words when he says them.

Hearing Yuuki's voice seems to be at least reassuring though, as some of the tightness in Joshua's eases. "I'm glad. I'm glad you're okay," he says to Yuuki. "You know, relatively speaking."

Yuuki doesn't answer.

"So, the palace – what's happening with everyone?" Sam asks again. The light of her phone dims.

Joshua swallows. "Right, sorry. Uh, we're kind of in the middle of discussing that right now. But it looks like we're not going to be staying here long. After…after the threat we just received, Andy's now deemed the palace unsafe grounds. We're evacuating, or making plans to do so promptly, in Andy's words."

Kyle and Sam exchange a glance. "Evacuating?" Kyle repeats. "Where to? Back to the country house?"

"No, I don't think so. I'm not sure. I think Andy's still working that out – Dad's talking with him now."

"And what of *those men?*" Sam asks.

"The three of them ran off and disappeared once they realised they had lost their advantage. We don't know what they're up to, but they haven't shown up again. I gave them a warning shot when they realised Yuuki was missing, just in case they thought about using their guns on us. Seemed to do the trick."

"Wait, wait. Did you say *three?*"

"Yeah. Another guy showed up shortly after you got Yuuki to safety. He came in time for the, uh, 'negotiation', I think. Anyways, all I know is that we're making plans to leave."

"How soon?"

"Tonight."

Kyle stares at the phone incredulously. "Wait, what?"

"Look – we made a *horrible* mistake. Everyone's realised that now. We should've trusted Yuuki's intuition and taken his warning seriously. I

196

mean, we should *know* by now that we can't just sit around doing nothing, but…" Joshua exhales sharply. "Yuuki, you're still there, right? I just…. I am so sorry. We should've realised. We should've done something or –"

"You did," Yuuki interrupts.

"What? No, I mean we should've been doing something *before*. This all happened because we weren't proactive enough, and now you're freakin' suffering because of it."

Kyle expects Yuuki to counter that it's not their fault, that Joshua doesn't need to be apologising for it, but instead he's silent. Kyle's not sure what that means.

"So what should we do?" Sam asks, purposefully changing the subject back. "We've set up camp, but it won't take us long to pack up. Will there be someone waiting for us when we get back down there or…?"

Joshua sighs. "Right. Uh – no, stay out there. Unless you think you could get back here in less than half an hour?"

"Not likely. Unless one of the tarpaulins we packed happens to be a magical flying carpet."

"Unfortunately not. You have that map on you, right?"

"Yeah?"

"Do you think you can find your way to the last hut we stayed at on the way here?"

"Checkpoint D?"

"Yeah."

"In daylight, maybe. Or with night vision goggles, but not in the dark."

"Okay, good. That's good. If you can find your way to that hut, you should be able to find the rest of the trail easy enough. There's a trail that branches off from the main one at Checkpoint C. It leads to a road. Andy says we can pick you guys up from there."

"So you don't want us coming back to the palace at all?"

"Yeah, don't. Remember, we're leaving here for a reason."

Yuuki swallows. The tension in his shoulders eases slightly.

"The hut still has supplies in it," Joshua continues, "so you'll be fine in that regard. When you get to the top of the ridge tomorrow, call Dad so he can give you an update on what's going on. Once you start going down into the valley you'll lose reception, so make sure you call while you're at the top."

Sam hums. "Got it."

"What happens if we can't reach him?" Kyle asks.

"Just call any of us. If you can't get a hold of Dad for some reason," Joshua says, "call me, or else Mum or one of the others."

"And if we can't reach any of you, just go on ahead and hope for the best?"

"Yeah, pretty much. Maybe stay at the hut and make a trip up to the ridge the next day to try call again if you're unsure."

"Okay."

There's a rustling on Joshua's end of the line. The sound of other voices filter in, including Susan saying something in the background. "Seems like we're about to leave," he says. "I gotta go."

"Alright," Sam murmurs. "See you on the other side?"

"Yep. Take care guys."

"You too."

With a bleep, the call ends. The night is plunged into silence again.

Sam groans. "So I guess…we're going for a hike tomorrow."

An impromptu hike right after a big scare like the one they've just had sure doesn't sound appealing. Kyle wouldn't be so fazed if the circumstances weren't so dire, and if all three of them weren't dealing with things ranging from mild sleep deprivation to flat out trauma.

"Good thing we're more prepared this time," Kyle murmurs.

"We shouldn't have to have been."

"I know."

Sam's quiet for a moment. "I don't get it. How come this keeps happening? We've been under attack for *months* now. It's ridiculous."

"We got in their way, that's why."

Something about those words has Yuuki's breathing quicken. Kyle can't see the connection and he knows Yuuki's not going to be willing to explain it, so he doesn't ask. With a steady hand, he rubs Yuuki's back, slowly, up and down over the raincoat, in the hope that it'll help ground him.

"Hey, Kyle," Sam says. "Can I ask you something?"

He hums in question.

"How much do you trust Andy?"

"…Andy?"

"Yeah."

"I trust him. Why?"

"I don't know. Maybe I'm just stressed." Sam's clothes rustle as she shifts. "But I've been wondering…what if he's behind what just happened tonight?"

Uncertainty washes over him and Kyle realises his hand's stopped. He frowns into the darkness and resumes the motion. "I don't understand."

"Think about it. He knew where Yuuki was taken last year. That's how we were able to rescue him, because Andy sent us the coordinates. He wouldn't have had access to that in the first place if he weren't one of them – the bad guys."

"Yeah, but Andy *saved* him. He wouldn't have..." Kyle swallows. He hates having this conversation when Yuuki's literally right here listening to them. He really doesn't need any more reminders of traumatic experiences right now. "If Andy hadn't done that, he wouldn't be here right now. And Andy saved me when Jeff caught me. He shot both Deborah and Jeff dead, like, right in front of me."

"You're missing my point. He was working with them, Kyle."

"I know that. Jeff called him a traitor."

"Well, there. Proves my point."

"Does it, though? I saw him after what he did – his hands were shaking. What you're trying to say is that you think Andy was a part in organising *this*, right? Why would he do that when he's been working with us ever since he joined us?"

Even in the darkness, Sam turns to fix an intense questioning stare in his direction. "Have you considered that he might be working on two fronts? He could be a double agent. He was pretty quick to shut down Yuuki's concerns about personal security. He wouldn't have done that unless he had someone he was wanting to keep hidden."

"Not necessarily."

"If he was working with them, then he probably knew all along who was involved in the Ninao incident – in other words, the very same guys we saw tonight. Andy would've known who they were."

She makes a good point, Kyle thinks. *But…* "Even if he did, and even if he knew they were here, that doesn't mean he was in on what they were going to do. Maybe that was why he warned us not to go investigating? Because he was afraid we might motivate them?"

"And what about that guy who saw us leave the palace the other night? The person who told that other guy about us leaving? Can you say for certain that wasn't Andy?"

"Can you say for certain that it was?"

Sam opens her mouth to argue but stops herself. Her brow creases.

"I'm sorry," Kyle says tightly. "I don't mean to say you're wrong. I just…I don't know, the idea doesn't sit comfortably with me. It's unfair on Andy. We don't even have any definite proof. Also…" he trails off, not sure he's prepared for the emotions that are about to follow what he's about to say.

"Also?" Sam prompts.

He swallows. "Even if we had 'proof', who's to say our interpretation of it is correct? I ended up in prison because my fingerprints are on that knife and because I was the only one at the scene. I get how they came to the conclusion they did. I get it. And there's nothing wrong with questioning these things – we need to. But I think Andy's a good guy and he's done so much to help us. I don't want to doubt him."

Sam is torn, he can tell. Torn between wanting to pay heed to the caution in her mind and wanting to respect Kyle.

"Your Dad trusts him," Kyle says gently. "That has to mean

something. He's a judge, after all."

"Dad's been wrong before. Just because he's a judge doesn't make him a perfect judge of character."

"None of us are. I know we're in a really bad situation here. We don't want to be putting trust in people who may turn on us, for sure. But I'd have died in a cell if your Dad hadn't given me a chance. If Yuuki hadn't. If you hadn't. You all gave me the benefit of the doubt and it saved my life."

"You're saying it's best to give Andy the benefit of the doubt, too?"

"Yeah," Kyle says. He lets out a heavy sigh. "Maybe I'm just looking at things too personally, I don't know."

Sam emanates conflicted energy. "Can I ask you something? It might be a little personal, though."

"Go ahead."

"The Village Park incident wasn't the only time, is it? Where something bad has come of someone accusing you?"

The question stabs Kyle through the centre. He narrows his eyes against the memories. "No, it wasn't."

Pressing her lips into a tight line, Sam hums in acknowledgement.

"I got in an argument with my foster parents," he says, deciding he may as well tell her. "They thought I wasn't taking school seriously, that I was slacking off. I wasn't – I just can't study like other people do. One night, I needed to go outside for fresh air since I was finding it hard to concentrate but they wouldn't let me go out of the house because 'discipline'. It upset me. When I tried explaining to them, they said I was making up excuses. It made me feel trapped and I knew I needed to get outside before it got too much.

"But when I tried to move past them, my foster father thought I was about to pick a fight with my foster mother instead and so he suddenly stepped in front of me to try stop me. I thought he was going to hit me. I flinched backwards and tripped. Fell. Landed badly and basically ended up rolling into the fireplace."

Sam stares at him, dismayed. "I remember there was that couple of weeks or so where you couldn't do any PE. The teachers gave you a hard time about it, and then they just stopped all of a sudden. The rest of us never knew what happened but we figured it was sensitive so we never asked."

"Yeah." Kyle sighs. "That was what that was about. Don't worry – it's okay. The worst burn is on my hip, so while it hurt like hell every time I moved, at least I was able to hide all the bandaging. Though I'm not sure what hurt worse: the burn, or the fact that my foster parents kept saying it was my fault I got hurt because I overreacted."

"You never should've had to go through that."

"They left me alone after the fireplace incident."

"Weren't you able to move houses?"

"They were my third foster family. The first could only have me temporarily. The second didn't work out. I felt bad for wanting to move a third time.

"Honestly, I did try talking to my social worker about how I was hurting, but she wouldn't listen. She wouldn't believe they were hurting me because there was no physical abuse involved. It was me, not them, she said. She said I was taking things too seriously and that I just needed to man up and be more resilient. She even tried persuading me go see a counsellor, as if it was me who was the issue and not the situation.

"In the end I gave up. I thought as long as I could last until I was eighteen, it would be fine. Once I left school and left that home, I wouldn't be so bound up in all that. I'd been with that family a year already, so what was another two and a half?

"Turns out I got to leave sooner."

It takes Sam a moment before she hears the implication in his tone. She doesn't say anything, but her heavy silence speaks in itself.

Kyle exhales sharply. "Anyway, enough about me. Long story short, I don't think we should be too quick to get suspicious of Andy. I'm not saying you're *wrong*, it's just…I guess what I'm saying is that I want to believe Andy is good. Even if he was once a part of whatever and whoever these bad guys are, I want to believe he's not anymore. He made his allegiances clear when he saved me, and when he saved Yuuki. That's how I see it, anyway."

Sam taps her phone and squints at the numbers shining on the screen. "Hmm. I feel really called out here."

Kyle winces. "I'm sorry. I don't mean to make you feel bad about it."

"No, you bring up a good point. I mean, I basically argued exactly what you are when I was talking to the others about your case, while you were in prison. I'm just feeling majorly hypocritical right now, is all."

"Now's not exactly a good time to think about things," Kyle murmurs.

Sam grunts. "Yeah, probably not."

"Maybe we should get some sleep."

"If we can. Do you want to take turns keeping watch?"

Kyle feels safer just thinking about it. "Sounds good to me."

"You haven't been feeling so great, have you? I'll take first watch. I won't be able to rest with my mind going crazy like this. I need some time to clear my mind. Besides, you need more rest than me. You're still recovering from your head injury and you're also going to be supporting someone else's weight for a lot of the time tomorrow. No offence, Yuuki."

Yuuki doesn't show any sign of even hearing her. He seems to have drifted off to sleep ahead of them. His body's gone slack in Kyle's arms, or as slack as the stiffness in his muscles will let him. His breathing's evened out and he doesn't stir when Kyle moves them so that they're lying down on the ground.

"Alright. Wake me up when you want to switch," Kyle murmurs over Yuuki's shoulder.

Sam hums.

They settle in for the night, Sam moving to Yuuki's other side to guard his back. With Kyle on Yuuki's right and Sam on his left, they form a protective barrier around him. It's reassuring to know there's no way Yuuki can be stolen from them this way. Even the cold will have a harder time getting to him like this.

Kyle cradles his head against his chest as he shifts to lie on his side. He tucks the edge of the sleeping bag around his back and then wraps his free arm around Yuuki in a loose hug. His arm lifts with every breath Yuuki takes. *Yuuki's safe with us,* it says.

As weird as it seems, it's the reassurance Kyle needs to finally allow himself to sleep.

23

"Do you think it's possible to win this fight?"

Though she's looking out the window at the hazy orange glow of city lights in the distance, Amelia feels Timothy glance over at her. He's quiet for a moment, likely sharing a look with Susan who's sitting in the back seat behind her.

"It's not impossible," he says finally. Amelia expects him to say more; he doesn't.

Susan coughs. She clears her throat and murmurs, "We'll find a way."

Out here on the open road, half way between the palace they've just fled from and the northern reaches of the city, it's hard to believe. They're constantly being chased, attacked and forced into helpless situations. It's easier to feel like they can do something when they're on the move like this, but all it takes is a second to remember that leaving the palace wasn't a strategic move so much as a survival one and the whole hopelessness of the circumstances they're facing comes crashing back down again.

"And what if we can't?" Amelia asks. "What if we can't find a way?"

Timothy taps the steering wheel with his index finger. "Yuuki and I wondered the same about Kyle's case, too. It was rigged against him from the get-go. It made finding concrete evidence in Kyle's defence extremely difficult to find."

"But you still managed to get something."

"Your guys' statements were what we needed. Without them, I don't think either me or Yuuki would've been able to find enough evidence in time. And though we technically haven't formally won that fight yet, we were still legally able to get Kyle out of prison."

"Albeit only *after* he ended up in a critical condition," Susan adds dryly, her voice low.

Amelia remembers that day clearly. It's not a time she likes to remember. She's tried to put it to the back of her mind – the images and the sounds and the lingering emotions she hasn't yet fully processed – but guilt still plagues her. When she'd seen Kyle that day, she'd thought she's indirectly killed him. It was her own witness statement that helped put him away, after all.

If that's the weight of power her words carry, then how can she bear the responsibility of ruling the kingdom?

She can't handle it. She hasn't even officially reclaimed her title yet and already so many people have died around her – Daniel, almost Kyle, potentially almost Yuuki, Taularh and Deborah and Jeff and whoever else lost their lives in the past few weeks because of her.

And then tonight, Yuuki…

I did this, Amelia thinks. It's not the first time she's thought it. Charlie has told her over and over again it isn't, that it's not her doing but Taularh, Deborah, Jeff and whoever else made the decision to act in such a manner who is accountable here. Charlie's an attorney; she should believe him.

But as of tonight, after *she* was the one who was given the ultimatum, and after seeing Yuuki used and hurt and hurting so horribly in front of her, how can she say doesn't have a part in this?

"It's not your fault."

Amelia startles. She shifts uncomfortably in her seat.

Timothy grunts. "You had the same air about you now that Yuuki has when he blames himself."

"Oh."

"Don't feel as though you have to take full accountability for everything that's going on. We're as much a part of this as you are." He sighs. "I'm sorry you have to be put in this position, Amelia. You didn't choose this. You're young; this kind of weight isn't something you should have to bear at your age."

Susan hums in agreement.

"It doesn't matter," Amelia murmurs. "It's always been who I am. I can't hide away from my identity."

"You're a person before you're 'the Princess'," Susan says.

Something in Amelia's heart gives way. She stares at the length of road ahead of them, not really seeing it. These last couple of months, she's been so overwhelmed by all her doubts and insecurities about herself. How she's not cut out for this role she was born into. How she's been Laura Smith far longer than she's ever been Princess Amelia.

She doesn't know *how* to be Princess Amelia.

But Susan's right, and maybe that's it. Maybe she's been doing it all wrong. She's been so stressed by the expectations she has of herself to fit the character of Arkala royalty and leadership that she's been caught up in seeing only how inadequate she is. But 'Princess' and 'Queen' are not simply titles or roles with duties to fulfil; they're positions, and with positions comes power to do things.

Nervousness flares in her chest, accented by some strange sense of newfound courage. It comes with a realisation: the people around her aren't getting hurt because she's the Princess; they're getting hurt because she isn't.

To Arkala, the Princess has been dead for years now. She's Laura to them, and to those who have been hunting her down trying to keep it that way, she's a hindrance. While that doesn't change, people are going to keep getting hurt: those hurting them don't want her becoming the Princess – they don't want her becoming Queen.

Why? Because she'll have greater power than them if she does.

And that therefore means, ultimately, if she wants to protect them and save them from further harm – if she wants to make sure Yuuki doesn't get taken again and Kyle receives the acquittal he's due, and if she wants to make sure no one ends up having to experience the degree of suffering they've had to in all this – she can only do that by truly becoming the Princess.

Amelia clears her throat. "I want to stop all this. I really can't bear to see anyone get hurt again because of me – because they're after me. Kyle got sent to prison a-and Yuuki's been hurt badly over and over. And you all had to give up your livelihoods for my sake. But none of this will stop unless I become the Queen, will it?"

"Or we die," Timothy murmurs.

His wife reaches forward and jabs him in the shoulder.

"What?" He glances at her sharply in the rear view mirror. "We've discussed this. They won't let us off with surrender. If we don't succeed, death is basically our next best alternative. We're threats to the entire Kingdom in anyone's eyes; they're not going to let us off with a simple apology for felling the current ruler and raising a ruckus. They're being lenient already just letting us pull together a chance for a speech."

Susan grimaces. "In answer to your question, Amelia, it may or may not. Certainly, we'd be able to secure more safety for ourselves, but that doesn't mean we're not going to see any backlash after that. We might end up eliminating the current threat that opposes us, but if you become Queen we're going to have to be prepared for whatever might rise up in its stead."

Amelia nods slowly. *Right, politics and whatnot. Everything I am definitely not ready for.*

"But that's something we tackle when it comes. No use worrying too hard about that now when there's more urgent matters to be occupying our thoughts." She sniffs. "And as doom and gloom as our present situation basically is, who knows what's around the corner? This is either where we fall and fail – and run ourselves to the ground simply trying to stay afloat and survive – or else this is where things start changing. Y'know, the darkness before the dawn. That kind of thing."

Timothy grunts, a wry grin tugging at the corner of his lips. "Forgive us, Amelia. We get like this when things get tough; we start talking all philosophical."

Turning her gaze back out the window, Amelia allows herself to smile briefly. "I think we'd be struggling without it. It's hard not to be pessimistic these days, but staying positive doesn't feel right either. I just..."

"We're allowed to have mixed feelings about things." Timothy reassures. "Emotions are complex things."

"As is our situation," Susan adds.

Timothy takes a moment to consider his wording. "The fight is bigger than us. We know that for sure. Yet as long as there's a pathway that lets us keep moving forward, it's not checkmate. We have to fight until we no longer can. And if there ends up being no more pathways available to us, well…we're going to have to find a way to create one."

Amelia thinks of Joshua, and the look he gave her when she was struggling with the ultimatum. She hadn't understood it then, but there had been a subtle confidence in his eyes and a determination in the set of his shoulders. She'd been prepared to surrender back there. The moment those two men took to hurting Yuuki as a method of persuasion, she'd been about to.

But Joshua had asked her not to give in, not to accept the threat of Yuuki being harmed and the pressure to surrender as the only two options available to them. She hadn't known it at the time, but it was because Joshua had been creating a third – a third pathway.

A third option in a two choice ultimatum.

Here they are, somehow still going and Yuuki gone from hands that would have harmed him more. It's like Timothy says – it's not checkmate. They've been making it through impossible fights because none of them have ever been alone on this chessboard.

It gives her the courage and a confidence she's been lacking.

24

Darkness lifts at the end of Kyle's second night watch. Kyle doesn't need to be able to see that Yuuki's eyes are open to know he's not sleeping. He's too tense for that.

Maybe he's not retaining much warmth after all.

Yuuki's trembling has died down, but it's still present. While the emergency blankets and the three of them huddling under the sleeping bag is undoubtedly a lot better than having none of that, it is still cold. It doesn't help that they didn't bring beanies; raincoat hoods don't quite suffice. It also doesn't help that Yuuki's dealing with yet another heavy blow of trauma – the shock of that alone is dangerous.

During the night, it wasn't as easy appearance-wise to tell just how shaken up Yuuki is. Come daylight, it's a different story.

Yuuki's face is drained of colour. His hair's unkempt. There's dried mud smeared over his clothes and bits of twigs, leaves and dirt clinging to them. When he lifts his head, there's a blankness to his expression and an unsettling lack of focus in his eyes. The shadows beneath them are darker. On his chin there's still a line of dried spit they missed while wiping the rest clean with water earlier.

He *looks* roughed up, not just on the inside but on the outside as well.

The dark bruise on his temple just visible at the edge of his hairline and the way he sometimes winces when he moves suggests that he likely was. And he looks haunted. Kyle could feel it in the tightness in Yuuki's shoulders and the overall air of despondency about him, but it's a lot different to be able to see it. Kyle's glad Sam's not up yet and no one else is around to see his expression. It's a lot to process.

He feels the urge to press Yuuki to drink more water and or eat something. Dehydration and hunger will only be making him feel worse. But Kyle's experienced it before, the way traumatic stress messes with the body's functions. Finding ways to work around those difficulties is more important than trying to force them.

It's just hard to know how to do that.

Kyle's afraid of screwing up. Yuuki's fragile. No, he's past that – he's absolutely shattered. When Kyle had been in prison, and in the few weeks after, Yuuki had kept him together. He'd been breaking, but Yuuki saved him.

But can Kyle be the same kind of person for *him*?

The three of them start getting ready to go just after sunrise. It's when they start moving that helplessness begins to attack.

The climb uphill to the ridge drains both Sam and Kyle's energy and ability to support Yuuki. Kyle finds himself feeling light-headed before they've even walked half an hour. His chest feels tight, his throat closed up. He's not even supporting Yuuki's weight here; Yuuki's walking by himself.

An hour in and Kyle feels downright nauseous. Yuuki regards him

213

with a gleam of understanding in his eyes, though he doesn't voice what that is and Kyle doesn't follow. This nausea doesn't feel fatigue associated. By all means, Kyle shouldn't be feeling this sick, should he?

It's not until the minor headache he's experiencing turns into one that slices and throbs that he has an idea of what's going on.

Sam realises then, too. "You hit your head somewhere around here, didn't you?" she asks as they stop to catch their breath.

It all makes sense: Kyle's irritability last night when they were talking about going uphill; the nausea right now and his vision doing weird things; the headache, and the anxiousness that just won't leave him no matter how much he fights it. "I think so," Kyle murmurs.

Nowhere they've walked has *seemed* familiar. Up until now, the bush they've been walking through and the ascending path they've been following has been nothing more than unvisited ground. But who knows? Kyle's memory surrounding his head injury is foggy at best. Maybe he and Yuuki had been here, if not the whole group. Beside him, Yuuki gives no sign of recognising where they are, but he might not remember it either – or else, there's also the possibility he doesn't want to.

Kyle tries his best not to think too hard about the whole thing.

The three of them continue on. They take frequent breaks, all of them out of breath and tiring. A couple of times, Kyle feels like he's bordering on having a panic attack simply from how the breathlessness simulates one. It happens a few times, too. He thinks he's overreacting until it happens to Yuuki.

By the time they finally reach the top of the ridge, Yuuki's eyes are glazed with exhausted and his face void of expression. The wind blows and he stumbles sideways.

Sam scans the area around them. Her cheeks are flushed, the tips of her ears red. She uses the end of her sleeve to wipe the sweat from her forehead. "We need to find somewhere sheltered, if we can."

With a nod, Kyle helps her in her search. It's hard to find somewhere less exposed when the ridge is exposed as it is anyway, but there's enough trees and rocks around that they're able to find a place to rest where the wind isn't quite so strong.

The ground is chilled and a little wet, so they lay down the tarp. Yuuki slouches heavily when they sit. Drinking water takes the rest of his energy out of him, and Kyle has to grab a hold of the water bottle before it slips out of Yuuki's grasp. He helps Yuuki lie down on his back after that, ignoring the headache he really ought to tend to while he does so.

"We're probably going to be here a little while," Kyle says. "So go ahead and nap if you need to."

Though he looks reluctant, it turns out he does need it. An awake nap, at least. Kyle takes an emergency blanket out of Sam's backpack and spreads it out over him, gently tucking the sides around him to keep it from blowing away in the wind. He stays beside him so he doesn't feel vulnerable.

Yuuki's brow furrows and he closes his eyes.

"I'm going to call Dad," Sam says.

Kyle looks over at her to find her tapping her phone. "Are you able to get reception?"

"Yep. It's not great, but I got some."

Without further ado, she presses call and puts the phone on speaker.

215

Timothy picks up after several rings.

"Hey, Sam."

"Hey, Dad."

"It's good to hear from you," Timothy murmurs. His tone is grave. "How are you all? How's Yuuki?"

"Uh…" Sam glances at Kyle, unsure.

"He's doing okay," Kyle supplies quietly. In other words, not well, but considering the circumstances, there are worse states Yuuki could be in than he is right now.

Timothy can hear the truth in his voice though. This, realistically speaking, already is one of those worse states. "Hi, Kyle. That's… good, I guess."

"So where is everyone now?" Sam asks. "Joshua said you guys were leaving."

"Right, yes. Andy decided to move everyone out. No one disagreed. What those two men did to Yuuki is statement enough that they're prepared to forego peaceful negotiations. We can't put anyone else at risk."

"Andy, Charlie and I have been sussing out some safe houses for the last couple of weeks in case we had to leave the palace. We got in contact with the three we were able to narrow down that were willing to take us. We're still waiting to hear back from one of them, but Andy's expecting they will within the next few days. The group's split between the other two at the moment."

Sam frowns. "What's up with the third house?"

"Resources. They can accommodate all of us, but we're kind of a big group – we're a lot of people to make sure there's enough supplies for all at once. The Peace Forces will be keeping an eye out for any suspicious activity, I'd say."

"So what, they're monitoring how much people spend at the supermarket now? Just so they can keep an eye out for us?"

"Any big supermarket spends," Timothy says, "or anything out of the ordinary that looks like someone preparing for having a bunch of people over. We're fugitives, remember, and it's not Christmas. Even with the group split in two, we're probably pushing it.

"Right now, the third house is organising a way for supplies to be delivered while keeping us all under the radar. I'm not sure how long we'll be staying there, but somehow I don't think it's going to be temporary. It's probably going to end up being our base for a while – at least until we figure things out, which is…much more of an immediate concern now."

"Are you sure we can trust these people?" Kyle asks, voice lowered. *Everything Timothy's saying makes sense, but…*

There's a hesitation before Timothy's answer, one that Kyle doesn't like. It's not present in his voice when he speaks, however. "Yes. And we're fortunate we have anybody at all we can go to. We wouldn't have been able to leave the palace if we didn't."

Sam's concern from last night replays in Kyle's mind. *"Do you trust Andy?"* It hurts his brain to try think about it. Even if there is some stuff about Andy that they could deem questionable, Timothy's right – they don't have many people they can trust as is. If they want to survive, then they have to be able to put as much faith in each other as possible. Given these circumstances, they don't really have a choice.

Timothy sighs. "Where are you guys now?"

"On top of the ridge," Kyle says. "We're just having a rest, but we're on our way to the last hut we stayed at on our way to the palace."

"Checkpoint D?"

"Yeah."

"Okay, good. Andy's going to come and get you. There's a road he'll pick you up from – you can get to it by heading east from Checkpoint C. Do you think you can make it there by dark tomorrow?"

Sam and Kyle exchange a contemplative glance. "I mean, hypothetically," Sam says slowly. "How far is it from Checkpoint C?"

"Two and a half hours?"

"At healthy-and-fit person pace, and without stopping or getting lost, right?"

"Oh, right – yeah. Andy reckons allow yourself four hours from Checkpoint C. That'll give you plenty of time for some decent rest breaks along the way if you need it. If you leave the Checkpoint D hut by mid-morning, you should be fine."

"And what happens if we don't make it that far by then? Will they come in and get us?"

"If you're not at the road by dark, he'll come in and get you. There's markers on the trees, so as long as you follow those as best you can and keep heading east, you won't get too lost. Andy said there's an emergency shelter about half way out to the road. Try to at least make it to there."

"Okay, we'll try."

"Cool."

"But seriously," Sam mutters, "how long are we going to have to keep running like this? Amelia was supposed to give her speech last night."

"I know. Andy even said we had a spot on the 10pm news channel. Don't worry, he contacted the broadcasting station to let them know what was going on. Obviously we couldn't give proof then, but we do have it: Joshua recorded evidence."

Kyle's stomach dips. "Evidence?"

"Of the rescue," Timothy says carefully, "and of those three's reactions to finding that they're plan fell through. He videoed the whole thing on his phone while he was up on the rooftop. Just like he did at Ninao."

Exchanging a glance with Sam, Kyle looks down at Yuuki. The older's breathing is steady and his face blank of any expression, but Kyle's not sure if he's actually asleep or if he's awake and still listening to the whole conversation.

At Sam and Kyle's silence, Timothy murmurs, "We didn't share it with the broadcasting station. We also copied the palace's security footage of the entire situation. That wasn't shared either."

Yuuki doesn't so much as twitch.

"In saying that, it *is* critical evidence. If our own word won't validate our situation, those recordings will. The content is, of course, very sensitive though, so if we are to decide to broadcast any of them it won't be without Yuuki's prior consent.

"But don't worry about that right this minute. Our priority is getting everyone back together safely. In the meantime, I think Amelia's making some alterations to her speech – updating it, rather – and…" A heavy pause. Timothy lets out a stressed breath. "Just get here safely, yeah? All of you."

"We will," Sam says solemnly.

Kyle nods. They will at least try to.

After finishing the call with Timothy, the three of them take a little while longer to rest. Getting up and going again is hard, but the prospect of a proper shelter to stay in is enough incentive to get moving again.

In spite of their pace being slowed by stiff, sore and fatigued legs, they arrive at the Checkpoint D hut in reasonable time. The front of the hut is awash in warm afternoon sunlight when they get there. They relish it. After spending some time soaking in the sunlight and resting, Sam goes inside to change and deal with female hygiene stuff. While she's doing that, Kyle has a brief quiet moment alone with Yuuki.

"You doing okay?" he asks softly.

Yuuki looks at Kyle in the corner of his eye, vulnerable, wary and mildly irritated. He squints in the sunlight. He says nothing. He hasn't spoken at all today, as if the cloth is still in his mouth and it's no use trying to get words out anyways. Kyle regards him carefully, increasingly worried, but is nonetheless respectful. Between the shock of the trauma and the exhaustion they're currently facing, he'd rather not force him.

Tentatively, Kyle lifts his hand. He makes sure Yuuki can see his movements, so he won't be startled and has plenty of time to move away if he doesn't want to be touched. Kyle places his hand on Yuuki's shoulder and lets it rest there.

With a downward pull at the corner of his mouth, Yuuki averts his eyes.

Sam opens the door then. The sharp clean scent of hand sanitizer taints the air. "We left a couple of gas canisters here last time we were here," she said. "I think they're almost empty, but there's probably enough in them for a few hot drinks, maybe a quick meal."

"What do we have for food?" Kyle asks, twisting around to face her.

"Uh, not much. At least, not much we can really have without water."

Well there goes that plan of staying here for long if we needed to. "We forgot to bring gas with us, didn't we?"

"Hey, it's never a tramping trip unless you forget something, right? Or bring a hitchhiker. Once I brought a carrot with me on a four day hike with my family. Never ate it. It sat in my backpack the whole entire time."

Kyle grunts, amused. "Oh well. Guess we just make do then."

The gas only lasts long enough to boil one pot of water. Sam sets the empty canisters aside by the backpack so they remember to take them back with them to dispose of. When they eat, Yuuki decides to try to eat only to throw up the small amount he had half an hour later. The most he's able to keep down is reconstituted juice.

It's worrying. Yuuki's lacking strength as it is. They've hiked a full day and Yuuki's barely been able to eat anything. Juice won't be enough to sustain him through yet another day's hike. But what can they do? Stomachs hold stress and Yuuki has fresh trauma messing with his system.

One more day. Tonight, and one more day – we've just got to make it through that, and then when can rest.

That's easier a prospect than it sounds.

The night passes much the same as the first. It's not quite as cold since they have better shelter, but Yuuki shivers more than he had the night before. When it's Kyle's turn for watch, Kyle tries to ease the tension and the shaking by rubbing Yuuki's back. Sometimes it works for a bit, other times it doesn't.

The next day is a blur. Kyle's vision is fuzzy at the edges and the colours of the forest are too contrasted. His movements feel automated, disjointed. His knees keep threatening to buckle.

Yuuki's seen the exhaustion taking hold of him, too. Kyle wonders if that's why Yuuki keeps rejecting the support Kyle offers him. It makes him feel guilty. Yuuki's exhausted right now; Kyle should be helping him. But then again, Kyle's exhausted too. Sam, too, has her own set of pain and tiredness to push through.

They make it to Checkpoint C in the passing showers of the early afternoon. Kyle keeps checking on Yuuki, who's become increasingly despondent. Yuuki only responds in glances, in small nods and in the aversion of his eyes.

Distress sparks in Yuuki's expression when they force themselves up to get moving again. It's masked again when they're back to walking, replaced by sheer exhaustion and vacantness. Kyle checks over his shoulder more frequently after that. Sam does too.

Yuuki's energy flags severely. He begins to list sideways, tilting to his left further and further as he walks as though he doesn't have the energy to counter the missing weight of his right anymore. Kyle and Sam help him through some tricky parts of the marked track they're following, but it's becoming clear that Yuuki's far *far* past his limit.

Shadows gather and swamp the forest as the sun sets, and the night begins to settle in again. They've just come in view of the emergency shelter Timothy mentioned when Yuuki's legs stop moving. His shoes scuff the ground.

Kyle turns. "What's…?"

Yuuki lifts his head with a sharp exhale.

"Do you want to stop for another rest? We can –"

Yuuki's eyes lose focus, and with a helpless sound he collapses.

25

Kyle lunges forward in time to catch him. His arms strain to hold Yuuki up, but Yuuki can't bear his own weight anymore and Kyle can feel him slipping from his grasp. Kyle tightens his arms around him and lowers them to the ground.

Sam's boots enter his periphery. The beam of her head light falls on them. "Is he..?" *Okay? Still conscious? Not able to walk any further?*

"Are you still with us?" Kyle asks. He tries to speak softly for Yuuki's sake, but he's too tense with anxiousness. "Yuuki?"

No response. Yuuki's been having difficulty communicating all day though, and yesterday too. Where he'd managed words in the few hours after they'd rescued him, now he's unable to speak at all. Kyle's experienced similar – he'd struggled with speaking in those first few days out of prison. Everyone had been patient with him. Caring. Accepting. And that had included Yuuki.

But Kyle's not Yuuki. He doesn't know what to say in situations like this. He can do his best to comfort him with hugs, but not with words. In the back of his mind, he feels like he should be saying *something*, if just to give Yuuki the sound of his voice close by to latch onto as an anchor, a reassurance.

What he doesn't realise yet is just how much reassurance he's already offering. To Yuuki, the physical contact with someone 'safe' is security. Right now, that's exactly the promise Yuuki needs.

"We should move to the shelter," Sam says. "It's only about fifty metres away. We can wait for Andy there."

Obviously they're not going to be able to make it to the road before dark. It's basically already dark. They've had to accept that they wouldn't make it ever since they got to Checkpoint C. It was probably unrealistic to think they could to begin with.

"Yeah," Kyle murmurs. "Do you think you could –"

Yuuki groans. Kyle waits, wondering if Yuuki's trying to say something. But then his muscles slacken and his body goes limp, and just like that he passes out in Kyle's arms. His head shifts and his face turns upwards. Yuuki's breath ghosts against Kyle's neck.

Kyle's stomach churns. *How hard has he been pushing himself?*

"I can help you carry him into the hut," Sam says quietly. She sets the backpack down, takes out the head torch and slips it on around her head. With a grunt, she shoulders the bag again. "Come on, before it gets really cold out here."

Kyle frowns. He's reluctant to let Yuuki go. "I could try piggyback him?"

"You're barely able to walk straight as it is."

"What? No, I'm –"

"You won't be able to walk while carrying him. Not unless you think your legs are strong enough to. Heck, even my legs feel like they're gonna go weak on me." She gives him a sharp look that reminds Kyle of Susan.

"Don't overdo it. We'll carry him between us."

Kyle finds he can't argue with that.

Dropping down into a crouch beside them, Sam helps Kyle manoeuvre Yuuki between them. Once they have his arm slung over Kyle's neck and shoulders, they brace themselves and then together they haul him up. Sam moves her arm around Yuuki's waist, supporting his weight from his right side. They pause to catch their breath and then start forward towards the shelter.

Behind them, Yuuki's feet drag in the dirt. Kyle winces at the sound of his shoes trailing over the dirt and sticks and stones. He wishes they could carry him better, but Yuuki is taller than him and Sam; there's little they can do about it. Sam also doesn't have an arm to hold over her own shoulders to help keep him upright. As it is, they're walking with Yuuki's weight unevenly distributed between them, with Yuuki mostly slumped against Kyle's side and Sam doing what she can to give extra support.

Sam's right. There's no way Kyle's going to be able to carry all of Yuuki's weight on his own. Even between them it's a struggle. They're also not exactly at their strongest. After two days' hiking, carrying someone is like tripling the muscle strain and making the achy tiredness burn and turn to lead. It reaches even to the muscles in Kyle's face, and judging by the way Sam's cheek twitches and the corner of her mouth twists downwards, it's also that much of a strain for her.

As they emerge into the small clearing surrounding the shelter, something sounds in the bushes ahead of them. Kyle nearly loses his grip on Yuuki. He freezes, as does Sam. She lifts her head to shine the beam of her head torch in the direction of the sound.

Something's moving towards us. The revelation comes with a fresh wave of adrenaline. His fingers tighten around Yuuki's wrist like a vice. The bushes wave ahead of them and Kyle tenses. Both he and Sam press themselves closer to Yuuki, eyes wide and fixed on what the light shows.

Light flickers between the branches and leaves. A moment later, two people step out into view. They're also wearing head torches, causing Kyle and Sam to be temporarily blinded by them. But the two torch beams turn downwards as soon as they hit the three of them, casting the ground in the bright light instead. When Kyle's vision clears of the lights' afterimage, a knot of tension in his chest unravels.

It's just Andy's rescue team, consisting of himself and a woman about the same age or older. They have a stretcher with them.

"You did well to make it this far," Andy remarks, eyes flicking to Yuuki slumped between them.

"I thought we were meeting you out at the road," Sam says. There's a hint of distrust in her tone. It's absent, however, when she squints through the lights and the darkness at the woman beside Andy and exclaims, "Wait, *Marina?*"

The woman raises her free hand, one corner of her mouth uplifted in a tired smile. "Hey, Sam. I see you lot managed to get yourselves wound up in trouble again, huh?"

Sam huffs. "I guess that's one way to explain it."

"In answer to answer to your question," Andy says, "Susan advised as to try meet you in a bit further. She and Timothy weren't confident you'd be able to get all the way out to the road." Before either Kyle or Sam can protest their efforts, he adds, "Considering the fact that two out of three of you are dealing with traumatic injuries, she made a just call. Traumatic brain injuries and PTSD share common symptoms and neither are to be made light of. I was told that you believed you could make it in time, but it's easy to get estimates wrong. The extent of Yuuki's injuries is, or was, also unknown to us. Hence why we decided to come into the bush early."

"And hence why we brought this," Marina says, gesturing with her chin to the stretcher. "Thought you guys might possibly need it."

The obvious doesn't really need to be stated: they do.

Marina comes forward with Andy and the two of them lie the stretcher down length-ways in front of Kyle, Yuuki and Sam. She straightens up with a sigh. "Not looking so great there, eh, Yuuki?"

Kyle tries to ignore the urge to pull Yuuki away from this person he doesn't know. Defensiveness automatically sharpens itself on his tongue. He knows any comment he makes right now is going to be some kind of hissed warning or else a nonsensical retort, so he grits his teeth and focuses on keeping himself and Yuuki upright.

Calm down, he scolds himself. *These two people aren't going to hurt Yuuki. They're Peace Force officers, but they're friends. They're not a threat.*

"He just passed out about five minutes or so ago," Sam informs them regarding Yuuki, her voice lowered and laced with guilt. "We kind of pushed each other a little too hard in trying to get here as soon as we could."

"Well, not long and you'll all be out of the bush," Marina says. "If you two want to go ahead and lay him down, we can have a short rest, make sure he's settled and then head onwards to warmer drier places."

Andy mistakes Kyle's hesitation to let go of Yuuki as being physically too exhausted and unsteady to do it. When he comes right up to them and reaches out his hands to help, Kyle almost fights him. Andy raises an eyebrow at Kyle in question, though not unkindly. Kyle clenches his jaw.

"You can let go," Andy murmurs.

Fear, fatigue and that last ditch survival instinct of fight make Kyle's blood run white hot and cool at the same time. Kyle's knees tremble. He's too afraid to let Yuuki go. Sam's not letting go, either. What happens if Yuuki gets hurt the moment they do so? Or if Sam's suspicions of Andy and Kyle's anxiousness around Peace Force officers prove to be a warning he didn't heed?

They're too on edge to trust anyone but themselves. It's made more so by the fact that Yuuki's unconscious and fully reliant on Kyle and Sam to keep him safe. They're scared of further harm coming to Yuuki, of not being able to stop it from happening if it does. Physically letting him go and handing him over to someone else is equivalent to letting go of control over the situation and lessening their ability to protect him.

Andy sees it now. He looks Kyle and Sam directly in the eye, a careful and remorseful gleam in his eye. "I'm just going to help you lie him down so you don't strain yourselves."

Carefully, Kyle eases his grip on Yuuki's wrist. Sam takes that as a signal and withdraws her arm from around Yuuki's back. With great care, Andy hooks his hands under Yuuki's armpits and eases his weight from Sam and Kyle's support.

Kyle's stomach dips as Yuuki's arm – the last point of contact Kyle has to hold onto him – slips off his shoulders. But Andy only sets Yuuki down right in front of him and Sam, laying Yuuki on his back with his head resting by Kyle's feet. The demonstration settles some of the anxiety residing in Kyle's body. Sam takes an emergency blanket out of her bag. Andy rises to his feet, slowly and takes a step back to give them room.

As Sam spreads out the blanket over Yuuki's still form. Kyle goes about gently tucking it around him, making sure that it's close to his body while still being loose enough to breathe and not feel restraining. The last thing they want is for Yuuki to wake up feeling tied down. They also don't want to risk him getting hypothermic, either.

Andy and Marina are the ones designated to carry Yuuki out on the stretcher. Neither Kyle nor Sam are comfortable with it, but it's something they're both subconsciously relieved about. They don't have the energy or the physical strength left that's needed to carry Yuuki; they can't object to the help they need. In any case, Kyle resolves to stay as near to Yuuki as he can.

The trek to the road takes just under two hours. Kyle and Sam aren't counting, but Marina checks the time and announces it when they arrive there.

A lone inconspicuous four wheel drive waits for them. The sight of the vehicle sitting there unattended unnerves Kyle. In normal circumstances, he'd just be seeing it for exactly what it is: the car that Andy and Marina drove here to pick them up in, left parked on the side of the road by the entry to the bush trail. But he finds his eyes darting back and forth, straining to see into the shadows beyond the other side of the road, ears pricked and listening for even the slightest hint of sound of approaching danger. There's been too much of it lately. So much so that it's hard to trust even the quiet.

Andy and Marina set the stretcher down. While they go about making room amongst the spare clothing, tools and emergency equipment strewn across the back seat of the car, Kyle and Sam take up protective positions around Yuuki. Kyle braces his hands on his knees and slowly sinks down into a crouch by Yuuki's side. His legs protest and his head throbs. He'd almost be happy if Andy and Marina pulled out a big tent and said they were all camping here. He's certainly glad they have the car.

Yuuki, on the other hand, doesn't share in that relief. He stirs with a disoriented whine, brow furrowing at the noise of the vehicle doors opening and shutting. Kyle realises it must've woken him but he doesn't give as much thought to it as he should. He's too distracted by his relief at seeing Yuuki conscious again. But when Yuuki opens his eyes to Kyle's shadow looming over him, Yuuki promptly panics.

His arm tears free of the emergency blanket. Yuuki shoves Kyle away from him with a kick – one that's weak but enough to make Kyle unbalanced. As Kyle falls sideways, Yuuki makes a desperate scramble to get away from him but his attempt at it isn't all that successful. His energy levels are depleted. He can hardly manage a crawl.

Kyle reaches out a hand to steady him but that only sends Yuuki reeling. Kyle's heart beats fast. He tries again but all that does is make Yuuki renew his efforts to get away.

No touching. Kyle's mind stalls. Calming via physical contact is how he's always approached helping him. It's the only way he knows how. He's not good with words, not in these situations, and he can't think of how words will be of any use when Yuuki's mind is overwhelmed with traumatic stress.

But it doesn't matter – Yuuki's panicking. He needs to think.

He doesn't really know what he's doing but he tries anyway.

Over and over, Kyle reassures Yuuki that he and Sam aren't going anywhere. That this isn't the vehicle he was kept in the other night. That the other two people with them are friends, not foes. That he's safe. That they'll be travelling to somewhere safer than the cold of where they are now. Kyle speaks slow and steady, meeting the fear in Yuuki's eyes with reassurance.

Somehow, Kyle's able to bring Yuuki out of it. Gradually the frightened sheen in Yuuki's eyes lessens, just a fraction. Yuuki's hyperventilating becomes a more controlled version of it. After that it's easier.

"It's cold out here, eh?" Kyle murmurs. He doesn't stop speaking to him. It's giving something for Yuuki to focus on. "I know being inside the car is probably going to be upsetting for you. That's okay. But I'll be right there with you. Sam will be too. We'll be staying together."

Sam gestures to the car in Kyle's periphery. *"We're ready to go."*

"Are you okay to go now?"

Yuuki shakily nods. He can't use words to communicate, and no one forces him too. Apart from Marina, they all witnessed the hostage situation. And then there's Kyle, who rescued him from it. They know enough to understand how this current situation might be triggering for Yuuki. They've seen enough to know how shaken Yuuki must be from it.

Though they're both stiff, Kyle and Sam manage to help Yuuki up. Gently, they prompt him to move forward. When Yuuki digs his heels into the gravel and tries to pull back, they don't force him to keep moving.

"It's okay," Kyle murmurs. "It's okay."

A long fifteen minutes later, Yuuki's finally able to move again. Each step is on autopilot. Sam goes first inside the vehicle first, taking the side of the back seat that Yuuki had been secured in. Kyle helps Yuuki step in and then settles in beside him. Though he closes the door behind him as softly as he can, Yuuki still flinches.

They don't make him wear a seatbelt. Kyle refrains from hugging him too, in fear of recreating the sensation of being restrained by one, or by rope. It's hard, especially when he wants to believe that Yuuki could really use the comfort of a hug right now. But it's not about what Kyle thinks is best, it's what's best for Yuuki. Instead, he keeps the offer of a hug open and lets Yuuki accept as much of it as he wants.

Marina drives them. As they head off, Andy calls Timothy to let him know they're on their way. Marina and Sam strike up a casual friendly conversation after that. Through it, Kyle learns that they became friends through their shared investigations about the Ninao incident. Marina and Sam don't linger on the subject of the Ninao Kidnapping case, for obvious reasons.

That topic of conversation doesn't help Yuuki but the easy way of their talking does. Curled up in the middle of the backseat, where he can see out the windscreen and have Kyle and Sam acting again as a protective barrier flanking each side of him, he gradually begins to lower his guard.

Yuuki pulls his knees closer to his chest and rests his forehead on them. His arm, wrapped around his legs, loosens slightly. When the car moves around a bend, Yuuki loses his grip on his legs and ungracefully unfurls. He slumps sideways into Kyle's side with the terminal velocity.

No move is made to pull himself back upright again. He stays as is for the rest of the journey.

26

Just a few nights ago, the city was too dangerous a place to go to. Going to the Harrisons meant acknowledging that. But accepting the high risk associated with being here had been a choice back then; it isn't so much so now. Reality is hard to keep up with.

The house they arrive at is, like the Harrisons', also in Two Lakes. At the end of a driveway that dips out of sight of the street, Timothy waits for them. Susan comes outside as they pull in. Warm light spills out the front door behind her.

"We can't stay long," Andy says when they stop. "As soon as you guys are out, we'll be taking off again."

"'kay. Thanks for picking us up," Kyle murmurs. His words are slurred with exhaustion.

"No problem."

Marina twists in her seat to look at them. "Are you okay getting out by yourselves?"

"We'll manage," Sam answers. "Thanks."

Yuuki remains slumped against Kyle's side until he's not able to. It doesn't need to be said that he's going to need help getting inside. Yuuki doesn't seem to be upset by touch like he was earlier, but Kyle asks him if he's okay with it just to make sure. At Yuuki's nod, Kyle takes his wrist and places his arm over his shoulders.

Sam gets out of the car first. She dumps the backpack on the driveway and comes around to help them. Kyle's grateful for her support. Both he and Yuuki are struggling to stay on their feet. Shivering overtakes Yuuki again within seconds, and Kyle and Sam soon after. The night is freezing. They're quick to get each other inside.

Inside, the house is flooded with warmth and light. Kyle's vision swims. Yuuki shudders. They let their eyes adjust to lighting as they take in the new setting. A lady they don't know – presumably the owner of the house – ushers them over to the couch. Before they can hesitate or protest in regard to their dirty outdoor clothes, she lays down some towels over the seats and reassures them it's okay to sit. Sam nearly trips over her shoes as she yanks her feet out of them. Kyle almost does the same. Yuuki doesn't have the energy to even try but no one forces him.

Timothy steps forward as though to reach out and give more support on their way, but Kyle shakes his head. He doesn't get the message straight away, though. He does, however, when Yuuki flinches.

"Sorry," he murmurs. Timothy reluctantly takes a step back, bewildered.

Kyle and Sam set Yuuki down on the couch between them and sit down on either side of him. Yuuki pulls his arm off Kyle's shoulders and leans forward to hold his head in his hand.

"Amelia's making hot drinks," Susan says, coming in with Sam's bag. She puts it down beside their shoes. "Are you all okay with hot chocolate?"

None of them can argue with that, although Kyle's already anticipating Yuuki's not going to want to drink any – especially not with the way stress has been affecting his stomach.

Timothy shuts the door behind them, muting the sound of Andy and Marina leaving. He flicks the lock. "Glad you got here safe."

The click of the lock has Kyle's hands growing clammy. Anxiety pricks the back of his neck. *No. It's fine. It's not dark in here – there's light. It's not cold.* But he's exhausted and on edge and not feeling well, and this doesn't have to be an actual prison cell to remotely feel like one.

The thought that he's not allowed to go outside is enough to make him feel trapped. Technically, he could: he could get up right now, unlock that door with his own hands and walk back out into the night. Kyle's not a prisoner here. None of them are. The only reason he needs to stay inside is because outside it's cold and not safe for them – it's because the circumstances they're in means that outside isn't safe, not because they're trying to protect the outside from *him*.

I'm not a prisoner here. We're simply taking refuge here.

Kyle takes a deep breath and tries to believe it.

But then he catches the lady who's place their at staring at with great wariness in her eyes and the effort crumbles. The lady turns away abruptly. She politely excuses herself under the pretence of helping Amelia carry over the hot drinks.

His heart sinks. *Right, that's who I am to everyone else – a convict. All that's associated with my name is either nothing or violence and death.*

"You shouldn't have been there in the first place." Yuuki's told him that many times before, as has Timothy. The others too, for that matter. Kyle tries

to tell himself that as well, that he shouldn't have been in prison to begin with. That being punished with a conviction and the isolation of solitary confinement wasn't at all fair when the very thing he was accused of isn't true.

But it's hard. Kyle had plenty of alone time in that cell to convince himself he did deserve those accusations and the confinement. That's not enough mentioning the sense of low self-worth he'd already been dealing with before that.

Before his thoughts can spiral, Amelia comes around the couch with two steaming cups of hot chocolate in her hands. She takes in Yuuki's bowed form as she lowers the cups to the coffee table. Her hands shake.

Kyle doesn't know what to say or how to reassure her, and he's too tired to get his brain to think. Instead he meets her eyes with a look he hopes conveys *'it's okay'*.

Amelia swallows. With a tight smile, she leaves for the kitchen to get hers and Sam's cups.

"So we're here," Sam says. "Where are the others?"

"At Andy's house in Ninao," Susan murmurs.

A small sound escapes Yuuki's throat. It's the Ninao district that's being referred to here, but Ninao is still how Yuuki and the Harrisons refer to the kidnapping in short.

"People won't be suspicious when they see he's home?" Sam asks.

Timothy grimaces. "Hopefully not. Andy and his family live rurally: there shouldn't be too much chance of them being seen. Our main concern is just whoever happens to recognise the cars on the road. We're hiding the vehicles we came here in there, in a garage."

Kyle frowns. "Wait, his family?"

"His wife and children." Susan says. She accepts the cup of tea the lady comes out and hands her with a small thanks. "He has a son about the same age as Joshua and daughter who's just graduated university."

"Oh…he must be seriously missing them. It's been weeks."

Timothy nods. Susan takes a sip of tea. The lady's eyes gleam.

"This is Hayley, by the way," Timothy says, gesturing to the lady who's hosting them. "We'll be staying here until Andy gives the go ahead to move out."

"To where, exactly?" Sam asks.

"That third house I told you about on the phone yesterday. Andy reckons Sunday at the earliest."

Kyle grunts. "What day even is it?"

"Thursday," Susan supplies.

"There'll be a lot of people out and about over the next two nights," Timothy says. "And Peace Force officers. If we want to avoid them, early Sunday morning is our best bet."

The lady – Hayley – clears her throat. "I know it's not for long, but please make yourselves at home. It's only my son and I here now. We'll be coming and going. Don't mind us."

"Thank you for having us," Susan says.

Hayley smiles, but it's grim.

Easy conversation is passed while the hot chocolates are consumed. Amelia kneels down on the floor beside Sam, the two of them sharing a hushed argument. From what Kyle can gather, Amelia feels responsible for what happened to Yuuki. Sam answers exactly what Yuuki would –

239

that it isn't her fault. Kyle's on the verge of adding that what happened to *him* wasn't her fault either, as if she's beating herself up about Yuuki's abuse then she's likely still feeling the same about his.

But he doesn't speak. Sam's the one she's confiding here, and Kyle doesn't want to interrupt that unless it's necessary. There's a reason why they're talking in low voices. Even if they can still be overheard if anyone chooses to listen in, the point is the sense of privacy it gives them.

Amelia has a lot to process. She deserves to have the time and emotional space to process it for herself.

Beside Kyle, Yuuki hasn't moved since they sat down. He stays sitting hunched forward, trying to hide his face from the light and likely also everyone else's view. His skin is off colour. Though the lights on in the house are warm, the shadows cast over his face only make his exhaustion look all the more awful. It doesn't take a genius to know Yuuki's not okay.

Kyle decides to intervene. He clears his throat, wincing at the flare of pain it causes. "Hey, um…would it be alright if we get some rest now?"

"You guys probably want to have a shower first," Susan murmurs.

A shower sure does sound inviting, but Kyle's not sure he has the energy for one tonight. It doesn't need to be questioned that Yuuki doesn't either. It's not for lack of will, but rather the inability to combat the dizziness taking over him. He can imagine how lethargic Yuuki is feeling right now, too.

He glances at Yuuki and, as if on cue, yawns. "Don't know if we can."

Susan hums. "That's fair enough."

"Well, I'm sure keen," Sam says, breaking away from her talk with Amelia. "But yeah, sleep is just as enticing as a shower."

"You can have one now if you want. There's spare towels in a basket in the bathroom. Do you have clothes to change into?"

"Yep. They're in the bag."

"I also packed some clothing before we left, so there's that also. Just so you're aware."

"Thanks, Mum." With an apology to Amelia, Sam gets up and eagerly accepts the opportunity for a shower.

"We'll all be sleeping down here," Timothy says. "Yuuki and Kyle, though, you guys can have the master bedroom." When Kyle opens his mouth to protest, Timothy reassures, "I've already informed Hayley that you two don't mind sharing a bed."

"One of my sons aren't around anymore," Hayley adds quietly, "so I'll sleep in his room."

There's nothing to be ashamed about. Societal norms would say it's weird or wrong that two guys would cuddle, especially when there's nothing romantic or sexual between them, but oh well. Platonic bed sharing might not be that common, but they're humans, and Yuuki's suffering.

And yet, somehow just being back in the city environment makes him flustered and defensive. Kyle wonders if part of that is because the last time he was in the city, he'd scarcely been a few days out of prison – one of which he doesn't remember since he'd been sleeping off hypothermia.

"What about you and Susan?" Kyle asks.

Timothy tilts his head in Yuuki's direction. "He needs it," he whispers.

Kyle nods solemnly. "Okay."

It's not just the physical support of the bed Timothy's meaning – it's the emotional support. Kyle remembers the night they all spent at Checkpoint B, how he and Yuuki had basically cuddled all night long after Kyle had been reunited with the group. It definitely had helped him sleep better that night.

They wait for people to disperse before moving. Kyle doesn't want to draw attention to Yuuki's state if he can help it. He knows Yuuki wouldn't like that one bit. Once Sam's in the shower, and Amelia, Timothy and Hayley are in the kitchen talking and washing dishes, Susan leads them to the room.

Yuuki's unable to keep his head up. He leans heavily on Kyle, his movements forced. The master bedroom, like the other two bedrooms in the house, is upstairs, and Kyle wishes he was strong enough to carry Yuuki up there. Maybe in full health he might be able to, but not at all right now.

In the end, Susan has to help them. Yuuki makes it up three steps before he can't lift his knees anymore. He stumbles back down one when Susan reaches out to take over from Kyle, but without the energy to make it up there on his own, Yuuki lets her. Even then it's still slow going, and Yuuki's practically hanging off her shoulder when they get to the top of the staircase.

Kyle flicks on the light as they enter. Susan sets Yuuki down on the edge of the bed and gently coaxes him into removing his jacket. She folds it up and puts it on the floor before easing the shoes and socks off his feet. After fetching the rest of the spare clothes from Sam's bag, they help Yuuki change into a fresh set of clothes.

More injuries are revealed in the process. There's bruises all over

Yuuki's torso and sides: signs of being punched, kicked and shoved. There's some on his legs as well. In an anger-tinged yet controlled tone, Susan ducks into a crouch and quietly asks Yuuki if they violated him at all. *They* meaning the men who kidnapped him.

Kyle swallows down the nausea that rises in his throat. He hadn't thought to ask Yuuki that.

But Yuuki shakes his head at the question. He winces at the action and presses the heel of his hand against his temple. He opens his mouth and then closes it, fingers curling to grip his hair in distress.

Susan gently pats him on the knee. "Okay. Hey, it's okay. I know you're finding it hard to talk at the moment. But if you need anything or you need to tell us anything, we're here." She rises to her feet. "I'm going to go down and find you some ointment for those bruises. And some painkillers. I'll be back."

In the stillness that settles after she leaves, Kyle sits down beside Yuuki. He tugs a blanket over to them, shakes it out and drapes it over Yuuki's shoulders. The worst of the bruises are on his upper body, so it's only there that's exposed, however the lesser layers of clothing may very well feel like less defences too. That's how Kyle interprets the way Yuuki has his arm wrapped around himself, anyways. He wasn't doing it before, so it's unlikely due to a stomach ache or injury.

When Susan returns, she first hands Yuuki a couple of painkillers and a glass of water. She then sets the glass down on the bedside table and starts working the anti-inflammatory cream into the bruised skin.

The touch sets Yuuki off. He doesn't startle, but with each bruise Susan rubs the cream into, Yuuki's trembling increases. Kyle watches as a sheen of fear glazes his eyes, his expression. He stares unfocused at the floors, and his fingers grip the edge of the blanket he's clutching.

Kyle doesn't know what he's seeing in his mind, or re-experiencing. He doesn't know what Yuuki felt when each of those hits landed, when each of those impacts was felt. He's experienced trauma, but he hasn't experienced Yuuki's, and he has no idea just to what extent Yuuki's been hurt. This is a shard of anguish driven into an already tormented soul.

Healing is going to take a long, long time.

Susan finishes applying the cream. She helps Yuuki pull on the clean black shirt she'd taken from his portion of the spare clothing, and then between her and Kyle, they help Yuuki lie down. Susan pulls the duvet and blankets up to his shoulders, and adjusts the pillow beneath his head.

She exhales slowly. "Same old story. Don't hesitate to call me if you need me. Same goes for you, Kyle, whether it's for Yuuki's sake or your own."

Bidding a quiet good night, she leaves.

Kyle sits back down on the bed. He groans, rubs a hand over the tightness around his throat. He should change too. As much as he just wants to let gravity take him now, changing out of worn-outdoors-tramping-for-two-whole-days clothes is enough incentive to hold out just a bit longer.

A tug on the sleeve of his raincoat. Kyle turns sharply, only to find Yuuki reaching out, hand clasping the sleeve.

"What's wrong?" he asks.

Yuuki struggles to keep his eyes open. There's a plea in his expression. *Please don't leave.*

"I'm just going to change. I'm not leaving, I promise."

The grip slips. Yuuki lets his eyes close and lies there, defeated.

Kyle gets up, closes the door and changes. He opens the door again afterwards – a reminder that they're not trapped here. Leaves the light on. This room is unfamiliar, and he doesn't wish it to become anything reminiscent of a prison cell or a shed. Or a blindfold.

He climbs into the bed and slips under the covers by Yuuki. The scent of the anti-inflammatory cream is strong but not overbearing. Kyle shifts over, slips an arm under Yuuki's side and pulls him up to rest against him. He remembers too late to double check if it's okay to do so, but Yuuki's already relaxing before he can stress too much.

After a few minutes of hugging, Kyle realises that Yuuki's body temperature seems more elevated than it should be. Frowning, he raises a palm to Yuuki's forehead. His skin burns. With a concerned hum, he brushes Yuuki's hair back into place. *Definitely a fever.*

Kyle's stomach twists with guilt. He should've checked sooner. He wonders how long Yuuki has been dealing with this, but his brain won't let him think. Exhaustion brings his thoughts to a standstill before he can even try.

Yuuki's slipping asleep before long. Kyle is soon to follow. Above them, the warm glow of the light is consoling.

27

Many unprocessed emotions follow Kyle down the stairs in the morning. He doesn't want to acknowledge them, not if it means disrupting the calm for something ugly. Perhaps that's why he's ignored them so blatantly until now and why he continues to do so.

It can wait till later, he reasons. *Everything's overwhelming as it is without exhausting myself crying.* He's had enough of the exhaustion brought on by tears, and by experiencing emotions strongly in general. Recovering from this head injury has worn him out, as has adjusting to how his imprisonment's affected him. And then there's everything that's happened to Yuuki because he came to Kyle's defence.

Things keep happening. They won't stop happening, not until this is over and maybe not even then. In the midst of it, have they become stronger or more broken versions of themselves? Is there any way to repair the damage that's been done? Can they ever escape these circumstances in the first place?

Downstairs, the scene before him is calm and familial. Sleep hangs heavy in the air. The morning sunlight lighting up the curtains a gentle gold gives the illusion of safety. The slumbering forms lying on the floor, on the couch, look at ease. It could almost be mistaken for some kind of family gathering sleepover.

But it's not. They're fugitives, chased out of every refuge they've established and pursued to the point it's hard to find one. They thought it would be over as soon as Amelia made her claim to the throne but they were wrong. They were so, so wrong.

Amelia has so much pressure on her now. This probably isn't what she had in mind when she'd prepared for the fact that one day she would have to reveal who she is. It should've been a choice of her own to make, when she was ready. Instead, her identity as the princess has been forced upon her.

How much more will we have to give up? How much more will we have to lose?

Kyle shakes the despair from his mind before it takes root. Yuuki got him out of prison when Kyle never thought he'd be free again; he was hope where Kyle had essentially none. In the same way, hope has to exist here.

Without it, there's no way forward.

Hair damp, Kyle sits with the others at the table, fresh from a shower. Yuuki's asleep upstairs. Rain falls steadily outside. The ambience it creates is soothing.

"You've gotten close, you and Yuuki," Susan comments.

Kyle hesitates, unsure of the connotation. "Is that a bad thing?"

"No, not at all. It's good you two are able to be there for each other."

"I'm sure you've noticed Yuuki's pretty reserved," Timothy says. "He doesn't let just anybody in. Besides us, he doesn't really have any friends as such. Well, I mean, there was Lee – his flatmate – but he never really…

247

has been very understanding of Yuuki's perspectives, or PTSD." He glances at Susan as he says it at she grimaces.

"Yuuki's the first friend I've had in a while," Kyle murmurs. "I haven't had anyone I've been able to consider close since…" Since when, exactly? When was the last time he genuinely had someone close to him? "Since my Dad passed away? There's you guys now, but…"

Sam leans into the table. "So you really had no one at all? At school or anything?"

"I got to hang out with you in the library at lunch times sometimes."

"Yeah, that's not exactly 'hanging out with friends' material though."

"It was enough for me. We often were sitting at the same table in our classes, so it was nice to have someone chill and familiar nearby, I guess?"

Amelia frowns. "I'm sorry. We should've taken notice and invited you to join us."

"You didn't know me back then." Kyle studies the mostly melted aromatherapy candle in the middle of the table. "It's okay."

"Still."

Sam nods. "We all need to have some group bonding sessions, I think. You have friends around you now."

Friends. Definitely not something Kyle had imagined would come out of his stay in isolation.

Amelia glances between Kyle and Timothy, brow creasing in thought. "I really don't know how to ask this, but Yuuki…I notice he doesn't spend much time around us. Have we been excluding him at all?"

Kyle shakes his head. "He prefers to be alone, I think. Part of that's because I think he's ashamed of his PTSD. He doesn't want other people to see it. He doesn't want other people to be affected by it either, so he's been isolating himself, for both those reasons."

"So how do we include him then? When he's better?"

There's an uncertain pause in the conversation. Kyle's not sure how to answer that, and when he looks to Timothy for help, and then Sam and Susan, he realises they're in the same boat.

"I guess… creating opportunities for him to be included in?" he offers.

"It doesn't help that we've been on the run all this time we've been together as a group," Susan says. "Limits what activities we're able to do in our down time. Otherwise we could do things like have movie nights or go for walks or something."

It sounds so good. Something resembling normality, although Kyle's version of what's considered 'normal' isn't something he wants to go back to. That's another black hole of despair he doesn't want to be sucked into.

"It's hard to think about, eh," Timothy murmurs. "Going back."

Kyle startles, but Timothy's not looking specifically at him. *Oh, right.* It's on everyone's mind, going back.

None of them look overly optimistic about it. They're not simply going to be returning to the physical places, jobs and studies they left behind, after all, and they'll be going back with varying degrees of trauma – all of them, regardless of how directly caught up in things they've been.

Kyle starts getting caught up in how he fears going back. He fears getting left behind. That once this is all over, everyone will go their separate ways and Kyle will be on his own again. A huge part of him fears and anticipates having to go back to prison. If not there, then he might be forced to stay with another family of strangers or otherwise left literally on his own to figure things out.

Sure, Timothy's already said that he's welcome to stay with them, as is Yuuki, but what if they change their minds? What if they decide Kyle's not worth the effort, or he's *too much* effort when Yuuki needs the help they're offering to provide more than he does?

He tries reminding himself that his troubles are also valid, but it doesn't quell the shame burning away at his self-worth. He needs a distraction, or rather something else to preoccupy his thoughts beside this. Sitting here mulling over them isn't going to do any good.

"I'm going to go check on Yuuki," Kyle says abruptly. He pushes the chair back and stands, then without another word leaves the table.

Timothy's words follow him up the stairs. *"It's hard to think about, eh. Going back."*

Yes, Kyle answers in his mind. *It is. It's why I deliberately try to keep myself from thinking too hard about it.*

Yuuki's asleep when he gets there. Sunlight has the room awash in comforting light, but the atmosphere fails to absorb the vibes. Yuuki's sick, that much is clear. Crumpled up tissues lie in a growing pile beside the tissue box. Yuuki shifts uneasily, uncomfortable in his sleep, still huddled beneath the covers yet in the process of shoving them away. Kyle opens a window to let some fresh air in, hoping it'll help.

There has to be something else he can do. Kyle frowns, considering. His eyes fall on the empty glass of water on the bedside table, the painkillers gone. Yuuki must've woken up at some point and taken them. There'd only been a couple left in the packet – Hayley was apparently going to get some more today – so he's not concerned to find the packet lying empty on the floor.

He walks over to Yuuki's side. Leaning over, he places his hand on Yuuki's forehead, flips it over so it's the back of his hand resting there instead of his palm. Kyle then feels his own temperature, and his stomach dips.

Was it like this last night, or has the fever gotten worse? The muscle aches Yuuki's experiencing – how much of them are due to dehydration, stress and fatigue and how much are due to the fever? How soon had it started setting in after they'd rescued him, or had he been coming down with it before that all even happened?

Regardless of how long it's been, Kyle's concerned Yuuki won't have the energy to fight it. He's been fatigued and emotionally spent as is. Traumatic stress will only make it worse, as will the last two days' of hiking they did. It's no wonder he collapsed. But that means he likely barely has any energy left over, and his body will be taking every last scrap of it to combat the fever. In other words, they need to do what they can to keep the fever down lest it overwhelm and drag him down with it.

"I'm going to get Susan," Kyle murmurs. He takes the empty glass as he stands. "I'll be back."

He doesn't get as far as Susan, let alone the staircase.

Nothing could prepare him for what he sees emerging from the room at the other end of the hallway. His fingers twitch. The glass slips out of his hands to land on the wooden floor with a loud *thunk*.

Unbidden, a cry springs from his throat. It's Daniel's ghost. Staring at him.

"Kyle?" asks the ghost.

He's seeing things, right? Hearing things? Daniel's not alive anymore. *Yeah,* sneers the voice in the back of Kyle's head, *because you killed him.*

No. No, I didn't. I didn't. He –

Daniel gestures for Kyle to go ahead of him. Kyle can't move, won't move. He unconsciously finds his eyes on Daniel's hands, on the pockets in his school jacket, scanning for anything that resembles the shape of a knife. There's nothing. Daniel – no, not Daniel, but his twin brother Ben – doesn't look about to attack him like that night at Village Park.

… wait, Ben?

Only then does Kyle realise whose house they're in.

28

"I didn't kill him," Kyle chokes out.

Ben frowns deeply. His expression is pinched, hurt. "I never said –"

"I didn't do it, I keep trying to tell you!"

Vivid memories of glares filled with anger get pulled to the front of his mind. That anger simmers as he pleads not guilty and continues to do so.

Invalidation. No one listens. *Your words mean nothing,* the voice in the back of his mind reminds him. The house morphs into the courtroom. This isn't the hallway downstairs, but the hallway he was led down in handcuffs with a sentence ringing in Timothy's voice through his head. Kyle covers his mouth, takes a step back, then another. He didn't do it.

I didn't kill him. I didn't kill him.

And then the judge materialises in front of him. Kyle heard him coming up the stairs but he knows already there's nowhere to run, and that running will only get him into more trouble. They'll never believe he's innocent if he runs. His only exit – down the staircase – is blocked, anyway. He's trapped; it's not like he could run if he wanted. He could flee into the room where Yuuki is, but that's not an escape. Yuuki was his escape, and Yuuki's incapacitated and trapped here with him.

He can't even hide anywhere…

"Kyle, it's okay," Timothy says, his voice low and urgent. It's quiet and concerned, not formal.

The Timothy who steps between him and Ben isn't wearing judge's robes. This Timothy is taller than him, stronger than him. He has *far* more legal power than Kyle has, and he is, at the end of the day, the one who put Kyle away.

Kyle takes another step back. "I didn't do it."

Timothy glances over his shoulder at Ben and jerks his chin toward the staircase. With a slow understanding nod, Ben ducks his head, glances once more at Kyle and then disappears down the stairs.

"Kyle," Timothy says, turning back. "They know the truth, okay? They know you're not guilty."

Why would they believe I'm not? I basically killed their son, their brother.

"What happened wasn't your fault, you know that."

My hand was on the knife when it stabbed Daniel. I didn't kill him but my actions resulted in his death, therefore it is my fault.

"Someone came after you and you fought to defend yourself. You acted in self-defence. It's not your fault."

It is. You ruled yourself that it is.

"They know you're not guilty."

I'm not guilty, but it's still my fault.

If it were Yuuki talking to him, perhaps it wouldn't be so hard to calm down. Yuuki wasn't there at the trial. He wasn't the one who declared Kyle guilty, or gave the order to have him silenced. He wasn't one of the people sitting in the courtroom satisfied with the punishment Kyle was given.

That's one of the reasons why Kyle decided to give Yuuki the benefit of the doubt when Yuuki came to him in detention, saying he wanted to help. He hadn't trusted Timothy, but even though it was Timothy himself who asked Yuuki to privately investigate, Yuuki hadn't condemned or shamed him in any way, shape of form.

Now, Kyle trusts Timothy, and he trusts his judgement here. That doesn't diminish the overwhelming sense of betrayal clutching at Kyle's insides. It screams at him that he's been tricked, that he shouldn't give Timothy another chance. The willing part of Kyle wants to be able to trust him, however.

He's simultaneously grateful and hurt that no one bothered to tell him that this is the Wilson's house. Susan would've known as well, and Amelia, that this is where Daniel lived before Kyle killed him. No, before Kyle's self-defence – his struggling to save himself – killed him.

Isn't that the same thing though? taunts the voice. Kyle swallows hard. Stress grips his stomach and he's nauseous. His mind whirls. Kyle's thoughts confuse and contradict. He staggers sideways. *"Not guilty,"* he'd pleaded, and yet here he is questioning again – maybe there's a part of him that is?

Kyle shakes his head against the thought. No, he won't go there again. His head's been messed with enough recently as it is. Instead he takes a shaky breath, lets it out with just as much shakiness, and snaps his focus to Timothy.

"You knew," he grits out.

Timothy maintains eye contact, steady. Accountable. Resigned. Guilty.

"I did."

"For how long?"

"Andy told me once he'd confirmed it. Less than a week ago."

"All this time, you knew we'd come here and you said nothing. You just went with it?"

"We needed options for refuges. We were still finalising others, so it wasn't as though we anticipated this being the one we'd – *you'd* – end up in. We could've swapped and gone to Andy's instead of the others, is what I'm saying. The Peace Forces aren't going to immediately come here looking for us and I'm quite certain I don't need to explain why. Hence why I say this is the safest place you could be right now, given the circumstances. It's also, by extension, the safest place for Amelia and for Yuuki."

"Yeah, okay. Fine. I get that. But why didn't you say anything?"

Timothy looks conflicted. "We wouldn't have come here if we believed they would harm you."

There's more than physical ways to harm someone. "You know what I did to them. To *him*. Why the heck would you bring me here? You say it's safe, but it sure doesn't feel safe to me."

"I can understand why you feel that way. I'm sorry. I should've talked to you about you."

Kyle forces his anger back. He doesn't like being upset like this. It all feels wrong. He swallows. He understands now why he's seen no family photos around at all. They must've taken them down in advance when they heard Kyle was coming.

"How long are we going to be here for, again?" he asks tightly.

"Tonight and tomorrow night," Timothy says. "But look, if it is too much for you, I'm not going to try force you to stay here. It's not fair on you to ask that."

But that means leaving Yuuki, and Kyle's not comfortable doing that while Yuuki's in such a vulnerable state. Even if Yuuki were to go with him, Kyle's not confident in his ability to help him the way Yuuki needs. Three out of four of the Harrisons – who were by Yuuki's side throughout his recovery from the Ninao kidnapping – are here. Amelia is a non-threatening presence.

Going to the other group would also mean being thrown into yet another unfamiliar environment, and having to adjust to the dynamics of the other group. As far as Kyle's concerned, it's not worth the energy. He'll just have to work hard at suppressing his anxiety in the meantime.

"Will you be okay?" Timothy asks.

Kyle stares at him, incredulous. His upper lip quivers.

"Right. Right, sorry."

A *thud* from behind makes him jump. Timothy's gaze goes sharp. Kyle spins around, and the alarm heightens when he sees Yuuki sprawled on the floor halfway out into the hall.

Timothy moves past Kyle and hurries over. Kneeling down, he feels Yuuki's forehead, then places two fingers to the underside of Yuuki's jaw. He bends over.

"He's got a fever," Kyle explains.

"Yeah," Timothy murmurs. "He sure does. Hey, Yuuki. Can you hear me?"

Yuuki forces his eyes open a fraction. He mumbles something

incomprehensible.

"Sorry, I didn't hear you."

"Heard…fighti'g…s-so –"

"Kyle's fine. You heard him, right? Something startled him, is all. He's fine. He's safe. Is that why you came out here? You were trying to get to him?"

Yuuki groans. He tries pushing himself up off the floor, but all he succeeds in doing is rolling onto his stomach and lying with his head turned painfully to the side, resting on his arm. He closes his eyes.

"Did you understand what I just said?"

"Hnngh?"

Timothy grimaces. He sits back on his heels, head bowed. "We should probably get Susan. Kyle, would you mind?"

Kyle hesitates. "I, um…" He knows he should. He knows he can. But his muscles lock up at the thought of going downstairs. That's where Susan is, yes, but that's also where Ben is, and the woman who turns out to be Ben and Daniel's mother. He sends an anxious glance over his shoulder, at where Ben was standing. "I don't think I can."

Seeing Kyle looking in that direction, Timothy catches on. "Right. Okay, that's fine. Then do you want to help me get him up?" He lays a hand on Yuuki's shoulder. "Yuuki, we're going to get you up now, okay? Get you back to bed."

"'m fine here," Yuuki murmurs.

"You're not sleeping on the floor. Come on."

With great effort, and with assistance from Kyle, Timothy hoists Yuuki onto his back in a piggyback. Yuuki lets himself be carried, arm hanging limply over Timothy's shoulder. Kyle places his hands on Yuuki's back as Timothy stands, supporting his weight.

They walk the few steps over to the bed and Timothy turns, setting Yuuki back down. Kyle helps him gently ease Yuuki back into the support of the pillows and mattress.

"I'll go downstairs and talk to Susan," Timothy says as they lift Yuuki's legs onto the bed. "Hayley's home now, so I'll see what she got from the pharmacy." He pulls the covers over Yuuki's body, right up to his shoulders so it's only his head that's visible. "You were going down to get water, right, Kyle? I'll get that for you, so you don't need to worry about coming down."

He stands up straight again with a sigh. "And don't worry about the Wilsons. They won't bother you."

Kyle keeps his gaze fixed on Yuuki.

"You'll be alright, staying here?"

"It's fine."

It's kind of not.

After Susan comes and goes, and Timothy back down with her, Kyle's left alone to process the emotional aftermath. He sits on the bed cross-legged beside Yuuki, turning between a bowl of water on the bedside table and a wet cloth laid over Yuuki's forehead. Heat rolls off Yuuki's body in waves. Kyle reapplies the cloth, bows and touches his forehead to Yuuki's shoulder.

Kyle's throat hurts from struggling to keep the tears at bay. It's a losing game. "I'm sorry," he whispers. "None of this would've happened if you hadn't thought me worth saving."

"Don't blame yourself," Yuuki would've once said. But he's quiet. Too quiet.

"You keep getting hurt because of me. Because of all *this*. And I'm scared of losing you to it before this is all over. I don't know what's going to happen. I want to promise I'll stop you from getting hurt again, but I know I can't do that. But I promise I'll do everything I can to keep you safe. Okay? So just…hang in there, 'kay?"

Why he's talking so much, Kyle doesn't know. Maybe it's because he's anxious and too tired to internalise it. Maybe it's because he feels there's so little comfort he's able to offer Yuuki right now and it hurts. It hurts even more when he has a visual reference of how thoroughly the trauma has reached.

What he can offer isn't enough. *He's* not enough. He needs to be strong for Yuuki, not this. He's talking like Yuuki is going to get worse, like he knows that it's going to happen.

Kyle's not wrong, though; over the next twenty four hours, Yuuki's fever only gets worse.

29

The light is fading when Yuuki wakes. At least he thinks it is. Everything's blurry, out of focus. His head pounds. He can't tell if the ceiling is at normal ceiling height or if it's less than a hand span above him. Is that even a ceiling at all, or is it the sky?

His body aches horribly. His mind floats but the pain and tightness in his muscles are like weights. It keeps him tethered to reality enough not to drift off, but he wouldn't complain if the tide took him anyway. He can't think of any objections. If it were his choice, he would let it. But it's his health that's making the calls, not him.

That means he's trapped here. In this nauseating heat and the chills that rack his body. In this aching pain. In this confusion. Yuuki tries to stay calm. Becoming distressed only makes these things worse. He looks around, tries to understand where he is if simply to ground himself, but this place is unfamiliar and it disturbs him.

How did I get here? A gentle breeze stirs the curtains. It whistles through the gap in the window that's been set on the latch. To Yuuki, it sounds like the noise is coming from underwater. Unless…*he's* the one underwater.

Nothing makes sense. He needs to find something that makes sense.

Yuuki rolls onto his side. Getting out of bed is harder than it should be. He's awake enough to know that's a concern. Something falls off his forehead onto the pillow, but he's too distracted by the weird sensation in his right arm to bother seeing what it is. His arm is numb; he must've been sleeping on it. It feels like it's missing, but his nerves tell him that the limb is still there. The only explanation is that his brain must be fooling itself.

Everything spins faster the more he moves. Shadows flick in and out of his vision, morphing into shapes of people he remembers but vanishing before he can be sure he even saw them in the first place. Strange people with echoing voices. Unfamiliar surroundings. Feeling like he's been drugged. Who knows, maybe he has been. That would explain why he's sweating so much, right? Why his vision is so warped and he can't walk straight and his stomach's stirring uncomfortably like he might be sick?

Something's wrong. This place isn't safe. The floor slams into him. He knocks his head on the bedside table and groans. This escape isn't going well. They'll find him at this rate, he's going so slow. Who's they? Yuuki doesn't know. It's always that same question going around in his mind. *Who's they?* He has no idea. He's never found out. Until recently, that is, but now his brain's too foggy to recall that.

Feet appear in his peripheral but he doesn't know who they belong to. It startles him. He lurches backward, ramming into the bedside table. A glass is knocked over above him. The person vanishes. He sags in relief, but the relief comes too soon.

Pain flares in his right arm. He gasps. It kicks the air out of his lungs.

262

He coughs. His vision doubles. Yuuki looks up. He can't actually see her from here, but he *knows*. She's back again. That person who vanished was her and she's back again. Sure enough, it's her: there standing in the middle of the open doorway is Deborah.

Someone screams. Yuuki's throat hurts at the noise. He scrambles to his feet, stumbling, crashing back down, trying to pick himself up again and failing. His heart hammers inside his chest. The blood drains from his face as he stands and the pounding inside his head hammers harder too. Outside the door, the sound of feet pounding up a staircase grow louder. Deborah doesn't move from her position, though she has to have heard it too, right?

They're coming for me, he realises. That means he has no option but to attempt to fight his way out and run.

When the newcomers hurry into the room, they move right through Deborah. Like she's a ghost. Like she's not even there. They make a beeline for Yuuki, and that's when Yuuki really panics. This isn't a fair fight. He's cornered, weak and outnumbered which makes him utterly screwed, and they know it.

His body doesn't feel like his own anymore. Still, it can't be helped. Yuuki staggers sideways into the wall, pushes off it. His movements are uncoordinated but he puts up a fight as best he can. He lashes out, stumbles again. A hand reaches for him. He trips over his own feet and careens into another wall – or maybe it's the same one, he's not sure.

Deborah's no longer a ghost. She strides forward and goes to grab him by the shoulders. Yuuki shrieks at her. She flinches. One of the others stares at him with wide eyes. That other person stretches out an arm and hastily pulls Deborah back, both of them downright disturbed. They back away slowly.

Yuuki doesn't trust them. He keeps his eyes flicking to their hands, to their faces, watching for any sign of attack. The pain in his right arm pulses. He clutches at it. His hand slips from his bicep, finding nothing.

Arms wrap around his torso from behind. Yuuki's pulse spikes. He plants his feet and thrashes his way out of them. He darts out of their reach, but it only puts him closer to Deborah and the other guy. The other guy looks like Timothy, and up close Deborah looks like Susan, but none of that can be right. He knows a threat when he sees one. Right now he's surrounded by them.

The arms are back, this time around his chest. They yank him backwards. Reality tilts and he's falling. They – himself and the person holding him from behind – land hard on the floor. Yuuki takes the opportunity to try wrestle himself free, but the person's hold doesn't loosen. Instead they lock their hands around their wrists and keep him there.

Yuuki struggles. He writhes in their grip, kicks, tries tearing at the arms that hold him with his fingers. Nothing works. He can't breathe. He cries out. It's a strangled sound.

"It's just me," the person is saying behind him. "Can you hear me? Focus on my voice. It's just me."

Familiar. Something about this person speaks familiar.

"It's Kyle."

Yuuki's efforts to escape stall. Recognition sparks in his brain. Kyle. Kyle is familiar. But why is he here, in this wretched unfamiliarity? Why is he so calm when nothing makes sense?

"That's it, just focus on my voice. Just listen."

No, Kyle's not calm. His tone is too high pitched for that, but it's still his voice nonetheless. He's trying to be calm, for Yuuki's sake.

"You're safe. No one here will hurt you. If anyone tries to hurt you, we'll make sure they don't."

"Deborah was here," he tries to say. The syllables are all slurred and his voice thick with congestion, but Yuuki has to warn him before it's too late. "She was here, just before. In the doorway. You need to run."

"Deborah's not here," Kyle says with certainty. His voice trembles. "It's okay. She's not here. You're safe. You can hear me, right? You're safe, Yuuki. You're safe."

Safety is an illusion. But Yuuki trusts Kyle, and he knows that this Kyle is not an illusion. He can't see Deborah anymore either. Just the ceiling darkening as night falls outside, and the corners of his vision darkening along with it.

Eventually the arms around him loosen. It had anchored him, and Yuuki misses the careful pressure around him. Hands gently lift him up, move him. He's carried. Kyle's presence stays beside him, and since he saw them not long ago, his brain registers that the other hands supporting him belong to Susan and Timothy.

"'m sorry," he whispers. Yuuki's not sure what exactly he's apologising for, but it feels necessary.

A cool hand on his forehead. "Don't be sorry," Susan murmurs. "Just get better."

A warm and comforting weight settles down on the bed beside him, pulls him in. Those secure arms are around him again. Someone cries.

Just get better, Susan had said. Yuuki relaxes into the arms holding him. He drifts off before he can think of how to answer.

Kyle wishes he could erase this horrible memory – or at least prevent any more from happening. Yuuki's suffering is like an avalanche and it's unbearable to watch. He keeps getting hurt and it's all piling up, accumulating, getting worse. The more it does, the greater the distance feels between hurt and comfort.

"How do you guys cope?" Kyle asks into Yuuki's shoulder.

Neither Susan nor Timothy answer him.

Kyle's only caught glimpses of what he deals with in terms of his PTSD, and that's enough on its own. He wasn't even there with the Harrison's during the Ninao kidnapping and Yuuki's rescue and recovery from it; he doesn't know the full picture of his trauma. Then again, just because the Harrisons were there with Yuuki throughout the Ninao incident ordeal, that doesn't mean they know it either.

He can't hide how scared and upset he is for Yuuki. Kyle sobs, trying to keep it quiet but struggling to breathe when he does. He holds Yuuki close to him, not caring about any misinterpretation Susan and Timothy might possibly have. They probably don't have any, but even if they did, screw it. Yuuki needs a hug.

Kyle curls his fingers into Yuuki's shirt. "What else can we do for him? Yuuki's not well." Fear shoots through his stomach. "W-we're not doing enough."

"We're doing what we can," Susan says tightly.

Timothy puts one hand on his hip, rubs his temple with the other. "He needs medical attention."

"But we don't have the supplies on hand that he needs. We do at home, from when he last ended up with fatigue like this. Of course, all that's inaccessible right now though."

"When else did he…?" Kyle asks.

"After he was released from hospital after Ninao."

"He went back home initially," Timothy elaborates. "Even tried to go back to work so he had something to do, something to keep his mind preoccupied with. But he ran out of energy really fast and he kind of just…crashed. Couldn't work, couldn't sleep, was so dizzy he couldn't even get out of bed. We considered maybe sending him back to hospital, it was that bad."

Timothy's forced neutral expression wavers. "The Chén family have medical support equipment," he murmurs. "I sent Andy a message asking about it last night. He said they have a family friend who lives with them who has a chronic health condition. They have supplies on hand, in other words. One of the family is a doctor, too."

Kyle tilts his head. "Who's the Chén family?"

"The third safe house. They're also the ones to whom Yuuki transferred ownership of the Youth Rehabilitation Trust to. They're the ones offering us shelter as of Sunday – tomorrow."

Susan nods. "Yuuki just has to hang on until then."

"Don't make it sound like it's going to…" Timothy says, voicing what Kyle thinks. He can't finish. No one wants to finish that sentence.

"He was hallucinating just now. You don't hallucinate on a low grade fever."

"That doesn't mean it'll compromise him."

"It already has."

"Still –"

"He's worse than he was after Ninao," Susan says sharply. "Sure, I get it – there's a difference in that we could get help then and now we can't, but you know what I mean.

"The stress from the trauma has heightened his fever; his body is under too much stress to cope. His stomach can barely handle anything we give him – another hint that he's under too much stress. We also can't rule out the possibility that the fever struck because of a bacterial infection. I wouldn't be counting on the idea that that cloth had been freshly washed before they gagged him with it.

"It's too much for him." Susan's eyes are red rimmed. She sniffs. Her voice dips. "It's imperative we get to the Chén family's house tomorrow. Yuuki can't fight this on his own."

Timothy hisses. He turns on his heel and leaves, movements sharp and lacking composure. The silence that Timothy leaves in his wake is full of suffocating anger, stress and sorrow. It's a disturbing contrast to Timothy's usual state of calm and collectedness.

With a heavy sigh, Susan closes her eyes. She covers them with a hand. The tight line of her mouth wobbles.

We'll get through this, Kyle wants to say. Yuuki will pull through. He's strong. But how does he know that? Susan's right: this is too much. Kyle's been through 'overwhelming'. He's been through trauma. But this...what they're asking Yuuki to have the strength to pull through...

Susan follows Timothy out the door. Kyle watches the crack in the Harrisons' confidence widen as she goes. PTSD affects the whole family, and this who Yuuki is to the Harrisons: family. Kyle's beginning to understand other things too – that Timothy's capacity to help Yuuki is limited, that Susan must be far less okay than she lets on. There's only so much they can do no matter how much energy they put into actively trying to find a way to help Yuuki suffer less.

Gathering himself together as best he's able, Kyle gets up and sees to replacing the wet cloth on Yuuki's forehead again. Afterwards, he goes back to holding him. He only leaves his side for occasional breaks.

Kyle doesn't know what to do. He doesn't know what he can do except stay beside Yuuki like this.

"Please... *live*," he whispers. "Survive this." He hates the way his voice pitches and wobbles. "*Li kih kehn ha'arh.*" Keep your spirit strong.

Late that night, Yuuki's fever finally breaks.

30

Kyle lies in bed wide awake, one arm loose around Yuuki sleeping beside him. The music playing from a neighbouring house finally stops, and as much as he relishes the quiet he still can't sleep. His head aches. Painkillers only numb it slightly. His heart aches. That...won't be relieved any time soon.

Yuuki's fever broke a couple of hours ago but he has yet to wake. That's probably a good thing, since Yuuki needs as much rest as he can get. He's been severely stressed both physically and emotionally this week. Traumatised, again. And he's now got the struggle of recovering from that awaiting him, and Kyle knows from experience how much energy healing takes. Yuuki isn't going to be okay for a while.

Kyle sits up, covers his face with his hands. He groans. It's late; he should sleep. He wants to, but he can't. Ever since his imprisonment, sleep has been hard to come by. The head injury he sustained a few weeks ago only made it more difficult. The recent events, even more so. He's only been able to sleep these last few nights out of sheer exhaustion.

The more he thinks about it, the more Kyle wonders if it's because of something his brain's more aware of than his mind is. He'd thought it was because of how hard the nights were in the cell – dark, cold, long and full of opportunities for his trauma regarding the whole Village Park incident to get to him. But even with the light still on, and his body warm and someone else – someone he trusts – in the room with him, a part of him remains unnerved and reluctant to sleep.

Apparently he'd almost died in there. Maybe that's it. He doesn't remember it though, only that he didn't feel great and that it was colder than usual. He remembers simultaneously hurting and feeling numb, and waking up intermittently with Yuuki either holding him or waiting nearby. He'd been out of the cell by then.

Is this associated with hypervigilance? he wonders. Being awake means being awake, and subsequently being able actively escape danger. It makes sense from a survival point of view. Kyle hates being stuck in it though. As far as he's aware, he hasn't developed PTSD. It doesn't need to be said that he'd rather not. He's seen how much Yuuki suffers because of it. No one in their right mind would desire to live with that.

A soft groan sounds beside him. "Kai'irh."

Kyle jolts. He turns slowly, eyes widening. "H-how do you know?" He wonders if he heard that right, and plays what Yuuki just said over in his mind.

Yuuki just stares at him blankly through half-closed eyes.

"Kai'irh," Kyle repeats. "That's my Arkala'ana name."

Confusion washes over Yuuki's face, as well as a flash of attention that tells Kyle that this information is new to him. In other words, Yuuki doesn't – hadn't – known.

Realisation dawns. Kyle inwardly laughs at how stupid he is. "Sorry, don't mind me."

271

Yuuki wasn't calling him by his Arkala'ana name. He was simply slurring his English one, in the same way the name Kai'irh translates phonetically to Kyle, only in reverse.

"Your name is Kai'irh?" Yuuki slurs.

Kyle nods. He can't disguise his relief at hearing Yuuki speak again. He blinks back tears. "Yeah."

"'s a nice name. You don't –" He closes his eyes briefly. "You don't go by it anymore?"

"It sounds so close to Kyle, it's easier for everyone just to go with that. My Dad used to call me Kai'irh. That's why it startled me. No one's called me that since, and the only place it's written is my birth certificate – which I suppose you might've come across when you and Timothy were helping me with my case, but…"

"I didn't know," Yuuki says. After a pause, he asks, "Did you prefer to be called that?"

Kyle blinks. No one's ever asked him that before. "I…"

It's not like it's an overly personal or sensitive question, and he can't blame people for not knowing of his Arkalahn name. But somehow it matters, being asked this. His father was Arkala'ana and used to call him by his Arkalahn name. It's something Kyle misses. There's also the belittling he's had to face enduring months of people calling him by his last name instead of his first, which in Arkala culture is a sign of disrespect when an interaction has already been established between two people. He'd understand if all those situations were formal, but they weren't. Instead they all involved people trampling on him and accusing him and denying him his right to speak and be heard.

"I'm not sure," Kyle says in answer to Yuuki's question. "I guess I'm just used to being called Kyle now. I haven't really thought about it."

"Right," Yuuki murmurs.

Hearing Yuuki's voice again – in a tone that isn't fearful or panicked – is reassuring in a way Kyle can't describe. It's like a cool breeze on a hot day or warmth after being thoroughly chilled by the cold. It settles a nervous tension within him. Kyle hadn't realised how anxious Yuuki's nonverbalism had made him.

But though Yuuki's temperature is finally on its way down and he's able to communicate through speech again, he's definitely far from well. Exhausted, for one, and guaranteed to be feeling awful and achy, for another. Kyle frowns. He lays the back of his hand on Yuuki's forehead. He then moves it to the side of his face, and then the back of his neck.

"You're still sweating quite a bit," Kyle murmurs. Yuuki has been since his fever broke, really.

Yuuki turns his face into the pillow and hums.

"Do you want to have a shower? I think it will help you feel better, emotionally too. It's, like, past midnight already, so you don't have to worry about running into anyone on the way down."

"Don't think I can move," Yuuki mumbles.

That is, of course, a problem. "I can help. If you're okay with it, that is." Kyle grimaces, trying to think of how to word what he's trying to say without coming across as weird or accidentally making Yuuki uncomfortable. "Like when how you helped me after you got me out of prison? You did this for me when I wasn't well. If you're okay with it, let me do this for you."

Squinting against the light, Yuuki turns his head to look at Kyle. His eyes flick over Kyle's face, reading. It's not so much an analysis as it is a hesitant question and an ashamed confession.

"I'll help you walk," Kyle says. "I know you're not feeling great. I just need to know you're okay with me…touching you." He winces. "Sorry, wording."

Yuuki huffs – a small laugh lacking energy. "'s okay." A pause. "Thank you."

Kyle offers him an understanding smile. "All goods."

After checking to make sure the coast is clear in regards to allowing Yuuki emotional privacy, Kyle returns to the bedroom and helps Yuuki up. Yuuki has hardly any strength in him, and when Kyle finally manages to get them standing, Yuuki's legs struggle to hold his weight. With Kyle there supporting him he's able to walk, however, albeit unsteadily and off balance.

They take the stairs slowly. One foot at a time, using the rail to support them with each movement. Yuuki exhales slowly in relief when they reach the bottom at last. Kyle guides him down the hall to the bathroom before any of the others are alerted to their presence.

Once there, Kyle shows him the basket of towels Hayley left out for their group to use. He ensures Yuuki's able to stand on his own, then ducks out to fetch a clean set of clothes and give Yuuki some privacy to change out of the ones he's currently wearing. When he returns, he finds Yuuki hasn't moved since he left.

Are you okay? Kyle almost asks – a rhetorical question if there ever was one. Instead he closes the bathroom door again behind him and

274

tentatively asks, "Do you want me to help you?"

Yuuki can't look him in the eye, either in person or through the mirror. He seems to be avoiding looking in the mirror altogether. Kyle understands the reasoning: until recently, he hasn't been able to do it either. The first time he caught himself in his reflection had been an accident. That was less than two weeks ago, and since then he's only been brave enough to look again twice.

With that in mind, Kyle moves them away from the mirror's reflection of themselves before helping Yuuki undress. Kyle hadn't wanted to see who he'd become after his two weeks' imprisonment; Yuuki's not going to want to see the aftermath of his recent trauma any more than he has to.

The bruises all over Yuuki's body are once again revealed. Kyle's stomach churns. Some of them blotchy and an array of colours, others dark and painful. There's no question this harm was deliberate; someone – or some people – intended to hit Yuuki, and they fully intended on hitting him hard. The thought makes the hair on the back of Kyle's neck stand up.

His eyes catch sight of the scarring of Yuuki's amputated arm, yet another layer of visible evidence of abuse, and anger simmers in his blood. Yuuki should never have had to suffer this violence against him. It goes further than physical harm – this is also violence wrought upon Yuuki's mind and psychological state. In a way, that damage done by the latter is worse than the former since it's not so easy to heal from.

'I'm sorry' isn't helpful. It's not logical, no matter how much Kyle's mind likes to debate that. It won't bring Yuuki any sense of healing, comfort or closure. There's no words Kyle can think of right now for any

of that, but he doesn't need them. Yuuki doesn't need them; words can't promise him safety. What he needs is what he can consider a safe place to heal. Ironic, really, when he's both literally and metaphorically stripped of every shield.

For the sake of Yuuki's dignity, Kyle helps him wrap a towel around his waist. Yuuki keeps his arm across his stomach still and remains avoiding eye contact, even when they settle kneeling down on the shower floor. He hangs his head, whether out of exhaustion or shame, Kyle's not sure. Maybe it's both.

Sitting behind Yuuki, Kyle takes the shower nozzle and runs the water until it's warm. He's rolled his pants up so he's not worried about them getting wet. Once the water's warmed up, Kyle rinses Yuuki's skin and then sets about massaging the stress and fever sweat out of it. He's gentle with it all, avoiding applying pressure to the bruised areas and to Yuuki's head when washing his hair.

At some point, as Kyle's working some of the tension out of Yuuki's neck and shoulders, Yuuki starts shaking. Kyle stops, worried, and asks, "What's wrong?"

But Yuuki just hunches his shoulders. His breathing hitches, and his next breath is horribly shaky. It almost resembles the beginnings of a panic attack when Yuuki breaks down crying.

Kyle's heart breaks with him. He rubs his hand up and down between Yuuki's shoulder blades, feeling every sob that wracks Yuuki's body against his palm. The tears don't last long but the hyperventilating does. It takes a while for Yuuki's breathing to calm again.

"I'm so weak," Yuuki whispers harshly.

"You're so resilient," Kyle corrects. He moves around so that he's sitting more or less in front of Yuuki and, allowing him to see his movements, raises his hands and cups the sides of Yuuki's face. Gently, Kyle lifts his head.

Yuuki averts his eyes determinedly, shaking. Eventually Kyle wins out, and Yuuki finally meets Kyle's eyes. The pain in them is deep rooted and terrible, but unmasked. There's no faking he's fine here. No trying to hide just how much all this hurts him. He's just Yuuki, in his rawest self.

"You're tired," Kyle murmurs. He brushes Yuuki's hair out of his eyes. "You're tired and you're hurting, but you're not weak. It takes strength to keep fighting the good fight, especially when you feel like you don't have the energy to get back up again…and when you don't necessarily have the will to.

"You've survived so much already. The fact that you can still remain kind and not become cold after all that…that takes someone strong." He leans forward and briefly kisses his forehead. "You're a survivor, Yuuki. That's not 'weak' at all."

Yuuki closes his eyes and shudders.

This is the most vulnerable Kyle's seen him. It's probably the most vulnerable Yuuki's ever allowed himself to be, consciously, his walls torn down and even the physical layers shielding him removed, and he's entrusting Kyle with seeing him exposed like this. It's something to be beheld with the utmost care and reverence.

They finish up with the shower. Kyle reapplies anti-inflammatory cream over the bruises and, considering how stiff and sore his own legs are, massages some into Yuuki's legs as well. He cringes every time Yuuki winces. He washes his hands and helps Yuuki dress, and then head back upstairs with Yuuki visibly looking more comfortable than before – clean and wearing clothes that are comfy and not so close-fitting.

Beneath that appearance, Yuuki's broken. The fractures run deep and to Yuuki they probably seem irreparable. He can't live as though they don't exist; they're there and he has to learn how to breathe through the pain they cause. What he's already learnt he'll have to relearn. Things that helped may not anymore.

It's not possible for Kyle to promise Yuuki that he'll protect him. He can't say something like the things that have just passed won't happen again – they already have – and both of them know all too well how uncertain tomorrow is. One day at a time is all they can manage, and that's enough for now.

31

Everyone's getting ready to leave the Wilsons' when Kyle brings Yuuki downstairs in the morning. Thankfully no one stares, but glances are often cast their way. Kyle ignores them and sits down on the couch with Yuuki leaning against him while they wait to leave.

There's a shift in atmosphere among the others, Kyle notices. It's most noticeable around Ben and Hayley. Of course, it's not limited to them either. Kyle can't pretend he doesn't see the emotion Susan tries to hide or the redness around Timothy's eyes as he hugs her. Amelia treads softer around them and Sam is quieter in general.

Oh…they heard. Kyle doesn't mention this realisation out loud. Yuuki doesn't need to know that his breaking down wasn't as private as he'd thought. Telling him that everyone heard will only be a slap of humiliation. Yuuki's had far too much of that lately; he doesn't need any more shame.

Daniel's mother regards Kyle with a deeply apologetic gleam in her eyes. Ben does as well. It doesn't sit well with Kyle: he saw how they looked at him in court. Hate had burned in their gaze with every word he tried to speak his innocence in. Their grief isn't heated like that anymore, but that doesn't mean it never existed. Kyle can still feel the scathing pain it caused.

They judged Kyle too quickly. It cost him. Kyle might now be redeemed in their hearts, but that doesn't warrant forgiveness. No apology is going to make up for the emotional trauma he went through. Daniel attempted to take Kyle's life at the park that night and in surviving Kyle was arrested and taken into custody as a murder suspect; Kyle had been trying to process almost being killed, out of the blue, and he'd been convicted as a reward for surviving. He pleaded his innocence and no one believed him. He'd been humiliated and sentenced and everyone had been happy.

On the way outside, Hayley and Ben verbally apologise to Kyle. Kyle doesn't say it's fine. He can't say he forgives them. That doesn't mean he'll begrudge them, but the hurt they caused him can't be dismissed so easily. Kyle can't forget the animosity the Wilsons showed him in court. He's been hurt too deeply for that. They invalidated him, although it might not have been their intention to do so. Had they given him a chance, had they *listened* to him, Kyle wouldn't have had to go through the extent of trauma he did.

He's relieved when they leave. He doesn't feel safe there. In truth, he doesn't feel safe anywhere anymore.

Andy drives Timothy, Kyle, Yuuki and Sam to the Chén's place. Amelia and Susan go with Hayley.

Yuuki spends the forty minutes pressed against Kyle's side, tense. Since it's daylight and he's surrounded by 'safe' people, he's not as stressed about being in a vehicle as he was when they came out of the bush, but he's still unnerved by it.

They arrive at a large rural property on the northern side of Lake Kano. Kyle feels subconsciously safer simply having the lake between them and the city – or more specifically, right now, between himself and the Wilsons. It's not a complete defence, but it's somewhat a geographical barrier nonetheless.

The house is out of sight of the road. The native bush on either side of the driveway creates a feeling of protection. Here, the *amelia* flowers are starting to bloom in the trees. A symbol of peace after hardship, and Amelia's namesake. Kyle's the type to find hope in that.

"Looks like the others are already here," Andy remarks as they pull in. "Marina's car is here."

The peaceful quiet, broken only by birdsong and breeze, is reassuring. The sunshine is warm, though the sky doesn't promise it'll last long. Rain clouds are building over A'o again and the wind that's picking up is threatening to sweep them over. Having spent the last two days essentially stuck indoors, Kyle wouldn't have minded if it had been pouring with rain when they stepped out of the vehicle anyways.

The front door opens. Kyle's helping Yuuki out of the car when it does, and he winces, imagining the entire group coming out to say hi and hound Yuuki with 'are you okay?' and concerned looks. But the man in the wheelchair who comes outside is alone, and no one follows him. Relieved, Kyle murmurs reassurance to Yuuki as he helps him stand.

Timothy hears this and frowns, pondering. "Hey, Sam. Would you mind going in and keeping the others at bay?" In other words, tell them not to overwhelm Yuuki.

"Sure thing," Sam murmurs. She goes ahead, pausing to ask directions from the man, and then disappears inside.

The man in the wheelchair rolls out into the sunshine, long dark hair flying in his face. He tucks it behind his ears when he stops. "*Sakerh*," he says, greeting them in Arkalahn. "I'm Minharh. Since we'll all be interacting a lot, let's not worry about acquaintance formalities. Just call me Minharh."

Kyle doesn't miss the Arkala'ana accent. It reminds him of his father, only this Minharh's voice is husky where his father's wasn't. Nevertheless, his heart pangs. It's been a while since he met anyone Arkala'ana.

"That's absolutely fine by me," Timothy says, shaking the hand that Minharh extends. "I'm Timothy. This is Kyle, Yuuki and my daughter, Sam, who just went inside. Guessing you've already met Andy?"

Minharh inclines his head, gaze flicking over each one of them as Timothy introduces them. "I have. Nice to meet you all. Although it could be in better circumstances."

Andy murmurs in agreement.

Kyle notices that named Minharh's gaze lingers on him, observing with a strange look in his eyes. His expression is reserved, masked. Kyle tries not to think too hard about it. He's already received that sort of emotionally weighed stare at the Wilsons; he'll just have to get used to ignoring people's judgement of him as best he can.

"So Andy informed me prior to you coming this morning that one of you isn't well," Minharh says. He looks at Yuuki, leaning heavily against Kyle looking like he'd be content to lie down on the grass right then and there if it weren't for his arm draped over Kyle's shoulders. It doesn't need to be pointed out that it's Yuuki who's the one being referred to.

"Are you alright walking in? We have a spare wheelchair. We can bring that out for you if you'd like."

Yuuki leans a little heavier against Kyle. He keeps his eyes downcast.

"No, it's fine," Kyle answers for him. "Thanks."

Practically speaking, it's a better idea. It would be less exertion for Kyle too, since wouldn't be having to support Yuuki's weight like this. But he gets it – if Kyle were the one having to choose between forcing himself through the motions of walking or being seated in a wheelchair, more exposed, in a more vulnerable position, he'd be feeling awfully anxious. It's better for Yuuki, mentally, to be supported by Kyle and walk.

Kyle feels guilty thinking about all this while standing before Minharh though. He doesn't get the same choice that Yuuki has.

"How about I carry you in?" Timothy asks Yuuki quietly. He comes over and gently lays a hand on Yuuki's open shoulder. "That way neither of you are straining yourselves trying to walk. Kyle, I know you want to help, but you shouldn't be overdoing it either. You've both got injuries to recover from."

Yuuki's eyes slip out of focus. He stares at the ground without seemingly really seeing it, and after a moment he ducks his head and whispers, "Okay."

They go about it easily, not wanting to make Yuuki uncomfortable or feel like a hassle. Timothy crouches down in front of Yuuki, back open. He gestures for Kyle to lower Yuuki onto his back, and he does so. Yuuki tenses at having to let go of Kyle but lets himself be supported by Timothy the moment he realises he's not about to fall.

Andy waits outside for Susan and Amelia when Minharh leads them into the house. In comparison to the other day, Yuuki's lucid where he wasn't last time Timothy carried him on his back. They meet no one along the way, but Yuuki hides his face in the collar of the shirt Timothy's wearing regardless. His knuckles go white where his fingers are gripping Timothy's shoulder. Judging by how tense Yuuki's shoulders are, he's probably trying not to be sick.

Kyle walks beside them, a hand placed in the middle of Yuuki's back – a reassurance, a point of physical contact to let Yuuki know he's right beside him. It's not necessary, he knows, but Kyle's personally found comfort in knowing Yuuki was near after things had happened. *An anchor,* he remembers calling it, that feeling grounded by one's presence. Kyle hopes he can help lessen Yuuki's stress through it.

They get Yuuki settled in a room with large windows and sunlight filtering in. It looks to be a converted study. There's a garden directly outside the window, creating a sense of peacefulness and privacy. The air coming in through the open window is fresh and cleansing. It's enough reassurance for Yuuki: the tension in his body loosens soon after Timothy helps him lie down.

Timothy lays a hand on Yuuki's shoulder. "Susan's going to be here soon," he says. "Are you okay if she comes and sets up an IV for you now?"

Yuuki's brow furrows. He's struggling to keep his eyes open. "Yeah. Why?"

"Her presence upset you quite badly yesterday."

"What d'you mean?"

With a questioning glance at Kyle – to which Kyle's not sure how to respond – Timothy clears his throat. "Your fever was really high. You thought she was someone else."

Yuuki groans and shifts, wincing. "…don't remember."

Concern and relief simultaneously wash over Timothy's face. He gently squeezes Yuuki's shoulder. "That's okay," he murmurs. "It's probably best you don't."

Neither Timothy nor Kyle elaborate. Yuuki's not awake and with it enough to question it either, and for that Kyle's glad. Timothy's right; it's probably best Yuuki doesn't remember that whole experience or what he hallucinated. It won't help Yuuki's recovery to learn that he mistook Susan for Deborah.

Yuuki forces his eyes open. He seeks out Kyle, lets his eyes slip closed again and exhales slowly. His head lolls against Timothy's hand. He mumbles something indiscernible for how slurred the words are.

Kyle and Timothy stay with him for a while. Susan does, too, even after she's come and finished getting Yuuki hooked up to the IV. It's in the crook of his arm this time, various fluids now dripping into his system. Shortly after, he drifts off to sleep and the discolour in his cheeks eases slightly.

No one speaks. No one needs to. The last word spoken was by Minharh when he left soon after Susan arrived. A native owl hoots from a hedge of trees in the garden. The warm aroma of freshly cooked food drifts in the open door. Yuuki breathes. Susan sits in a chair on his left side, holding his hand in both of hers. She rubs her thumb back and forth across the back of his hand.

Kyle tries not to let the atmosphere break his efforts not to cry, but fails.

Timothy stands behind Susan, hands on her shoulders. "I'll go see the others," he murmurs. He pats her shoulder, glances at Kyle with a small nod and takes his leave.

Eventually Kyle leaves too. Yuuki's got someone with him and Susan's showing no desire to move from her seat at Yuuki's bedside. Sorrow emanates from her like the pressure in the air building from the incoming storm outside. Her ability to keep it contained snaps like a dam breaking as soon as Kyle's stepped out of the room.

Before Kyle finds himself swept up in Susan's grief as well as his own, he turns and follows the hallway to the living room.

32

Joshua comes up to Kyle the moment he steps in the door. "Can I give you a hug?"

It's so out of the blue Kyle isn't sure how to react. Joshua's sudden leap off the couch he'd been sitting on has drawn the attention of everyone, and now almost everyone – Sam, Avi, Logan, Amelia and Charlie, and Andy and Marina – are staring at him. Timothy is elsewhere, and the Chinese couple standing with Minharh are locked in too deep a conversation to pay heed to Joshua's essentially announcing Kyle's arrival.

Joshua is still waiting for permission, eyes shining.

Kyle lifts his shoulders in an uncertain shrug. "Um…if you want?"

The hug is fierce but not restraining. Not wanting to make Kyle uncomfortable by prolonging it, Joshua releases him but leaves his hands on his shoulders. "Thank you for saving him," he says firmly. "I forgot to say it when I called you guys. Sorry it took a few days."

It takes a moment for Kyle's mind to click as to what he's talking about. "Oh, I…"

"You saved him," Joshua repeats. "Also Sam says he's been down with a really bad fever these last few days. She says you basically stayed with him the whole time."

Kyle withdraws, wraps his arms around himself self-consciously. "I'm sorry. I don't mean to be clingy or anything."

"What? No, you're not. You're fine. What I'm saying is, I think you might have saved him twice. Just in the last week."

Unintentionally, when Kyle averts his gaze it lands on Sam. Her expression is serious, Amelia's too. Their body language speaks of pent up nervousness not yet fully processed. Beside them, Avi, Logan and Charlie regard Kyle intensely, though in a solemn, inquiring way.

All I did was change a wet flannel on his forehead and hug him, Kyle wants to protest. But the fact is that Yuuki's fever had been getting dangerously high, if it wasn't already so. Kyle doesn't feel like he 'saved' him, but maybe in a way he did. The implication that Yuuki was in serious danger isn't one Kyle likes to think too hard about though.

Susan, who slipped into the room a few moments ago, hums. "Speaking of which," she murmurs, and makes a beeline for her son. Kyle hastily steps out of the way. She barrels into Joshua and embraces him with the same fierceness Joshua had hugged Kyle with, only less careful.

"Ack! Mum, please!" Joshua exclaims.

"I've heard you were the mastermind behind the rescue."

Joshua holds his hands up. "What? Oh, not really?"

Susan's frown is wobbly as she pulls away. She raises an eyebrow.

Sam tsks. "It was you."

Kyle confirms.

"C'mon guys, it wouldn't have been possible without all three of us." Joshua glances between them. "Or are you trying to get me to take full accountability here? Is that what this is?"

"Actually," Andy says, coming forward with a cup of coffee in hand. "Before you start worrying, I'd like to commend your efforts. Accountability doesn't mean just being held accountable for the negative consequences. And don't worry," he says to Susan, "I've already had a talk with him."

Susan narrows her eyes. "So we can spare you a lecture then?"

With a wince, Joshua mutters, "Please."

Marina chuckles. "He's proven his case already."

Kyle tries not to let those words trigger a bitterness inside him at his profound inability to prove his own.

"You did well, all of you," Andy says. "I want to call it foolish, but given that we had no forces to attempt a rescue besides ourselves, and that the outcome of not performing that rescue would've been… devastating…"

Marina carries the sentence on. "The fact that you carefully planned and carried out a critical high risk operation successfully is to be commended. Especially in regards to how short a time frame you had to construct a plan and the limited resources you had to implement it."

It feels a bit much, receiving such acknowledgement from the two Peace Force commanders. Kyle's caught in a web of anxiety, waiting for the criticism to follow, for the niceties to wear off and the accusations to begin. But there's none of that. Apparently Andy's already had a talk with Joshua and doesn't find there to be any necessity in lecturing Kyle and Sam. They knew the risks going into it and Andy's aware of and satisfied with that.

Nonetheless, Kyle still feels like he's standing waiting in court, about to be tried. Timothy coming into the room right then doesn't help with that thought.

Joshua clears his throat. "Well, in that case, Amelia deserves some credit there too."

Amelia meets his gaze, bewildered.

"When Yuuki was…I know it must've been awfully hard to not do anything," Joshua explains to her. "You didn't know what we were planning on doing but you trusted us anyways. Thanks for giving us a chance."

Amelia's brow furrows. "I don't understand. Why are you thanking me? I'm the one who put him in that situation in the first place."

"Circumstantially, yes," Andy says, "but you had no part in making the decision to do what they did. You didn't make any agreement with them, before or during that situation. Since you waited and didn't agree to the mens' terms, Joshua, Sam and Kyle were able to get in there and get Yuuki out. Subsequently, we were then able to get ourselves – as in all of us here – out of there too."

Marina sidles over to where Amelia's standing by Charlie. "You played a big part in enabling the mission to be a success." She reaches out and grasps Amelia by the shoulder. She offers a reassuring smile. "You did great."

Charlie nods in agreement.

No more is said about the hostage situation after that. Kyle's glad. It puts him on edge and out of kilter remembering how he'd felt during the whole experience. He wasn't the hostage, but he was part of the group Yuuki was used as leverage against, and Kyle's experienced second-hand some of what Yuuki did through simply trying to help him through the aftermath.

But of course, while the hostage situation itself is not talked about further, there's still a matter everyone's hesitant to touch upon. It's Avi who finally addresses the elephant in the room. "And Yuuki? How's he doing? I mean, Sam said to give him space and all, and that he's not been doing well – which is, of course, completely understandable – but...?"

Everyone's eyes fall on Kyle, Timothy and Susan to answer, but none of them do. Their silence becomes answer enough.

"He's not doing well at all," Logan says slowly, "is he?"

There's no point in lying and saying he's doing okay. The group were there when Yuuki was recovering from his arm amputation at the country house. They heard his nightmares. They've seen his distress. They've seen how Yuuki's been struggling recently, before the hostage situation. In other words, Logan and Avi aren't asking yes or no – they already know the answer. Rather, they're asking for some sort of reassurance: a reassurance that Yuuki can recover from this. In truth, the Harrisons need one too.

"He's getting through it," Kyle murmurs. The answer is left at that.

Everyone falls into casual conversation among themselves. According to Andy, the next few days will be spent compiling what evidence they have to support themselves and considering how best to present that. Amelia's speech is at the forefront of that.

But while making plans and figuring out how to navigate all the challenges they face is indeed critical, right now everyone's just relieved to be back together. Speech practise can wait. Accumulating evidence can wait. The hostage situation back at the palace scared them all. To have made it through that in relatively fortunate circumstances is something that needs some down time to process.

Not knowing where he should be and not having the energy for much talking, Kyle decides to join Timothy standing by the door, content to simply observe. He pretends not to notice how Timothy's eyes are somewhat red and puffy.

The atmosphere is comfortable but it doesn't quite reach Kyle's heart. Neither does it reach Timothy's, probably, if the lack of relaxation in the man's posture is anything to go by. Both of them can, however, identify with the worn undercurrent of a vibe emanating from everyone; they're all in varying states of tired. The reunion at least gives them some solace in spite of it.

The living room – the entire house and property in general – is so nice that Kyle feels out of place in it. He doesn't belong in a place like this. Seeing everyone talking with each other and not knowing how exactly he fits into that only reinforces that, and as soon as Kyle questions where it is, then, that he belongs, a vivid image of his isolated prison cell flashes in his mind.

He grits his teeth and breathes in deep. *Don't think about that.* He distracts himself as best he can by concentrating on the sensations and visuals of the here and now around him. The image of the prison cell remains superimposed over the scene before him, but it helps.

Nearby, the couple Kyle hasn't met yet is casually talking to Minharh about something. Since they're speaking in Mandarin, Kyle doesn't understand what they're saying but for what he can gather by their tone of voice and body language. Minharh looks stressed. The couple appear supportive yet their tone suggests they're insisting on something Minharh is increasingly uncomfortable about.

Whatever it is they're talking about must be important. Kyle can't shake off the feeling that it involves him.

The man in the couple catches sight of Timothy and Kyle standing quietly nearby. He parts the other two with a comment and joins them.

He approaches Timothy and Kyle and greets them with a bow. "Hello," Minharh's friend says to Kyle with a polite bow. "My name is Chén Jié. You can call me Jié." He turns and gestures to the woman continuing to speak in stressed, now hushed Mandarin with Minharh. "She is my wife, Chén Xiùyīng."

Kyle nods. "Uh, hi."

"Good to see you again," Timothy murmurs. "I believe it's been over a year now."

Jié smiles lightly. "Yes, although it would be more fortunate if our meetings could be in better circumstance."

"Your friend said the exact same thing. And that it sure could."

Kyle remembers then what Timothy had said yesterday: these are the people to whom Yuuki transferred ownership of the Youth Rehabilitation Trust to. It allows Kyle a much greater sense of trust in the shelter that's been offered to them than he'd felt at the Wilsons'.

"I have something I want to talk with you about later," Jié murmurs to Timothy. "It's about the A'o Fire case."

Kyle feels the blood drain from his face. The A'o Fire case. That's the very fire that his father died trying to contain as a firefighter.

Timothy leans back against the wall with a sigh. "That case has always bothered me."

"Why do you want to talk about that case?" Kyle asks, bewildered.

"The prosecution suspected arson," Timothy explains. "More evidence was discovered that strongly pointed it being so, but material was insufficient." He raises an eyebrow. "Am I right in guessing you know something else about it?"

"You are. We found evidence," Jié explains, "when we were dealing with the fire... the, uh, the case, that is. The nature of it left us in a dangerous position. This is why we haven't been able to inform you formally on the matter." He pauses, opens his mouth to add something else and then hesitates. Quietly, he resigns to say it anyway. "Minharh had to leave his son because of it."

Minharh turns to his friend, jaw clenched. His gaze hardens. "We talked about this."

Jié winces and mumbles an apology. Clearly it's a sensitive area.

"What did you find?" Kyle asks, trying to steer the topic of conversation back to safer grounds. He internally flinches when Minharh's eyes sweep past him, stopping with a careful examination of Kyle's expression before turning back to Xiùyīng. It seems like both of them have bad memories associated with the A'o Fire case.

Jié opens his mouth to reply but is interrupted by something his wife says to Minharh. He sighs. "Excuse me," he murmurs, and heads over to mediate.

Xiùyīng seems to be trying to get a point across to Minharh, and vice versa. Minharh appears distressed by the topic at hand, and Jié, who openly winces at a particular line his wife says, sees it clear as day now too. Minharh sends a glance sideways as Jié cuts in with a comment, and his eyes lock on Kyle's. Dread rooted in fear creeps across his expression. He narrows his eyes and looks away.

Oh, Kyle thinks. Shame washes over him. *They're talking about me, aren't they?* He can't distinguish between their tones, but because of Minharh's timbre of voice and Arkala'ana accent, Kyle hears when he pronounces his name as Kai'irh. Or at least, close enough to it as pronouncing Kyle in Mandarin tones will get.

Xiùyīng is probably upset she has a convict in her house. Or maybe it's Minharh who is, and Xiùyīng is trying to argue that I'm not who everyone says I am. That would be more accurate, right? Minharh does get a strange look about him when he looks at Kyle, and just now Kyle saw plain as day how Minharh looked at him with anxiousness scrawled across his face – anxiousness that increased as a result of realising Kyle caught him looking. While he can't know for sure, to Kyle it's high enough a possibility that his criminal record is the subject of conversation.

It upsets Kyle more than he anticipates.

On further reflection, he understands why: it's because Minharh reminds him of his father. Watching Minharh argue about him with that fearful apprehension in his expression feels like watching his father acting the same way towards him. Minharh is not his father, he gets that, and Kyle could be wrong about what exactly the Mandarin language conversation is about. He still can't help but feel off put regardless.

"Kyle," Timothy says. "You alright?"

Shaking himself out of his reverie, Kyle forces a smile. "Yeah. I'm good."

"Is something bothering you? Your head injury acting up again?"

"Oh, no, it's not that. I, just…Minharh reminds me of my Dad," Kyle confesses quietly.

It's already been five years. Kyle feels like he should have learnt how to move on by now, and yet he still can't help but miss him like his passing was only yesterday. Kyle knows there's nothing wrong with missing someone, but for some reason other people always had a problem with it. "*He's in a better place now,*" people would always say. "*Missing him won't bring him back.*" The latter had been Ben a few months after Kyle had become orphaned – and right before Kyle had punched him.

Kyle digs his hands into his pockets. "I was just…missing him, I guess."

Across from them, Jié makes a point that brings the debate to a standstill.

Timothy hums. He casually crosses his arms and leans back against the wall beside him. "Your father's name was Sa'a, right? Sa'a Kindall?"

Kyle blinks. "How did you…?"

"The A'o Fire case was one of the first I processed as a judge."

"Really?"

"Hmm. I hadn't put two and two together until recently – that your Dad was one of the victims in that fire. I'm sorry that happened to you."

"It's fine."

"I'm not so sure."

Kyle opens his mouth to argue, but can't find the words. The truth hits close to home. His Dad was his only family, and until recently his only friend. Since his mother died shortly after giving birth to him, he never knew her, and any family he might've known through her all lived overseas. As for his Dad's family...

From what he'd understood of how his father had told it, his Dad had disagreed with the political perspectives among the family. They'd supported the same views as Taularh, and they'd been very close-minded about it. His Dad had been a liberalist, like King Fahlu, whereas the rest of his family had been conservative. Such modern views aren't aligned with traditional Arkala culture, especially not Arkala'ana culture.

It's what led Taularh to usurp the throne and succeed in establishing power the way he did. It's why no one challenged him – because he brought conservatism back to Arkala, and stricter law enforcement. *More like unforgiving and somewhat corrupted law enforcement,* Kyle thinks bitterly.

Politics aside though, the best that can be said of the situation is that Kyle has no place among his father's family. He was disowned automatically from the moment his Dad simultaneously removed himself from his subtribe's social environment and been outcast from it. When his Dad had died fighting the fire, none of the family acknowledged wanted to know him – hence why Kyle had ended up having to live with a foster family, though there was no 'family' about it.

The A'o Fire burned in more ways than the fire itself alone ever could have.

Jié comes back over to Timothy and Kyle. Minharh calls out sharply to him in Mandarin, protesting. With a grimace, Jié turns and dismisses the concern, although Minharh still watches him warily out of the corner of his eye.

"Everything alright?" Timothy asks.

"Actually," Jié says, glancing at Kyle. "That conversation might be better to have later."

Timothy's frown is heavy. "I don't know what this has to do with what you want to tell me about the case, but if this is about Kyle's conviction, I will tell you now that it was an unfair trial. He's not a criminal. Might I remind you, too, that this is coming from the judge who held him guilty as charged to begin with. I'm responsible for charging him, so I should know."

In that moment, something loosens in Kyle's chest. It's like a cord that's been binding him has snapped. The edges of his vision blur and grey. He hates how desperately he needs those words. He hates how it knocks the air from his lungs, makes it hard to remember to draw in more. Makes it hard to think.

"You never deserved to be there in the first place," Yuuki's said so many times. Kyle wants to believe that, too. He did believe that, once. But the constant condemnation has messed with his mind and made him doubt what he knows to be true. It's also done more damage to his self-worth that he realised. As is if hadn't already been low enough.

"It's not that," Jié reassures. "It's something else."

Xiùyīng inclines in her head. "Don't worry, Kyle. We don't think of you as a convict."

"But you were talking about me just now, though," Kyle says sharply, "weren't you?"

Minharh rolls up and cuts in before either of them can answer. "What we were talking about is personal." The masking of his emotions is slips back into place as he speaks.

"If you're talking about me, then that makes it personal for me too. Do you have a personal vendetta against me or something?"

"No, I don't. None of us do."

"Then what? I saw the way you looked at me just before. You view me as a threat, don't you?"

Minharh locks his jaw. The mask fractures.

Xiùyīng passes by with frustrated mutter. She glances at Kyle, evaluating his expression. There's no accusation present in her body language. The exasperation in her eyes is reserved for Minharh.

"I'd rather not talk about it," Minharh grits out. "Not yet."

"Or," Kyle says quietly, "you'd rather not talk about it while I'm present." His stomach sinks and a cold weight settles there. "Fine. I'll leave you to it."

He doesn't want to walk away, but he does. It feels pathetic, childish. Like some kind of grumpy emo teenage attitude, or at least that's what his foster father used to call it. Kyle's chest tightens further at the thought. He clenches his teeth and breathes through his nose, trying to maintain as much appearance of control as he can until he's out of sight.

Kyle veers towards the front door the second he steps out of the living room. It's closed; he fumbles with the door handle, his right hand choosing then to seize up on him. With a distressed groan, he hastily switches hands, shoves his weight against the door and stumbles outside.

33

Outside. Not trapped. The door shuts behind him. No voices out here to condemn him. Space all around him reassuring him that's not because he's locked in isolation. He breathes, however shakily. He tells himself it's fine, that this is just how it is; there's nothing he can do about people's perception of him and he's just going to have to learn to deal with being labelled as a criminal and a convict and kid who should be in prison.

Kyle's less okay with that than he wishes he could be.

He lingers out in the fresh air, breathing through the residing waves of emotional backlash. After however long, Timothy comes outside to stand beside him. Kyle's shoulders tense, anticipating a lecture or a speech of meaningful, well-intended words that will instead make him feel worse. But Timothy doesn't say anything, instead just letting his presence speak for itself: there will be none of that here.

"I feel so permanently incriminated," Kyle confesses after a few minutes.

Timothy murmurs, "Part of that's my fault. I'm sorry."

"You were just doing your job as a judge. They set you up too."

"I'm still responsible for the decisions I made. I made a ruling in spite of the doubt I had and you suffered for it."

"You asked Yuuki for help," Kyle says, "and you both worked to prove my innocence and revoke that decision. I'd rather you held yourself responsible for that. If you'd questioned too much during my trial, you'd have ended up with a target on your back. In that video you were looking at back at the country house, Jeff had a gun, didn't he?"

Timothy stares out into the distance. He exhales slowly. "I know. I've thought about that too. Though I think it was actually intended to be a threat more than anything. A show of arms. A warning not to be quiet if I'd started challenging the prosecution during the trial. He'd have been stupid to fire in the courtroom. That might've been one of the only things preventing him from eliminating the risk of us accidentally spreading word about Amelia."

As he talks, Timothy's tone shifts deflates into something much more tired. He's mentally and emotionally exhausted by it all, Kyle realises. Being a lawyer or a judge is a high stress job as it is without having corruption laced in cases and personal trauma aka the Ninao incident to recover from.

"Do you think you'll go back to being a judge?" Kyle asks. "Once this is all over?"

Timothy frowns. The lines beneath his eyes seem to deepen right then and there. "I don't know. The more I think about it, the more I dread it. If I'm honest, I'm not sure I'd be able to handle it now. I struggled to keep up with things after the Ninao incident, and what with trying to make sure Yuuki was doing okay…" He sighs. "Guess I'll see when the time comes. They might not accept me back in anyways, since I've violated the law and all. Might be the excuse I need to get myself to leave that career before it ends me."

The wind stirs the trees. A small bird flits up and down the outer branches of one, chirping.

"And what about you? Anything you have in mind that you want to do after?"

Kyle grunts. "I don't feel like I have a future."

"You do have one. We'll get you acquitted, don't worry."

No, it's not just that, Kyle wants to argue, but he holds his tongue. He doesn't know how to explain that it's more than just his conviction weighing down on him. This is an overall and overwhelming sense of a foreshortened future he's experiencing. Like he has no tomorrow. Like he'll get an acquittal only to wind up in some other incident shortly after. Like all roads into the future lead into nowhere but dark, swampy *suffocating* places, all places where the shadows lurking there will find one way or another to end his life.

Timothy, however, isn't aware of the extent of Kyle's helplessness. "Your birthday's less than a month away, too," Timothy reminds him. "You'll be eighteen; you'll legally be able to live and work where you want. There's also the option of overseas?"

Kyle scoffs. "I'm a threat to national security, aren't I? They won't let me into another country."

"They will with an acquittal."

"If they listen to me in the first place."

Unable to provide a good enough counter to that, Timothy avoids commenting. Instead, he says, "Yuuki did that, you know – he moved overseas to Arkala from Japan when he was nineteen. Came here on a scholarship to Arkala Police College through which he was granted residency after graduating. I met shortly him shortly after he moved here."

Kyle blinks. "I thought he'd grown up here."

"Until he was about seven or eight, I think he once said, then his family moved to Japan. He's only been here the last...what is it now, six or seven years?"

"Wait, how old is Yuuki, again?"

"Twenty-five. Twenty-six at the end of the year, in December."

Somehow it stuns Kyle to relearn that. Yuuki has the demeanour of someone older in age than he actually is. If he'd paid closer attention to the details mentioned in the newspaper articles of the Ninao kidnapping, he might've remembered it but these days Kyle's memory fades stuff out easy.

Trauma, he reminds himself.

"We crossed paths frequently while out running in the mornings," Timothy says. "Struck up conversation and ended up becoming friends from there. He shared his heart for wanting to help kids caught on the wrong side of the justice system. I've seen a lot of it myself, how easy it is for the current judiciary laws to ensnare people. You've experienced first-hand how unfair it can be."

"And so that's why you guys created the Youth Rehabilitation Trust?"

Timothy hums. "It was Yuuki's idea. But he needed a lawyer to navigate the legal side of things, and since we shared a common vision I decided to help him with it personally. We did it; we got it set up. June 5, last year."

"The same day as the Ninao incident."

"Yep. The day we officially established it was the day that happened. All that hard work we did, only to have to sign it off to someone else to manage because the circumstances screwed us over…"

"These guys here took over it though, right?" Kyle gestures to the house. "So not all of that hard work was lost."

Timothy smiles bitterly. "Relinquishing the Trust was easy in comparison to what we lost." Taking his phone out of his pocket, Timothy opens his photos folder and starts swiping. When he finds the photo he's looking for, he holds out the phone.

The photo on the screen is of himself and a slightly younger looking Yuuki. Bold writing on the certificate in Yuuki's hands reads, 'Qualified Security Officer'. Yuuki's graduation from Police College. In the photo, Yuuki's skin tone is darker, healthier. Glowing, even. His eyes are bright even in spite of the mild tiredness in them. And he's smiling, genuinely. Kyle's never seen him smile like that.

The graduation year is 10-Tau – only three years ago.

"He's trying so hard," Timothy murmurs. The screen flicks off. "He's making such a decent damn effort to keep picking himself back up. Now if the world would stop beating him up and just let him be already…"

Kyle throat constricts. "I don't want to lose him."

"We'll do everything we can to protect him."

"What if that's not enough?"

Timothy swallows hard, sets his mouth into a firm line that curves sharply down at its edges. "Then it isn't, and we'll have to deal with the consequences."

Kyle folds an arm across his chest, props his arm up on it and covers his eyes with his hands in time for the tears to start. He bares his teeth against the burning sorrow this hardship brings, against the severity of it.

It's the bitter truth, what Timothy says. They've seen enough. Yuuki's been hurt enough. Is it selfish, wanting him to stay alive when each day is filled with so much suffering? Of all of them, Yuuki's been hit the hardest and most destructively. There's no telling what tomorrow will bring and the freedom they're fighting for is nothing more than a glimmer of hope on the horizon.

There's a chance Yuuki might not last until the end of it. There's a chance he may not even want to.

"Is it alright if I hug you?" Timothy asks softly.

With a sob that wracks his body, Kyle nods.

Timothy's arm settles around his shoulders, a warm and steadying weight. Kyle's drawn into the embrace offered. It gives a sense of security, though he knows Timothy's confidence is fractured too. Timothy's hand gently rubs his back. A high pitched cry escapes Kyle's throat.

It feels like déjà vu, this. At the country house, Kyle had a similar heart to heart with Timothy. They'd talked about similar things. Yuuki was recovering from a recent injury then too – a new layer of trauma, another wound cut into his heart to scar, another onslaught of stress to wreak havoc on his brain…

How much of this can Yuuki withstand before he can't? And if even if there's to be no further incidents, what about the aftermath?

"We'll do what we can to support him and help him heal," Timothy murmurs. There's a gravelly edge to his voice when he says quietly, "We'll give what energy we have spare to help him live."

Kyle hopes that'll be enough.

34

As dusk sinks into night, Kyle returns to Yuuki's room. Yuuki's awake, lying on his side and gazing absent-mindedly out the window. Kyle lightly taps on the door as he enters. At the sound, Yuuki turns his head, though only as much as necessary to look over his shoulder.

"You're looking a little better," Kyle murmurs as he walks in. *Contrary to how painful it looked for you to move just now.* He turns on the light before the room's plunged into darkness with the outside.

Yuuki blinks slowly. "S'ppose that's a good thing."

It doesn't have to be explained that it's a good thing. Even since Kyle was last in here, napping on the mattress set up on the floor for him, Yuuki's looking and sounding slightly better. *Much better than what he was last couple of nights, at least.* His words are still slurred and his skin still off colour, but there's still an improvement. He's also more aware and his fever is gone. It'll take a lot of resting before he's well enough to be up and about again, but fortunately he's got the IV now to help with that restoration while he does.

With a sigh, Yuuki drags himself wearily into sitting upright. He slumps back into the pillows. "How long's it been?"

"Since when?" Kyle asks, sitting down on the bed. "Since we got here or…since the day we were last at the palace?"

Yuuki's brow creases. "Both?"

"It's been five days since the night we rescued you, and about…" Kyle mentally does the math. "…nine hours since we left the Wilsons'. I don't know how long you've been awake, but you've been asleep pretty much since we got here. Here's the Chén's, by the way."

"Haven't been 'wake long. Thought I might've slept through a whole entire week or something without knowing, though. That's a relief I haven't, I think." Yuuki's eyes narrow. "Wait…*who*?"

"The Chén's? The people you signed off the Trust to?"

"No, the other one. Where we were before."

"We were at the Wilsons'," Kyle says quietly. He's too honest around Yuuki now to bother disguising the stress in his tone. "As in, Daniel Wilson's family's house."

It takes a moment for that to fully register in Yuuki's brain. When it does, his mouth pulls downwards and he groans. "Urgh, Timothy. I'll talk to him."

"It's okay. I understand why he and Andy chose there."

"I need to talk to him."

"You don't," Kyle quickly interjects. "We already talked – *argued* – about it, me and Timothy. It's fine."

"No, 'bout something else." Yuuki's tone is heavy. "Something he needs to know about. Sorry, my mind's all over place. Actually, no place at all would be a better way to describe it. I don't know."

Kyle frowns. He puts his confusion to the side. "Do you want me to get him for you?"

Yuuki stares tiredly out the window. "I gotta figure out how on earth to tell him first."

"Might I ask what it's about?"

"Ninao." After a long pause, Yuuki elaborates. "I figured it out."

"Figured…what out?"

"Why it happened."

"It didn't happen because of the Youth Rehabilitation Trust, did it?"

"No, it didn't. That was just an excuse to close the case and bury it."

Something cold settles in Kyle's stomach. He remembers the night before the hostage situation, when Timothy had brought Yuuki in half-drunk and looking utterly emotionally exhausted. The weird expression in Timothy's eyes as he recounted what they'd been talking about – the look that told Kyle that Timothy didn't like the idea of what might await them at the end of Yuuki's train of thought.

Kyle frowns. "Why are you making yourself think so much about it right now? You're dealing with enough as is. You shouldn't be stressing over this."

"Too late. Besides, it's given me something to keep my mind preoccupied with."

Instead of giving his mind an invitation to think about other things against his will. Kyle pulls a leg up onto the bed and sits on his foot. "Okay, so what you just mentioned, about Ninao – do you want to talk about it?"

"I don't even want to think about it, if I'm honest."

"Then –"

"But Timothy needs to know. And, well…I guess you should too." After a long pause, Yuuki's gaze blanks and he continues, "They, um…when they caught me, they said some things. They said I kept getting in the way of things. That it was…that it's my fault I get hurt because I keep getting in the way."

"That's just an excuse to justify deliberately hurting you."

"I don't think they ever intended on doing so."

"How does that make sense? They freaking kidnapped you, tied you up, held you hostage, made you lose an arm – and you're saying that happened without them intending on doing any of that?"

Yuuki winces. "No, as in the way they said it was like they've never been after me in the first place. Sorry. I'm sorry. I can't think straight. My mind's all fog and…" he groans. "Words."

Kyle frowns hard, brow furrowed. "I'm sorry." Maybe he's being too impatient here.

"S'rry, can't really think clearly. Asked Susan earlier and she gave me some kind of sedative to help me not think so much 'bout…about what happened. 'Cause I'm sick."

"And yet you're thinking."

Yuuki grunts.

"You need to rest as much as you can."

"Can't rest with this on my mind."

Kyle hums sympathetically. "That's fair."

"Besides, it didn't come to me all at once. It was more like… slow realisations, over the last however long. Things clicked, subtly, and then it all just whirled into something that made sense. Can't lie and say it hasn't hurt my brain trying to untangle my thoughts on it though."

With a nod, Kyle shifts where he sits. "Well, if you want to keep on talking about it – to help you process it – then we can. What did they say exactly? The men who captured you?"

"Something about me getting in the way all the time," Yuuki mutters, "and that it's my fault I keep getting hurt. Uh…I can't remember it precisely."

"In any case, you believed them?"

"They were saying it to taunt me, Kyle. To get at me."

"That doesn't change the fact that what they said is a lie. None of it was your fault."

"I know."

"*None* of it. Not what happened at Ninao, not your getting shot when you looked into my case and they almost got away with kidnapping me, and most definitely not them taking you hostage – unless you volunteered. You didn't volunteer, did you?"

Yuuki gives him a look that says, *what do you think?*

"Rhetorical question. You get my point."

"You're not getting mine, though."

Kyle regards him carefully. "What do you mean?"

"They weren't after me. Not now – since they were targeting Amelia – and not when they shot my arm off either, because they were wanting you…and not even at Ninao."

"But you were the target of the Ninao incident. They kidnapped you from there. They *kidnapped* you and left you in that shed because –"

"I was collateral," Yuuki interrupts. There's a certain defeat to his tone. His whole body language speaks it too. His voice is getting scratchy with fatigue now and he swallows with difficulty. "Have you never asked yourself why they didn't kill me? Why they locked me up in that shed instead of...whatever?"

Kyle's palms grow clammy. He doesn't like where this is heading.

"It wasn't me they were after; it was Timothy."

"...what?"

"Think about it: for what reason do you think they held onto me?"

Something clicks in Kyle's mind then. A pattern. Another parallel. Horror blooms in his chest, just as cold and twisted as he'd anticipated. "They were gonna use you as a hostage?"

"Makes sense, right? They had me, they wanted him. When they blew their chance to get Timothy, they had to rethink since the mission objective wasn't achieved. Keeping me as leverage was a way they could attempt to get him again, only they had to think of how best to do it. Using me would've been their best option had they done it right. But they had a time limit on me, and then Jeff got distracted chasing the Princess and Andy used that as an opportunity to send the coordinates to where I was so I could be rescued..."

"But why would they want Timothy? Are you sure it's not just that they wanted *both* of you for starting the Trust?"

"If they did have pre-determined means for me, they could've made use of the time they had me instead of just...sticking me in a shed and leaving me there."

"So you're thinking they had Timothy in their sights exclusively?"

Yuuki hums. He lifts his hand to his face and rubs his forehead. The IV line shifts. "I don't know why. It's taken enough just to realise all this. My guess is it's likely something to do with a case Timothy had input in.

He's a judge, after all; it wouldn't be hard for him to make enemies."

"You're not sure of the case, though."

"Yeah."

Kyle doesn't know what to say. In the silence that falls between them, he realises that Yuuki probably only was able to come to this conclusion after being held hostage. Having the concept fresh in his mind probably helped see the similarities between his treatment during the Ninao kidnapping and the hostage situation back at the palace.

If what Yuuki says is true, then that does truly mean that of all the times Yuuki's been taken, bound, hurt and traumatised, none of them actually featured him as the subject in the mission objective. Instead it was Timothy, or Kyle, or Amelia, and Yuuki was simply a tool for getting them.

He hates how they're going to have to relay this news to Timothy.

Kyle lets out a long sigh. "Gosh, Yuuki."

Yuuki grimaces.

"And you've been doing all this mental processing on your own? I thought you said Susan gave you some stuff to help you not think so much. That you didn't want to."

"Welcome to PTSD," Yuuki says dryly. "Sometimes you ain't got a conscious choice."

They decide to approach Timothy together later that night, after Yuuki's had more rest and Kyle's had time to process everything Yuuki told him. Better to tell him while they have the courage to.

This time Yuuki accepts the offer of using a wheelchair. It doesn't take too much to figure out how to transfer the IV from the stand to the wheelchair, and once that's sorted and Yuuki's seated, they mentally prepare to leave. Before they do, Kyle drapes a large blanket over Yuuki's legs, covering him from waist down and giving him some sense of lessened vulnerability as they move out of the room.

They go slow. Kyle's not up to walking fast and Yuuki's uncomfortable in the unfamiliar surroundings. Kyle catches a glimpse of Yuuki's scowl as he tries to adjust the blanket without disturbing the IV line or irritating the area of his arm it's feeding into. Yuuki's eyes dart back and forth, flicking to every doorway and shadow, every window and possible pathway someone could approach from.

Kyle tries distracting him with small talk about the house and how the group's doing. He only briefly mentions the people hosting them, since Yuuki apparently already knows them and Kyle's metaphorical feathers are still ruffled from his exchange with Minharh.

But then Yuuki starts having difficulty breathing. The sedative has his breathing slowed and his chest's heaving with the effort of trying to get enough air in for fight-or-flight. That in itself triggers him. His eyes are wild, anxious, only half-focused. Each breath is too shallow, too strained.

"Do you want to go back?" Kyle asks.

Yuuki looks torn. His fingers tighten on the blanket.

"I think you'll end up having a panic attack if we keep going like this," Kyle says evenly. "I'll take you back."

"He needs to know," Yuuki grits out. His fist shakes.

"Not at the expense of your health. I can tell him. You need to rest. Okay?"

Too distressed to argue, Yuuki resigns to let him. "Fine."

It's a good call to make. Yuuki's worn out. His energy crashes even as they're moving, Yuuki's head dropping onto his chest and making him sag forward. Kyle has to reach out to steady him before he tips out of the chair.

Back in the room, Kyle sets the IV back in place. He leans forward and slips his arms around Yuuki's torso, careful of Yuuki's arm hanging limp over his. He gently draws him to lean against him. Kyle locks his hands together, braces himself and hauls Yuuki out of the chair. The blanket slips off his lap and Kyle has to be careful not to trip on it.

Getting him from the chair to the bed seems easy, but it's not. Yuuki doesn't even have the strength to try take some of his own weight. Kyle strains under it, blood draining from his face. The room tilts and his head feels light, throbs, reminds him of the head injury he's still recovering from. With a grunt of effort, he gets Yuuki turned around and seated on the edge of the bed.

From there, fortunately, it doesn't take as much to get him settled.

"'m sorry," Yuuki slurs. His eyes slip closed. "…was a stupid idea."

Kyle adjusts the covers over him, mindful of the IV line. "You don't need to be sorry. Do you still want me to get Timothy?"

"Yeah. I jus'…just want to tell him, at least."

"Get it off your mind."

"I don't want him to think I hate him for it."

"Timothy wouldn't think that." Would he?

"He's got survivor's guilt, I think," Yuuki says hoarsely. He coughs, forces his eyes open again. "'cause of Ninao."

"Because he and Joshua escaped and you weren't able to?"

"Hmm."

"And when he knows everything you went through was because they were trying to get him...?"

Yuuki's mouth twitches. "It'll be worse." His brow furrows. "Don't want it to be worse."

"I'll go let him know," Kyle reassures. "You just rest. I'll go find him and ask him to come here for you."

With a mumbled acknowledgment, Yuuki's eyes shut on him again. He looks like he's fighting to open them again, but his mind won't connect with the action. Kyle waits a moment longer to make sure Yuuki's okay. When he's assured, he sets off to fetch Timothy.

35

Timothy's not in the living room or outside on the driveway, and since those are the only other places Kyle is at all familiar with besides the bathroom and Yuuki's room, he has no idea where to look. He could wander about, but he's too afraid of being caught and landing himself in trouble for being somewhere he shouldn't.

Just as he's settling with the idea that he'll have to go back and tell Yuuki he couldn't find Timothy, he hears Amelia's voice drifting from a different branch off the hallway to the one Yuuki's room is on. He starts in that direction but then halts in his footsteps when he hears Sam's voice too.

Must be the girls' room. Kyle doesn't want to be rude. He also doesn't want his actions to be misinterpreted if someone sees him headed in that direction. Maybe he wouldn't be so worried about it if it were just their group here, but it's not, and who knows what Minharh, Jié and Xiùyīng think of him. Particularly Minharh. And so he stands rooted to the spot, unsure of whether or not it's okay if he allows himself to show up at the girls' door or not.

Kyle's heart beats faster with the realisation of how much fear getting arrested has earned him. It might not even just be that, but also all the false accusations his foster parents would make based solely on presumptions as well. Saying he's procrastinating study when all he needed was a decent break. Saying he's looking for a fight when he responds to someone's unfairness with anger, as though being upset over something that hurt him is an unacceptable and impermissible human emotional reaction he's not allowed to display. He's anticipating getting in trouble with basically everything he does, in other words.

But then he hears Avi and Logan's voices too, and Kyle takes a moment to breathe. He'd been about to say better safe than sorry, turn around and go back without continuing forward. But if Avi and Logan are also there with Sam and Amelia, then the most he has to worry about is interrupting the group conversation they appear to be having. Reassuring himself it's fine to go now, Kyle walks the length of the hallway and arrives at the door.

Warm light pools outside the door. The atmosphere inside is also warm, and Kyle lingers in the shadows outside of it for a moment. He feels like he'll be disrupting the atmosphere. Amelia's practicing her speech too. The others are passing her constructive criticism on wording and tone of voice, all in an effort to get the essence of what Amelia's trying to accurately convey through her speech.

It sounds good, Kyle thinks. He'd heard Amelia practicing her speech before, back at the palace, but this is a revised version and it...it has a certain quality to it that makes it stand out. That makes *her* stand out, especially in regard to Amelia now essentially being a political leader. It's personal, what she's saying. It's not just about making herself look good in the public eye, it's about protesting all the hurt that's been done against them. It's about explaining why they've been on the run these past couple of months. The speech is honest. It asks respect, patience and empathy. It brings to light the injustice Kyle experienced with the Village Park homicide case (hearing it be called that with his name attached makes him realise why Yuuki never refers to the Ninao incident as a 'the Ninao kidnapping').

The speech also describes what happened to Yuuki, both in regard to the loss of his arm and his recent trauma. Sam points out that giving the detail about Yuuki's lost right arm might not be such a good idea, as it would make it easier for people to find them in a crowd if they end up having to go out into the city. Kyle finds himself nodding in agreement. Logan suggests simply calling it a severe injury instead. The group concede.

Distracted by his own approval of the decision, Kyle doesn't hear Sam's movement until she appears in front of him. He flinches. "Sorry, I- I'm not trying to eavesdrop or anything. I –"

"You just gonna keep standing out here or are you going to come in?" Sam interrupts.

Kyle swallows. "I…I didn't want to intrude."

"Pfft, you're fine." She grabs his wrist and drags him into the light inside. "Come join us."

Avi, Logan and Amelia welcome him. The invitation to stay and hang out with them is a wide open door, but Kyle feels somehow threatened by it. Or rather, undeserving. This is their small group; he doesn't belong here. And besides –

"Oh, I'm… I just came to ask if you guys know where Timothy is?

Sorry, you were practicing," Kyle adds, glancing at Amelia. "I didn't want to interrupt."

Avi waves his hands dismissively. "You're not. It's all goods."

Logan and Amelia nod.

"I think he's outside," Sam says, frowning. "My Dad, that is."

Kyle tilts his head. "I already looked. I couldn't see him."

"Did you check the other side? The lake side, that is?"

Kyle blinks. He hadn't thought of looking there. The curtains were all drawn and undisturbed when he checked the living room both times. Perhaps Timothy went out another door besides the sliding door in the living room?

"There's a conservatory on that side," Sam explains. "I think Jié wanted to talk to him about something."

Oh yeah, there was that. Kyle nods slowly. "Guess I'll have to line up then, huh."

"You needing to talk to him too?"

"Yeah." He fidgets with his hands. *About the Ninao incident.* "Well, actually it's Yuuki who does. I said I'd get Timothy for him, but if he's busy, then…"

"Nah, I'd just go. Worst comes to worst, you could just ask him to come by once he's finished."

Avi glances between them. "Do want one of us to go sit with Yuuki while you go get him?"

Kyle's heart warms at Avi's thoughtfulness. He flashes him an appreciative smile. "No, it's alright. He's okay resting on his own. Thanks though, Avi."

"Okay. No problem."

Sam comments, "Yeah, when he's not well, there's few he'll let near him. He'll get stressed otherwise. Happened to me and Mum when he was recovering from Ninao too – he hated anyone being around him except Dad and Joshua, but I think that's because they were the ones who found him. But eventually came to trust us. Obviously, now he trusts Kyle also, and likely trusts him the most. He may eventually open up to you guys as well, but in the meantime he'll heal better if he knows that the only people who will be around him while he's in this state of vulnerability are people he's decided he can trust. Emotionally trust, too."

"Charlie had great difficulty back at the country house trying to help him because of that," Amelia remarks.

"Yeah, we've learnt that Yuuki doesn't like people touching him unless they're close or he's the one initiating it. There's an emotional element to feeling comfortable with it, too."

Avi nods. "That makes sense."

Sam's insight is good. Kyle also thinks about how reserved Yuuki is in general, and how in all the times he's been hurt badly it's involved a good deal of manhandling. He thinks of how good Susan is with the way she approaches helping with injuries, and how considerate and caring Sam, Joshua and Timothy all have been when Kyle and Yuuki have been experiencing various hurts – knowing how to approach helping them without encroaching on their boundaries. That has to have been something learnt through much trial and error, and much, much patience.

Kyle suddenly has an even greater respect for the Harrisons.

On that note, he clears his throat. "I don't think I've ever verbally expressed it, but I, uh…wanted to say thank you to you all. Timothy – your Dad – told me about how you and Logan, and Amelia, all went into the Peace Force station to speak up for me. And Avi." His tone twists with emotion that comes unbidden. Stress from his helplessness in defending himself threatens to turn into anxiety. "T-thank you for what you did for me."

"Did Timothy also tell you I was the one who made that witness statement against you?" Amelia asks quietly. Her expression is shadowed.

"You went in and adjusted it. You realised you mistook what you saw at the park, and about me, and you went in to fix it. You did something about it when you realised you might've made a mistake."

"I *did* make a mistake."

Kyle grimaces. He doesn't intend to make an example of his low self-worth here. "Anyways, you still fixed it." *I'm not okay with how that mistake affected me, but that kind of doesn't need explaining.* He meets her eyes, serious. "You acknowledged that you were wrong, and when you did you did something about it. That's one of the reasons why I think you'll make a great leader."

Amelia's face falls into bewilderment. Clearly she'd been expecting Kyle's reaction to be different than *this*.

"Plus everything Joshua said earlier," Sam adds. "You're probably concerned about how the public may view you because they'll be looking for any negative thing they can find about you. But don't forget that they'll also be looking for positive things too. The media might be portraying you in a negative light, and people may subsequently view you in such, but that's the point of this speech – to tell everyone the truth of what's been going on here, and to let them know who you are and what your political standpoint is."

"You'll have a better chance of being listened to than me," Kyle murmurs.

Avi nods at the paper in Amelia's hands. "Give yourself a chance at it."

Amelia glances between them. She smiles nervously. "Thanks, guys."

Leaving them to continue practicing, Kyle excuses himself. He takes a deep breath as he walks away down the hallway. A lot of their hope is in Amelia's speech. Kyle's not so hopeful about how the Arkala nation will receive it, but it's something.

Hopefully.

True to Sam's directions, Kyle finds Timothy in the conservatory on the lake side of the house. He doesn't know where to find the door connecting it to the house though, and he doesn't feel scouring the house to find it, so he goes out the sliding door in the living room and approaches along the smoothly paved pathway along the side of the house.

He's in the dark as he moves. Kyle can see where he's going since the conservatory lights are on, but the ones on the side of the house are not and so while he can see Timothy and Jié, and Xiùyīng standing beside them, they can't see him. It gives Kyle a sense of privacy, a moment to himself to work out how he's going to broach the subject.

Fortunately or not, the job of doing so is already in the process of being done.

"You really have no knowledge of it?" Jié asks.

Timothy shifts on his feet. "All I know is what was handled with the case. Beyond that, no – nothing."

A fourth person lets out a heavy breath. "And nothing ever crossed your mind?"

Apprehension stabs Kyle in the stomach. *Minharh's here too.* He fights the instinct to turn back. Jié and Xiùyīng seemed fine with Kyle being around when he went to talk to Timothy earlier, but Minharh, on the other hand...

"Personally," Timothy says, "I think the A'o Fire case should be reopened. But I'm a judge not a prosecutor, and I'm not technically a lawyer now. It's not like I can go looking for additional evidence myself. That's why I had to take a different approach to look into Kyle's case when I became suspicious of it."

"You commissioned your friend Yuuki to investigate, eh?" Minharh asks.

"Yeah. He could do it – and we could go about the investigating legally – because of his qualification as officer in security. That's not to mention he was working as a warden at the detention centre Kyle was sent to. I was able to investigate through him, in other words. I didn't have any such options available to me in regard to investigating the A'o Fire case."

Jié exchanges a knowing glance with Minharh. His mouth quirks. "Well, now you do."

Timothy frowns. "You have something?"

"A witness."

Expression tight, Minharh tilts his head. "I can't really tell you much at present. It…" Jié's hand lands on his shoulder, and Minharh grimaces. He clears his throat. "Besides, it's…it's more a speculation. We aren't able to provide solid proof for it."

"That's why we haven't been able to tell you," Xiùyīng explains.

"We've also kind of been in hiding because of this information."

Timothy nods slowly in understanding. "That's why you had to leave your son?"

Minharh hums. He sounds broken when he murmurs, "Yeah."

Kyle's close enough to see how conflicted Timothy is – wanting to know more but wanting to respect Minharh's boundaries. Kyle wonders if now's a good time to be asking Timothy to hear about the Ninao revelation. He has enough going on, and Kyle would only be interrupting this conversation. Again, he contemplates leaving, but something urges him to stay.

For Yuuki's sake, Kyle decides to remain where he is. He'll just wait until the serious conversation is over, or at least until the tension of this part of it dissipates before he approaches.

However long that might be…

Timothy breaks the lull in the conversation. "You were worried something might happen, weren't you?" he asks quietly. "If the people who committed the arson found out about you knowing the reason why?"

Minharh gives a small nod. "Our concerns were proved correct last year, too, when the Ninao kidnapping happened."

Timothy unfolds his arms and puts his hands on his hips. "You're saying that the people who attacked us – who kidnapped Yuuki – were involved in the A'o fire case too, huh?"

Xiùyīng's brow creases. "Too? The Ninao kidnapping happened *because* of the A'o fire."

At Timothy's confusion, Minharh grunts. "No, of course you didn't know."

"I don't understand," Timothy murmurs. Perplexed, he glances between them with concern. "What do you mean Ninao happened because of that?"

Minharh leans forward in his wheelchair, rubs a hand over his face. "This gets more messed up the more we try find answers."

"We've been researching about the Ninao kidnapping case, too," Jié says after a moment of gathering his thoughts. "We found it strange that hardly any investigating was done, and what was done was pretty much given up on half way. Just like with the Fire case. We thought there might be a connection, and there was – is."

It all clicks. Kyle's eyes widen. "They were after you because they thought you knew about the evidence."

His heart skips a beat. *Oops.* His face burns as everyone's eyes fall on him. Having given away his presence, Kyle has no choice but to emerge from the shadows. He avoids all eye contact but Timothy's. He's fully expecting to be shamed for eavesdropping, but there's not even a hint of irritancy in the atmosphere.

Beside Kyle, Timothy looks at Xiùyīng, at Jié, then at Minharh. He raises an eyebrow, his mouth open in an argument he doesn't trust his own point-of-view in anymore.

Minharh hums in confirmation of Kyle's statement. "The objective of the Ninao kidnapping was to take you," he says to Timothy, "find out how much you knew and then dispose of you."

"Just like what they tried to do with me," Kyle whispers. *At least, the latter part.*

The words hang in the air like a smog. Timothy turns to stare at Kyle, then at Minharh, eerily still. His face drains of colour as he tests the revelation in his mind. "...but you said they thought I knew about this evidence. I didn't. I still don't."

"Like how I didn't know about Amelia," Kyle points out.

"But..." Timothy raises a hand to his forehead. "If they wanted me for *that* – for having handled the A'o Fire case – then why the hell did they kidnap Yuuki and do what they did to him?"

"They were holding him hostage," Kyle says. *So much for letting Yuuki handle the revelation.* "You got away with Joshua, and they had him and not you, and they wanted you."

"How do you...?"

"Yuuki told me; he figured it out earlier. He wanted to tell you. That's why I came here, actually: to get you for him. He wasn't feeling up to coming out here himself."

The gears turn and the pieces fall into place in slow motion. Timothy's body language protests, but his expression conveys that his mind has already established the fact that this is not a theory they're speaking of.

"You tried to have the case reopened," Jié explains. "They – who we're still unsure of – thought you knew about what is was that they destroyed with the fire. They didn't like that." He casts a weary glance at Minharh. "Perhaps they worried not all trace of what they were trying to cover up was gone."

Timothy stares, stressed. "But that new evidence was found insubstantial anyways. The case stayed closed as with insufficient evidence; it never ended up being regarded as arson."

"You still suspected it."

Nausea rises in Kyle's throat. "So what the Ninao incident really was about was them trying to silence Timothy like they tried to silence me. I didn't know actually know anything with my case, either."

Xiùyīng nods.

"Timothy," Jié says, "when you got away from them during the Ninao kidnapping, they were likely going to attempt to recapture you by using Yuuki to draw you in."

"What they wanted to cover up was highly sensitive information," Minharh murmurs. "They had to keep it hidden at all costs, and part of that meant dispatching anyone who might have come across it."

"*Anyone?*" Kyle asks.

"Anyone."

Kyle nervously swallows. "So then...my Dad – he was one of the firefighters who tried to put out that fire. Did that include him?"

Minharh looks him in the eye, his face solemn. He nods.

"So it definitely was arson?" Timothy asks.

Minharh confirms. "Yes. They deliberately lit the fire to cover up evidence, and when the firefighting crew got there to put out the blaze, they targeted the gas line by gun. That caused the explosion, thereby

THE REDEMPTION OF KINDALL, K.

taking out anyone who might've seen the evidence."

Kyle's cheek twitches.

"So the puncture in the gas line being at fault is still true," Timothy murmurs, "however it was intentional and didn't actually start the fire so much as encourage it. Is that what you're saying? And how on earth did you come across this information?"

Minharh's face contorts. He tilts his head, takes a deep breath. His fingers twist in the hold he's got on his jersey. Narrowing his eyes, he steadies himself and goes to reply but then catches himself. With a grimace, he shakes his head. "I'm sorry, I don't think I can speak of it right now."

"Right." Timothy hisses at himself. "You were a witness. Sorry."

Kyle's heart softens. He knows that kind of distress too well. He asks quietly, "May I ask…is it because it brings up bad memories for you? Of what Jié said earlier, about having to leave your son behind?"

Locking his gaze on a spot on the floor in front of him, Minharh nods. "Yeah."

The exchange sparks *something* in the back of Kyle's brain. If Kyle's seeing it correctly, Minharh remorseful – and in a way that's directed at *him*. It feels like there's something Minharh isn't telling him, but in the moment Kyle can't determine exactly what that is or why. He finds himself nevertheless unnerved by it.

"It's okay," Timothy says. "We don't have to talk about it now. It's all goods."

"We'll need to at some point," Xiùyīng points out.

Minharh takes a slow, controlled breath. He shoots his friend the same anxious stare he'd had when arguing with her earlier. "I just… need…time…"

Kyle can sense Minharh's words ringing through Timothy's aura as well. It ripples out from a place deeply penetrated, shaken to the core. A silence falls on the conversation. There's too many questions to ask, and the ones that have been answered leave a gaping hole in the places that should've brought closure.

After a few minutes, Timothy heads back inside without a word, face awash in emotions. Kyle catches a glimpse of them has he goes: anger, terror, frustration and other indistinguishable things. Denial. The logical piecing of things together. The want to shatter that logic with some other reasoning besides this.

The Ninao incident was wrought with more horror than they anticipated.

36

Not wanting to hang around in the awkward and unsettling wake Timothy leaves behind him, Kyle excuses himself from the conservatory and leaves Jié, Xiùyīng and Minharh to return to Yuuki's room. Kyle's not expecting Timothy to be there, so it's no surprise to find he's not come by.

Yuuki's drifted off to sleep while waiting, but he stirs when Kyle walks in. "s he coming?"

"He knows," Kyle murmurs. "At least, now he does."

"You told him already?"

Kyle sits down on the edge of the bed with a sigh. "No, he…the guy you handed the Trust over to, Jié, he mentioned earlier that he wanted to talk to Timothy about something." He grunts. "It was about this. Turns out the Ninao incident was a parallel of what happened to me: Timothy was suspected of knowing something he wasn't supposed to know, and so they tried to get rid of him."

"Like you with the Princess?"

"Yeah. Only this was about the A'o Fire case. Whoever 'they' are, they thought Timothy was going to prove it was arson and they didn't want that. They wanted to check that Timothy hadn't told anyone of what they thought he knew, hence why they chose to kidnap him first."

"And why they kept me on hand, in that shed. So they could get him back."

Kyle nods solemnly. "Yeah."

"...how did he react?"

"Timothy?"

"Yeah."

"I think he'd prefer to believe it happened because of the Trust. I guess it's good that there's that better explanation for what happened to you now, but..."

"He's not going to be coming in here for a while then, huh." Yuuki groans. "There goes telling him not to hate himself because he had to do with what happened to me. Urgh."

"He probably just needs time to process it. To accept it."

"Hmm."

Kyle catches himself wringing his hands anxiously. He grimaces. "I, um...I also found out that my Dad was a victim of it too – the whole covering up thing, I mean. I told you he was a firefighter? Yeah, he was called out that night to fight the blaze and he never came home."

Yuuki watches Kyle's expression, but he doesn't have the energy required to think of how best to offer any consolation. Instead he simply hums in acknowledgement.

"I want to know what is that they so badly wanted to keep secret. Apparently Minharh knows something, but he's not ready to talk about it yet. It has to be something serious, right? Otherwise they wouldn't have gone to such extremes to get rid of anyone who knew or knows about it. And if it had been about the Princess, Minharh could've said so already."

Kyle huffs out a disbelieving breath, only it's less disbelief and more bewilderment. "It's like we're all caught up in this net of interconnected plots and whatnot. We try untangle it and it becomes even *more* tangled and messed up in the process..."

He's venting. Frustration and anxiety, exhaustion from being emotionally wrung out by everything – it's all wound up tight inside of him, and Kyle's struggling the process it. It's compartmentalised for now, put aside in a mental-emotional box where it only needs to be brushed on as much as necessary. It'll overload what he's capable of processing if he opens it now.

"Sorry," Kyle murmurs. "You need sleep and I'm keeping you awake."

Yuuki exhales slowly. "'s okay."

"...I forgot to ask, but are *you* coping with it okay? With the Ninao revelation, I mean."

Yuuki looks away. Swallows thickly. "Not really."

Kyle hadn't expected him to be, but the honesty of Yuuki's answer catches him off guard. "Is there anything I can do to help?"

It's such an open offering for a closed question. Kyle's waiting for Yuuki to say 'it's fine' instead of actually requesting anything, but instead Yuuki stares at him, his gaze conflicted. Kyle's stomach dips. A chill runs down his spine and makes it tingle. This honesty and allowing him in unexpectedly *hurts*.

"What is it?" Kyle asks.

"Is it okay if you...I mean..." Yuuki grimaces. "Do you mind sleeping here tonight? As in, like...here." He means the bed. "It's okay if you don't want to. Besides, I'm still sick, and there's not really enough room for two people to sleep on this bed, anyway, so…"

In a seemingly selfish way, Kyle's relieved. "Of course I'm fine with that." If he wasn't, he wouldn't have spent the last five nights doing so.

Of course, sleeping separately would be fine, but he's come to find great comfort in the close proximity. It's reassuring – the simple calming of shared body warmth, the certainty that Yuuki's right beside him and that nothing bad has happened or crept up on them while Kyle's been asleep. And put simply, they're both traumatised humans who need comforting hugs.

Once he's ready for bed, he lays down beside Yuuki, shifts in close and gently pulls him into a loose embrace. Kyle reaches over to check that the IV line isn't going to catch on anything. Yuuki's tense, as though he expects Kyle to change his mind at any moment, or find it's too much all of a sudden and change his own mind.

But when Kyle relaxes, gradually Yuuki does too. For the most part, at least. The muscles of his neck and shoulders remain tight, his jaw clenched.

"What's bothering you?" Kyle asks quietly.

Yuuki blinks slowly. "'m afraid…"

Kyle hums.

"…of many things. Not just about what else might happen to me, to us – to everyone… I…"

He trails off and doesn't speak for a few minutes. The tension in his shoulders remains. Kyle waits, giving him space without prompting, giving him the option to withdraw from saying the latter half of the sentence if he's too uncomfortable with saying it.

Yuuki curls his fingers into a fist. He turns his face to hide against the material of Kyle's jersey. "I'm afraid of who I'm becoming," he whispers.

The confession, fragile as it is, goes through Kyle's heart like a spear.

"I can't feel anything anymore. 's all just… numb and achy, or adrenaline. Nothing else. Sometimes both."

Kyle swallows. He knows that feeling, or rather lack of; he's experienced it himself. That essentially emotionless void that had hollowed him out while he was locked up in isolation isn't something he likes to think of.

"It's a survival mechanism," he says, "remember? And you're surviving. When you start to heal, you'll also start feeling again."

Yuuki grunts.

"We'll help you feel again, 'kay?"

"…how?"

"In small steps. Like…like being outside in warm sun if it's cold, o-or a refreshing breeze after being inside for a long time. In good coffee. I heard Susan say they have a really good coffee machine here. Um…"

A tear slips out of the corner of his eye. Kyle tries to keep it internalised, but the stifled cry ends up jolting through his chest. He bends his elbow and brings his hand to rest on the back of Yuuki's head. Smoothing Yuuki's unkempt hair down, he unconsciously settles into the repeated motions of stroking it. It's as much a self-soothing action as it is intended to comfort Yuuki.

"Do you think I can get better?"

As much as Kyle wants to say yes to that, he and Yuuki both know that it'll take an incredibly long time for Yuuki to consider himself recovered. Considering the hurt he's suffered, it almost feels wrong to expect him to recover. Some hurts don't heal properly – they scar, and as Kyle is physically reminded of by the burn on his hip, the pain and complications they bring may not necessarily fade in full.

"In time," Kyle says instead, "I think you can. But you don't have to pretend to be getting better. You're allowed to be hurt; you don't have to hide it from us. I know it's got to be…humiliating, thinking of everyone seeing you like this. That's okay. You don't have to force yourself to be around us all.

"But don't hide yourself either. We're not going to shame you if you're having a bad day, no matter how many you might have in a row. We're not going to invalidate your efforts and say you're not trying hard enough to heal if you're not showing any signs of getting better. Healing isn't linear and it can't be forced.

"I know you're hurting terribly. It probably seems like this suffering won't end – that things will keep happening and it'll just keep getting worse." Kyle's breath hitches. "But surely not all the things that'll happen to us from here will be inherently bad. That's not to say they'll be what we can call 'good', either, but I want to believe we can experience good things again. All of us. I can't believe it now, but I want to fight so that maybe someday I'm able to. And so that you're able to, too."

Yuuki grunts. "What do we even have to fight with?"

For all the words Kyle had before, now he has none.

"Amelia can only do so much," Yuuki mutters. "All we do is keep running, but what other choice do we have? Everyone in this country is going to favour the Peace Force's word over ours. We don't have any way of fighting back like this."

Kyle inhales slowly. Contemplates. His heart pounds. He lets the breath out again. "Actually," he murmurs, "we do have something."

"What?"

"Evidence."

"They won't believe it."

"Hard evidence."

Yuuki's brow furrows. He closes his eyes. "But we don't…"

"No, we do."

"If you're talking about trying to explain it using the Ninao revelation or your case or my missing arm as an example or something, they won't –"

"Joshua recorded the hostage situation."

Yuuki's sudden silence makes Kyle sick with dread. *What on earth made me think it was a good idea to tell him that? As if his reaction to seeing the photo evidence of Ninao wasn't enough warning. You really think Yuuki's wanting to hear this now?*

After a minute, Kyle can't take it. Yuuki hasn't said anything or moved since spoke. The tension is unbearable, and if Yuuki has a panic attack right here and now, Kyle doesn't know if he has the emotional energy to be able to bear staying with him long enough to help him through it.

It surprises him, therefore, when Yuuki finally does speak. His voice is eerily steady when he quietly asks, "How much did he get?"

Kyle takes a deep breath. "I'm not sure, exactly. He went up to the rooftop after Sam and I went out to get you. So probably everything from as soon as he got up there?"

"But nothing before?"

"He said he also got a copy of the palace's CCTV footage."

"It wasn't damaged?"

"You mean the cameras?"

"No, the data. Well, both."

Kyle realises what Yuuki's thinking about. "No, Joshua made sure to get it before it could be tampered with. Andy was thinking that we could broadcast it along with Amelia's speech. I think he's already checked to make sure it's fine. It's not like my case, don't worry."

Yuuki swallows. His shoulders tremble.

"But, hey, listen to me: everyone's on the same page here – we aren't going to do that without your permission. If you don't want us to, we won't, okay?"

"Use it."

Kyle stills. "What?"

"Use the videos," Yuuki whispers. The steadiness in his voice cracks. "I don't care. They need to know. Arkala needs to know. They have no idea what's going on here because everything keeps getting buried. Or erased, or else ignored, like your case. We might not be able to prove what's going on by using your case, but we can use mine."

"But Yuuki, that's –"

"We have a chance. If you're looking for permission, this is it. Don't let this opportunity go to waste. Please."

"Okay, but you can change your mind whenever. It's your trauma we'd be broadcasting. No one's going to show those videos without your definite consent."

"I told you already: you have it. Promise me you'll get them to use it."

Kyle lies his head back against the pillows. Maybe they don't have it in them to overcome the fight ahead of them, but if they can survive then that's sufficient. To do that, they're going to need to use the evidence they have of Yuuki's abuse. "Okay. I'll let them know."

While Yuuki's relief is palpable, there's no smile accompanying it.

Kyle wonders to what extent this fighting will go on. How far will they have to go and how much of this will they have to endure before they can rest? Before they can have a proper chance at healing?

Yuuki and Timothy did their best to keep within legal parameters when they starting this fighting back, but it's become clear that this fight isn't one they can win through legal means alone. They can't defend themselves with something that's rigged against them.

At this rate, they may have to go to war.

37

Later that night

In the wake of Yuuki's revelation about the Ninao incident, Kyle starts to feel his own consciousness being prodded.

It starts faint at first. The revelation is no more than a hint of something on the brink of being discovered, like a shadow without enough light yet to reveal it. It's there, but it needs more thought.

Kyle mulls over it. It lingers in the back of his mind, has him on edge in a way he can't explain. Too awake to sleep, he gets up and takes out his knife – the one his father gave him of his mother's treasured collection. He stares at it as though writing will magically appear on the hilt or blade, offering him the answer he needs. Kyle gets why Yuuki never said anything about his own revelation while he was processing it. It's confusing, and he's not sure he's going to like what he learns when the realisation comes.

And so he continues to doubt it, out of nervousness more than anything – even when he *knows*. The signs are all there and it doesn't take much to piece them together. But Kyle still hesitates to believe it.

He needs this confirmed by someone else – specifically one person in particular.

On the hope that they're still up, Kyle seeks that person out. He's relieved to find that person's alone, sitting in his wheelchair drinking tea by a window in the living room. Kyle's stomach churns. Judging by the vibrant deep red-orange of the tea, it's rooibos.

His father always liked that tea.

"Your name's Minharh, right?" Kyle asks, feigning forgetfulness.

Minharh looks up, startled. Apparently he hadn't heard Kyle come in. "Yeah, that's my name."

"Can I ask you something?"

Minharh looks at him, a certain vulnerability behind that failed guarded look of his. "Uh, sure?"

Before he asks it, Kyle fixes his eyes on Minharh's, analysing every emotion and thought he sees refracted in them. At worst, he'll come across as silly, maybe somewhat delusional if he's wrong. If he's right, though…

"Kyle?"

Pain stabs him in the heart. Kyle knows he's right. The answer he's looking for is in the way that Minharh says it – the way Minharh says his name. His voice is different, raspier. Husky as one's voice might get after being damaged by smoke inhalation. Slightly louder than necessary in the quiet of the room, perhaps due to partially damaged hearing – something that isn't uncommon after being in proximity to an explosion.

Kyle takes in the other confirmations in front of him, like the wheelchair – a necessity due to an injury from an experience that potentially almost took his life. Minharh is older, his hair longer and his

341

face more worn, but such things happen over time.

Time which Kyle thought had stopped for good five years ago.

Resigned, Kyle commits to the question, though he already knows the answer before he even asks it.

"My Dad didn't really die in the fire, did he?"

Acknowledgements

Thank you to everyone who's been awaiting this book since *The Case of Kindall, K.*! Special thanks to Katy, for your unfailing support and love for this story; to my friends around the world who helped me keep going when circumstances made writing difficult; and to all of you who expressed your enjoyment of the first – and excitement for this second – book of the series.

See you for the third part of the story!

The Deliverance of

Kyle Kindall

The story continues in the third book in the Kindall K series...

After much struggling and suffering, Amelia's group are finally being received. The fight for Kyle's acquittal continues. The promise of freedom is tantalising...

There is still a high risk involved with every step forward they take, however. New evidence surfaces to support and explain the recent events, but Yuuki and Kyle are nonetheless troubled by the uncertainty of the future that lies ahead. In the midst of it all, Kyle deals with a revelation of his own. It ought to bring joy, but the trails of grief left in its wake only bring a shattering sense of betrayal.

Meanwhile, with numbers dwindling and time running out, it's not long before the last remaining members of a certain group of individuals each start going about things in their own way....

Published July 2020
ISBN-13 (paperback): 9780473527990 | ISBN-13 (hardcover): 9780473630539| ISBN-13 (Kindle): 9780473528003 | ISBN-13 (ePUB): 9780473578992

RENEE NIELSEN

Appendix: Arkalahn glossary

Amelia (name): an endemic flower of Arkala. Flowers bloom in late winter, historically marking the beginning of Arkala spring. The flower is a symbol of promised peace after hardship and is the main feature of the Arkala national flag.

Arka (country): the indigenous name for the geographical territory of Arkala. The Kingdom of Arkala – or the nation state in general – is known in short as "Arkala", however it is referred to as *Arka* when spoken in Arkalahn.

Arkala (ethnic subgroup): *lit. transl. the people of Arka*. The collective term used for the indigenous people of the Kingdom of Arkala. Among the indigenous people, however, *Arkala* traditionally refers to descendants of the Polynesian group that established livelihood on the island. The Arkala nation's monarchy are descendants of this group.

Arkala'ana (ethnic subgroup): *transl. the cave-dwelling people of Arka*. A minority group of indigenous people. They arrived earlier than the group that arrived from Polynesia (the Arkala). Their preference for living in the caves became a source of discrimination from the Arkala who made their dwellings on the surface. Since the Arkala'ana are a minority, they are often simply called Arkala by non-Arkala residents.

Arkalahn (language): *transl. the language of Arkala.* The common language spoken among the Arkala. A slightly different dialect is spoken among the Arkala'ana, adapted from the language of their ancestors to adjust to the sound dynamics of the caves. Arkala'ana words are sometimes stressed for clarity and are identified in writing by an 'h' written before or after a consonant – like in *kai'irh*.

Arkalan (nationality): general nationality of Kingdom of Arkala citizens.

Kai'irh (phrase, name): *lit. transl. "tides alternate".* The ebb and flow of the sea tides. It is Kyle's Arkalahn name.

Li kih kehn ha'arh (Arkalahn phrase, spoken in Arkala'ana dialect): *lit. transl. your spirit strong remain.* "Keep your spirit strong." Also spoken as a prayer of health and an expression of farewell when parting ways with someone for a significant duration.

Sakerh (Arkalahn greeting, verb): *lit. transl. paths crossed; an intersecting.* A greeting like "hello". Pronounced sah-KERH. The ending 'h' sound of both syllables is more heavily pronounced in Arkala'ana dialect.